INFINITY CHARGE

INFINITY CHARGE

TYLER H. JOLLEY

JOLENE PERRY

*Thank you Keaton for
brainstorming everything with me*

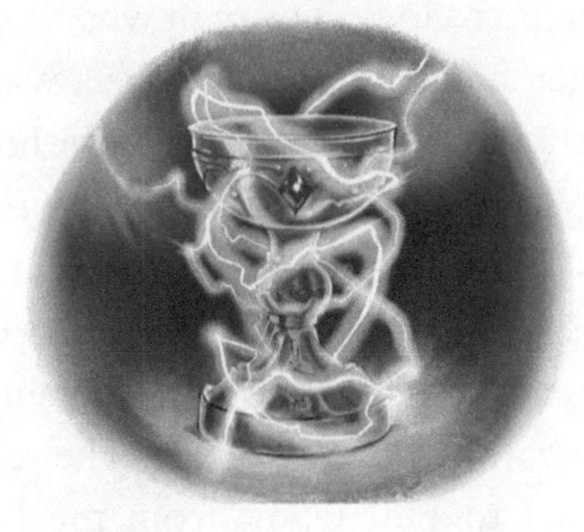

PROLOGUE

· · · · ·

Hayrah clutched the shoulder of her six-year-old son, knowing the risks, and understanding she had no choice. Her white hair sat braided over one shoulder—a testament to her heritage as a soil charger rather than a human. A man stood next to them—a man she would pretend was her husband. He was the man who had failed once at saving the world they lived in.

Fahren stood in front of the three of them, sympathy written on the wrinkles of his forehead and around his mouth, but when she looked deeper—looked beneath the outward features of the face belonging to the leader of the humans—she saw what they would all need to cling to.

Hope.

Her son peered up at her, determination on his young features. Her heart broke further. She had never asked for her name to be written in history books—or the name of her adopted son—but success or failure would be noted. Remembered. Just as she knew of Tel'el's failure. The man she would pretend to love. The man who would teach her half-soil-charger, half-human son to be a warrior.

Hayrah felt the stranger's gaze bore holes into her. She and Tage were his chance at redemption. Humans suffered in terrible conditions every day due to the soil chargers across the Saptex Sea—soil chargers like himself. They weren't all bad—but the leadership was rotten to the core, spreading lies and deceit. The second the soil chargers learned to pull water from the latex sea and no longer needed the humans, they'd all be slaughtered. Tel'el refused to allow that to happen. Fahren gave him a slight nod. A show of understanding that he was once again putting the fate of the human race in Tel'el's hands.

Hayrah's heart cracked as they left their leader's room together, knowing her future would be nothing but planning, subterfuge, and possibly saying goodbye far too soon to the boy she'd raised.

Tel'el likely saw nothing but his chance at redemption, the scars on his body a testament to his last failure.

For good or ill, they were a family now, leaving for enemy territory. Hoping for a day when enemies no longer existed.

10 YEARS LATER

• • • • •

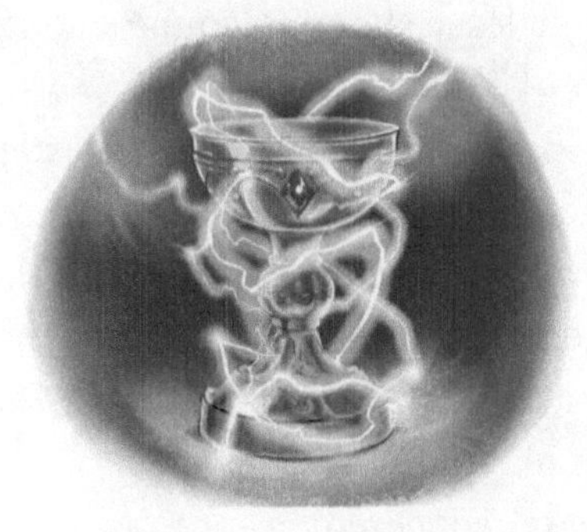

CHAPTER 1

• • • • •

Every piece of playground equipment was an opportunity to improve strength and dexterity. Tage grasped the bar above the swings, threw the weight of his legs back once, forward once, then swung his legs up and over his head until his waist was even with the bar, his arms flexing to hold him upright. In another easy move, he slipped one leg over and straddled the wide metal bar.

Even now—even when he didn't try—Tage could feel the hum of power in the soil below. Though only half soil charger, there were times when he swore he could feel the vibrations of electricity more easily than his friends.

"Dude!" Lumen called up. "How did you make that look so easy?"

A corner of Tage's mouth lifted. His father had shown him. Well, his adoptive father. The only father he'd ever remembered, anyway. He flipped his white hair over his shoulder and grinned. "Hop on up, Lumen."

"I got it." Capacity's smile made his heart flip. Again. She hadn't been part of the plan. She was never part of the plan. But at least she was young enough that she'd forget him after he died.

Her lithe body hopped up as she stepped on the wobbly swing and she reached for the bar overhead.

The playground sat empty aside from them. The two suns had started to drift low in the sky, casting crisscrossing shadows across the empty streets. Tall apartment buildings. The playground.

Tage's heart squeezed as he watched. Capacity grasped the bar and swung her body back and then forward, slowly gaining momentum. She could have made it up in two swings, just like Tage, but she'd always been a hair more cautious than her capability.

"You got it!" Lumen called. Her long white hair was folded into intricate braids. Lumen was far too athletic to deal with things like her hair getting in her face.

Another swing back and then forward, and Capacity pulled her feet up into a near pike position, just barely touching the bar. In a flash, Tage reached forward, grasped her calf muscle, and tugged, helping guide her to rest on the curve between the top of her thighs and her stomach.

"Made it!" She laughed, full and strong. Leaning forward, she quickly slipped one leg over the top, resting the bar between her legs and facing Tage.

When Capacity laughed, it lit up every feature of her delicate face. Bright blue eyes. Pale freckles. White hair.

Capacity lightened Tage's serious heart.

Her lips touched his, sparking a whole different kind of electricity through his body. The scent of lavender lingered in the air around her. Always did.

His smile trembled as he stared at her. He never should have allowed himself the luxury of feeling so much for someone. Of allowing her to feel something for him. But the days before his mission were growing few, and when she first pressed her lips to his, he decided he'd allow himself this one selfish indulgence. But now . . . months later, he was realizing that all he'd done was guarantee her heartbreak. He'd brought another person into his destiny—she just had no idea.

Shouts called from below.

Lumen gave her best friend a fist-pump, and Impulse tiptoed his giant body lightly along a balance beam. The guy was huge, but he moved like a cat—stealthy and swift. The last bits of sun glinted off his bald head. Every soil charger was born with white hair or no hair; Impulse fell into the second category. Tage's category was half human who had to bleach his hair to fit in. As far as he knew, he was the only one in that category.

Even shouts and marching steps snapped Tage's attention to the street, and to the small platoon of Surge Knights. They stepped together in a two-by-six arrangement, their shields, metal finger and arm bands, and red spinal lights on full display. Lumen and Impulse had already been drafted. Tage had signed up, putting him one step closer to his mission.

Their mouths were closed as they marched, but as one adjusted, Tage could just make out the metal denture of the man's teeth. Their white hair hung in similar fashion—aside from the one without hair. An involuntary shiver ran down Tage's spine. Soon, that would be him. Altered, used, and abused, until he could make his move.

Two weeks left.

"I can't believe we all just put up with this." Lumen crossed her hands over her chest, peering at the empty playground, the dirty streets, and the mostly dark windows on the gray brick building. "I remember when we used to have block parties and the playground was always full . . . not that I'm complaining." She deftly jumped up, grabbed onto the critter bars, and swung her way, hand over hand, from one end to the other.

"Yeah, well . . ." Impulse paused, folding his thick arms. "When everyone knows that the humans are going to come across the desert and take us out, we can be convinced to do almost anything."

Tage itched to tell them that the humans weren't the beings to be feared in their world, but he'd listened to how the soil chargers mocked their own who would stand on street corners shouting that very thing. They'd disappear into prisons, just like the soil chargers who were caught trying to find a life outside of the city. Or food in the small oases in the desert. Worms that could feed a family for a day. Tage had done enough wandering in the city at night with Tel'el to become familiar with most of the ins and outs that led from the city to the desert. Some of the entrances to the utility tunnels were under the surface of Currentgrad, but they had to find them all.

"Maybe we should sneak out of the city and become nomad soil chargers," Lumen teased. "Get ourselves some big, strong ursogen and ride off into the sunset. I hear they never tire."

Everything tired. No matter how fierce the creature and no matter how easily they picked up a charge. Even the broad, muscular ursogen, with their large teeth and deadly claws. Tage stayed silent.

Capacity ran her black-tipped fingers over the top of Tage's hand, the extra webbing of skin between their fingers showing their soil-charger genetics. His gaze connected with hers again. In these moments, he wished he could tell her who he really was.

Impulse stood high on a piece of equipment, and Tage watched as he glanced at the top of the swing set.

"You going to—" But Tage hadn't finished when

Impulse made the leap, easily swinging his thick legs to grasp onto the bar where Tage and Capacity sat.

But there he hung. Arms on one part of the bar. Ankles hooked over another part of the bar. Mostly defenseless.

"You having fun down there?" Tage laughed.

Lumen's snorts turned to laughter, too, as Impulse slowly lowered his feet and then dropped to the ground.

"I gotta head home." Impulse stretched his neck one way and then the other. "Mom needs help."

Impulse was one of a lot of kids. His dad had been arrested for coming back from the desert with food. They hadn't heard a thing from him in almost three years. Probably why Impulse had been drafted.

Lumen gave him a slap on the shoulder. "You're one of the best mommies in Currentgrad," she teased.

Even without the draft, Impulse had no choice but to become a Surge Knight—it was his best chance of saving his younger siblings and his mother. With the Surge Knight stipend, it would immediately thrust them into some semblance of wealth. They were barely scraping by, and had been in that position since long before his father had been arrested.

In one easy move, Tage swung down and dropped to the soil, immediately feeling the ripples of energy beneath his feet.

"Nice." Lumen held her fist up in the air, and Tage immediately tapped his knuckles against hers.

"See you tomorrow," Impulse said as he ambled toward home.

"See you," Tage called.

Watching Impulse's hulking form shuffle along the street, no one would guess how nimbly he could move when he wanted to.

"Okay." Capacity stared at Tage and Lumen, biting her lower lip. "I wasn't thinking about getting down."

"You got it," Tage told her. "You made it up there. Just swing down in the same way."

"Jump it," Lumen said. "Use that soil-charger strength."

The crackle of lightning broke across the darkening purple sky—another dry storm was rolling across the desert. They'd been happening more often.

A light laugh bubbled from Capacity. "I don't think so."

Tage walked underneath the swing set. "I got you. You got this."

Their eyes connected for a moment, and he felt the intensity of her deep in his gut. Saying goodbye would be torture—he could only hope that he could change this world for the better, and she'd find happiness with someone else. He couldn't conceive of a scenario in which he'd get to keep her.

Shifting, Capacity leaned forward, allowing herself to hang upside down. Grasping the bar, she untangled her legs and dropped to the ground. She stumbled twice, and Tage grasped her before she lost her balance, pulling her into his arms.

"Hi," she said with a smile.

"Hi," he said back, tightening his arms around her waist.

"Gag," Lumen teased. "I'll leave you two to walk home together. I get enough PDA from my brother and his wife. I swear, they'll never get their own place."

"Not with the overlord's high taxes," Capacity said through a laugh—a standard joke anytime any one of them tried to prepare for the future.

With a wave, Lumen disappeared into the darkness.

Lights began flickering on in the buildings around them, a sea of apartments from here to the Voltaic Dava—the overlord's palace—in one direction, and the science research buildings in the other. Even the wealthier soil chargers had money only due to research skills, in which case their homes were next to the research facility, or they worked for the overlord and lived in the palace.

"Want some light?" Capacity grinned before showering them both with White Sparks from her fingertips. The spots of fizzling electricity rained around them like a halo, popping against his skin.

"I wonder if I'll ever learn how to absorb another's ignition?" Tage held out his hand, but Capacity hadn't put too much charge in the flickering balls of electricity, so they only stung a little.

"Surge Knight . . ." Capacity trailed off. "You've always had strong ignitions, putting out more sparks and bolts than the rest of us."

Tage shrugged. "I practice a lot."

Releasing a small sigh, Capacity peered up at him again. "You'll be able to switch from sparks to bolts without discharging everything between . . . I bet there are some things you'll love."

That might be, but the transformation process wasn't something he looked forward to.

So few days left.

Tage tucked Capacity against his side, and they started the walk to her apartment.

Chanting was followed by a group of four Surge Knights moving toward the city wall, their red spinal lights glowing in the dark. The ground shook with thunder, but even Capacity didn't flinch. The storms were common. The energy was something they all craved.

Capacity leaned closer against him. "I can't—I can't

believe how many there are now. How many of us are so willing to alter ourselves . . ."

"Remember," Tage told her. "That'll be me soon."

"Only because you need the protection. Your family needs the money. I can't imagine what the taxes on a full home would be, or how scary it would feel to know you could lose your family's house." His narrow home was sandwiched between others, forming a row of more than a dozen identical houses.

So many lies made up Tage's life. And the money or the reasoning weren't why he was joining the Knights at all. But then, most of Tage's life was a secret—even from the people he spent most of his time with.

"Yeah," he agreed, because there was nothing else to do.

It wasn't like Tage could tell her that his father wasn't actually his father, but a failed assassin. Or that, because of his half-human genetic makeup, he'd been chosen by the humans at the age of six to carry out a plan to assassinate Overlord Koax. That an undetectable poison had been painstakingly harvested for years by his mother. That they were just a few days away from having enough. That if Tage failed, it could be years before another attempt could be planned.

There was no way for humans to take the soil chargers by force—especially with most of Currentgrad being part of the overlord's defense. Any assassination would have to be cautiously planned. Only one attempt had been made since Tel'el's failure. Tage had lived in Currentgrad at the time, and it was all anyone talked about. The rogue human had failed, of course, and resulted in another draft of soil chargers to become Surge Knights, as well as a lot more propaganda from Koax about the evil humans. The humans couldn't afford another failure.

Their world needed them to succeed. Tel'el had been hinting at Overlord Koax's horrific plans to take over not just the human settlement, but other terraregions as well.

Tage had no choice but to succeed. To hope that once the veil of deceit so carefully cultivated by Overlord Koax was lifted, that a new peace could be established between the humans and soil chargers. Tage had lived in both places. There were good people in both places.

Capacity squeezed his hand. "You're quiet tonight."

"Yeah," he answered. "It's getting closer . . ."

He didn't need to say to what. His transformation was knocking on his life's door. That was something they both knew.

"It'll keep us both safe," she whispered in the dark.

Tage glanced to his row home to see Tel'el watching him from the window. He was known as Array here, but it was a name Tage only used when friends were over, and in public.

Tel'el's mouth dipped into a frown. Capacity was a distraction, a weakness—at least in Tel'el's eyes. In Tage's eyes, she was more motivation to be smart and cautious and to succeed.

Her eyes drifted to the window. "Your dad hates me."

They continued to walk. He wanted to make sure she got home safely before returning back to his house.

"My dad doesn't want me involved . . . with anyone."

She laughed a little. "Sounds like my dad, I guess. You know . . . before he was arrested."

Their situations weren't the same at all, but there was no way to explain that to her. There were so many things she could never know about him. Maybe her anger when she learned the truth would help her get over his death. He had very little hope that he'd be able to succeed at both his mission and keeping his life. But as he felt her body next to his, he desperately wanted to.

They stopped at her building, and he walked her up the steps to her door. They had so few of these nights left. Far too few. The familiar fruits and vegetables hanging in bowls of water were another testament to how very poor this city had become. Most everyone had hydroponics instead of traditional window-coverings. There were shortages in the stores far too often for a family to not at least attempt to grow food at home.

For a moment, Tage wondered how much of his human home in Ohmstave would be the same if he was able to return.

He wrapped his arms around Capacity and buried his face against her neck. "I'll miss you."

She held him back, her thin arms stronger than anyone would guess. "Your Surge training won't last all that long. I love you too much not to wait for a few weeks."

There was a lightness to her voice that he couldn't force himself to feel. "Good night."

She kissed him. "Night."

He breathed her in, feeling every piece of her lips sliding across his as he pulled away. Allowing himself to get this close to her had been a terrible mistake, but he couldn't give her up. Not now. "Night."

The walk home was cold, and Tage focused on the low hum beneath him, buried under layers of concrete. He flexed his fingers, the tips blackened from the charges he released. Once he was outfitted as a Surge Knight, he'd be able to fully take advantage of the charge in the soil around him. That would be something to experience.

"Tage," Tel'el greeted him from the doorway. "You know I don't think Capacity is a good—"

Tage held his hand up, swallowing down the disappointment of a future he couldn't have. "I know. I'm going downstairs to train."

His mother frowned as he moved aside the furniture and rug and tugged on the ring that led to the hatch.

"Our tomatoes are nearly ready," she said as she pulled her long white braid over her shoulder. "We could share one when you finish."

Tage glanced at the bowls lining their windows, the blinds closed for the night behind them. "No, thank you."

The closer he got to his mission, the longer his mother's looks lingered on him. She knew what they all did—chances for survival were slim.

He took another step down toward the familiar training space.

Goofing around on playground equipment was good practice, but it wasn't the same as really focusing on individual skills.

"I'll need to bleach your hair in the morning," his mother said. "Just a light touch-up to make sure you continue to blend in. Won't take long."

He nodded before descending the stairs to the room his family kept a secret.

Maps of the palace—the Voltaic Dava—covered one wall, and plans rested on a long and narrow table. Weapons hung neatly on another. Bars, small holes used as makeshift windows, balance beams, and a weighted bag occupied the room.

Tage wrapped his hands and immediately sideswiped the weighted bag, forcing it to swing wildly. These weren't the kind of hits he needed to practice.

Slowing his mind, focusing on the abhorrent conditions that both the soil chargers and humans lived in, Tage jumped to the floor. Push-up, push-up, push-up, jumped to his feet. Left, right, left, right punches to the bag. Jumped to balance beam one, ducking below the ceiling as he leapt to balance beam two. Landed on the floor in push-up position again. Repeat. Repeat. Repeat. Repeat.

If he didn't fail—if he was able to kill Overlord Koax—there was still a chance he could survive and live to see the world change. And a chance he could kill the overlord was a chance they had to take.

If he didn't? Not only would the humans' fate be sealed, but also his mom's and dad's. Death. Or worse: the powerline. Heck, anyone else close to him was in danger. Not that living a life as a Surge Knight was really a life anyway.

Failure wasn't an option.

He just had to work hard enough. Be strong enough. Fast enough.

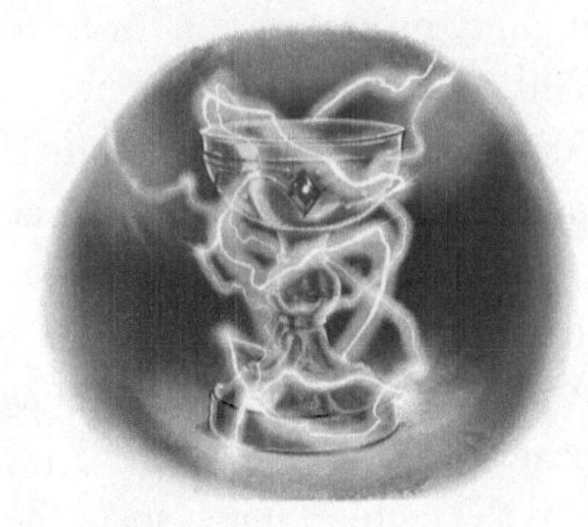

CHAPTER 2

• • • • •

Sun filtered through Tage's living room, highlighting the worn floor and sparse furniture.

Tears ran down Capacity's face. "What am I going to do?"

"Do?" Tage shook his head. His mind was spinning with information too quickly for him to formulate a response.

"How can they put my mom in jail also?!" Capacity yelled. "She didn't do anything!"

Her face twisted from anger to sadness. More tears flowed, and she buried her face in Tage's chest, soaking his T-shirt. He wrapped his arms around her and sucked in a deep breath through his nose. Lavender. He was going to miss her smell.

"Seriously," Lumen said as she readjusted on the small couch, "they already threw your dad in jail forever ago. Now your mom? This is total bull—"

"I know, Lumen," Tage interrupted. "I'm so sorry, Capacity." He stroked her hair, unsure of what to do.

He already felt guilty by association for her dad, Aeocag, going to jail. This only complicated things.

"They said"—she choked on another sob—"that since I have nowhere else to go, and I'm of age, I'm going to be drafted into the Surge Knight Program." A fresh eruption of tears broke Tage's heart. He hated seeing her like this. And worse, her life was no longer her own. Forced to dedicate herself to the overlord.

"Welcome to the club," Lumen spat. "Now we're all drafted. Go us." She twisted a small braid around her finger. "Except you, Tage. Remind me again why you volunteered? Keeping the family house seems a bit weak, as far as motivation goes. You were one of the few smart enough to enter into research rather than being stuck as a Knight or some kind of grocery or garbage worker."

"Stop, Lu," Impulse said. He folded his hands in his lap and stared forward.

Impulse had only one choice. His grades weren't nearly high enough to allow him in research, and his family needed the protection they could gain by him being a soldier.

"I thought I had escaped," Capacity said. She lifted her chin and stared at Tage with her big brown eyes full of tears. "It was going to be perfect. You'd serve as a Surge Knight, work your way up, and you'd come home to me every single night. We were going to get married and live together and have babies and . . ." Burying her face in Tage's chest again, her body continued to convulse in sobs.

Of course, Tage had known that would never be their future—at least it was a very unlikely future. But the thought of such a positive way forward had helped her hold on to hope. Now . . . she'd be forced to be transformed with the rest of them.

"How can he do this?" Lumen asked. "I hate him. I. Hate. The. Overlord." She gritted her teeth.

Hayrah walked in after unlocking the door. She paused, taking in each face in turn. "What's happened?"

Capacity lifted her tearstained face but said nothing.

"Oh," Hayrah said, her mouth tugging into a frown. "Capacity, I heard about your mother. I'm so sorry."

"It's crap, is what it is," Lumen said.

Hayrah glanced out the window and slid the blinds closed, shutting out the shafts of light.

"Shush," Hayrah said, turning a stern glare on each of them. "Please, you cannot speak like that. If anyone hears you, you know the consequences."

"Good," Capacity answered, setting her jaw. "Maybe I can share a jail cell with my mom."

An awkward silence fell over the room. Hayrah stepped into the next room, set down her things, and stood between the living room and kitchen—once again looking at each of them. Tage caught his mother's eyes, but there was a determination there he wasn't sure he'd ever seen before.

"Tage." Hayrah clasped and reclasped her hands. "Perhaps you and your friends should discuss this in the basement?"

The basement? He thought of all the precautions they'd taken over the years to make sure no one knew of the space beneath their house.

Tage shook his head slightly before a nervous laugh skittered out of his mouth. "Very funny, Mom."

"You have a basement?" Impulse's eyebrows pinched together, and he tilted his head toward his left shoulder. "I've been coming to this house since I was six. I didn't know you had a basement."

"Oh," Hayrah said. "We have more space in this home than what is apparent."

Capacity glanced around as if the door would suddenly appear. "Really? Is it a whole floor or . . ."

"Mom, what are you doing?" Tage gently pushed Capacity away, stood, and walked over to his mother.

Hayrah ignored him, moved a rug, and revealed the latch in the floor. "Go on and check it out," she said, lifting the trapdoor. "Tage will be down in a moment."

If they went down there, they'd know. They'd know who Tage was. They'd lose the opportunity to be ignorant of his plans. "Mom! No."

Lumen leapt up and stood at the top of the steep staircase. "Whoa."

"Don't go down there," Tage warned.

Lumen snorted and grinned. "Since when do I listen to you?"

Their eyes locked for a moment—Lumen's full of energetic curiosity.

"Please," Tage whispered.

But of course, Lumen trotted down the stairs.

"It's soundproof," Hayrah said as she ushered Capacity and Impulse down. "Go."

"No," Tage urged, unsure if he should be convincing his mother or his friends. Them knowing wasn't okay. His best friends being put in danger didn't sit well with him. He was doing this in part for them. "Please don't go down there . . ."

"This is wicked." Lumen's voice echoed up from the bottom. "Now I can yell all I want! Hey Overlord Koax, suck . . ." But she'd gotten deep enough that Tage couldn't hear the rest of her sentence. He knew her well enough to know the last word was "it."

"Okay," Capacity said. She wiped her tears with

the back of her hand. "We can speak freely down there. Maybe figure out a solution, you know?"

Her eyes were rimmed with red and full of desperation. Tage tried to smile, but it faltered.

"Sure," he said. "I'll be right down. Just . . ." They were about to see the plans, the people involved, maps of the Voltaic Dava, the city . . . Were there hints as to his heritage? "Don't judge, okay?"

Impulse was already halfway down the hidden stairs. Always the gentleman, he held a hand out to help Capacity, not that she needed it. It felt not like his friends had gone into a hidden room in his home, but that his whole being had been flayed open for them to inspect. His destiny, his past, his fears, his plans.

Tage grabbed his mom's wrist and led her to the kitchen.

"What are you doing?!" Tage stared at the open trapdoor. "That was our secret in case things went bad. You're going to ruin everything." He ran a frustrated hand through his brittle white hair. "The plans! They're down there alone with all the messages from the humans in Ohmstave, the layout to the assassination . . . everything!"

"Tage, calm down." Hayrah put a hand on his shoulder, using the soft, lowered voice they nearly always used at home. "Your father and I have been considering this for some time now. Currentgrad is not the same place it was when the plan was hatched. No one could have predicted Koax's paranoia would become this intense or that the Surge Knight Program would be so vast. You're going to need some help inside the castle. There are far too many Knights for you to accomplish this task alone. We've been talking about when we could possibly bring in your friends, or find someone sympathetic to our cause.

The problem is that speaking to the wrong person could have resulted in failing before we've begun."

"You want me to tell my friends who I really am?" They saw humans as savages. Beasts. Monsters intent on destroying—they'd seen enough evidence. "I should have known this was a possibility. You and Tel'el should have talked to me."

"You wouldn't have agreed." Hayrah took his hands. "Especially once you and Capacity started dating. But Tage . . ."

He blinked. Took in her worried face.

"You four have played and worked and gone to school together for years. You know one another. As your mother,"—her voice cracked—"I want to see you come out the other side of this alive. It was never fair to put this on you."

"I was the best chance," Tage argued. "Being half of each. Being raised how and where I was." Not for the first time, Tage wondered how his soil-charger birth mother had fallen in love with a human. Tension between the groups was almost as old as the history of the Saptex Sea. Though there were a few soil chargers amongst the human population—two of them had come back with him to parade as his parents.

"I've listened to you four talk," she continued. "They hate the overlord as much as the humans. And now that he's enslaving Capacity, I think this is our very best opportunity."

"My friends are not an opportunity." Tage shook his head. "Capacity is not a means to an end. We can send them home now and tell them to forget everything they saw."

His mother's face didn't change, and part of him knew he'd already lost this argument. He glanced out the back window of the house at the endless city, and the Saptex Sea beyond. The desert clung to Currentgrad from every other side. People were starving in Ohmstave, the human city, as well as here. Lives could be made so much better—everyone just needed a chance to see beyond the lies. Killing the liar was the simplest way to do that.

"Tage, be reasonable." Hayrah's tone had changed from loving to stern. "This gives all of them a chance to make a difference. And when you're successful, you and your friends and their families can flee with us to live among the humans or rogue soil chargers. It is more of a life than they would have here. We both know this is true."

He leaned over the counter, holding his head in his hands.

"Enough with the drama, Tage," she said.

Tage stiffened. She'd never spoken like this.

"I love you more than life, but you knew your life here was temporary. School, friends, girlfriends—all of it was to assimilate, become a Surge Knight, and kill Koax. If your friends mean that much to you, you'll recruit them to help."

"I don't know," Tage said. He took a deep breath but was interrupted.

"What would they say if given the choice?" Hayrah folded her arms.

Well, curses, she had him there. They both knew it. Lumen would be in without a second thought. Impulse would do anything to save his family the horror of the life in Currentgrad, and for all his quietness, he'd been the most outspoken in his hatred of Koax. Even more than Lumen—though Impulse had more family to watch suffer than the rest of them combined. Capacity . . . she was a different story, and with the complication of who her father was, would that make her more or less likely to help? He couldn't be sure.

The front door opened, and they both froze. Had his friends spoken too loudly? Had someone heard something before his mother had come home to bring the Surge Knights here?

They'd left the trapdoor open. Tage leapt toward the front room but skidded to a stop when he heard Tel'el.

"Anyone home?"

Tage released a long breath. Thank the suns it was just his dad.

"We're here," Hayrah said. "In the kitchen."

Each minute he spent upstairs with his parents was another minute his friends had to snoop around in the basement.

Tel'el walked into the kitchen and stopped short. "The door to the basement is open. Everything okay?" His attention fell on Tage. "Tage, my boy, what's wrong?"

But Tage hadn't quite found the words to express what it meant for his friends to see so much of him—all the details he'd kept hidden for most of his life. Nearly all of the life he remembered.

"Tel." Hayrah stepped forward, resting a hand on his arm. "I told him. His friends are already in the basement."

"Perfect," he said with a curt nod. "We were running out of time." He turned to Tage. "I need you to know that we've put a lot of thought into this decision. There is just barely enough poison to kill. Only a drop or two extra. And while we're aware there are other methods . . ." Tel'el sighed. "They've resulted in worse conditions for everyone involved."

At the base of everything, both his parents were saying, was the basic fact that they didn't think he could succeed. After all the work, all the late nights and training, they still didn't think he could complete the task.

"Thanks for the vote of confidence," Tage said as he moved for the trapdoor. He couldn't leave his friends alone in there for much longer. "You didn't even give me a chance."

"A chance?" Tel'el grabbed Tage by his shoulder, swung him around, and stared at him. "This isn't a game, Tage. If you fail, you die. The only reason I was allowed to live is so Koax could tout his power in front of the humans—send my broken body back to them as a warning."

Tage had heard the stories about Tel'el riding an infant ursogen into Ohmstave as a warning against future attempts. His heroic escape through the stained-glass windows in Overload Koax's palace. One faster move, a little more training, could have been the difference between him being caught or not. The scars on his face, across his back and arms, his hands—all told the story of his failure and survival. Now, he wore prosthetics not just to mask his appearance, but to cover his scars. In ten years, Tage could be Tel'el, willing to infiltrate and raise another warrior to succeed where he could not. But he would succeed. He'd trained in ways that Tel'el knew he would need to be able to accomplish their goal.

"I was lucky," Tel'el said slowly. "And that was before Koax ramped up his Surge Army. We have one chance, and one chance only. They're on the verge of a breakthrough with the drudges' brains. If the patched-together beasts can learn, if the scientists continue to make steps forward, soon they'll figure out how to extract water from the Saptex Sea. That makes humans useless, and they will kill them all. The latex isn't dangerous to the drudges like it is to us, and even if it were, he'd allow them to die if it meant water for him. The drudges aren't just defense, they're also slaves to the scientists. Right now, the only thing saving the humans is that the soil chargers can't be exposed to latex that long."

But Tage could—the human side of his body didn't react to the liquid latex at all.

Tage shuddered as he thought about the drudges—the beings made from leftover parts of deceased soil chargers, and Currentgrad's front line of resistance. Completely expendable, barely conscious, with just enough thought process to follow two-step orders. Move. Kill. Stop.

Tage turned away, but Tel'el held his chin, forcing Tage to look at him.

"No one, not even the most loyal Surge Knights, want the drudges to gain intelligence. If we kill the overlord, the creation of drudges ends with his rule. The humans and soil chargers can live freely."

"And what if my friends don't want to help? Huh?" Tage asked. "Then what?"

Hayrah leaned against the counter. "Stop acting like a child."

"I've never had a chance to be a child." Tage crossed his arms.

A flash of sadness crossed his mother's face before her gaze turned toward the floor.

Tel'el took a step back. "If your friends won't comply, we will keep them hostage in the basement until it's over. We'll release them after the overlord is dead. Right before we've made our escape. This is not up for discussion." Tel'el walked out of the kitchen and toward the stairs.

This was how Tel'el ended every argument that he had a real stake in. Say how things would work, and then walk away. Tage was reminded nearly daily of his father's military background. But even he had to admit that it would be better for his friends to be locked below than to be subject to the overlord if there was any indication that they knew of the plot. Also, he didn't think his friends would turn him in, but each of them was desperate in their own way. Unfolding a plot would save an entire family—possibly for generations.

"Plus, there's something I haven't told you," Tel'el called behind him as he started down the stairs. "It's about the powerline. Follow me. It's not wise to discuss this so freely."

The powerline. Rumors were horrific, but without entering the desert themselves, rumors were all they had. Getting caught sneaking out wasn't a possibility—not with so much on the line.

Another crack in the sky lit up the windows for a moment. Tage paused before following Tel'el down the stairs. Hayrah closed the trapdoor as she brought up the back of their three-person line. A pit formed in his stomach, as if he'd swallowed a lump of latex. He rounded the corner and saw his two friends and girlfriend standing over the long wooden table, mouths agape, staring at the carefully crafted plans.

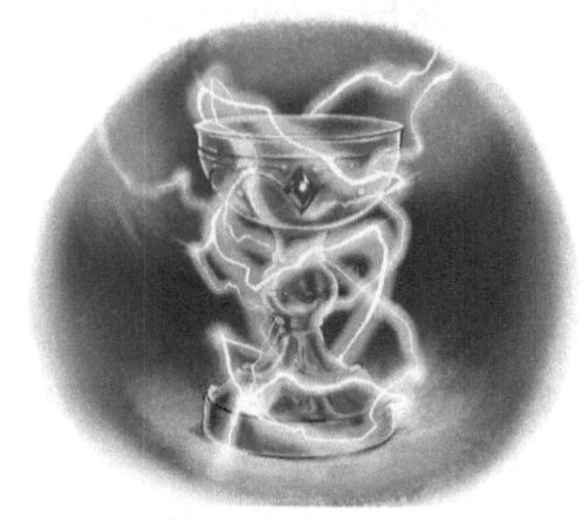

CHAPTER 3

• • • • •

Tage swallowed. He knew they hated Overlord Koax, but he was unsure of how much. Enough to help? Enough to understand why his family would have to lock them up if they didn't join him? And would Tage argue for them to join, or beg them to take a few weeks and hide in his basement? Tel'el would take every precaution to make sure his possibly trapped friends weren't able to communicate with anyone on the outside. He wouldn't hesitate to turn Tage's friends into prisoners. The mission was too important. Tage should have fought harder to keep them from going down the stairs.

"Hey, guys," Tage said, trying to keep his voice light. None of them looked up. "I see you found our plot to kill the overlord." The pitch in his voice went up an octave at the end of his sentence, as if he were telling the punchline to a joke. He cleared his throat. "Guys?"

Capacity finally raised her head and stared at him. "Is this real?"

"It is," Tel'el said as he strode toward them. "And we'd like to invite you to help."

"Whoa," Lumen said, taking a step back. "I hate that sack of crap and all, but kill, like actually murder him? He basically lives in a fortress populated by his own minions. No way."

"That's fine," Tel'el said. "No one is forcing you. But please, hear out the plan before you say no."

"I'm in," Impulse said, his eyes still on the map of the palace.

"Really?" Tage took a shocked step back. Impulse had so much to lose. So much family to care for.

"Yes," Impulse said, chin up, shoulders back.

"Before you decide . . ." Tel'el said. "Do you three remember the story of the imposter Surge Knight who tried to assassinate the overlord many years ago? Not the human who bungled his way through town before being caught, but the one who was in the palace."

Capacity's gaze moved between Tel'el and Tage. "Yes," she said carefully. "Everyone has heard some version of the urban legend."

"It wasn't a rumor." Tel'el began peeling off his rubber facial prosthetics.

Lumen gasped.

"That was me. My name isn't Array. It's Tel'el. I aligned myself with the humans after I discovered what the overlord was doing to them. Hunting them, like wild game. Forcing them to stay within the confines of their city. Killing anyone who stepped foot in the Charged Desert . . . and worse. I'm not the only soil charger who has left Currentgrad." He shook his head, gaze fixed on the floor, and peeled another prosthetic off, revealing his half-missing ear. "Ever since then, the Surge Knight army has exploded, and the overlord has become paranoid, to the point of insanity."

Tel'el finished by removing his nose.

"What are you doing?!" Lumen yelled. "That's disgusting. I think I'm going to be sick."

"Lumen!" Capacity scolded.

"What?" she asked. "He just removed his nose from his face."

"It's fake," Tage said. "Look, it's a disguise. The humans helped design it, out of latex. He's Tel'el. Come on, surely you guys have heard about him. Right?"

Tel'el so often wore his prosthetics that even Tage stared at his father's scars for a moment longer than normal.

"Yes," Impulse said. "Legend has it he broke through a stained-glass window to escape the castle and stole an ursogen from a stableman to leave the city."

Everyone turned to Capacity.

"No." Capacity shook her head. "No, no, no! My dad." Her voice cracked. "You did this! You're the reason my dad is in jail?"

Tage's heart sunk into his stomach.

Capacity's attention flashed to Tage. "Did you know? Did you know my dad's in jail because of—of . . ."

Tage just swallowed again. Of course he knew.

"This is your fault, Array, or Tel'el, whatever your name is!" Capacity yelled. "You're the reason I grew up without a dad. You!"

"I'm sorry," Tel'el said, heaving a long sigh. "I never wanted anything to happen to Aeocag."

"And you knew?" she screamed at Tage. "You pretended to care about me this whole time when you really just felt sorry for me?"

"No," Tage said. "Yes, I . . . I felt terrible, but I didn't know you were Aeocag's daughter until a few years ago. And we'd already been friends for years. I'm sorry. I'm just so sorry, about all of this." He turned to his mom. "I told you this was a terrible idea. They shouldn't be involved."

Capacity's father was the exact reason they should involve as few as possible.

"Capacity," Hayrah said, "Tage is not responsible for Tel'el's actions."

Capacity covered her face, and Lumen put an arm around her.

"I think we should go," Lumen said.

And just that fast, the girl Tage loved turned to someone else for comfort. He glanced up at his mom, who now sat on the stairs.

"Hear me out," Tel'el said. "Capacity, your dad was a part of the plan. He wanted to take down the overlord. He knew the risks. He gave me the ursogen from his stables and this." He pulled out an old dagger from his desk. "Take it, it was his."

Capacity stopped crying and took the dagger. She slowly turned it over in her hands, studying the weapon. "I don't believe you."

"Don't you think it's an odd coincidence that the overlord waited until you were sixteen and just a few days before the next Surge Knight Ceremony to charge your mom with a bogus crime?" Tel'el asked. "Leaving you to be orphaned and drafted into the program? He's still punishing your family. He won't stop."

"What does he have to gain by lying?" Tage asked, wishing he could force her to see the truth. "And I didn't know it was your dad who had helped Tel'el for years. You don't talk about him much, and when you did . . .

there was no way to explain to you without putting you in danger by telling you who I was."

"Is that all?" Capacity whispered, squinting her eyes and cocking her head to the side.

"Who are you in all of this?" Impulse said slowly, his light eyes focused on Tage.

Allowing them into the basement was exposing, but not like this. Tage never thought he'd have to tell his friends that he'd been lying since they met.

"No, no, no." Capacity sniffed. "Please, I can't take any more."

Tage took her hand in his, the familiar softness of her palm resting against his. "I'm a soil charger . . . but only half."

"Half," Lumen said flatly. "Oh gods of charge, please don't start peeling your face off, too."

"Very funny," Tage said, continuing to rub Capacity's soft hand. "I'm half soil charger and half human. Before you say anything, I know, it's not supposed to be possible. But it is, I'm living proof. I can take up the charge like you, but I can also touch latex completely unaffected like the humans. My hair is naturally black. Mom bleaches it white every few days."

Capacity continued to stare at the floor. Impulse sat back, as if mulling over the information. Lumen's eyes narrowed as she stared at Tage's head.

"I grew up in the desert and in Ohmstave," Tage said slowly, allowing them to take in the idea that he'd been partially raised in a town they'd been taught to fear. "It's a peaceful city. All they want is autonomy. They deserve that, and so do you and your families. No one should be forced to live in Currentgrad."

"You were planning this? The whole time?" Capacity pulled her hand away from Tage and wiped her nose on her sleeve. "This is too much for me. I have enough on my plate."

"It was never up to Tage," Hayrah whispered from her spot on the stairs. "It is his destiny. The first and only live birth to date. We've pinned our hope on a new future for Hadrain on my son."

Tage's shoulders slumped, and he released a long breath. "I didn't want to lie, but this—this plan—it was created by those who want better for everyone. Who believed I was the best chance of success. My whole life has been this plan, and you all gave me the small bits of normalcy that have kept me determined to succeed."

They all sat in silence for a moment. Impulse's pale brows were halfway up his forehead. Lumen scowled. Capacity still stared at the dagger in her hand.

"When he was born, his mother died," Hayrah said. "The rogue soil chargers I lived with didn't want him in their clan. His father was later murdered for courting a human. But before they could get to Tage, I took him away from the clan. We lived in the desert for a while before we went to the humans in Ohmstave and I begged them to take us in. They showed him mercy. If the overlord or any soil charger knew of his existence, he'd be murdered just for being different. Keeping his identity secret was of the utmost importance."

His mom sometimes talked about these people, Tage's birth parents, and they never felt quite real to him. Mom was real. Tel'el was real. He had no memories of any of these events—only trips to the desert with Hayrah, and the wooden boards beneath his feet in Ohmstave.

"Oh." Lumen slapped the top of the table. "That's why you're so good at school!"

All eyes turned to her.

"What?" She shrugged. "I'm just saying, everyone

knows humans have bigger brains and IQs to make up for sucking at basically everything else."

Tage's mom laughed lightly.

"We have friends in the city," Tel'el said, still focused on the task. "Soil chargers willing to help keep your families safe."

Impulse nodded slowly, and Tel'el nodded back.

"I'm sorry for lying to you guys," Tage said. "I hope you get why I had to."

"I understand," Impulse said, his brows twitching. "And I'm still willing to fight with you. No one here is living. We're only existing. Remember a few years ago when my brother died during the Surge Knight Ceremony? Death has become so common, no one mourns. No one matters. Lives are meaningless. He was forced into the program, and the overlord's carelessness killed him. My younger brothers and sisters have a few years before they can be recruited. I need to act before they're drawn in too. I'm ready for this."

Tage opened his mouth, but nothing came out. It was the most he'd ever heard Impulse say at one time.

"Well, I'm not in." Lumen sat back and shook her head. "You guys go do your crazy mission, I'm out. Let's go Capacity." She headed for the stairs, but Mom stood, blocking her path. There weren't many times when Tage remembered how incredibly strong his mother was, but as she stood blocking the stairs, sparks dripping from her fingers. He was fairly certain that her training could keep the two of them down here without anyone's help.

"There's more," Tel'el said, and the two stopped. "The powerline. You've all heard the rumors, I assume?"

Capacity and Lumen stood together at the bottom of the stairs. Tage knew his mother was ready to bring the hatch down if they tried to run. They knew too much.

Tage would never be forgiven—by either of them—if that was how they had to move forward.

"The powerline rumors are true," Tel'el said. "The overlord convinced the other two terraregions it was time to harness the power from Anoths and Cathos, and to stop giving it away for free. By creating a powerline that connects these two poles of Hadrain, they can suck up all the power, and distribute the charge equally to the regions. But the respective overlords can distribute it as they see fit. Tax it. Limit it. Do whatever they want. It gives them control, and Koax is trying to sell the idea. Once the powerline is finished—and they're close—the three overlords will have power over everything. Conditions will worsen. Once they learn how to get water from the humans' Saptex Sea, a whole race of people will be destroyed."

"What does that have to do with me?" Capacity shifted her weight and her arms loosened across her chest. She was at least beginning to consider Tel'el's words.

"It's everything your dad was fighting against," Tel'el said. "They're enslaving humans."

Enslaving humans? This hadn't been brought up before. Not once. Tage thought he had been fighting against keeping them in horrifying conditions and living in fear. But the people of Currentgrad were living in the same oppression.

"What?" Tage asked. "How? Why?"

"So, he keeps secrets from you too?" Capacity asked. "This family is nothing but a bunch of liars."

"No, Overlord Koax is the liar," Tel'el said. "The Surge Knights are hunting humans, putting them into a powerline, their bodies hooked to each other, legs plunged into the sand. The bodies of the soil chargers who have displeased Koax suck up charge from the desert, then pass them from person to person. He's building power storage facilities at both Anoths and Cathos—both of the planet's poles as well as smaller storage banks at specific points between. His hope is to attach the opposite poles, which would put him in control of all of the power on Hadrain. Koax sold this idea by telling the other overlords that the humans have volunteered their old, sick, and criminals to the line. It's an eternal prison, and they're in a trance, mildly aware of their hell."

"No way the humans volunteered," Tage said, horrified. "How could anyone believe that someone would sign up for that kind of torture?"

Hayrah sighed. "Remember, it's not just humans. Soil chargers who step out of line are also placed along the powerline. Koax has promised that once the powerline is complete, and Anoths and Cathos are connected, the charge will be removed from the soil, and plants will flourish like they do on other planets. Rich grains and fresh fruits and vegetables."

"Is that true?" Impulse asked. "We'd have our own farms? Not just hydroponics? Like . . . we'd be able to plant in the actual ground?"

"I don't know," Hayrah said. "And neither does the overlord. His goal is to keep the humans under his thumb, toss away the difficult soil chargers, and sell the electricity emitting from the soil. Think about what life without charge beneath you would feel like."

Tage couldn't imagine.

"I don't believe for one second he'll distribute it to the other terraregions for free," Tel'el said.

Tage's frustration built into a knot. This was why he'd agreed to his assignment. Even at six, he'd known that life had to change, and that resolve had only grown as he experienced life in Currentgrad after also experiencing it in Ohmstave. "If he finishes the powerline and connects Anoths and Cathos,"—Tage shook his head—"that will make him the only ruler of the planet."

Each terraregion could pull some charge from the soil to power the cities, but the regions near Anoths drew from there, and the regions from Cathos drew from Cathos. If Koax tied that energy together, those regions would have to come to him for electrical power.

"If he's capturing humans this way," Lumen said, "is that why they're always withholding water? Why we always have shortages?"

"There are no water shortages." Tel'el's jaw twitched in a way that made Tage know he was doing everything he could to not yell. "It's all made up by him to make soil chargers hate humans."

Lumen sat back. "But we've been dealing with shortages for years. And now you just want us to believe that it's all been some big lie to make us hate the humans? We've barely held them off for years."

"More lies." Hayrah shook her head slowly. "The humans may be known more for their ideas and technology, but when you teased Tage and said that's all humans are known for, you're not far from the truth."

Tage had known this bit, at least. But brains only allowed a culture to go so far when their other needs were so miserly delivered by Koax.

"But the raids early on in Koax's reign. Us being safe because of the rise of the Surge Knights . . ." Capacity trailed off.

Tage ached for the confusion in her eyes. This was a lot to take in all at once. He'd always known the true nature of both soil chargers and humans, having the benefit of growing up around both.

Capacity's tear-filled eyes trained on Tage. "Is this

true?" she whispered. "The humans are weaker? They're not withholding water?"

"Yeah," Tage answered.

Impulse sighed, still staring at the map tracing a corridor of the Voltaic Dava. His bald head glistened with sweat in the dim-lit basement.

"Why didn't you say anything sooner?" Lumen demanded.

"Oh, come on." Tage shoved his hands in his pockets. "You've heard the occasional soil charger on the street corners talking about how we're being lied to. Then what? They disappear."

And now Tage knew they had probably been placed in some grotesque form of a living powerline.

"And you couldn't risk drawing attention to yourself," Impulse said quietly, before tapping the table and the plans. "Because of the plan."

"Exactly," Hayrah said.

"How are you both so involved?" Lumen asked. "You're soil chargers. How did you learn the truth?"

Lumen was still sorting through all the information. Probably trying to decide if they were lying to her or not.

"I used to spend a lot of time in the desert, and like I said, I watched how horribly the humans were treated," Tel'el said. "I finally decided I was going to do something about it. I aligned with the humans, became a Surge Knight, and then failed at my mission."

"So you're making Tage try and right your wrong?" Capacity asked. "You have prosthetics. Why can't you go in and do this?"

Tel'el shook his head. "I'd be discovered almost immediately."

"But he's like a son to you," Capacity said. "I can tell. How could you risk him on this—"

"He *is* my son," Tel'el spat.

"I chose this life. This plan." Tage looked at each of his friends in turn. "I choose this still now. And he's right, he has trained me but also been a father to me. Hayrah is the only mother I've known."

"I grew up in the desert," Hayrah added. "Lived with the humans for years. They've lived in conditions much like Currentgrad is now, but for many years longer."

None of Tage's friends spoke for a moment.

"Overlord Koax needs to be stopped," Impulse said. "I'm in."

Lumen twisted a finger around a thin white braid. "I have a lot to sort out, guys. I just . . ."

"I'm being forced to be a Surge Knight no matter what," Capacity said. "Unless . . . can you get me out of the city?"

Tage's heart stilled. *Could we smuggle her out?* As soon as the thought entered his mind, he knew they couldn't risk being caught doing something so rash. Especially not so close to carrying out his plan.

"You can hide in our basement until this is over," Tel'el offered.

Capacity swallowed.

"I can't do nothing." Lumen's gaze moved around the room—from the plans to the weapons, to the crude bars and balance beams Tage had been using for training. "I never liked him; I just never realized how evil he was."

"You have a better chance with more of you," Tel'el said. "The more of you who agree to help, the better everyone's chances are."

"Only Tage has years more training than we do," Impulse said.

"Yeah." Lumen snorted. "Because he's half wimpy human."

Impulse cracked a smile, and Tage took his first real breath since walking down the stairs.

"Let's get food and go over details," Tel'el suggested.

Tage's attention rested on Capacity. Her attention rested on the floor. The best option for her would be to stay in this basement until they'd succeeded. Failure wasn't an option.

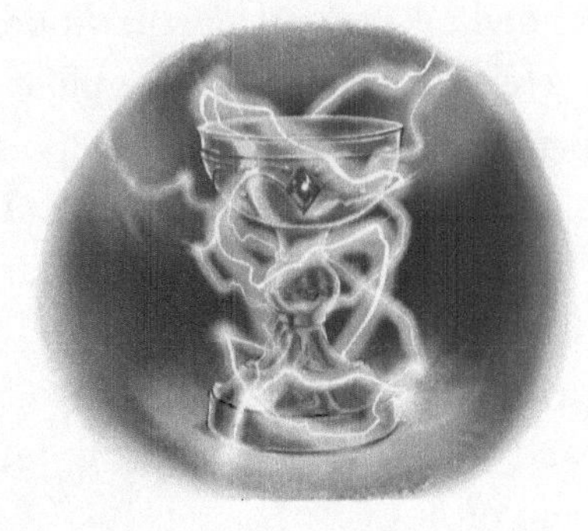

CHAPTER 4

• • • • •

Tage stared at the bowl of protein porridge that Hayrah had brought down. His stomach couldn't settle enough to eat. His mission had faded in and out as a thing that would actually happen. Moving from theoretical stages, to planning stages, to contingency plans, and now this: laying out the plan for his friends. They'd reached a new level, and the importance of Tage's mission was truly becoming real.

"Capacity," Tel'el said quietly, "I'm sorry again about your parents. Once the assassination is over, I vow to break them out of jail."

"And if Tage fails?" she asked quietly.

"He won't," Tel'el said.

Impulse scraped the bottom of his bowl with his spoon. Tage was about to hand his friend his own bowl. "There's always a chance for failure." Impulse's eyes met Tage's. "But I'm in. I said I was in. After learning more, I'm still in. More people allows for a better chance of success. Let's take him down."

Capacity's bowl hit the table as she stood and walked to the wall where more details of the palace hung. The room where Tage hoped to distribute the poison. The different ways in and out of the kitchen area. The servants' passages. The main hallways. He could redraw the map of the Voltaic Dava in his sleep.

"Take your time," Hayrah said. "But Capacity, you have talents and strength, and they're recruiting you whether you help or not."

"Unless I'm held here," she responded.

The room fell silent. Tage glanced up at Lumen, who gave him a small shrug. If Lumen couldn't follow her friend's reasoning, Tage surely couldn't.

"Give me a second." Capacity paced back and forth in the small room. "I think . . . I don't know, I mean . . ." She pulled her hair free from her ponytail and rubbed her hands through her long white hair. "Ugh!" she yelled. "This is not how I'm supposed to be living my life."

Tage tried to touch her hand, but she yanked it away.

She turned to him. "Everyone I love is in jail."

He swallowed, allowing her meaning to fully wash over him. He wasn't in jail. She no longer loved him. Was this the inevitable end, when they could have had weeks still? Possibly more if all went to plan?

"He must be stopped," Impulse said as he drove one fist into the other.

"Okay." Lumen leaned forward, placing her elbows on the table. "What's your grand plan, anyway?"

"Poison," Hayrah said. "I've spent the last ten years extracting it from shock worms."

"Whoa," Lumen said, raising an eyebrow. "No wonder you had to wait ten years. It must have taken that long to get enough from those slippery little suckers."

"It has," Hayrah said. "And we have barely a little more than necessary to kill just him."

"It's true," Tage added. "After we become Surge Knights, we'll automatically be assigned to night shift until they find us a permanent post. Every night, the overlord has a drink and snack before bed. We'll need to wait and watch until we see his meal left unattended. That's when we'll strike. We'll slip it in his chalice, he'll drink it and die in his sleep. We'll hang around the Voltaic Dava until they confirm it, then we'll sneak out of the castle and out of Currentgrad before they make the announcement the next day. If we run right away, our guilt will be obvious."

"Where would we go?" Capacity asked.

"The humans have offered us safe haven in Ohmstave for as long as we'd like," Tel'el responded.

"Wait." Lumen sat back. "I don't think I want to live with humans." Her attention shifted to Tage. "No offense."

"Then you can live on your own in a different terraregion, or try to find a rogue soil-charger camp," Tel'el said. "You'll have help."

"Those are my only choices?" Lumen asked. "So I'm going to risk my life, but know for sure I'll have to leave Currentgrad?"

Hayrah sighed. "Lumen, the fallout after the overlord is killed could take a while to simmer down. Your families will go into hiding, and we will get them out. There will be a struggle to know how to move forward with power plays in the works, but we're sure that without Koax, we'll be able to make the soil chargers here listen to reason. And another thing: We will have to figure out a way to balance the charge with the desert."

Lumen rubbed her eyes.

"My family," Impulse said softly.

"Impulse," Tel'el said, leveling his gaze on him, "we will do everything we can to keep your family safe. I promise that after what's happened to Capacity's family, our sympathizers will make all of your families a priority. They'll be safer with our protection than moving forward without it."

"Unless I'm seen as a loyal Surge Knight," Lumen said, but her face immediately fell. "But knowing what I do . . ."

"Lumen," Tage said, "do you want to stay here? And be a Surge Knight forever? I know I don't."

"No." Lumen anxiously twirled a thin braid. "No, I guess I don't."

"You guess?" Tel'el asked. "If you're not completely positive, then don't do it."

"No," she said. "I'm in. My parents already said their goodbyes to me. They're positive I won't make it through the Surge Knight transformation." She stared at her nails dismissively. "But whatever, they're probably right."

"You're one of the toughest people I know," Tage said. "You'll make it."

"When?" Impulse asked.

"The Surge Knight Ceremony is in one week," Tage said.

They all already knew this, of course. The date had been looming for a while.

"We'll train together," Tel'el assured them. "And we'll make sure your bodies are as healthy as possible before transforming."

Tage had taken years to come to terms with the way the new biotech implants would be shoved into and onto his body. So had Impulse. The idea was slightly newer for Lumen, and he could imagine it was shocking to Capacity. He could only imagine what it would feel like to be drafted into being a Surge Knight, when you'd spent a lifetime believing you'd never follow that path.

"After we're . . . altered," Tage said carefully, "we'll take some time to heal. In that time, we can memorize the guard change, watch the kitchen and servant staff. Hopefully within a week or two, the overlord will be dead, and we'll be gone from Currentgrad until a more sane leadership has formed."

Lumen nodded; her smile twisted into a sly grin. "Poison the old bastard!"

"Okay, then." Impulse clapped his hands with a grin. "Let's bring on this food that's supposed to make us bigger and stronger." He lifted his bowl. "We could start with second helpings?"

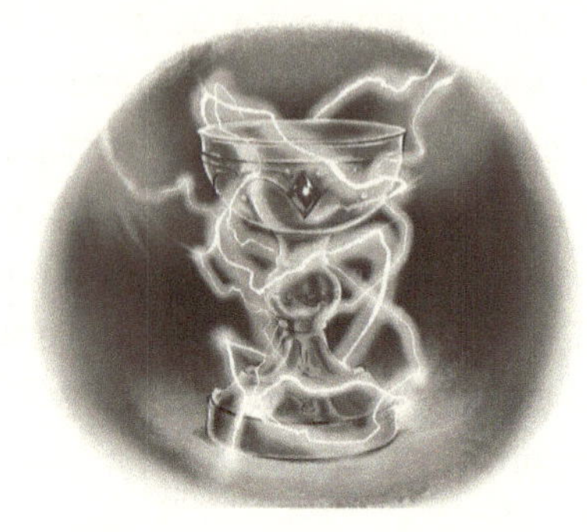

CHAPTER 5

· · · · ·

Tage sat with a burlap robe draped over his half-naked body. The moist air in the basement of the castle made his skin clammy. He shivered. He had volunteered to go first. Since he'd nearly always known what his fate would be, he'd been preparing for longer than his friends. Lumen tapped her feet, her eyes darting around the small room. Her burlap robe hung to the floor, the hem sitting in a small puddle of water. Impulse's robe was too small, so he sat like a twisted tree trunk, with his legs crossed tight. Capacity sat next to Tage, not making eye contact.

The past week had been filled with tense meetings, brutal workouts, and contingency plan after contingency plan. But they all knew once the poison had been placed, it was just a waiting game. Ten years of painstakingly difficult work would rest in a single cup.

Rows of small doors held Surge Knights' uniforms. Ursogen leather made up the sleeves, with clasps over the back and neck. This left the back exposed so they could wear a rubber back piece. Each Surge had a custom piece made from rubber. If they died on a mission, it made them easier to identify. Everyone had twenty-four red LED lights screwed into their spine that could be seen through small holes in the rubber back piece. They wore suede pants with tufts of ursogen hair and were protected at the front by breastplates made of stiff leather, steel, or a combination of the two.

Tage tapped his foot, and tugged at the burlap robe. They'd been silent for longer than he could handle. He'd just opened his mouth to speak when Lumen shifted on the bench.

"This castle is so drab. Vol-ta-ic Da-va." Lumen drew out her words. "More like Voltaic Crapa. Who names their castle, anyway?" she huffed.

Capacity rested her head on Tage's shoulder, and he felt his heart swell.

Her lavender scent and lithe body calmed his nerves, and he was selfishly glad she was with them. He wished they could have a lifetime together. And in just mere days, that could come true. Maybe.

"How are you feeling, Tage?" Impulse asked. He rested a boot on the bench and sat his elbows on his thighs as he leaned forward.

"I'm okay," Tage answered. "I'm a little nervous to go first, but I've been preparing for a long time." He paused for a moment. "I hate that I dragged you into this."

"We were all coming anyway," Impulse said as he straightened. "At least for the transformation part."

"Your butt puckering from fear yet?" Lumen asked with a smirk.

Tage rolled his eyes.

"That's so crude," Capacity said, stifling a giggle. "Do you have to be crass all the time?"

Her voice was about two notes higher than usual—a testament to how afraid she was.

"Crude's my middle name," Lumen said, twisting a tight braid with her finger.

Tage's leg bounced. He was shoeless, and the cold, damp rock floor sent a shiver up his body. The foundation for the castle was made of the dark pulse-dune rock. Sitting on the equally cold stone bench in the middle of a locker room, his feelings were once again mixed—grateful his mission was finally beginning, sad to know a whole chunk of his life was now over.

Tage stood and walked to his assigned locker. He removed the back piece from the locker and ran his finger over the detailing.

"Wow, that's . . . what is it?" Impulse asked. "Did we see this already?"

Tage immediately lowered his head and felt his face warm.

The outburst from the normally quiet Impulse made him laugh. "Here, take a closer look." He handed it to Impulse.

Lumen grabbed it out of Impulse's hand and ran her fingers over the surface. Small bolts of electricity jumped from her to the surface and back again. "That looks like a piece of crap. Congratulations, you're going to have a giant turd covering your back."

"Come on now," Tage said. "You don't like the design?"

"No," Lumen said flatly.

Capacity shook her head and sighed.

"You know," Tage said, "you're lucky we like you, Lumen, or you wouldn't have any friends."

"I'm an acquired taste." She lifted her chin. "Just like your hideous back piece."

He had taken great care to stain the rubber backing dark brown to match the other ursogen leather pieces on the uniform. Most people didn't bother with that detail until after their first year of service. Tage wouldn't have a year. As soon as the poison was delivered to him at the barracks, he'd need to move forward. To have it discovered before he was able to act was unthinkable.

Impulse scratched his bald head and pointed to the back piece.

"How did you think of that design?"

"I saw it when I was a kid," Tage replied. "It was in an old book the elders of Ohmstave kept under lock and key."

The animal had talons and held a dagger in its left foot. It had two wings and a beak that was open, as if it was frozen in the middle of screeching.

"I can't remember exactly, but I think it was called an igle or eagle or something. Yeah, eagle. That's it!" Tage said. "It *was* a bird of some sort. I think it represents freedom."

"Newsflash," Lumen said, then rolled her eyes, "they probably still exist on some other planet."

"I've never seen one," Impulse said. "Good job, Tage. I didn't do anything fancy on my back piece. I only engraved my name on it."

"Me, too," Capacity said.

Down the sides where his midback would be ran two corrugated pillars that bent at the end toward the hole.

"Hmm." Capacity put her hands on her hips.

"What?" Tage asked.

"Nothing," Capacity said, frowning. "It draws attention to you. Is that really what you want? Considering . . ."

"Whatever," Tage snapped, "it's fine."

He took the back piece and shoved it in his locker. Then he flipped a dangling suede pant leg back into his locker before slamming the door.

He plopped onto the stone bench again and let the thick, awkward silence settle in. He didn't want to fight with Capacity. But he assumed she was still mad, and coupled with the impending ceremony, he knew he couldn't win. Admittedly, he justified it as nervousness. The last thing he wanted was to blow the whole plan just before the assassination.

"Sorry," Tage mumbled.

He breathed deep through his nostrils and sighed. His slumped shoulders itched under the burlap robe, fueling his level of irritation. A well of emotions burst and he leaned over, propping his elbows on his knees, squeezing his fist on his right hand.

"No." Capacity grasped his hand in hers. "I'm sorry."

She had tears in her eyes. He'd seen her cry more in the last week than he had in the ten years he'd known her. He squeezed her hand, reveling in the feel of her skin against his.

"It's okay," Tage said. "I'm just trying to fight off my nerves. This is going to suck."

"It will be worth it," Impulse said.

"We'll get your parents back, Capacity," Tage whispered softly. He tilted her chin up with his index finger until he met her eyes. "I promise."

Her nod was faint as she leaned closer and pressed her lips to his. Tage breathed her in as he pulled away.

He glanced back at the other group of four that had entered—one girl and three guys, huddled on the other side of the room.

"Hey, we don't want them to hear," Tage whispered, moving his brow toward the other group of kids.

Impulse sat next to Capacity, and Lumen sat next to Tage. They all put their arms around each other.

"We're going to get through this together," Lumen said.

"Our lives are about to change forever," Tage said. The transformation was just the first piece.

"I wish we didn't have to get all twenty-four LED lights inserted at once," Capacity mumbled.

"It's the lamest thing ever," Lumen said. "It seems like a little overkill."

"I think it makes the whole system work. One for each vertebra," Tage said. "Linking up the charge cells like that is how we will be able to shoot all three ignitions with one charge. I agree, though, it seems like a lot. But there's no way around it."

They were far past the point of being able to change their minds without going to prison.

Or the powerline.

The room opened, and a drudge shuffled in, scraping the soles of its feet across the uneven stone floor. It had two eyes, although they weren't evenly spaced or aligned on its face. Its skin sagged, except for around its snub nose, which had been pulled high and tight, like a pig. A sign surging with electricity spelled Tage's name. Behind the drudge were two more drudges pushing a metal gurney.

"We'll stay with you as long as possible," Capacity said.

He stared at her for a moment. Her pale skin. White hair. Worried eyes. "I love you," he whispered, as his heart thumped in his ribcage.

She kissed Tage softly on the lips before they pulled him away.

"Are you ready?" Impulse asked with a sideways smirk.

"Always," Tage answered, while inside, he screamed. *This is it! This is it! This is it!*

• • •

The overlord's drudges wheeled Tage down an uneven stone hallway. He had been strapped face down, and his cheeks dug into a wooden, U-shaped face rest. The burlap robe draped open, exposing his back. Another shiver ran through his body, covering his skin in gooseflesh.

The wheels squeaked and bounced along the uneven stone floor as the abominations pushed him. Their bare feet slapped as they maneuvered the gurney. Tage stared at one of their feet—six toes. The additional appendage jutted unnaturally off to the side.

Lumen, Capacity, and Impulse would all have to go through what he was about to endure. He cringed.

His heart raced, and fear prickled across his skin. Blinking hard, he pushed away his trepidation. He'd been made for this. Trying to get comfortable, he squirmed under the straps. *Why'd they strap me down? I'm here voluntarily.*

Tage tried to look around, but the head strap prevented any such movement.

"You've got this, son." Tel'el's voice came from somewhere to his left, but his head couldn't turn far enough to see him. Tage wondered how and why his parents were allowed in the hallway on the way to the ceremony.

"We love you," his mom whispered from even closer. His gaze darted around on the floor, but he couldn't catch a glimpse.

His stomach churned. He wasn't sure if it was from

the nerves or being facedown while being wheeled into the room. Sweat dripped from his naked armpits and pooled near his chest, his very own cesspool. As soon as they entered the center of the operating-room amphitheater, chatter from the audience stopped. He tried to look up, but only succeeded in straining his neck.

Blinking, Tage tried to find his parents in the crowd, but his head couldn't move enough. He couldn't see past the persons on either side of him as the drudges slogged their way to the center of the room, towing Tage along with them.

"Welcome," the overlord's voice boomed, echoing through the room.

Tage silently winced.

He had witnessed the creation and transformation of Surge Knights in the past. The amphitheater was one of the larger rooms in the castle, not only big in square footage, but also multiple stories tall. But like most rooms in the Voltaic Dava, it had no windows. The dark room was bright with sizzling artificial light. The entire operating room was a half-circle shape that had four tiers of dark pulse-dune stone seats with backs made from the wood of rubber trees.

"We have a full house tonight," the overlord said. His voice bounced off the walls in the massive room. "Thank you for coming to support the Surge Knight Ceremony. And drudges, please properly position our subject."

Alone, Tage suddenly felt colder, more vulnerable. Again, he pushed those thoughts aside. This was an opportunity. Once a Surge, he'd have physical access to the overlord. The ruthless leader was giving him the key to his assassination.

Tage's heart beat faster. He breathed quick, as if he'd been running for hours.

The drudges situated Tage's operating gurney in the middle of the stone room and secured the wheels with rusted chains bolted to the floor. A long, rectangular wooden box the length of his gurney sat underneath. Sawdust plumed as Tage released a pensive breath. Dried blood stained the sides and the bottom. Tage's stomach contracted the second he inhaled the putrid smell of dried blood left over from previous ceremonies. He tried to breathe through his mouth, but the smell of death was too strong.

Another shiver came over his body as he focused on holding still. The last thing he wanted was to become paralyzed like so many had during the surgery. A horrible way to live out life in Currentgrad.

Tage closed his eyes.

"We are gathered here today to induct more Surge Knights into the courts of the Voltaic Dava," the overlord said, his voice booming throughout the room.

Such a large voice for such a frail man.

Tage pictured Overlord Koax's pale skin and thin arms waving at the audience while he stood on frail, bony legs hidden under an elaborate black and silver cloak.

"I'm eternally grateful for all the faithful soil chargers that support this righteous cause. We must stay one step ahead of the humans."

This garnered a small eruption of applause from the audience.

Tage gritted his teeth. He couldn't believe the falsehoods the overlord had spun over the years. Everyone in Currentgrad followed the crazy ruler in blind obedience. And those who didn't found themselves in prison, or worse. Thoughts of being stuck in the sand to help Koax gather and conduct electricity strengthened his resolve once more. He hoped that Impulse would think of his family during the procedure, that Capacity could think of freeing her parents, and that Lumen could use her stubbornness to help fight off the fear.

"Today, we will be performing the life-altering procedure on Tage Gradient, son of Array and Hayrah Gradient."

Tage's back muscles tightened as the overlord stroked the skin there. His sharp, black fingernails traced a line down his spine.

"Drudges, if you please," the overlord said, "let the ceremony begin!"

This time, loud and excited cheers filled the cavernous room.

To Tage's right, he heard squeaking wheels. The front part of caterpillar tracks from a machine stopped directly under his face. He'd seen this as a spectator. He knew it was the menacing machine that assisted the insertion of the LED lights. All of the research and recon was coming to life for him.

He imagined the steps he had seen at other Surge Ceremonies. First, a wooden arm with a steel blade at the end would hum with turning pulleys. This would cut the skin and notch each bony vertebra, allowing the LED charger cells to fit snugly under his skin. This part scared him the most, even though the LEDs were small. If he were to become paralyzed, the mission would fall to his friends.

The machine cranked to life.

It had begun.

Tage clinched his fists and clenched his teeth together so hard that he thought his molars would explode into powder.

Each slice on his tender skin ignited every nerve in his body. Sweat pooled around his face. But he didn't move. He knew what came next. Time to implant the lights. A clunky machine with a wooden arm that held a screw-driver on the end was wheeled inches from Tage's table.

He heard the whir of a spinning screwdriver moments before he felt the overlord part his skin, exposing his spine for the machine. Every nerve in his backbone awak-ened, and a cold draft felt like red-hot needles stabbing into his exposed flesh. He could hear his bones creaking as the light was twisted into his spine. The pain was fan-tastic. His vision clouded—a sign of passing out. Blood dripped down his neck, through the U-shaped face rest, and accumulated in the sawdust box. In that moment, he focused on it as the trickle became a constant flow. The copper scent of his own warm blood sent a wave of nausea through him.

By the fourth vertebral LED, Tage had started count-ing his inhales and exhales to even his heart rate. Just as he counted to eight, the drill arm wrenched and screeched to a stop. The smell of smoke filled his nose. *Bone dust?* Tage thought. *No, machine oil . . .* The crowd gasped, which made his already fast-beating heart thump even harder. Murmurs ensued as the overlord rushed past him, his robes painting cold blood along the skin of Tage's rib-cage.

The drill slipped forward, cutting the strap holding his head and nicking his ear. He lifted his head. Coming out of his pain-induced trance, his eyes darted from side to side, trying to figure out what happened.

"You imbecile!" the overlord yelled. He pushed aside a group of drudges as he made his way to the back of the machine.

Blood from Tage's nicked ear dripped into his right eye. He blinked wildly to clear his eye of blood, then he turned his head to his right.

"That drudge is getting electrocuted!" a spectator yelled.

That isn't part of the plan! What's happening?

Panicked, Tage twisted his face at the sight. He squinted, trying to get his brain to process what he was seeing. A drudge had been plugged into the machine, powering it. Its body tensed and lurched as it was overloaded with electricity. Tage planted his face back into the cradle, away from the carnage.

"Are you paralyzed?" the overlord asked Tage.

Tage tried to answer, but words didn't come. *No, I can't be. I'm close to the end.*

The overlord rushed to him and leaned down. "Can you breathe?"

Tage took a deep breath. His eyes were wide.

"Good. Are you paralyzed?"

With a dry and shaky voice, Tage found the words. "I . . . I don't know, Overlord Koax."

"Drudges!" the overlord commanded. "Unstrap the right leg."

Cold, callused hands pawed at his calf as the drudges unstrapped his leg.

The overlord leaned down again, his thin, white face filling Tage's vision. "Lift your right leg."

Doing as he was told, Tage lifted and bent his leg at the knee.

"Exquisite!" the overlord said. "Not paralyzed! Back to work!" The overlord cleared his throat.

Hayrah gasped from somewhere in the audience.

The drudges could now hold charge? Koax had come a long way with them—or his researchers had. Time was definitely running out. He needed to be stopped.

"Drudges," the overlord said, "please remove Hayrah

Gradient. She may return once she has her emotions under control."

Tage's trepidation turned to rage, and he vowed to get through the ceremony. He wished he could be there when the poison took effect. A small smirk crept onto Tage's face as he imagined the overlord writhing in pain before he died.

The overlord left Tage and grabbed the trembling drudge behind the machine. Tage watched in horror as the drudges restrapped his leg again. Then, Overlord Koax yanked the dying drudge from the chair mounted to the back of the contraption. He ripped a thick plug from the drudge's chest, a six-inch-long forged metal spear sparked as the drudge slumped. Lifeless. Throwing the plug onto the floor, he grabbed the drudge's throat and pulled. Its trachea sparked in the overlord's clenched fist. He discarded it to the floor, and it came to rest near the live plug. He lifted his slender leg and pushed the drudge out of the seat. The servant flopped as its skull cracked on the rough stone floor.

The drudges weren't just holding a charge—they'd become small, portable generators.

The overlord pointed to a drudge standing on the edge of the operating amphitheater and beckoned it to approach with the twitch of his bony index finger. It shuffled toward the overlord. Overlord Koax picked it up by the straps holding its chest armor and threw it into the chair.

"Stay!"

He scooped the plug up off the ground, and with the quickness of lightning, he jammed it into the drudge's chest directly through the armor. Sparks cascaded from the charred chest hole to the ground. The abomination squealed as it thrashed violently. The overlord grabbed its shoulder and shoved it back into the chair of the machined contraption. In the end, it did what it was told and sat in the chair.

Tage turned away. The spectators quietly chatted amongst themselves.

"My apologies," the overlord said. "Sometimes one's creations don't do exactly what they were created for. But on the bright side, you all got more of a show than you were anticipating."

Tage hoped Capacity's transformation would go far more smoothly.

"Tage, do you wish to continue?" the overlord asked. "Afterall, you volunteered for this program."

Tage turned toward the overlord, this time resting his cheek on the headpiece. A wave of nausea washed over him. He took a deep breath and made hard eye contact with the soulless man. "Let's finish this."

The overlord snapped his fingers at two drudges grouped where the last one was. "You and you, come hold his head."

Tage turned back and stared straight into the blood-soaked sawdust box as silent tears streamed down his face. He'd do anything for his friends not to endure what he just had. His only consolation was the thought that once Koax was dead, the ceremonies would cease as well. He had to focus on the mission.

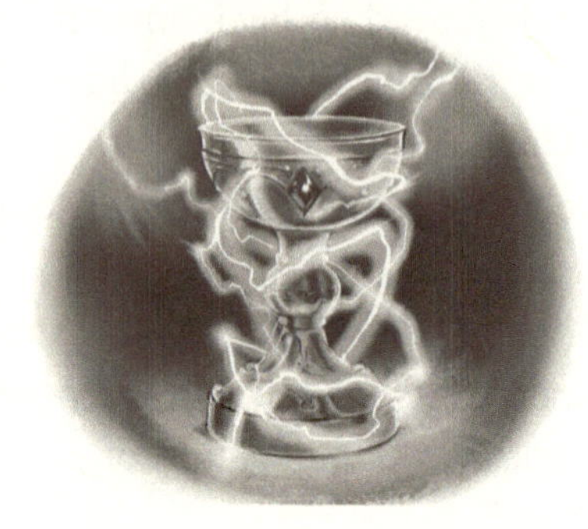

CHAPTER 6

• • • • •

Once all the LED charging cells were inserted, the same machine stapled up the back skin incisions, leaving twenty-four tiny, indestructible red bulbs exposed down Tage's spine. He took deep, even breaths, trying to calm himself.

The drudges held his head, unstrapped his body from the operating gurney, and flipped him onto his back. Pain shot through his spine in sharp spikes of fiery heat. His back arched, and he bit his lip, stifling a scream. There was no precedence, no clue as to how a half human would handle the implants. He regretted talking his friends into this. The sacrifice should have been his to bear. He held onto the thought that his friends were with him no matter how they came to this horrible ceremony.

"Sit him up," the overlord yelled. "Idiots."

They positioned him seated, with his feet dangling over the side. Electric charge tingled his legs and pulsed through his palms. A familiar sensation after charging from soil. He scanned the crowd. At some point, his mom must have returned, because she sat next to Tel'el, eyes rimmed with red.

The overlord slowly approached Tage. "The rings." He opened his hand, exposing a pale palm, but never broke eye contact with Tage. A drudge deposited forged silver rings into his hand. "Young Tage, you've come so far. Now, we must enhance your ability to draw charge from the soils of Hadrain."

Of all the details to run the city, the overlord was always present as new Surge Knights were transformed—a sadist to the end.

He pushed a ring onto Tage's index finger, but his skin bunched at the knuckle, preventing the ring from continuing down his finger. The old ruler forced it over the skin, filleting apart layers of flesh. Fresh drops of blood dripped off Tage's fingertip, and he finally cried out through clenched teeth, in both shock and pain. He squinted, then forced himself to relax his face. Show no expression.

Overlord Koax continued to stare him down with a wicked smile, metal denture teeth framed by thin purple lips, all while forcing rings onto each finger. This was no mistake. They'd taken measurements of his fingers when they'd outfitted him for the uniform. This bit of torture was a powerplay. A show that the overlord could and would have his way.

While Tage was able to maintain his composure outwardly, his chest rapidly rose and sank. Would there be a point when the overlord would see through to his half-human self? A sign that would show his true nature?

Long wires dangled from the rings, adorned with a small, barbed hook at the end. The overlord finally broke eye contact. Tage followed his gaze to his own hand. The old man twisted the wire around his finger, then untwisted it, as if he wasn't sure what to do with it. Then, he struck as quickly as a shock worm, plunging the barb into the soft skin on the top of his hand, thus connecting the ring to his body. Tage sucked in a sharp breath. More blood trickled down the side of his hand and dripped onto the floor, as if it had been dipped into red candle wax.

The overlord rubbed a fresh blood spot on the coarse stone floor with his bare foot and said, "Pity. The drudges forgot to move the blood collection box."

He harpooned the next four fingers on Tage's hand quickly. Each time, he pressed on the fresh wound, almost eliciting a scream or curse word from Tage.

Tage stared at his pierced hand in disbelief. The LED lights, he expected to hurt. But this? No way could he have prepared himself for the fresh hell Koax had unleashed upon him. Would Tage's friends be treated the same? Or had Tage's reputation as a stellar student preceded him, encouraging the overlord to be harsher to the kid who had graduated at the top of his class?

"Have you had enough yet?" he whispered to Tage.

"No," Tage said through gritted teeth. "I've dreamed of this day my whole life."

"Excellent!" Overlord Koax beamed. "I trust it has lived up to your expectations."

The overlord grasped a barb on Tage's left hand and plunged it in above his pinky knuckle. Tage's body began to shake, and bile rose in his throat, yet his face still remained calm. *I want to scream, but I won't. I want to pass out, but I can't.* Then guilt overwhelmed him. *How will my friends get through this alive?*

"There," the overlord exclaimed. "Look at those beautiful hands. Drudges, outfit his feet, will you? I want this done in two minutes so we may move on to the next."

Four drudges converged on him, shoving rings onto

each toe, then harpooning the wires into the top of his feet. This time, Tage welcomed the drudges and the agony. While they were clumsy, they were quick, and that mattered.

The overlord approached him one last time, took him by the hair, and lifted his head. "Now for the final step in young Tage's conversion." A drudge presented the overlord with the denture atop a velvet purple pillow. The prosthetic was polished to a high sheen, and it gleamed in the artificial light.

"What does it do?" Tage whispered. "How will it enhance my charge?"

"It won't." The old man tightened his grip on Tage's hair with bony fingers. "It keeps the charge flowing. Think of it as a circuit breaker. Without it, the charge breaks and is useless."

Tage half opened his mouth as the overlord shoved his clammy, slender finger between his lips and pried it open wide the rest of the way. His thick, long chipped fingernails cut Tage's gums.

Warm blood pooled around the base of his tongue. The metallic taste of his own blood was too much. He fought the urge to swallow. Just before the metal teeth were placed, he caught a glance at the small pins that would pierce his gums once the steel denture was shoved into his mouth. He closed his eyes, and darkness dragged him down.

He was jarred back into consciousness as he was jerked up by his wrists and ankles while the table was pulled away. Suspended in the air by only his limbs, he couldn't fight it—he folded in half, back now facing the ground, wrists kissing his ankles above his head. He squinted and gritted his bulky denture.

A drudge manipulated the archaic machine, pushing and pulling levers with its three-fingered hands. The abomination pressed and stomped on pedals holding the straps hooked to Tage. The drudge was like a puppet master, and Tage was its marionette. Bolts of electricity coursed over its gray-pink skin. Sparks fell.

Suspended in the air, Tage smiled to himself. The transformation was finally over, he'd done it. The machine pulled him up to the third story, then toward a wall with a false door. He vaguely heard applause from the crowd as the smell of herbs overwhelmed him. The relief was brief when compared to the knowledge that his friends would soon face the same fate.

The apothecary. He'd made it. Now, all he had to do was heal.

Then, kill the overlord.

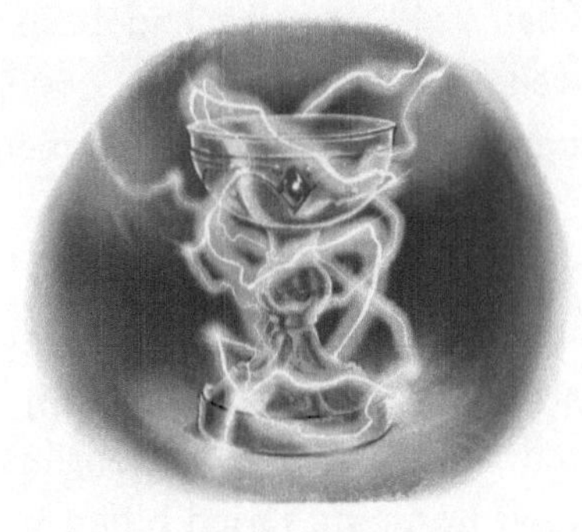

CHAPTER 7

• • • • •

The jarring feeling of being lifted woke Tage. He squirmed like a fish on a hook, but the tugs on his body were a reminder that he was still tied to the drudge's contraption. Taking a deep breath, he relaxed, safe in the apothecary. Relatively safe. Of all the places where his heritage could be exposed, this felt the most likely. If an apothecary couldn't tell, or didn't care, Tage would have covered another hurdle of his transformation. One step closer to his goal.

Rich thyme, piney rosemary, flowery lavender, and other herbs filled his senses. The comforting smell of herbs was like being in paradise compared to the scents he'd experienced in the amphitheater. He had seen the apothecary on his tour of the castle while in school, and it meant one thing: The horror was over.

The stone-walled apothecary was loaded with medicinal concoctions and hanging dried herbs. Humming from a castle worker at a long counter soothed Tage's soul.

"Friends," he whispered, trying out his voice. "My

friends . . ." Their last moment had been a short hug before he'd been strapped down and taken away. He should have spent more time in that moment, but it was too late now.

"How are you feeling?" the old soil charger asked, her voice slightly cracked with age.

Tage wiggled his toes experimentally, relieved he wasn't paralyzed. He tried to speak, but his swollen lips only allowed a weak moan. Dried blood from the metal denture caked his mouth.

"That good, huh?" she asked. "You did well. Let me look at that ear."

My ear? Oh yeah, I forgot about that.

A cool finger touched his ear, and pain rocketed through him.

• • •

Weaving in and out of consciousness, Tage hung from the straps like a sack of clothes waiting to be laundered. The soil charger pushed him around on tracks from long pulleys on the ceiling of the apothecary. She maneuvered him to a table covered with mortars and pestles, vials of liquid, and stacks of herb plants. She positioned herself on the other side and started dicing and crushing different herbs. Before long, she rounded the table and parted his lips. She shoved a pungent handmade pill into his mouth and used her thumb to push it past his tongue and into his throat.

"Swallow," she said.

Tage gagged, the pill stuck to the roof of his dry mouth. She greeted his lips with a glass of ice-cold water. The pill went down easily this time, but the taste of blood was still at the forefront.

She slathered paste on his ear that stunk worse than

the ursogen stables. "You'll have a piece missing, but most of your ear will heal quickly. Just think, not a lot of people actually leave a piece of themselves down there." She was interrupted by the clanking of a pulley arriving at the herb garret.

Someone was sobbing.

Capacity. I hope she forgives me. We'll kill the overlord and get her mom and dad out. Tage tried to move to get rid of his anxious energy, but instead he ripped his skin on a hook. *I didn't do this, the overlord did. This isn't my fault.* But he knew she could have chosen to stay in his parents' basement and avoid the draft. Wait it out. They would have fed her and kept her safe until this mess was over. Instead, she'd come. She'd chosen this, but he couldn't help feeling guilty.

She now had disfigured fingers and toes, not to mention the scars that would cover her spine. Then he thought of her gorgeous face, ruined with the disgusting metal denture. He would still love her. Nothing the overlord could do to her would change the way Tage felt about her. She'd stuck by him even after she found out he was a freak, and even after she learned that Tel'el was partially responsible for her dad being thrown in jail all those years ago. Their last days before their transformation had been strained, but they'd been together.

Soon, the soil charger in charge of the apothecary swung Capacity next to Tage. They hung like pieces of skinned meat. She cried quietly but didn't look at him.

Tage reached for her limp hand. "Capacity?"

She sniffed.

"We're going to make it," he said softly, watching her tears trickle to the wood floor.

"It hurts so bad," she responded, through gritted metal teeth.

"I know," Tage whispered, attempting his best soothing voice. "This nice lady will help you. There's a pill. It'll make the pain go away."

Tage turned his head, looking for the caretaker. "Hey, please give her that pill."

"I'm making it right now," the soil charger said gently.

Capacity sobbed again. "This was a mistake . . ."

"Hey," Tage said softly, the aches in his body growing with every word. "It could be worse."

"How?" Her speech was slurred, unused to the denture.

"You could be missing part of your ear like me," he teased. "I guess my modeling career is over."

Capacity laughed. "Stop it, Tage. It hurts worse when I laugh."

He held her hand, and she held his back, but let go almost as quickly.

"Don't look at me," she said.

He couldn't fully see her—his body wouldn't completely turn that way—but he could see her face contorted in pain. "You'll always be beautiful."

"I'm serious," she said. "This is not how I envisioned you first seeing me in my undershirt and bottoms."

"Oh, that," Tage said. He hadn't noticed how much of her skin was on display. Pain had overshadowed everything. "Right. Sorry . . . for everything."

"It's not your fault." Her voice was low. Heavy. "I said I'd come."

• • •

Another hour or so passed, and Tage's pain had mostly subsided. He felt more energized. Besides herbs and medicinal concoctions, the apothecary now housed Tage and his three friends, bent over strangely curved beds on their stomachs, as well as three of the other four who had joined them in the locker room. How long had he been here? Where was the fourth?

The startling realization that someone their age had maybe died that day began to creep into Tage's thoughts. Disfigured was better than dead. Pain was better than dead. Embarrassment at being hung from the ceiling in just his underwear was better than dead.

A spiral staircase wound through the floor in the corner of the herb garret like a snake. Tage hoped no Surge would come gather them. He wanted to be left with the woman healer for a bit longer.

"Hello?" Tage tried.

Impulse groaned.

He looked to his right. "Sorry, guys, I wasn't trying to wake you."

"I feel like a polished turd," Lumen said.

Footsteps echoed in the stone room.

"I'm here, I'm here." The woman strode up the staircase with ease. "Are you ready?"

"Ready for what?" Tage asked. He had only witnessed the insertion of the biotech, not the after care.

"This part of the ceremony is the most sacred," the attendant said. "Which is why it's kept secret. It's my favorite segment of the transformation. I get to see you for the first time in your Surge uniforms, and then I get to present you to the overlord."

Tage squinted his eyes.

"My name's Proxy," she said. "I'm the one assigned to run the apothecary. I think you've healed long enough. Let's get you out of those slings." She engaged a pulley system that lifted each one of them off the curved beds and uprighted them as if they were standing in the air.

Proxy tucked her white hair behind her ears, her charred, black fingernails a stark contrast. She seemed healthier than other soil chargers; her muscle tone wasn't depleted, and her skin was bright. She started singing a cheerful song and smiled. She had wrinkled skin surrounding deep blue eyes.

She slowly lowered Tage to the ground by rapidly pulling a rope through a triple-pulley system. He let out slow breaths until she unhooked him.

Proxy placed her warm hand on his shoulder. "Do you think you can stand?"

"No," Tage answered. "Why'd you leave us hanging like that anyway? Why were we on these weird beds?"

"It's so your vertebra don't fuse together. The pill I gave you expedites healing, and if you were flat, there would be a greater chance of spinal fusion."

"Well, I can't feel my arms and legs. Give me a sec," Tage said. He scooted over until he sat on the cold floor, slowly stretching out his legs. Blood rushed into his limbs.

Proxy gently let Impulse down.

"Here, let me help you," Proxy said. She pulled with thin hands and arms, and in an instant, Impulse was on his feet.

Tage took in the woman again. Large bun on the top of her head, wrinkles around her mouth and eyes. Thin and wiry build. "You're surprisingly strong," he said.

"That's what happens when you don't charge for over a decade," she said. "You actually use your muscles. First lesson of being a Surge Knight—or a soil charger, for that matter—is don't let the charge overtake you. As you know, you can use it for everything. Being a Surge Knight means you can stay charged longer than any other being on this planet."

Tage glanced down at her hands.

She unleashed Capacity, then Lumen.

"Also," she continued, "being a Surge Knight means you can use many kinds of ignitions. There are five. Most can only perform the main three, but you'll get creative with them. Don't get physically lazy and atrophied like . . ."

"Like who?" Capacity asked, slowly stretching her neck from side to side.

"Yeah, who?" Lumen said. "I could use a delicious bit of gossip right now." She linked her fingers together and tried a stretch above her head, wincing as she moved.

"I could use a delicious bit of painkillers," Tage muttered.

A short chuckle escaped Impulse's lips.

Proxy smiled. "You'll know when you see them. Excellent at casting ignitions, but if they were ever devoid of charge, they'd be as weak as a toddler."

"She's talking about the overlord," Tage whispered to Capacity. "All skinny and decrepit."

"Wait," Lumen said. "Five? Is this some sort of test? There are only three. I win. What do I win?"

"No test," Proxy said. "The other two ignitions are a bit of a myth around these parts. Our Surge Knights don't harbor them on a regular basis. Now, you need to grow your mind and your body. And remember, discharge once in a while. Remember this always. You aren't a run-of-the-mill soil charger anymore."

Impulse let out a deep moan.

Proxy raised an eyebrow. "Your herb pill is taking longer to kick in. You're such a big boy, it'll take a few moments longer for you to start feeling relief." She reached down and helped him up.

The assassination crew stood in the plain white underwear given to them upon arrival. They all looked like they had been run over by a shock craft and left to die.

Proxy's attention shifted to the three Knights hanging on the other side of the room. "They'll be out for a bit longer. If any of them stir, let them know I'll be right back."

Tage nodded once to show he'd heard. He flexed his hands, testing out the metal crammed onto his fingers.

Proxy disappeared around a corner. She returned shortly, pulling four hanging Surge uniforms across the tracks.

Capacity smiled, her metal teeth gleaming in the dull electric light. Despite the teeth, rings, and other trauma she'd sustained, to Tage, she was still beautiful. There was the same sweet determination in her eyes. She'd been traumatized, but she now stood tall and firm.

In fact, all of his friends wore the Surge biotech like a professional Surge Knight. Tage returned their smiles. This part was finally wrapping up.

Tage put the rough leather pants on, clasping them in the front.

Capacity helped him dress, first placing the back piece on him.

He grimaced.

"Sorry," she said.

Tage turned around and held her face, the rings on his fingers looking foreign to him. "You never need to apologize." He leaned in and kissed her lightly. Most of the swelling had gone down on his lips, but his mouth was sore. "I should be the one apologizing."

"I was drafted to be here." Her eyes filled with tears, and she looked down. "Let's finish getting dressed."

Tage turned, and she held the back piece in place while he strapped three straps across his collarbone area, right under his chest, and around his navel. She had to strap the back across his shoulder blades, under the flap of rubber covering the flying animal.

Proxy stopped Capacity and looked intently at the back piece. "That's an interesting design."

"Yeah, it's all right," Tage said quickly, then turned toward her.

Capacity helped him slide the hood piece attached to the apron covering his chest and thighs.

"I like it," Proxy said. "It's a unique design in a city that is all the same."

"Thanks," Tage responded, though standing out should be the last thing he wanted.

Capacity handed him the straps after crossing them in the back. He took the clasps and hooked them to a series of horizontal buttons running near his pelvis. The leather cowl hood flopped over his shoulder blades. With each movement, his body felt lighter, stronger, healthier.

Proxy helped dress the others, while Tage carefully helped Capacity, averting his gaze when necessary. She hardly moved, only shifted as he prompted, and said nothing.

"Capacity?" Tage asked.

Silence.

"Capacity, please look at me." He bent to catch her attention, but she stared at the stone floor. "I don't know what to say."

She didn't lift her eyes. "It's not you, Tage. Let's just get through the next twenty-four hours and heal, okay?"

"She's right," Proxy said. "The first day is the most difficult, but you'll grow accustomed to your new bio-tech. Soon, you'll begin to really feel the advantages you've gained."

"Can you give us a sec?" Tage said. He put his hand

on the small of Capacity's back and led her to the corner with the small staircase.

"I . . . I don't know what to say," Tage said again.

Tears streamed down her face. "It's all so overwhelming. The last few weeks."

He reached out and squeezed her hand. She blinked while staring into his eyes. Was it doubt he saw, or regret? He wasn't sure. But she squeezed his hand back, and that was all that mattered in the moment.

They stood in full regalia. He was so close. He'd wait for word that the poison had been placed for him to use, and then all he could do was pray that it worked.

Proxy ushered them to a rickety elevator that Tage hadn't noticed before. They squeezed into the small box, and she released a lever that pumped power to the machine above. It smelled musty inside the elevator and reminded Tage of the wooden buildings back at Ohmstave. He hadn't smelled that scent in a decade, and breathed in deeply. If all went to plan, he'd be back there soon. He looked up and watched the ropes loop through the pulleys as they descended. He had to orient himself within the palace, and fast. Place the map he had memorized with the walls and floor around him.

"Now, when we get in there," Proxy said, "there will be four large red pots full of charged soil."

Tage was familiar with them. Tel'el had walked him through what to expect and had spent the last week doing the same for his friends.

"Stand behind the pots and wait for the overlord to address you," she continued. "He'll want to see how your power flows through you. He will want to check your magnitude to charge as well. When he calls you, charge yourselves. It'll feel different than before your biotech was inserted. You can hold more power now, and you might think you'll electrocute yourself like the humans, but keep taking up current from the soil. You can handle a lot more now than you used to be able to. Truthfully, us soil chargers can overdo it, but the Surge Knights . . . well, just remember you can take up far more charge than a regular soil charger. Learn your limitations as quickly as possible. And when you do charge, always take the maximum amount possible."

"Anything else?" Impulse asked. His newly pierced fingers jingled as he massaged his bald scalp.

"When you are charged, he'll want to see the different ignitions. Run through them in any order that you'd like, but you must perform all three."

"Great," Lumen said. "'Cause no one has ever seen the other two. Three, it is!"

The elevator touched down on the main castle floor. When they exited, Tage quickly realized this was a service elevator that wasn't used by most patrons at the castle. This may prove a possible escape route if necessary. The three others who had made it out the other side of the procedure might help muddy the waters of new Knights in the castle—though, with poison, anyone and everyone near Koax could be a suspect.

"Here you are, my dears," Proxy said. "Just go through those doors and head to the main hall. The sixteen head Surge Knights will be waiting with the overlord." She held a thick swinging wood door open for them. Tage marched out into the main corridor renewed with confidence. He felt about fifty percent perfect. For now, all he wanted to do was get this portion over with and sleep. But there were so few steps left. No more years to count down to the assassination, just days. A week or two, tops.

They approached large, closed wooden doors. Two

drudges stood in full armor blocking them. The drudge armor was a mix between rubber, steel, and leather. It looked like leftovers, which was fitting, considering that was how drudges were made. In their right hands were vertical battle axes taller than them. They turned in unison and pushed the creaking doors open, exposing the main chamber. He'd have to discern how much more the drudges were capable of than they used to be. Now fully oriented, Tage snuck a glance up and down the hallway before he stepped into the vast room. He could place the servants' halls next to the room they stood in. He knew what was above and what rooms lay below.

Each corner of the palace matched with the plans in Tage's basement, and with every familiar corner, his confidence grew. The empty shaft actually held the elevator they'd just used. That was good information to hold on to. He'd trained. He was ready.

Tage looked up to see the gaunt overlord standing at the head of the table, his black robes draping to the ground. His friends helped him form a line facing the leader of Currentgrad, and soon, all of Hadrain if they didn't succeed.

"Welcome," the overlord said with a metallic-tooth grin. "Now to see who will survive and who will fail."

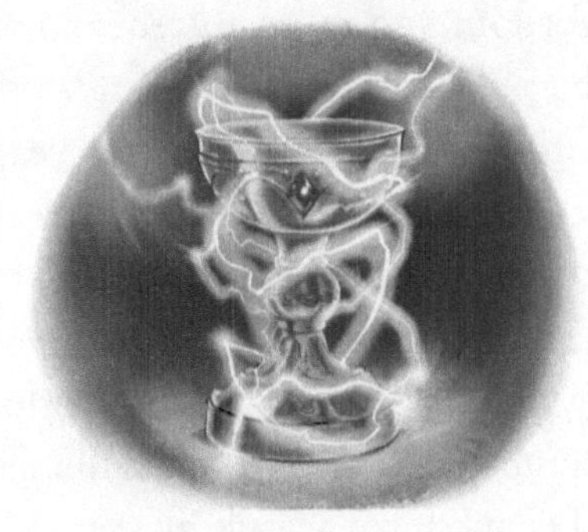

CHAPTER 8

· · · · ·

At the far end of the room, a feast was in progress at a long wooden table. Tage closed his eyes and inhaled the scent of savory foods, his stomach contracting. Opening his eyes, Tage scanned the room. He replayed the story he had been told by his father dozens of times. Of how Tel'el had failed.

This was the room.

He could imagine his father jumping on the table, trying to slit the overlord's throat. The cries of the Knights around him as they leapt to take down the man who dared to take Koax's life. That's why poison was the best answer—there would be no one to stand over the deceased body and claim victory. Tage's breath quickened. He imagined his dad crashing through the stained-glass window to the left. Saw in his mind the scars and bruises from his fall.

Tage and his crew stood taller. The entire table of Surges stopped eating and stared through slitted eyes, as if the new recruits were intruders. The table was adorned with rare mushroom and moss entrees only found in the caves under the pulse dunes. Platters of wormsteak were scattered over the entire tabletop. After years of protein porridge, only occasionally made better by the few fruits and vegetables his mother had managed to grow, this meal looked and smelled positively divine.

"Do come in. Don't be shy," the overlord said with outstretched hands, his filthy, long nails elongating his bony limbs. "Let me have a look at you. My new devotees."

Tage and his friends each took a spot behind one of the large red pots.

The sixteen Surge Knights ate in uniforms similar to what Tage and his friends wore. The overlord, on the other hand, sat in a dark cloth robe. He propped his elbows on the edge of the table, staining the material with food remnants.

The decrepit old man then folded his arms. "We would have you eat, but only full-fledged Surge Knights are deserving of such fine foods. Your final test will determine if you leave with a full belly, or on a gurney." He smiled, and his metal teeth shimmered.

Tage looked at each Surge Knight in turn. What would happen after Koax's death? Would one of them take his place? Were Tel'el, Hayrah, and their intelligence contacts correct in believing Koax's death would cause a chaos big and long enough for reason to be shown to the citizens of Currentgrad?

"We shall return to our feast shortly," Koax said, "but first . . ." He held his hand toward Tage and his friends. "I see Proxy has trained you well. Already in position behind the red pots. Let's get to the festivities. I want to see the show." Baring his metal teeth, he continued. "Tage, why don't you begin? Cast an ignition at anything in this room."

"Of course," he muttered.

Tage took a step toward the red pot and thrust his hands in the black soil. He waited. As a regular soil charger, he could only leave his hands or feet charging in soil for ten to twenty seconds. This time, a minute had passed, and he still didn't feel full. Heat coursed up into his webbed fingers, then to his wrists, and finally through his shoulders. He could feel each of the charging cells light up with a slight vibration, indicating that they were full. Silence blanketed the room. He looked at the table of Surges awkwardly. Sweat ran down the sides of his face; the Surge uniform was hotter than he'd imagined.

"I hope you all realize how lucky you are," the overlord said, breaking the silence.

Tage managed to smile.

Small lightning bolts coursed up his forearms while he waited with his hands in the pot. The nerves in his body swelled with electricity. Proxy's words echoed in his mind. *Always take the maximum amount.*

The overlord stood abruptly. "Tell me, young Tage, why is it taking so long to fully charge?"

"I don't know, Overlord Koax."

Tage stared at the soil and his newly metalized hands, wishing for the charge to come more quickly.

"Check him!" the overlord ordered.

Two Surges stood and were swiftly at his side. They stood behind him.

"Lean your head forward, boy!" The Surge's deep voice echoed in the stone room.

Tage complied. His pulse quickened when they started to mess with his hood flap.

Panic flooded Tage. *What if there's a stray dark hair?*

Or worse, what if the procedure didn't take? What if they learn I'm human? Do my friends know enough to take over if I am found out?

He felt as exposed as a human in the Charged Desert. One of the Knights pulled on his collar and looked into his back piece. Tage's back wrenched in pain.

"Don't remove your hands from the pot," the female Surge said.

Every nerve on his back jumped as they touched his fresh wounds. Anger coursed through him as they carelessly examined his back. He bit down on the metal denture, clamping his mouth shut.

"Number twenty-one just lit up," a deep voice said. "We've only got three left over the cervical spine, then he'll be at full power."

The Surge scooped up a handful of the black dirt. "But the soil is out of charge. He drew it all up."

Silence blanketed the room for a moment.

The overlord sat and shifted in his chair, his gaze fixed on Tage. "This has never happened before."

Tage shook his head.

"Move him to the next pot!" The overlord rounded the table and slinked toward Tage, his hands folded behind his back.

Tage looked frantically from his friends to the overlord.

"Go get another pot for the other candidates!" the overlord ordered a drudge standing in the corner.

The two Surge Knights pushed Tage to the next pot. Capacity dodged out of the way. They shoved Tage's hands deep into the soil. "Hold still!" the female one said.

Tage looked at his friends. Capacity's eyes seemed darker and were wide with concern. Impulse and Lumen stood behind her, watching with intrigue. A trickle of sweat trailed down Tage's spine. Perspiration dotted his forehead. If he couldn't fully charge, would he be dismissed? Killed? Locked up? Discovered as half human?

The Surges continued to hold Tage's back piece away from his neck; the cowl was flopped up on the back of his head. He felt a soft zap and warming sensation as two LEDs lit up before they announced it to the overlord.

"We have one more to go, Overlord Koax," the female Surge said.

The last LED flicked on near the base of his skull, and Tage felt an immediate change. A euphoria that he had never felt flowed through every nerve cell in his body, like he was fully awakened for the first time. The current pulsed through power-sensitive cellular conductors throughout his entire body.

He closed his eyes and leaned his head back. Sucking in a deep breath through his nostrils, he could smell everything from the feast to the wooden table to the drudges and the stone floor. Stretching his back, he sensed each muscle fiber, ready to bend to his will. In this moment, anything was possible.

He shivered when the Surges readjusted his hood. Even the touch to his skin was heightened.

"My, my," the overlord said. "You're quite the Surge Knight. I've never seen someone take up that much charge before. Bravo, young Tage. I have a feeling you will prove to be quite useful."

Lumen stifled a laugh.

Tage did hope to prove useful—just not to the Knights in front of him.

The overlord eyed Tage. "How do you feel?"

Tage slowly removed his hands from the dirt. The specks of soil fell from his fingertips as he straightened his back. He flicked his hands over the top of the pot, ridding himself of any granules of soil. Small sparks shot back into the pot.

"I feel strange," Tage said, staring at his palms.

"Strange?" Overlord Koax frowned.

"Not b-bad," Tage stuttered. "I just feel different. But I'm not in pain anymore."

"Ah, how are your senses? That's one of the blessings of being a Surge Knight."

Tage stared into the overlord's dark eyes. "They're amazing."

"Wonderful to hear," the overlord said. "Spin and let me look at you." He made the motion with his index finger.

Tage slowly turned, holding his arms out. Small sparks rained down from his fingertips as he did a full revolution. Tucking his hand across his midsection, he bowed as a courtesy when he was finished.

"We got a suck-up in the castle," Lumen whispered.

Capacity squinted. "Stop."

The overlord retook his seat at the head of the table. Settling back in his high-back dinner chair, he said, "Show us what I've created."

Tage looked up and shot White Sparks from his right hand onto the ground. They were thicker, brighter, and held far more power than he'd ever been able to do with White Sparks as just a soil charger. Twisting sideways, Tage threw a Bolt Ignition with his left hand at the rafters. No more discharging or recharging to do a new ignition like a regular soil charger. The bolt was sharp and jagged, just like the lightning that rolled through with the storms.

His aim wasn't that good, but he hit some of the wood, causing it to smolder.

"That's it," the overlord said, widening his eyes. "Now show me the Current Ignition."

Tage pushed a thick column of current through his fingertips at the stained-glass window, emitting a wavy cylinder of current toward the designs. He wanted to break the glass so badly, just like Tel'el. He dropped his hands, suddenly wary of causing damage to the overlord's palace. Tage's job was to prepare for the assassination. Garnering too much attention would not help his cause.

"Everyone goes for the window." Koax laughed. "It's been altered, unbreakable." He clapped. "Very good. Welcome to your new life as a Surge Knight, Tage. Next!"

Impulse stepped forward. "How am I supposed to beat that?" he whispered.

"Come on, big guy." Tage smiled. "You'll do just fine."

Impulse thrust his hands into the pot of soil and waited. It only took him thirty seconds to charge, and he didn't use two pots like Tage, but when the overlord bid him to cast ignitions, he stepped on the lip of the large pot and used it to launch into a backflip. While flipping, he shot all three ignitions wildly like a spark wheel at the carnival. The sparks hit one rafter, the bolt charred another, and the current sizzled on a third. His aim was stellar.

Tage watched the overlord.

Overlord Koax clapped his hands together and said, "Impressive moves. Next." He waved his hand, ready for Lumen. The Surges pounded the table with their fists, creating an almost drumlike sound, as Lumen readied herself with charge. Clearly, they were liking what they saw. This could work to their advantage and give them access to more places in the palace, or the shifts that would best help them kill the target.

Lumen took up current from the pot in front of her

and stood back. She did an interpretive sort of dance. Spinning then leaping, all while casting ignitions. While her power wasn't on full display, her ability to move definitely was.

"Acceptable," the overlord said.

Lumen turned a feverish shade of red. Tage grabbed her hand to lead her back. She was shaking.

"Not now," Tage whispered.

Capacity sucked up power and immediately shot a bolt to her right, then sparks to her left, then blasted a wormsteak out of one of the Surge's hands midbite.

It exploded, and chunks of meat splatted all over the Surges in the vicinity.

Tage shot a glance at the overlord and back to Capacity. His jaw went slack. Capacity had always been more capable than she believed, and he loved that she'd taken a moment to show off.

All the Surges stared at her and the overlord.

"Outstanding." Koax stood.

"You're going to let her get away with that, Overlord Koax?" one of the Knights asked.

He walked toward Capacity, and scratched his neck. "I never granted you permission to resume eating," he said, without looking back at the Knight who had spoken.

Koax's eyes took in Capacity's form from top to bottom, and Tage's fists clenched at the way his dark, beady eyes drank her in.

"I'm sorry, sir," Capacity said, but her gaze never wavered from his face. "I think I'm just overly excited with the new charge."

"Of course you are," the overlord said. He placed a fingernail under her chin. He stared at her, examining her face.

Capacity's jaw ticked, and her fists clenched.

"You are in a class of your own. The most accurate Surge I've seen in a long time. Just think what you'll be able to do for me once you've had more experience."

The overlord walked back toward the table.

Tage let his shoulders sag, though the picture of Koax's hand on Capacity's face would not be leaving his mind anytime soon.

"Thank you for participating in our final phase of the Surge Ceremony," the overlord said. "Remember, retaining massive amounts of power and heightened senses sets you apart from all other soil chargers. Don't be foolish and don't take it for granted. Being able to cast the three main ignitions off one charge is key to the success of the Surge Knights. Thank you for your willingness to be converted to the program that is most near and dear to my heart. You may be dismissed."

They turned, and Tage felt relief, like he was floating on a cloud.

"Tage! Stop!" the overlord yelled from behind them.

They stopped and Tage slowly turned. The overlord pointed at Tage's feet and rushed toward him. "You're Arcing."

"Look!" Capacity said.

Tage looked down. He was elevated a couple of inches off the ground, with a current emitting from the soles of his bare feet.

"What the . . ?" Tage said, floating on a narrow cushion of power.

"I haven't seen this in many years. Charuss is the only one who can Arc in this court of Surges."

Charuss, the head Surge Knight, cleared his throat and stood. Tage recognized him from his training. Charuss was to be feared, no doubt.

"Although, he has been unable to perform such a

mystical ignition in years." The overlord knelt next to Tage. "We're going to have to practice this ignition, so you can master it."

He stood and placed both hands on Tage's shoulders, and the Arcing stopped. Tage immediately felt every imperfection of the cold, irregular stone floor with the bottoms of his feet.

"You are going to be my most powerful Surge yet," Overlord Koax said. "I have big plans for you."

Stone mugs stamped on the table in a clomp-clomp rhythm.

Overlord Koax smiled. "Today was a very good day for Currentgrad."

If he only knew.

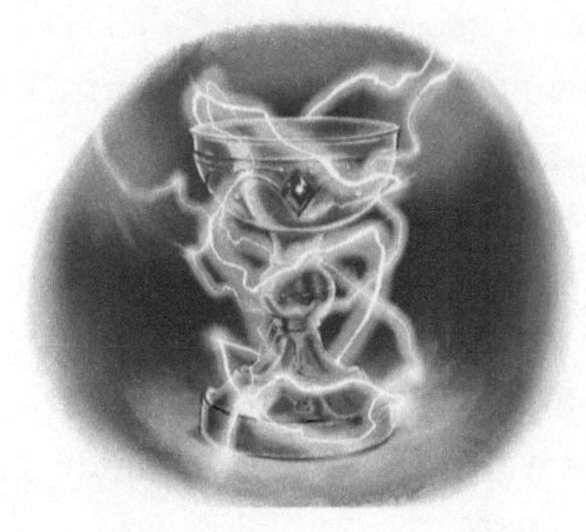

CHAPTER 9

· · · · ·

The group of seven new Surge Knights followed a Knight with several years of service as he walked swiftly through the hallway, forcing them to nearly run to keep up. "Dorms for new recruits are this way. All approved Knight clothing has been put in the locker near your bunk. You're responsible for your back piece, as it's custom to your spine. Lose it and don't bother showing your face in the Voltaic Dava again."

Tage stole a glance at Capacity, but she walked next to him, facing forward.

"Your families have been invited to your morning meal," the Surge said, his voice quiet but barking in the way of the Knights. "Your official training will begin after that point, but you will be expected to cover shifts guarding the palace almost immediately."

None of them spoke, not Tage's party, and not the other three who had been altered on the same day. Time had begun to blend together, and Tage's healing body was both energized and exhausted.

"Female new recruits there." The Knight pointed left. "And male new recruits here. Your name is on your bunk."

"Well—" started Tage, but the Surge cut him off.

"Lights out in ten minutes." He finally turned, his jaw set in the way of far more loyal Knights than Tage. "Don't start off on the wrong foot."

The Knight walked through the middle of their group, forcing them to part.

"He's a load of fun," Lumen whispered.

"I suggest you find your bunks!" the Surge barked just before he disappeared around the corner.

Tage reached out and gave Capacity's hand a squeeze—her skin was still silky soft around the rings. She squeezed him back, but her eyes never caught his.

His heart dragged as he followed Impulse's hulking frame into their room.

"Sleep on your stomach," one of the other recruits said, as he tapped his name card and crawled into bed.

"Your friend?" Impulse asked. "What happened?"

"Can't feel her legs. She'll be . . ."

There was no need to finish. There were almost no suitable jobs for those who became paralyzed. She would most likely end up in a ration center, stuck on a mechanical cart, filling orders and getting yelled at by families not receiving enough food.

"I'm glad she's alive," Tage said quietly.

One of the guys scoffed. "If you can call that living."

As Tage found his bed, his stomach rumbled. The lack of food was probably to help keep their minds sharp. But as he rested his head on the flat pillow, he ran through the events since they'd come to the palace. Thank the suns that Capacity still had the use of her body.

If all went to plan, Tage's father would most likely

bring him the poison the next day, and then . . . then it was just a matter of opportunity. Ten years had led up to this. Tage was so close.

•••

Ten bangs against the dorm room door snapped Tage awake. He expected to feel sharp, shooting pain like yesterday, but instead he felt full of energy and was pain free. Tage sat straight up—still no pain. He swung his legs off his bed. "Impulse?" His voice sounded like gravel running down a corrugated metal sheet.

"I'm good," Impulse mumbled from the bunk below.

The other male recruits made their way to the locker room. As Tage pulled on his pants, he felt a small tube in a strange pocket. The moment his fingers touched it, he knew someone had deposited the poison for him. Tel'el really did have help. How much help they'd be remained unknown, but for now, Tage was happy to have the precious liquid in his possession.

A few wordless minutes later, Tage, Impulse, Lumen, and Capacity all walked together to the cafeteria. Capacity had no family to come visit, so she walked with Tage to where his parents sat waiting.

His mother's face wore a smile that didn't reach her eyes. Tel'el's eyes were red-rimmed, and he kept his head mostly down, his white hair covering half his face. If Tel'el were to be discovered . . . Tage couldn't even consider the implications.

Tage's mother grasped Capacity's hands over the table.

Tage dug into his meal. Sweetened wormsteak.

"You look tired," he said to his father. As he sat,

every muscle in his body felt tightened, honed, ready for anything. He'd never felt so strong.

"I haven't slept," Tel'el replied. "How are you? How did your exhibition go? I believe every upper-level Knight was present."

"Tage Arced," Capacity said. "I've never seen anything like it."

One of Tel'el's brows danced upward. "My boy! It is just as we hoped. Your . . . particular traits are well-suited to the changes."

Of course Tel'el had to be cautious as to what he said within the palace walls.

"You're special," his mother whispered, finally grasping one of Tage's hands.

"Tage," Tel'el said. "It could prove to be useful. But don't use it until it's necessary. Drawing attention to yourself won't help anyone."

"I don't want to draw attention to myself," Tage said quietly as he scraped his plate. "I didn't even know I was doing it."

"Did you get your uniform okay?" Tel'el asked, a question in his eyes.

Tage resisted the urge to run his hands over the small vial. "All set, yes."

Hayrah dabbed at her eyes, and Tel'el swallowed and nodded once.

"Time's up!" a loud voice boomed. "Recruits will meet in the yard for their briefing and day one of training."

Hayrah stepped around the table and wrapped Tage in her arms. "I love you, my son. Gods of charge be with you."

Her hug was followed by Tel'el's. "Proud of you,

son," Tel'el said, loud enough that Tage was sure a few of the Knights heard.

He hadn't been recruited, so the illusion of his faithful parents was paramount to not drawing attention.

"You are very brave, Capacity." Hayrah pulled her into a tight hug, and for the first time since their transformation, Tage saw some of the tension ease out of her face.

The room cleared out, and Tage and the other recruits walked to the yard situated on the side of the Voltaic Dava.

Capacity's shoulder bumped against his as they walked, and he allowed himself a smile.

"First step is checking the guard-shift schedule," she said, looping a pinky through his for a brief moment. "One step closer to the goal."

That's why Capacity had come. She wanted Koax dead as much as Tage—he'd taken far more from her than he'd taken from Tage.

So close. They were so close.

Tage couldn't stop the feeling that live baby shock worms had hatched and started to swirl in his stomach. But uneasy wasn't what he felt. It was more apprehension and excitement. The whole ordeal was almost over. Outcast or not, he longed to be back at Ohmstave.

Sparks fell from Capacity's fingertips, like a mini electric storm, as her arms swayed from the brisk pace they walked. Nerves, Tage thought. But even now, her sparks were impressive, and she wasn't even trying.

"You okay?" Tage asked Capacity.

"I'm all right." Her voice was shaking and her teeth chattered.

Tage grabbed her hand. "I'll be here for you."

She nodded to him, then asked, "How about you, Impulse?"

He nodded. "Okay."

"I'm not okay," Lumen said. "I'm so worried. What if we screw up?"

The large, open yard spread out in front of them, and Tage immediately felt the charge in the dirt beneath his feet.

"We can't mess this up," Capacity said. "We won't. Too much is at stake."

"Come on!" one of the other new recruits shouted from across the yard. "Don't be late on day one."

"It's in my pocket," Tage said. "Just don't let the nerves get to you. We've gone over the plan over a dozen times, and I know we all got this. We need to be spot-on with our ignitions and pacing while we go through the castle."

They all nodded. They'd been over and over and over the plan.

"We can't disrupt the flow of things too much tonight either," Capacity said. She nervously picked at her black nails.

Tage put his arm around her. "Agreed."

"Tonight?" Lumen whispered.

"Once we know the schedule and where we'll need to be," Tage answered. "No matter what, be quiet, careful, and stick to the plan."

Energy pulsed through his body. Strength wrapped up his few spinning doubts into manageable portions. They would not fail. They could not. He'd given his life to this; he would give his life for a chance at a new future for the citizens of Hadrain. Tage would kill Overlord Koax. Ten years of training could not be for nothing.

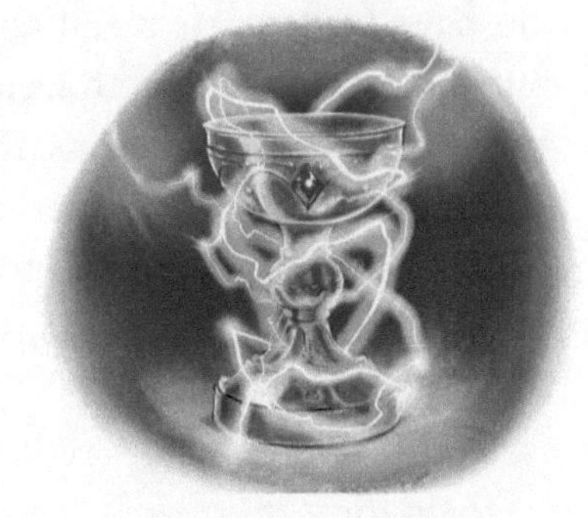

CHAPTER 10

• • • • •

Tage and his friends found themselves under the bright suns, in full regalia, listening to a Surge Knight barking instructions at them. Sweat covered Tage's body and dripped down his face. He breathed steadily. The courtyard was open to the Charged Desert, and charged black soil covered the entire area.

"The Surge Knight is the most esteemed on Hadrain," the Surge said. "With the blessing of Anoths and Cathos, and the overlord's brilliant biotech, we are the most powerful of all races."

"Infinity charge!" they all chanted in unison.

"My name is Surge Knight Flux, and today, we are going to talk about ignitions. There are five, three of which you will use readily and with ease," he continued. "The fourth, the Arcing Ignition, is for the strong, and the fifth, the Volt Foil Ignition, is unheard of in this day and age. In my lifetime, I have never met anyone who can cast a Volt Foil Ignition. As many of you know, the Surge Knight can do all ignitions on one charge, unlike soil chargers, who have to dedicate a full charge to one ignition." He smiled, metal denture teeth gleaming in the sunlight. "We can switch between ignitions at will on one single charge. It is a glorious thing the overlord has provided to the few elect." He spread his arms toward them.

"These uniforms are so hot," Lumen whispered. "I'm about ready to rip this leather off."

"We'll get used to it," Tage whispered. "Plus, we'll only need to wear them for a short time."

"Today, we are only going to do the three common ignitions. But first, let me tell you a little bit about each."

Lumen rolled her eyes. Capacity sighed.

"First, the Bolt Ignition. It is the longest range of all ignitions. Cast the Bolt Ignition at those targets over there."

Along the far wall of the courtyard were burlap scarecrows stuffed with ursogen hair.

Tage lifted his arm behind his ear and threw his hand forward, extending his fingers. Three bolts fired from his fingertips in rapid succession.

Every recruit cast the Bolt Ignition over and over, chanting, "Infinity charge!"

"Again," the Surge Knight said.

They all cast the ignition.

"Again!" Flux yelled, followed by the recruits complying.

The burlap dummies were engulfed in flames. Drudges came out and doused the flames with water before retreating to the edge of the courtyard.

"Again!"

"Infinity charge!" they all screamed.

The Knight held up his hand. "Stop! Good. Okay, take twenty steps forward."

They marched in a line toward the burlap forms.

"Next is the Current Ignition," he said. "This is used for shorter range, but it's still very effective."

Tage stared at his black fingernails. So much power. So much voltage. He contemplated Arcing again, but didn't want to draw any attention to himself in front of the other recruits.

"Shoot the Current Ignition now!"

"Infinity charge!" the group shouted.

Tage cleared his head and held his fingers out. Lightning current sizzled from the tips of his fingers. He concentrated. The current wasn't strong at first, but the more he focused and the more he pushed his nerves to expel voltage, the stronger and stronger the current became. He backed up a step or two while aiming at the dummies. Once again, they became consumed with flames.

"That's perfect!" Flux said.

All the inductees stopped and waited for further instructions.

"The last one we will do today is the White Sparks Ignition." He held his hand in the air and blasted a short column of sparks above him. Crackling fizz echoed through the area as the recruits stared. The brilliance of the White Sparks Ignition was something to behold. The sparks cascaded down upon him as they fell back to the Charged Desert. "I love this one. Not only is it extremely effective for close counter-combat, but it is the most beautiful ignition we have."

A girl off to the left of Tage raised her hand too eagerly. The Surge Knight raised an eyebrow. "Yes?"

She cleared her throat. "Can you learn all five ignitions?"

The Knight shook his head. "Four you can learn, but no one has seen the Volt Foil in generations. Some think it's just a legend."

With that, she bowed her head and stepped back.

Tage thought it was a good question, and he had wondered that in the past. He shrugged his shoulders, letting the wonder fade away.

"Step close to the burlap dummies," Flux said. "Remember, this is for close contact. The closer, the better."

Tage realized the dummies were human mockups. That didn't sit well with him. His pulse quickened, and he concentrated on making the burlap forms the overlord. He didn't want to lose it and blow his cover now.

They all approached the dummies. One for each Surge apprentice. He pictured the gaunt overlord's face etched into the charred marks on the oval head of the mannequin and blasted sparks squarely onto the area, burning a deep hole into the ursogen-hair filling.

"Good, good!" the Surge Knight said over the constant sizzling sound. "You are all doing amazing. But you have a lot of work ahead of you. I need to go to a meeting of the Knights, but I want you to still practice. Do any of you have questions now?"

"I do," a taller boy said. "When do we get to learn absorption, like the overlord can do?"

The Surge Knight approached a box behind the row of dummies. "Years, many years. You're not ready. It takes years and years to learn. A Surge Knight has to learn to empty charge milliseconds before any ignition is absorbed. If you don't, then you can die. Overload your system, so to speak." He lifted multiple rubber suits from the box. "Any other questions?"

All the inductees looked at each other, anticipating another question, but none came. They shook their heads.

"Good. Please put on these cribriform chest plates and helmets we acquired from the humans. Practice on each other. These will protect your chest, neck, and head." Flux stepped away from the pile of rubber gear and walked toward the Voltaic Dava.

Tage, Capacity, Lumen, and Impulse each donned the rubber chest plate and helmet.

Capacity and Lumen practiced on each other, while Tage and Impulse wrestled on the ground, spraying White Sparks onto each other's rubber helmets. Sparks bounced off their face shields and trickled onto the black sand. Tage kicked Impulse in the chest, pushing him back, then sprung to his feet. Impulse shot a Bolt Ignition at Tage. He rolled out of the way, but Impulse was patient and shot the second bolt just as Tage was standing. They both laughed. The other recruits hooted and hollered. Practice was going well until the taller boy who had asked about absorbing ignitions took off his rubber armor and let it drop to the black sand.

"Do it!" he shouted. "Shoot a bolt at me. I want to see if I can absorb it."

Tage rushed over to the small group formed around him. "Hey, I wouldn't do that if I were you."

"It's going to be nothing," the boy said. "I just want to see what's going to happen."

"Um," Lumen said, "you could die."

"I'm not going to die." The kid held up his hand and commanded one of the other Surge Knight trainees to cast an ignition at him. "I can take it."

"It doesn't matter how much you believe you can do it," Impulse said. "We haven't learned how to do it yet."

"Stand back, it'll be okay. I'm a Surge Knight now, I can take it!" he said, readying himself for the blow.

A recruit still clad in rubber armor stepped back and threw a Bolt Ignition at the kid and missed.

"Come on!"

The recruit pulled her arm back again and cast the ignition in the boy's direction.

Time stalled as the boy flew back in an explosion of sparks and sand. Tage propelled himself forward to check on him and was soon surrounded by the other five recruits. Tage knelt by his side, but the kid was unconscious and barely breathing. He knew from the humans that shallow, quick breaths meant close to death.

"Hey!" Tage yelled. "Help!"

From near the dummies, three pig-snouted drudges with staple-skin faces waddled toward the commotion.

Tage shook the boy. "Can you hear me?"

No response.

The drudges pushed the small group aside and grabbed the boy. With unbelievable ease, they hauled him to the Voltaic Dava like one of the burlap dummies.

The girl who shot him started sobbing. She removed her helmet and sniffled as tears streamed down her face.

"It'll be okay," Capacity said, putting her arm around her. "Here, let's get this chest plate off you." Capacity and Lumen unhooked the back and let it fall to the Charged Desert floor. The others removed the rubber protection armor also. Impulse and Tage collected the pile of rubber pieces and deposited them in the boxes behind the dummies.

In an instant, another drudge snorted next to the girl.

"Sheesh," Lumen said. "Where'd that thing come from?"

As quiet as a Bolt Ignition, the drudge snatched the girl's wrists, jammed a barbed prong connected to a wire into her hand, and threw the other end of the wire into the ground. The spike on the other end stuck into the soil with precision, then the drudge stomped on it with its cracked and callused, three-toed foot, driving the wire deeper. The poor girl didn't have a chance. In an instant, she went limp. Not only was she drained of charge—it seemed as if she was switched off. The moment she buckled at the knees, the drudge flung her over its bulbous shoulders and shuffled off.

"No!" Capacity screamed. "It wasn't her fault!" She tugged at the lifeless girl, but the drudge ignored her and kept walking. Tage pulled Capacity back to the group.

Within mere seconds, it was over.

Tage watched the barbed prong rip from the girl's hand before it fell to the ground. Tage stared in horror. Drops of blood flowed from her wound.

What would be the fate of those two?

Once seven, now down to five. The overlord wouldn't care. Next session, another handful of hopefuls would be forced to become Surge Knights.

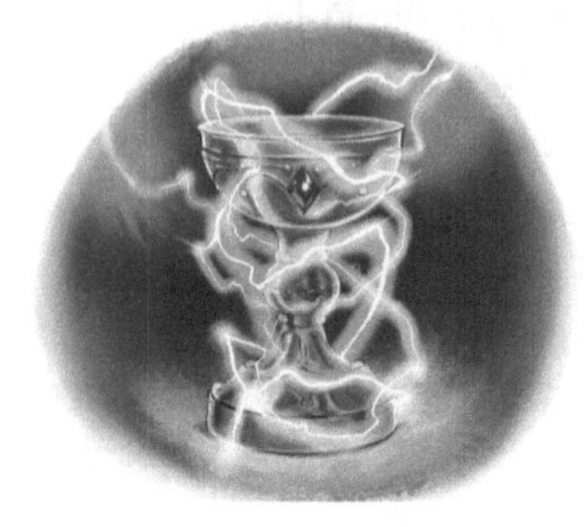

CHAPTER 11

• • • • •

The dark purple skies were alive with lightning and gray clouds, like soapy water swirling down a drain. The marketplace bustled with people slowly gathering their rations and scrambling with change for a luxury item or two. A guy, not much older than Tage, wheeled by in a decrepit and rusty chair, the back of his neck still scarred from an LED. When had he known he could no longer feel his legs? He slipped behind a booth with a sign that read Approved for Desert Goods—meaning he, or something he worked with, had permission to go outside the walls of Currentgrad. Tage's stomach churned. Without Overlord Koax, implants could be done cautiously, giving soil chargers the power without the danger. Such a simple change could affect so many. The overlord was sick.

Impulse stretched his large arms above his head, scanning the square.

For three days, the four friends had watched Overlord Koax closely. Double-checked each shift that guarded the castle. Gone to the kitchen each night through an old service entrance and waited, hoping that Koax's evening snack would be left alone. And while there were far fewer persons about at that time of day, his food or drink had yet to be left alone.

Patience.

Tage reminded himself of this every hour of every day.

He had been given the "honor" of moving from palace duties early if he continued to impress. He'd laughed to himself. He would be long gone before he'd be promoted for loyalty. The poison still weighted a small pocket near his knee.

"It feels so good to be outside of the palace." Capacity's shoulder bumped Tage's as they walked through the bustling marketplace. This was the place they loved to hang out. This would likely be the last time they walked the streets of Currentgrad—at least possibly for years to come. They would leave the memories of their childhood on the worn and dirty streets and flee to Ohmstave. Home for Tage, but another wholly new experience for his friends. They'd get out. He'd make sure of it. He'd had nearly five days with his new tech, and he'd never felt stronger.

Hayrah and Tel'el promised they would have a herd of ursogen waiting for them at the appointed place. There was a specific tunnel entrance that Tel'el had told Tage to use. If they moved downhill, they'd be deposited in the correct location. Tage knew his parents would wait for the signal of White Sparks out of the west spire window.

Tage couldn't wait to spend time with the ursogen— the big, deadly creatures would be the easiest way to travel the desert without interference from any desert-dwellers. Tage still worried that the humans wouldn't welcome his friends with open arms. They had teased him relentlessly for being different when he was a boy. But his parents had assured him that things would be different after they assassinated the overlord. They would be considered heroes.

Capacity paused, and Tage turned toward her. "I love you," she said.

"I love you," he said with a smile. "I wish . . . I wish we could have had that normal life you talked about."

"Maybe"—she lifted onto her toes and placed a soft kiss on the corner of his mouth—"we still will."

He breathed her in. The familiar scent of lavender had been replaced by the smells of the castle, but he loved being close to her just the same.

"We ready?" Lumen asked quietly, determination in her voice.

"Ready for change," Impulse responded.

The castle stretched above them as they neared the front entrance, darker and more foreboding than it had ever been.

Tage nodded as they passed the sentry drudges stationed outside. A muscle in his jaw ticked, and he swiped his damp palms on his leather pants. They had full access to the castle and wouldn't be questioned, but still, his mouth went dry. All he could think about were the demented metal dentures. He wanted to rip them out. He couldn't find the saliva to swallow.

The closer they got to the area of the castle that would lead to the back hallways of the kitchen and the overlord's chambers, the more cautious they had to be. Being seen wandering to and from the barracks was one thing— being seen near this part of the castle would make it clear who had killed Koax. And they *would* kill him.

"Let's hope it's tonight, hey?" Tage whispered as they stepped inside.

The castle halls were quiet.

"So far so good," Lumen said.

They walked quickly into a room and shut the door behind them. They stood in an antechamber with three doors: one they'd come through, one led to a staircase going down to the kitchen, and one led to the hallway connected to the overlord's chambers.

"Kitchen or bust?" Tage joked.

"I'm always in for a meal," Impulse joked back.

"Are you guys ready?" Tage whispered. He looked at each of them in turn. "If we get a chance to drop the poison, there's no going back. And with any luck, we'll slip it in, head to our guard duty, and feign shock and dismay when his death is announced."

Lumen rested her hands over her stomach. "I feel like I'm going to puke."

"Me too," Capacity said, her voice trembling.

"We should be good," Tage said. "The shift change is just about to happen. With even more Knights at the castle, well, we've seen how relaxed they've all become. We have a small window, and we're wasting it."

Lumen nodded toward the door.

He opened the door leading to a stairway, and they descended. Tage took two steps at a time. He cracked a narrow wooden door open, and the hinges squeaked. Impulse had his finger to his lips, telling him to be quiet. Tage nodded. He looked around the kitchen through the crack in the door. The cook added a covered bowl to the tray with the overlord's chalice and late-evening meal.

There was no one else in the room.

Tage only needed a minute.

The cook brushed his hands down his apron and stepped out of the room.

"Drudge-free zone," Tage said. "We have maybe a minute."

"Huh," Lumen said. "I guess the plan is in our favor."

They rushed in and stared at the chalice, which had lightning bolts zapping a white, sparkling stone. Tiny streaks of electricity coursed back and forth across the surface of the liquid and then disappeared and reappeared again.

Tel'el had said that the overlord believed this drink was what had kept him so strong during his older years. Tage smiled at the idea that this very thing would be his undoing.

He removed the vial from the small pocket sewn into his pants. His hands shook. He quickly placed the glass vial on the thick butcher's block. With his thumbnail, he wiggled the cork free.

"I'm watching the door where the cook left," Impulse said. "Let's get this done."

Capacity peered in. "Looks tasty."

Tage smiled and gingerly poured the poison into the goblet. His stomach dropped at the reaction of the liquid. "You've got to be kidding me!"

"Oh, no," Capacity whispered.

The three of them surrounded the cup and watched. Impulse glanced over a broad shoulder and groaned quietly.

"The little lightning bolts disappeared completely," Tage said.

Capacity stood back and put her hands on her hips. "Do you think he'll notice?"

"Of course he will!" Lumen said. "He's paranoid. And, as it turns out, for good reason."

Impulse wiped his forehead. "What are we going to do? Remake the drink?"

"Even if we did," Tage said, "we don't have any more poison. I dumped the whole thing in there."

He couldn't have failed this quickly and this simply.

Please let this not be the end.

"Hurry," Impulse hissed. "I heard voices. They're not moving now, but it won't be long."

"Let me try something," Capacity said. "I'm over-charged anyway."

She dangled her fingertips above the drink. Small bolts of electricity dripped off her fingertips like drops of water. They immediately dissipated in the red drink.

"Hurry," Impulse whispered. "The voices are moving closer."

"Come on," Capacity whispered.

Tage's heartbeat drowned out even his breathing, which he was sure echoed in the vast kitchen.

Lumen ran to the far door, holding it open for a faster escape.

More bolts dripped down, this time with force. Tage's eyes widened. Capacity's hand swirled in quick circles. A small tornado of lightning bolts hovered above the drink, some falling in, sizzling, but a few remained.

"I think she's got it," Tage said softly as he squinted at the glass.

"It's not the same," Capacity said, "but it's close."

"Go, go, go!" Impulse bolted for the door and raced across the kitchen.

Capacity sprinted behind him and Tage took up the tail, spinning the door almost closed just as the cook re-entered the room and set something else on the tray.

Way too close.

Tage turned, walked up the now-empty stairs, and stopped behind the door with his friends. Lumen had a hold of the door handle and eased the door open a crack. "Looks clear."

"Go," Capacity said. "They'll be using this stairway any second."

"We're late for our shift," Impulse whispered.

Capacity slipped out the door. "We'll just pretend like we're not. Like the plan."

It hit Tage as he stepped out of the small antechamber that he'd done it. He'd dropped ten years of painstaking work into the chalice. The poison shouldn't have caused that reaction. If he hadn't had Capacity there, would he have thought to recharge the drink?

Every nerve ending rested on edge. Tage pulled his shoulders back, but also attempted to keep a loose swing in his step. How would he ever repay his friends for taking this risk with him? Could he protect them if they were caught?

They'd gotten through the first step of becoming Surge Knights. Then the second step of learning the guard schedules and timing that with Koax's small nightly meal. After imagining doing that very thing for so long, now that the third step was behind him . . . all he had to do was wait to see if they were successful and then run. Tel'el and Hayrah would be ready to hide as soon as the news broke. Ursogen waited near their exit. The tunnel was near the service entrance of the castle.

"You all remember where to go if we're split up?" Tage said softly.

His three friends nodded.

"I can't believe we just did that," Lumen whispered on a breath.

Neither could Tage. The action almost didn't seem real.

So close. He was so close to success.

At the end of the upper hallway, a thin, weathered Surge Knight greeted them.

"You're late."

"Are we?" Tage glanced around, as if there would be a clock just on the wall. "We were told ten fifteen. I think we're actually a few minutes early." It was dialogue he'd rehearsed once he knew the schedules.

They'd just dropped the poison. Ten years of cautious collecting from pulse dunes sat in a glass in the kitchen.

"Ten fifteen?" The Knight furrowed his brow. "That's absurd."

"That's what I was told," Lumen said. "We've been on time every day. We've always come when we've been told to come."

Impulse nodded. "Sorry, sir. We didn't intend to be late."

"You too?" The Knight looked at Capacity. "All four of you were told the incorrect time?" He shook his head. "I'll be notifying—"

"Is this because you Arced at the ceremony?" Lumen interrupted.

Tage shook his head as warmth raced up his neck.

"I'll bet it is." She rolled her eyes. "Someone's trying to make you look bad because they're jealous."

She was brilliant.

"You Arced?" the Knight asked. "Impossible . . ."

"Oh yeah," Lumen said. "He did it without even trying. Charuss seemed pissed off. I bet he told us the wrong time on purpose." She turned to the Knight. "You know, payback. Doesn't want to be outshined."

"How?" the Knight asked.

"Like this." Lumen folded her thumb around her fingers, making a talking face out of her fist. "You four report at ten fifteen," she made the hand say.

Impulse tapped his foot.

"I didn't mean to," Tage said, ignoring Lumen. "I

just took up too much charge, I guess. I—I haven't tried since."

"Interesting," the Knight said. "Regardless, that doesn't excuse your tardiness."

"Uh, yeah it does," Lumen said. "Remember? Charuss, jealous, told us the wrong time." She used her hand to mimic speaking again.

The Surge turned his attention away from them, then turned back. "I've got my eye on you, young lady. What's your name?"

"Capacity," Lumen said. A wide smile framed her face. "That's C-A-P-A-C-I-T-Y."

Capacity shot her a look.

"We're really sorry," Tage said. He put a hand on the Surge Knight's back and led him away. "Now that we know, it won't happen again. I promise."

The Surge Knight stopped and looked over his shoulder at them. "Just this once." He pointed his index and middle fingers at his eyes, then at Lumen's. "I'm watching you."

He rounded the corner, and Lumen erupted into quiet laughter.

"Very funny, Lumen," Capacity said. She shook out her hands. "I'm still trembling."

"Tell ya what," Lumen said. "I'll take your punishment if we're still around."

"Speaking of," Impulse said softly as they walked, "how long should it all, you know . . . take?"

"I don't know." Koax's food was delivered at the exact same time every night, but Tage had no idea if he ate it right away or savored it. "It should work quickly, though. My parents said we needed to stick around until we've heard for sure. We have to stick to the plan. If we leave before shift, we'll for sure be outed."

"I just want to run," Capacity whispered. "Can't we just run to the tunnel now?"

"If we're discovered missing," Impulse said, "everyone's routine in the castle would be thrown off. The chances of him drinking what we left for him would probably get disrupted with our departure."

"Way to be smart, big guy," Lumen smirked.

Tage tucked his arm around Capacity, and for the first time in a while, she cradled herself against him for a moment. "I'm so sorry you were dragged into this, but we couldn't have done it without you."

She nodded before pulling away.

Their assignment came moments later.

Tage met each person's gaze before they marched to the archive room door. They knew where to go.

The time passed at the pace of a feral stuck in liquid latex. Tage paced back and forth. The door they were guarding had remained vacant. He counted as he walked. At six hundred paces in, he felt like he was about to crawl out of his skin.

Commotion and yelling to their left was followed by Charuss rushing down the main hallway from the Surge Knight chambers; his frail body moved at an unnerving speed.

"Gather everyone!" Charuss called as he moved through the hallway. "Overlord Koax has been poisoned!"

Tage's eyes widened. This was wrong. He was supposed to fall asleep. Die silently.

"Is he okay?" Tage finally asked.

Charuss led a handful of Surges into the antechamber. "No, follow me."

Every Surge Knight in the building ran behind Charuss, who sent ten of the more experienced Knights to surround the outside of the castle.

That would make escape tricky, but to run now would be to seal their fate. Tage had to worry about more than just himself.

Capacity stopped in the hallway. "Let's get out of here. Let's pretend that we thought we were asked to guard outside and then run."

"We can't." Tage grasped her hand. "We have too far to travel to get outside the city. Once they know which tunnel we're in, they could seal us off outside our tunnel entrance, and kill the chargers who have risked everything to help us."

"We're fast," Lumen offered.

Not fast compared to Knights who had trained for years.

"We need to show that we're not guilty," Tage responded. "And then we can sneak out."

"He's right," Impulse said. "To go out now is to put a sign over us that says we're guilty."

The pulse in Tage's ears thumped. Normally, the feeling of current surging through his body felt comforting, but now, it was unsettled in his body—zapping and spinning, setting him on edge. They entered the antechamber and paused. No other Surge Knights could be seen in the dim light.

"This way," Charuss said brusquely.

The four friends closed in together and moved through the doorway Charuss had indicated. Tage knew the layout of the castle—this was a large but unused room. His heart beat harder.

His breathing echoed in the vast, dark space. The door clanged shut behind them.

Tage's heart dropped to the floor. He should have

allowed his friends to run. He should have stayed to distract so they could get away.

"Why did Charuss close the door?" Lumen asked.

"Maybe to keep the death a secret," Tage said. He hoped. "Imagine if it got out that the overlord had died without a controlled announcement. There would be mass chaos."

"Why would they have us come up here?" Lumen asked. "We're new. We're too new to be guarding the overlord."

"I don't know." Tage backed away. He should have never allowed his friends to be involved. "Maybe you're right. Let's go."

They turned together when a voice echoed in the room. "Going somewhere?"

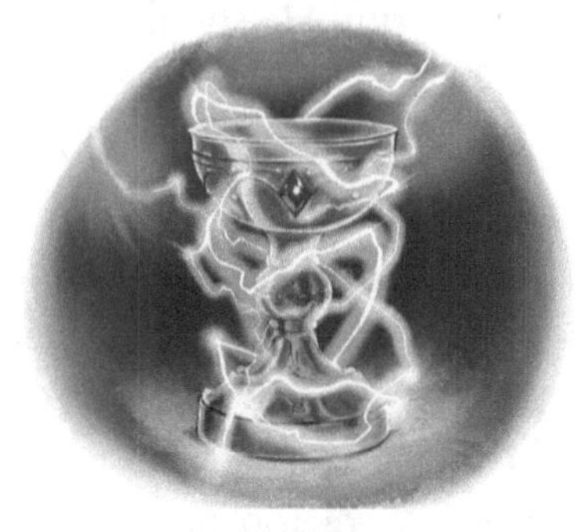

CHAPTER 12

• • • • •

Even though it was completely dark, Tage could feel the enormity of the room. The window on the opposite wall cast dancing shadows on the ground from the lightning storm outside. The aroma of spices and musk filled his nostrils.

Coughing came from the wood-and-steel, four-poster bed near the window. This wasn't an empty room. This was the actual room of Overlord Koax. The room was marked in a different space on the map. Maybe he changed where he slept.

Capacity sidled up to Tage.

"Welcome," a deep, raspy voice said from the shadows—like the grim reaper greeting them to their demise. "I rarely have my newest Surge Knights in my chambers, so this is a special occasion."

Panic bubbled up in Tage's throat. His stomach swirled with acidic froth. Capacity had silent tears streaming down her face. Lumen's eyes were wide with shock, and Impulse stood unmoving.

"Pull it together, Capacity," Tage whispered. He grasped her hand.

The curtains around the four-poster bed slid open. The overlord sat on the edge of his bed, hands clasped in his lap.

Decidedly not dead. Tage swallowed. Ten years of planning. Who knew how many hours of labor. Surge Knights marched into the room, positioning themselves near the exits.

Koax poured the liquid from the chalice onto the ornate rug next to the bed. Then he hurled it at Tage and his friends. Tage ducked and spun, taking in the room. Drudges guarded the doors, with spears and battle axes at the ready. Surge Knights stood between the bed and the window.

Capacity sniffed next to him. If Tage could keep calm, could convince the overlord someone else had dropped the poison, there was still a chance of escape. He couldn't have failed. Not after so much work.

"Why the confused faces?" Overlord Koax asked. "Do tell me how this little plan was going to end."

"Plan?" Tage asked. "What plan? Charuss said you'd been poisoned. We came up here to help." His voice sounded smooth and even—years of training and planning coming to good use.

"Help? Help what?" The overlord scoffed. "Finish me off?" He stood on the liquid-stained rug, and within a flash, had his hand around Tage's throat. "Young Tage." His dark eyes traveled over Tage's face as he gasped for breath. "You showed so much promise. Pity."

Tage kicked his legs as the overlord lifted him in the air. He'd had no idea the frail-looking man still had so much strength.

"This is going to be fun," the overlord said.

Tage kicked wildly and landed a foot in the old man's ribs, feeling the energy within him pulse through his body. Koax dropped Tage into a crumpled pile on the ground, his armor taking most of the impact. Tage gasped for air, his vision blurred. His windpipe throbbed.

Koax stumbled back with a look of astonishment on his face. "My, my, aren't we a powerful little Surge."

"We don't know what you're talking about," Lumen said.

"Please," Capacity pleaded, "listen to her. She's telling the truth."

The overlord clapped slowly, his long, black fingernails clicking sickeningly.

"And here I was going to save you for last," the overlord said. "Capacity, is it?"

"Yes." She bowed her head. "Happy to serve you, Overlord Koax."

"Yes." He approached her and lifted her chin with a bloody finger, staining her face red. "You fools. You should have paid more attention in school."

Tage tilted his head in confusion, his throat still aching from Koax's brief attack. He racked his brain then stiffened, eyes wide. They'd screwed up.

"Ah," the overlord hummed, "it seems young Tage has figured it out. Each cast leaves a piece of you behind. An electric fingerprint of sorts. It takes years to understand how to read it; most never master the art."

Tage clenched his fists. *How could I be so stupid? This is my fault.* All he'd felt was horror when the chalice's electricity had disappeared, and then elation when Capacity's current reformed it.

"As I settled in for bed, one of my loyal Surges informed me the four of you were late. Never in my years have four Surge Knights shown up late during their first months. As I was contemplating your punishment, my evening nightcap arrived. Troubled as I was, I noticed the drink was different. Felt different. The lightning bolts had been disrupted. The usual voltage signature was gone."

Capacity's silent tears had become sobs.

There would be no way for them to recover from her blatant show of guilt.

"Normally, I would have used a drudge to test it, but I was in such disbelief, I placed my own finger in my drink." He held up the same burned and bloody finger he'd placed under Capacity's chin. "Shock worm poison. Nearly ten years without a single attempt on my life, until today. You can imagine my utter surprise when I felt the charge, the disrupted bolts, had come from Capacity. Although, I shouldn't be too surprised—aren't both your parents in jail? Criminals."

"No," Tage yelled. "They are not criminals."

"And now," the overlord said, ignoring him, "I must make this right."

"I . . . I . . ." Capacity collapsed to the floor.

Tage glanced around the room. They were outnumbered in both physical persons and experience. Some of these Surge Knights had been training for decades. Tage and his friends had worn their biotech for mere days.

A drudge ran toward Capacity. Tage opened fire upon the drudge and rushed to her side. He pulled her up and stretched out his arm, throwing White Sparks at the approaching Surge Knights as he and his friends sprinted for the door. The White Sparks rolled and bobbled across the armor of the Surge Knights until they absorbed the charge. He couldn't hold them off. They also couldn't lose.

Lumen and Impulse both threw bolts, but the Knights soaked up shot after shot. This wasn't a skill they'd practiced yet. Once the practiced Knights began throwing ignitions, they'd be hit.

"Capacity," Tage said. "You have to fight."

She lifted her hands, slight sparks dancing on her fingertips. "I'll try."

Tears streamed down her cheeks. Then, she shot a Bolt Ignition out of each hand. Zaps of electrified light shot out from them. One drudge collapsed with a charred hole where its torso had once been. The other drudge's head exploded into hot, steaming chunks.

Lumen sprinted to another drudge, casting a Current Ignition at close range.

A drudge leapt at Impulse, and Impulse kicked the beast into oncoming Knights. The abomination staggered, then Impulse shot White Sparks at its snout-nosed face. The metal staples holding pieces of skin together split open under the heat, leaving scorched skin tags.

Tage kicked the burnt corpse on the way to the door. Just a few feet away, his mind raced. He had no idea what awaited them outside the chamber doors, but it had to be better than this. Grasping the door's metal handle, he released a pensive breath.

He pulled on it, but nothing happened.

The overlord laughed as if he were watching a jester put on a show. "What a dream come true." He almost seemed giddy. "My bedroom has become your tomb." He sat on the edge of his bed, and sparks leaked from his fingertips. He clenched his sheets as the bed coverings singed.

The Surge Knights converged on the assassination crew. Tage stood against the door, the hinge pressing into his back. Nearly out of charge, senses dulled, he could still smell the static in the air as the Surges approached. Charuss snarled like a wild animal with metal teeth. Others squinted as small bolts ignited and coursed around their hands. Just waiting for Koax's order.

He couldn't have lost. Not so fully. So completely. Losing his life while taking Koax's life would have been a trade, but this . . . failure on all counts . . . How could it even be possible?

Tage glanced up. The rafters were too high, but the window might work.

"Dearest Tage, it would seem you are the ringleader in all of this. Before I place you in my powerline, please, indulge me. Nothing would delight me more."

Tage's face drained of all color. At this moment, maybe all he could do was make Koax believe he'd forced them to help.

The overlord's grin was filled with delight—as if he'd planned the entire show for his own amusement.

"Are you working for the humans?" Koax asked. "Or do you have another agenda?"

"No plan. No dealing with humans." He put as much coercion in his voice as he could. Tage rubbed his hands down his face, trying to find another way to prove their innocence. "We thought we were early for shift. We were hungry. The cook wasn't in the kitchen, but we saw your tray. The lightning disappeared from the cup. Capacity just tried to fix it. That's all."

"Grab her," the overlord said.

Three Surge Knights jumped forward

"No!" Tage yelled as he leapt in her direction, but the Knights picked up Capacity as if she were nothing. She struggled and wiggled to free herself, but it was no use. They placed her in a chair, and the overlord approached.

"This one"—he stroked her hair—"is your girlfriend? You love her?" He tugged on a forged ring on her pinky.

"Ah!" Capacity screamed. "No, stop!"

"Tell me." The overlord pulled just enough to create a small tear in her skin, then stopped. A small trickle of blood pooled around the finger ring.

Capacity bit her lip and stared at the ground. She shook her head back and forth; only through clenched teeth did she scream.

He pulled again, widening the rip, and released. "Who are you working for?"

"No one," Tage said. "I swear. If your meal was left unsupervised, you may want to speak with your cook. Perhaps he left on purpose upon hearing us in the hallway."

"Oh," Overlord Koax said, "the cook has been disposed of. He was simple-minded anyway. Not nearly clever enough to work with anyone patient enough to collect poison in that manner."

Tage swallowed.

"What a shame. Because I swear this is going to be unpleasant." He yanked on the ring once more, this time ripping it and the wire from Capacity's skin. She screamed in pain, and tears flowed. "Nine left, and that's just the hands." He flicked the ring on her thumb. "I like to work my way to the center. Maximizes the pain. I wouldn't want you to go numb."

Capacity screamed as he freed the metal ring from her thumb. It released with a sickening pop. Blood trickled down her hand.

"Please," Tage pleaded. "Stop." He stared at the glass window. Heat rose up into his chest. What could he say? That he'd forced her? Would it make a difference? He opened his mouth, but Koax cut him off.

"I will." He yanked another ring out. "When." Again, he tore out another. "You confess." And with that, the fifth ring was forced from her skin. The top of her hand was filleted. She whimpered.

Tage started forward, but every eye of every Surge Knight in the room was trained on Tage and his friends. If there was any hope of escape, it would be to convince Koax to let them go.

"Tel'el," Lumen said. The word dropped from her mouth so quickly, Tage wasn't sure he'd heard her right.

"What are you doing?" Impulse growled between his teeth.

Koax stepped back from Capacity. "What did she say?" He stomped toward Lumen.

"We were commissioned by Tage's parents. Hayrah and Tel'el," Lumen said. Her chin was lifted, her gaze very specifically not on Tage. "Please, let her go."

"Where did you hear that name?" The overlord gritted his teeth.

"No," Tage said. "Everyone just stop." He shook his head. "Let me think!" If he could just find a new angle . . .

"I'm sorry," Lumen said, staring at the floor. "Array is Tel'el. He's been hiding in Currentgrad since he tried to kill you."

"Impossible," the overlord said.

"It's true," she said.

"Lumen, no!" Capacity cried.

"He's killing you!" Lumen yelled. "I had to give him what he wanted. Make him stop!"

"My, my," the overlord said. He tapped his blood-stained fingertips together. Capacity's blood. "What a delicious turn of events. I had already planned on putting you four in the powerline, but I suppose there's room for two more. That is, if Tel'el survives my interrogation."

"No," Tage whispered. He stared at Lumen, then the overlord. "This isn't happening." At this point, his training said that he was to blame Tel'el for everything. That he was to say he was forced into action by a man bent on taking down the overlord. That Tage had been a prisoner, trained and forced into action. Or . . . or Tage should attack Overlord Koax with every bit of power he had left. Closing his eyes, he tried to tap into the pieces of energy still sparking within him, but he had nothing left. A few sparks bounced along his arm and sputtered to a stop at his fingertips.

There was no winning now. Tage would turn in his parents, his friends, or both. And they were all on the line now. The evil smirk on Koax's face said he would destroy every one of them.

"Charuss," the overlord said, "please round up Hayrah and my long-lost friend Tel'el. I can't wait for our reunion." He clapped his hands in excitement. Small bits of blood dotted his face.

The room swirled. Tage couldn't warn his parents, but he had to try and save his friends. At least Impulse and Capacity. And anyway, Tel'el and Hayrah had help. They had a way out of the city. A basement to hide in. They knew the plan would go into motion at any moment. He had to hope their preparation and planning would keep them safe.

The words were bitter in his mouth even before he let them drop off his tongue. He had to focus on his training.

"Let us go," Tage said. "I know you have unfinished business with my dad, but let my mom go with us. Banish us to the Charged Desert, and you can carry on. We won't say a word about the powerline to anyone. You'll have Tel'el. He's . . . he's . . . he's held me since my youth. Forced my friends to comply. He—"

"Your entitlement is incredible," the overlord said. "It's truly—"

"Run!" Tage said.

He ran toward the window. Clenching his fists, he jumped—or rather, faintly Arced with his last bit of charge. Crossing his arms in front of his face, bracing for impact, he closed his eyes.

Thud.

His head spun as he slid down the unbroken window. Blood erupted from his mouth and nose. He'd known he didn't have enough charge, but he'd hoped.

The overlord stood over him. Tage shifted, but felt a foot on his chest. "You really are Tel'el's son. That's the same escape he did. Unlike you, we learn from our mistakes. That window has been fortified. As I said during your exhibition, the glass in this castle is unbreakable. Surges,"—he turned toward them, then back to Tage—"gather up the rest. And you, the little ringleader of this pathetic crew . . . I can't wait for you to see what I have in store for you."

Tage turned his head toward his friends and saw them being rounded up, eyes filled with terror, like animals being taken to slaughter.

"They were forced!" Tage yelled. "I forced them! You want me! You want Tel'el! Not them!"

A boot to his face led to a crack and a snap, which dislocated his jaw. Searing pain surged up the side of his head. He opened his useless mouth, unable to let out a proper cry or command. Red-hot pain spun the world out of focus.

His body slumped lower, and hair wet with sweat clung to him. He had nothing left to give. His eyes caught Capacity's for a mere moment as she was dragged from the room. Desperately, he crawled toward the door before another kick to the face knocked him on his back. Staring at the high ceiling, he tried to make sense of the chaos.

A frustrated tear ran down the side of his face. This defeat wasn't how any of this was supposed to happen. The whole point of bringing in his friends was to help him escape at the end. To help the chance of success. When Hayrah first opened the basement door, Tage should have fought harder. Begged more. Chased his friends from his house. If he'd done that, he may have failed, but at least it would have only been himself on the line.

A vibration on the floor signaled someone approaching.

"Guess you're not so special, are you?" Charuss sneered.

The toe of a boot directly into his temple sent him into darkness.

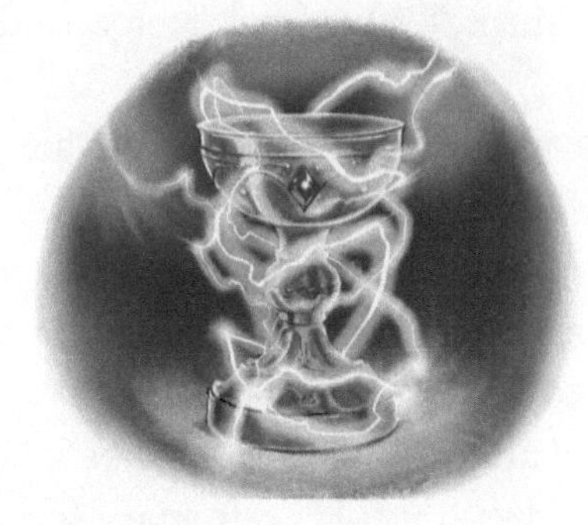

CHAPTER 13

• • • • •

Tage blinked wildly as his bare heels scraped on the porous stone floor. Pain from the rough surface jostled him awake, and a deep ache shuddered through his entire body. For a moment, he thought he was dreaming. But the floor was too cold, the pain too real.

Through walkways and servants' entrances they moved, Tage's vision blurring in and out of focus. The scent of blood and sawdust filled his nose. They were back in the amphitheater, and his heels were rubbed raw. Closing his eyes with more purpose, Tage searched his body for a charge—examining each of his limbs, veins, muscles—but found nothing. Unable to cast an ignition or even struggle. His vision blurred again.

"Hook the traitors up to the cradle," the overlord said.

Tage blinked again, attempting to fight the fog in his head. He turned to the side and saw his friends all strung up like him, just as they'd been during the ceremony. It didn't make sense. They were already Surge Knights. Why were they in the amphitheater?

"Look at them," Overlord Koax said. "Pathetic, really."

Something about the casualness in his voice sent a chill through Tage.

Straps were secured around Tage's ankles and wrists just as they had been before. His head flopped forward, with his back toward the ceiling.

Tage kicked and screamed. He yanked, hoping one of the straps wouldn't hold. He felt again for a charge but was empty—like desperately trying to get a drink from an empty canteen.

"Let us go!" he said through gritted dentures.

"Hmm," the overlord said sarcastically. "But what about the audience? They'd be eternally disappointed if they didn't get a show."

The overlord frowned and pretended to pout, reminding Tage of a look Lumen routinely gave him. Tage lifted his heavy head to see the amphitheater sat empty. Every single seat, vacant. He tried to move, do anything to orient himself. Without windows, he couldn't tell if the purple skies still covered the evening sky, or if they'd given way to a lavender morning. How long had he been passed out?

The overlord turned to the empty seats and made an announcement to the vacant room. "You're all in for a special treat tonight. We are going to do this the old way. No fancy machines. No drudges to help. I'll be performing the entire thing with my bare hands." He held his skeletal hands up.

Had the overlord lost his mind? The procedures had already been purposefully crude and painful. Why the mind games?

Koax waved his bloody finger in front of Tage's nose. The same finger he used to test the poison in his cup. Tage stared at it, disgusted. He never dreamed he'd fail so spectacularly. Koax alive. Him trapped. Helpless to save his friends. What was left of his life?

The overlord rested his digit on Tage's upper lip as the old man continued his announcement to the empty theater.

Tage opened his mouth and bit down. All the pent-up rage finally had an outlet. A bone cracked against his metal denture.

The overlord jumped up and down, trying to free his finger. Tage let up for a moment, just long enough for him to try and pull it free. Instead of pulling away, Tage managed to bite his index and middle fingers. The soft flesh against his mouth unleashed something primal. He bit until blood ran down the corners of his mouth, and he was certain he'd crushed the bones. Surge Knights convened on him, but the damage was done.

The overlord stepped back holding his wrist, blood dripping down his arm. He sucked through clenched teeth, then he whipped his gaze back to Tage. Sweat streamed down his face.

Both of his fingers were still in Tage's mouth. Tage smiled, then he spit them on the floor.

Walking over to a red pot of charged soil, the overlord shoved his good hand inside. He tipped his head back and quickly regained his composure. His robes swished as he walked back toward Tage. Tage could almost see him using the charge to dull the pain.

"Was it worth it?" the overlord asked. "You'll pay for that dearly. If you thought transforming into a Surge Knight was painful, wait until I turn you back into a soil charger and insert you into my powerline."

The overlord scooped up his missing fingers, wrapped them in a handkerchief, and gave them to a drudge. He started to hum a menacing song as he ripped Tage's uniform away from his back.

Tage arched his back as he felt an LED cell being ripped from the top of his neck. Searing pain engulfed his frayed nerve endings. Muscles tore, and his skin was filleted once again. He gritted his teeth.

"Oh, too bad," the overlord said. "This one is stuck."

Tage felt him wrench it from side to side. His stomach lurched and bile crawled up his throat. "Just take it out!" he growled.

One by one, Koax savagely plucked all twenty-four LED charger cells from Tage's back. Blood dripped down like rain. A Surge pulled the box of sawdust over to catch the drippings. The overlord kicked it across the room, scattering sawdust everywhere, and continued to hum.

"No, his blood shall stain the floor. A permanent mark of his failure."

Pain blinded Tage's vision.

He screamed.

Instead of pulling out his forged rings like he'd done to Capacity, Koax gnawed each metal ring off Tage's fingers like a ravenous animal attacking prey. Tage's back arched in pain, and he was barely able to stifle another scream. The overlord's lips and chin dripped Tage's blood.

When the final ring was ripped from his finger, Koax said, "Unfortunately, your body must be mostly intact for the powerline to function properly. Pity." He smiled, showing blood-stained metal teeth. "I wish I could have more fun with you, but I need you alive to connect Anoths and Cathos."

He bent down and worked on Tage's toes, this time with his hands. He slowly tugged each harpooned wire out of the tender skin on the tops of his feet one by one, tearing the flesh. Tage sucked in a breath through his teeth as he felt one of his toes dislocate.

"Whoops." The overlord smiled. "Good thing you won't need those. Walking will soon be a distant memory for you, my boy." He held up the bloody set of ten rings before tossing them to the ground.

"Why not kill me, huh?" Tage asked. "An eye for an eye."

"Trust me," the overlord said, inches from Tage's face, "the powerline is worse than death."

Capacity erupted into hysterical sobs.

"Bring it." Lumen's words were laced with rage.

The overlord flashed dark eyes in her direction. "Oh, you'll have your turn."

"You think you can make my life any worse than it was living in Currentgrad? Try it. Be my guest." She spat on the floor.

Overlord Koax backhanded her so quickly, Tage wasn't sure it had even happened until he saw Lumen's head sag.

"And now for my favorite, the metal denture." He summoned Charuss over. "Let's make sure we don't have another incident, shall we?"

Tage tasted remnants of charged soil under Charuss's fingernails as he forced his mouth open. Tage couldn't draw charge from the tiny bits of soil, but there was something comforting in the feel of something that once held power. The overlord pressed his thick, jagged fingernails into Tage's gums and Tage writhed, tossing his head back and forth violently. He felt his soft tissue tear as he twisted. The overlord hung on, and after what seemed an eternity, the set of metal teeth yanked free.

"Exquisite," the overlord said. Metal clanked against the bloodied floor as he carelessly dropped them. "I deem you excommunicated from the court of the Surge Knight." He tapped Tage on the nose with a bloody stump. "On to your cohorts."

Not his cohorts. His friends. Soil chargers who should have never been involved. He should have trapped them in his parents' basement once they'd hit the bottom. Kept them there until after his failure, and had Tel'el and Hayrah sneak them out.

All he could do now was hope that Koax would be kinder to his friends than he'd been to Tage.

Tage hung with his spine filleted open, trying desperately to catch his breath. But each gasp only brought a fresh round of pain and no relief. He stared at his blood puddle staining the floor. A mark of his failure. A failure for the human race. For everyone on Hadrain. His mouth filled with blood and he choked, spitting up the frothy, red substance.

He watched as the overlord performed the same gruesome procedure on his friends. The overlord waited for Lumen to wake before removing her biotech. Looking away was the best thing he could do, but nothing could shield him from the metallic scent of blood and the ear-piercing screams.

Capacity was whimpering. She was the last one; it must be over. She confirmed it with a primal scream, followed by the clang of her dentures hitting the ground. The ugly dentures that marred her face now bore her blood. Warm tears fell to the ground, mixing with his blood.

They should have never been here. For years, Tage had been an outsider, first as the only half-soil charger in Ohmstave, the human settlement. And with them . . . with Impulse, Lumen, and Capacity, he'd found what he thought a "normal" existence could be. And this—the pain and horror and defeat he felt—should have been his alone. Not his to share. Not with them.

After it was done, the overlord said, "Suture them up and get them ready to transport by the morning."

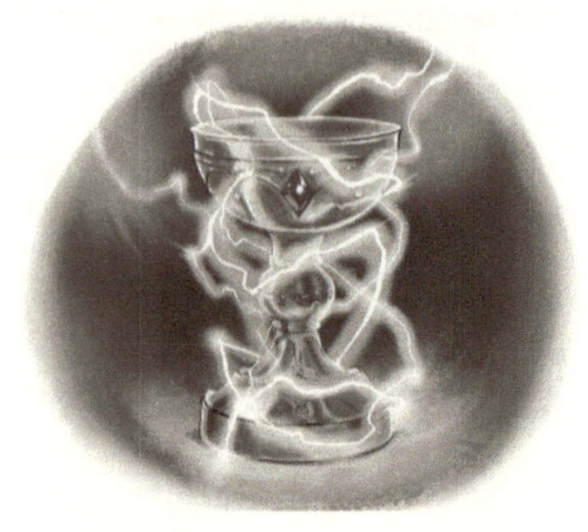

CHAPTER 14

• • • • •

Tage awoke when the fresh wounds on his spine scraped the black Charged Desert sand. He was still in the cradle just as he was the day before. His arms and legs were bound, held by ropes to the mechanism above. The metal limbs of the cradle were stark against the purple sky. His arms and legs had gone entirely numb.

He searched his brain. The last thing he remembered was when the charger who had helped after his initial transformation had come down to the amphitheater floor and made him choke down another pill. It must have been a sleeping pill. He swung between two of the biggest ursogen he had ever seen. Their dark skin was wrinkled at every joint, and their large claws clutched the desert sand—most likely drawing charge to continue to have the strength to carry him. The teats of both swayed limply near Tage's head. Nauseated with a stomach full of blood and the pungent smell of ursogen dung, he did all he could to stay awake.

Tage moved his heavy head to one side and then the

other, but Capacity and the rest of his friends weren't anywhere to be seen. He licked his dry, swollen lips, but got only coagulated blood off them.

"Water," he said, barely audible.

The two drudges leading the ursogen just looked back at him and kept walking. They had shock sticks that every now and again prodded the animal in one direction or the next. Voltage flowed continuously from the Charged Desert to the soles of the drudges' feet, begging to be absorbed. Tage watched as each step made a spark, a little lightning show just for his entertainment on the trip. If he could just get his hands in the dirt, he could heal himself enough to escape. He wished his back could take up charge. Hands and feet—those were the places on Tage's body that could draw charge, and they dangled above him, tied, numb, and useless.

He pulled hard on one of the straps and the ursogen bellowed in protest. The drudge on the right rushed to Tage, and he tightened his body, as if there was some way he could defend himself. *If I can grab the tip of the shock stick, maybe I can charge myself.* Instead, it only poked him, no charge.

"Ouch!" Tage said. "Come on! Can't you see I'm already on my last leg here?"

The day carried on, and Tage lapsed in and out of consciousness both from exhaustion and pain. His hands were a dark shade of blue; the blood had been cut off by the straps long ago. The way he hung, Tage figured he'd lose a hand or foot sometime soon. No blood supply, no appendage. The throbbing in his wrists and ankles was so bad, he almost hoped they would fall off.

Swirling clouds above did nothing to shield the sunlight from scorching Tage's face. The two drudges forced the ursogen to stop. They snorted their wide, black snouts, showing a bit of their sharp teeth as they did.

"There you are," the familiar voice of the overlord said. He sounded so cheerful, Tage would have thought they were old friends. "I thought you two had gotten lost."

The drudges grunted something that sounded like someone trying to gurgle with sand and water.

"Don't let his soles or palms touch the ground," the overlord said. "Like you did with the white-haired girl down the line."

The girl down the line . . . Which girl?

"Where are my friends?" Tage asked. His gritty voice was just above a whisper. The drudge poked him again.

The dark desert stretched in every direction; only slight pulse dunes and swells could be seen around the horrifying line. Tage strained his stiff neck and beheld the most gruesome sight he had ever witnessed. Humans lined up with their arms extended straight out to their sides. Bulbous steel grommets bolted one person's hand to the next. As if each person shared a metal mitten with the being next to them. Steel bolts with heads as big as eyeballs sealed the couplers' two halves together.

The humans were buried up to their knees in charged soil. All were dressed the same, and Tage looked down at his own clothes. Evidently, the uniform for the power-line was white shorts and a matching short-sleeved shirt. Undergarments. He lifted his head and looked down to his toes. As far as he could see, humans were linked together this way. They should have been charred to death. How was this happening? Humans couldn't touch the Charged Desert, let alone be submerged in it. Nothing made sense.

"Tage, this is my greatest invention," the overlord said. "I'm excited that you get to be a permanent fixture of it. But don't feel too special—you're not the only soil charger in this line. There are many. Once I gather enough bodies, I can link both poles of our planet together. I will control all the power. Sell it to the other terraregions. The ground will flourish, and we will farm it. But don't worry, I'll keep a few humans alive. Enslaved, of course. I will allow them to tend to the water. But they cannot be trusted. You're proof of that."

"The humans," Tage moaned, as he once again let his attention go to person after person, bolted together by their hands. No wires or cables, just bolted couplers and bodies.

"Yes." The overlord beamed. "They will be used in a more efficient capacity—Capacity." He laughed.

Tage tried to find the right words to yell but came up empty. This was his fault. He'd dragged her into the plan, and now Capacity, Lumen, and Impulse were doomed to the same fate as him.

"Capacity," Tage whispered. "My parents."

"Young Tage," the overlord said. "So foolish."

Koax waved Charuss over, his cloak billowing around his frail body.

Charuss wheeled over a horizontal platform and placed it under Tage. It outlined the position: outstretched arms and legs together. Another Surge lowered Tage from the saddle's slings onto the platform. Blood rushed back into his limbs. He tried to rub his hands together, but Charuss strapped his hands and feet to the T-shaped form.

The drudges led the ursogen away and left Tage lying on the platform, unable to touch the charged soil. He hadn't noticed before, but there was a large steel-and-wood crane machine off to the side. Three drudges were plugged into it, giving it power. They also maneuvered a hook on the end of a rope toward Tage. It swung wildly above his face. Instinctively, Tage closed his eyes.

When he opened them again, Charuss had hooked the thing to Tage's platform. He signaled to the drudges operating the machine to lift him.

"I guess being able to Arc didn't really matter in the end, now did it?" Charuss said, spinning the platform as Tage went up.

Tage swayed and twisted in the air like an animal caught in a trap. He attempted to free himself, but to no avail. The drudges lowered him in a shallow hole between two humans. He sunk just to his knees.

"Having a soil charger now and again in the powerline does wonders to boost the power!" the overlord yelled over to where Tage was being inserted into the dirt. "Don't worry about putting the insulating sleeves on his legs. These criminal soil chargers don't need them. Let him take up as much charge as possible."

The powerline was a monstrosity in the Charged Desert. A line of soil chargers and humans, attached at the hand, and strapped to a crude wooden cross.

As Tage forced his head to one side, he saw a woman's shoulders rise and fall in a slow breath that went in then out. This was what Koax had meant when he'd said that this was a fate worse than death.

The humans next to him weren't dead, but they weren't conscious either. They were in some sort of shocked trance.

The woman had fingernails that had grown long and curled. Veins had extended from her fingers into the nails. How long had she been here? Years? The man on the right had a mangy beard. A gray food substance matted down the wiry hairs. Tage looked to his left farther down the line to see if he could spot Capacity, but all he saw was a cyclops drudge with a filthy bucket that had gray slop leaking down the side. He carelessly shoved a crusty spoonful into each human's mouth as he shuffled down the line.

"These are your new neighbors," the overlord said. "Do be sure to make friends with them, won't you, dear Tage? They'll be here for you for the rest of your life." The overlord grinned. Sunlight glinted off his dentures. "And try not to die like the last person in this spot. It makes for such a hassle to add someone in the middle of the line. It's the least you can do, don't you think?"

But Tage couldn't answer. The pain, the sleeping pill, the exhaustion all dragged his mind back to a place where he couldn't hold onto a thought for long enough to make sense of it.

The drudge hooked Tage's left hand up. They intertwined his fingers with the woman's, her nail catching on his web between his first and second finger. The drudge pushed hard and her fingernail snapped. Blood seeped from the jagged stump onto Tage's hand. She didn't flinch, open her eyes, or even take a deep breath. She was utterly motionless. Then the drudge sealed the bond with the steel coupler over their entire hands. Bolts were screwed down near their wrists and along the border of the hand trap. It was like a sick wedding ceremony. Bonded together for eternity.

They did the same to Tage's right hand. He sunk deep into the soft, black soil, while the remaining drudges back-filled the hole he stood in. Sparks and sand secured him to infinite doom. Relief didn't come as he expected. Something was wrong—the charge felt different. Being linked in this manner made it so he couldn't draw up any charge and hold it within his nerves. It only passed through him, like a conduit. Pulled from the ground and shoved out the hand connected to the woman.

"The effect will only take a moment, then you'll be completely integrated in your new environment," the overlord said. "Enjoy your new life."

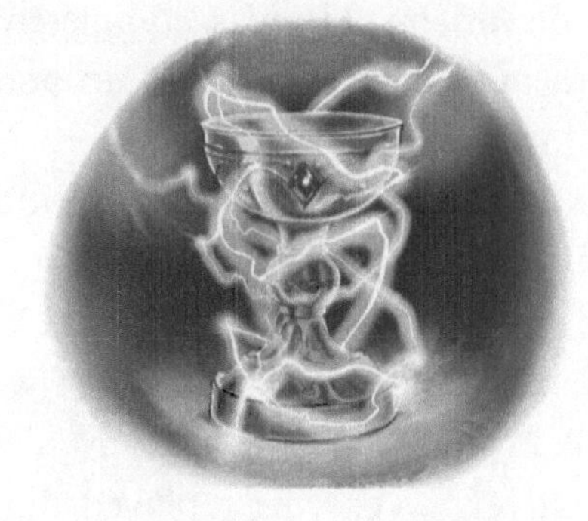

CHAPTER 15

• • • • •

The current was sporadic and uneven—like nothing Tage had ever felt before. It wore on his nerves, fraying them raw.

When he was a soil charger or Surge, taking up a charge was like drinking water. Smooth and fluid. This, on the other hand, was like having water burn your throat. Then came the choking and coughing uncontrollably with every attempt to quench thirst.

The pulses of power shocked his body with a jolt of pain day after day. He'd always loved electricity. The more voltage, the better, was his motto, but now he felt hatred and rage toward it. The current from his feet filled him to the core, then it was ripped from him and moved down the powerline to the next person. Simultaneously, power from the person to his left was being forced into his arm, across his chest, and out the right arm into a human. What kind of dirty power was this?

The charge must be collected in the storage units Tel'el and Hayrah had talked about.

This was his prison. He was completely paralyzed, from speech to movement. He could do nothing except be trapped in his head.

Feedings were infrequent. The sensation of starvation was always there. There was some realization of the world around him, but no power to act. He knew now that he was healed, but didn't know if it was from the current or time in general.

For the first few weeks, he replayed the trap in the overlord's chamber and how they could have gotten out.

He wasn't mad at Lumen for selling out his parents anymore. They had put them all in this situation. Besides, she was only trying to help save Capacity. And that had been Tel'el's advice for a final plan to maybe help set them free. They'd given Koax that information and then been trapped in this . . . hell.

Stuck half in the trance, Tage began to formulate a new plan. Steps that would normally take him an hour or two to sort out now took him days or weeks. But he had time. He had nothing but time. If he could force himself to work on this new time schedule—to learn that he could hold on to information if he didn't force it too hard—maybe he could find a way out. By his guess, about four months had passed. His hair now danced along his midback in the breeze.

If he could just muster enough energy from being plugged into the ground, he could blow the couplers off his hands. He attempted to suck up charge again and again, but it continued to seep out his left hand. He would have to find more patience than he'd ever had before. Energy pulses didn't have enough constant voltage for him to draw on. What charge he sucked up was immediately ripped from his fingertips—or so he thought. Until one day, he realized he could hold a drop of charge here and there. In a reserve somewhere in his nervous system.

Tage surmised that the couplers would rip the charge from him and send it down the line. He carefully held the droplets of electricity within his nerve cells. It took a lot out of him, but he felt the voltage growing inside of him. He'd been trying to bring the charge away from his feet. Now he tried something new and attempted to keep the energy in his legs.

The overlord may have robbed him of his Surge bio-tech, but he hadn't stolen his natural-born charge cells. Those were sacred. A gift from the gods. He spent the better part of a week getting enough energy stored up. Now that Tage knew he could store energy in his legs, he slowly let it rise up within him, allowing a small stream out to help keep the connection. As long as he allowed some power through, some power to join the line from the charge running from his feet, he could continue to store energy.

His body craved the charge. The pulse. Not just the power, but freedom. As he stored more charge, he felt more coherent. The thought that he could wake himself up from the shock trance surged through his nerves. His thoughts moved more quickly, allowing him to replay events and store them. To count the days more clearly.

After weeks of slow power draws, Tage had enough current to feel satisfied with his efforts. It was a pains-taking effort that took an immense amount of patience, one spark at a time, until he felt his natural charge cells becoming full. The pulses of voltage were like trying to fill a large bucket with small droplets of water.

But it was something.

He pushed all the power he drew up down his arms

and out his fingertips. *This is it. I'm getting out, or I'm going to die trying.*

In a shuddering pulse, every watt of energy Tage had drawn into his body released through his left hand—and he hung. Empty. His thoughts once again caving into nothing.

For another week, he allowed himself to hang. The daily protein slop shoved in his mouth was the only reminder that time passed. As another spoonful of the slop entered his lips, Tage once again forced most of the charge to stay in his feet. Then his calves. Several more feedings. Several more days. He was filling up again. This time, he'd have to be far more cautious as he attempted to use the energy. He'd have to keep channeling a small stream out his left hand and into the wire. If he could keep that connection, he could escape.

He'd held the bits of stored energy in his broken nerve cells, but now it was time to release it. Before the energy reached his shoulders and arms . . . before the powerline could steal his pathetic stored charge. Instead of casting an ignition, he'd throw the power as if he were discharging. If he'd calculated correctly, it might be enough to blow off the couplers covering his hands.

It would have to be.

Eyes closed, he imagined the power swirling around and gaining momentum in his body. He had to be quick. His chest warmed as the current worked its way up and out into his outstretched arms. He held the small stream steady, and then in a rush, like lava running through his veins, heat steadily rose up. His fingertips nearly burst from the pressure. Finally, the power shot through his fingertips, and he felt something he hadn't felt in months.

Warm sunshine on his hands. On his face. Chest.

Back. The warmth of the sun was followed by the acrid smell of burnt flesh.

He was free. Or almost free. He tugged at his hands. Shifted his legs in the sand.

Then, the alarms sounded.

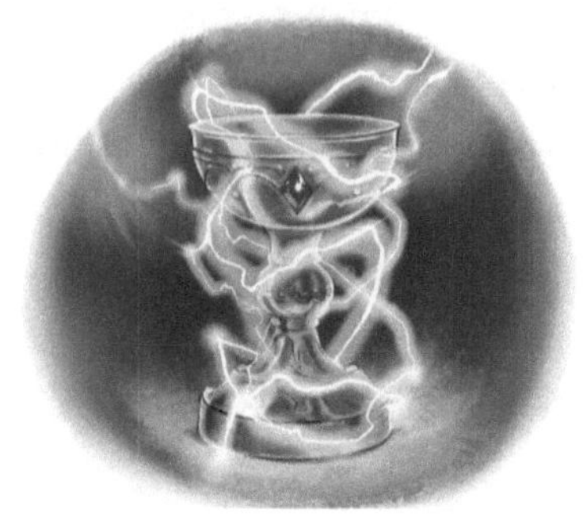

CHAPTER 16

• • • • •

Tage turned to the right, disoriented, finally free of the trance. But its hangover still lingered. Blinking, he could make out sand. The horrifying line of beings attached at the hands. The pain in his fingertips and palms after tossing all his charge and blowing the iron couplers that had been holding him still. He shook his head and tried to comprehend what he was seeing. Black sand. Rocks. The siren flared in his mind—a shocking wave of sensory input after months without.

He bent at the waist, tearing the bindings that had held him to the board, and plunging his hands into the Charged Desert. Sucking up charge without the leak to the powerline was like feasting after a long fast. He sucked in a deep breath through his nose. Suddenly, he was fully awake.

The alarm continued, but he could now set that noise into the background.

Placing his hands on the ground by his knees, he drew

even more charge, and then forced his buried legs out of the sand.

Free.

He looked to the left and right. Both directions of the powerline had collapsed on either side of him. His eyes widened, and his pupils dilated. Humans were toppled, bent at their knees, their delicate skin melted and smoldering on the Charged Desert floor.

Both the woman on the right and the man on the left had hands burned to crispy nubs.

He gasped. *No, no, no! How many humans did I kill?*

Tage was kneeling by a man. He lifted his head to look at him. The man's lips were burned away, exposing his teeth. The long beard was singed, and his eyes were empty orbs oozing orbital liquid down emaciated cheeks.

Tage crawled to him. "Hey!" He shook the man's shoulders. "Can you hear me?" He scooted to the next person in line. "I'm sorry! Please, wake up." Her eyes had burst as well, leaving clear gel pooled in the sockets. Her lips were also burned black.

He paused and looked at the leg insulator. White rubber encased the humans' legs, but small copper wires jutted out from every angle. *He forced electricity through them, without burning them alive. How?*

Tage rolled onto his back next to her and cried. The alarms continued; anxiety bubbled up in his throat. There had been an empty space here before Tage had arrived. He knew the line could be separated, but he couldn't fathom how to release everyone—there were thousands— let alone get them back to Ohmstave safely.

Over twenty humans in each direction lay flopped on the ground like discarded rope, still hooked to each other with metal couplers. Tage drew up power and tried to cast a current ignition directly at one of the steel rivets to free them. It sputtered, dangling from his fingertips until he shook it loose.

Squinting his eyes, he tried again. The putrid smell of scorched flesh filled the air around him before the rivet came loose.

The siren continued to blare.

He couldn't free them. Where would they go? They couldn't walk on the Charged Desert without the protective cribriform suit. Instead, he'd go back to Ohmstave and tell the elders to come get them, so they could rescue the living, and also bury their dead. They'd have the tools. He could strengthen himself to help—to make up for how wretchedly he'd let them down. He didn't have time now—the alarm made sure of that. He needed to create as much distance between himself and the powerline as possible.

But first, he had to find his friends and parents.

Tage tried to stand on wobbly legs before collapsing again. He took the opportunity to draw up more power. His muscles had atrophied; if not for the charge, he'd be done.

He searched feverishly, taking up charge every few minutes. Exactly what Proxy had told him not to do. But this was an emergency. He'd rebuild his muscles behind the safe gates of Ohmstave.

A crack of lightning flashed in the distance. He laid his forehead on the charged dirt, listening.

Beep. Beep. Beep.

He put his hands over his ears.

"Shut up!" he yelled at the alarm. "Just let me think!"

He ran east, searching for a familiar face in the powerline. Sprinting, using false energy on borrowed time, he saw long, tight braids on a girl.

Lumen.

He shook her. "Lumen, I think you can hear me. I'm going to blast off your coupler on each hand and get you out of here."

Drawing up a fresh charge, his hands shook. Overcharged. He stood a few feet away, aimed down his arm, and shot a Bolt Ignition at her right hand. Sparks bounced back and singed her hair and arm. The metal exploded and fell off her hand. Tage quickly grabbed the human hand next to her, cautiously resting the man's hand on the coupler. No way was he going to be responsible for another human death. He repeated this on the other side. Both humans were slumped against another human, but no skin was exposed to the desert floor.

"Tage?" Lumen asked, her voice groggy.

Beep. Beep. Beep.

"Lumen," he said. "Here, I'll help you out. But first, draw up a charge. We're weak."

"How?" She shook her head. "I don't understand. What was that noise . . . oh, my head." She cradled her head, then vomited bile down her front.

"Lumen," Tage said as he held both sides of her face. "You have to move now. I don't know what the alarm is, but it can't be good."

She reached down and plunged her fingers into the ground. Falling forward, Tage grabbed her shoulders and held her upright. Her frail, emaciated body didn't respond like it used to.

"Thank you," she said. "The charge, it feels wonderful. Now all I need is a hot bath and something to eat."

Tage dug at the sand by her knees while she recovered.

"Come on," he said. "Let's go. We have to move."

She stood on wobbly legs.

Tage instructed her to draw up charge as often as she

needed to stay strong. "I think you should head east, and I'll go back west. We've got to find Capacity and Impulse. Maybe my parents too. I'm not sure if they're here."

Lumen shook her head. "I think we should stick together. Get to the humans and get food and help."

Beep. Beep. Beep.

And then the dull roar of a ship.

"Do you hear that?" Tage pointed to the sky. "They're coming. If you see a shock craft, bury yourself in sand away from the broken powerline. It's the only way."

"Look," she said. "I'll trust you, but no one painted this as a possibility for us, okay? I figured worst case scenario, I'd be in jail or dead. Dead would have been better."

"Then let's get out of here," Tage urged.

"I'm going!" she yelled as she started the direction he'd pointed. "Even though you're the reason we're in this—"

"Fine!" Tage yelled. "I'm sorry, okay? I can't do anything about it now. This isn't helping. We need to get our friends and escape."

Tage turned and headed back west, where he'd originally come from. He had to find them. But Lumen's words rang in his head.

This was his fault. He was the reason. He hadn't thought quickly enough—not when his friends were first introduced to the plan or when they'd first been summoned by Charuss.

Running with false strength was like drinking ale to hydrate. It didn't make sense, but it worked in the moment, and he'd surely pay for it the next day. He'd passed his broken spot in the line and was careful to avoid looking at the dead bodies. After maybe a mile of running, he felt real thirst. His throat was drier than the desert. About fifty feet away was an outcropping of amp plants.

Beep. Beep. Beep.

He rested his hands on his knees, caught his breath, then walked over to the succulent plant. Pulling a long, thick, orange leaf from the base of the plant, he quickly brought it to his lips and let the thick, sour liquid coat his throat. His mouth watered. Normally, he'd gag at the thought of drinking the acidic water, but today it was his savior.

Not wanting to leave any evidence behind, and because he was starving, he resorted to eating the bitter leaf after he drained it of the water. As a small child, he'd hated it when they were forced to eat the rare desert plants. Now, he was grateful.

"That was less disgusting than I remembered," he rasped, wiping his lips.

Bare feet pounding the hot sand, he continued to run along the powerline. A tall, thin boy hung limply. How could anyone so young be part of this . . . wait. Tage slowed. He knew that bald head. His once-muscular brute of a friend had been reduced to a sad, slender boy. His heart sank.

"Impulse," Tage yelled. He ran harder than ever. "Impulse, I'm coming."

He tripped, skidding down on his knees, then jumped to his feet. Blood seeped out of his new wounds.

He lifted Impulse's face with trembling hands and said, "Hang on, buddy. I'll get you right out."

After freeing himself and now Lumen, he felt like he was an expert. Blast the coupler, grab the human, and turn them so they were resting on the person next to them. Lickety split.

Oh no . . . I forgot to tell Lumen how to free them.

Even now, he continued to fail his friends. Tage had to work harder. Better. Faster. Smarter. Moving through the same steps he'd used to help Lumen, Tage worked frantically. He couldn't take anyone else's death on his conscience.

After his hands were freed, Impulse collapsed to his side before Tage could grab him.

"Impulse," Tage said as he rolled him over, leaving his feet in the sand, begging him to pull a charge. "Impulse, come on, buddy." Tage shook him. "Wake up."

His eyes fluttered, then rolled back into his head.

"Get up," Tage said. He lightly tapped Impulse's sallow cheeks. "I know you're in there."

Impulse groaned and rolled his head from side to side. Tage kneeled on the ground and dug Impulse's legs up from the sand. The coarse, gritty texture worked its way under Tage's black fingernails and separated the nailbed from the skin. New pain shot up from his fingertips. He cursed under his breath. He put his arms under Impulse's armpits and pulled him out of the hole.

"Tage?" Impulse rasped. "I can't believe it." He put his hands up to his ears. "What is that noise?"

"It's an alarm. I broke free and . . . just, please, we have to go. Draw up a charge and cast a few ignitions until they feel right."

Impulse slowly dipped his hands in the charged sand. Tage stared at him. At the way his bones protruded where he used to have bulging muscle. He'd become so thin—like a ghost of who he used to be. Walking over to the amp plant, Tage broke off another leaf.

Beep. Beep. Beep.

"Get a drink while you can," Tage said.

Impulse snapped off his own leaf.

Color slowly flushed back onto Impulse's face, but his

cheeks were sunken in his new gauntness. He slurped the same way Tage had, and the two friends finished together. "I hated these when I was a kid," Tage said, wishing he could look at Impulse and not see the sickening way the powerline had drained him.

"I already found Lumen. She's east of here looking for Capacity. We have to go find her. I forgot to tell her how to safely free people . . . I don't want anyone else to get hurt."

Impulse nodded and they ran. The hot sun beat down on their weathered bodies.

"Wait," Impulse said as he fell to his knees. "I need to charge."

They both paused, shoving hands and feet into the current-ladened sand to draw more energy. If Tage had been just human, the charge would've killed him. Even without the desert charge, without the power they gained from the soil beneath them, the humans wouldn't survive. Tage knew small camps of humans and soil chargers lived together here—he just didn't know how.

"Okay." Impulse stood slowly. "Let's go find them."

Tage nodded and they continued on. The beeping was unrelenting—thank the suns that Koax didn't have the manpower to keep drudges or workers at every station. They'd be toast. If he hadn't put so many on the powerline, maybe he would have had enough. Again, Tage's feet felt numb as he traveled through the desert, but at least he was using his feet rather than having them strapped to a crude cradle between two ursogen.

They stopped to charge every few minutes. Being free, no longer part of the sick powerline, pushed them through any pain they had.

As they crested a small ridge, Lumen was running at them, waving her arms.

"This can't be good," Tage said. "I hope she didn't hurt anyone trying to free Capacity."

"Tage," Lumen yelled. She continued to sprint toward them. "They're coming!"

He stepped next to Impulse. "Who?"

"The overlord!" she gasped.

"Where?" Tage asked.

"Back there!" She pointed over her shoulder. "They're in shock crafts."

"Wait," Tage said. "Did you find Capacity?"

"No." She shook her head, just now close enough for Tage to see the tears leaking down her face. "I looked, but then the shock crafts appeared and I ran back toward you."

Tage looked to the purple, swirling sky. Lightning loomed in the distance, but nothing out of the ordinary. "I don't see anything."

"They're coming," she said. "I saw them in the distance. The alarm—they must know we broke free. What are we going to do?"

"I, um, let me think." Tage scanned the area. Nothing but sand as far as he could see. No pulse dunes, nowhere to hide. "We'll have to bury ourselves."

"Where?" Lumen asked as she swiped at her eyes.

"Here," Tage said as he dropped to the ground.

Impulse started digging with his bony arms.

"We're nowhere near our missing spots on the powerline," Tage continued. "Surely, they're going to see what triggered the alarm. They're flying overhead. They'll be looking for movement, or something. We'll stay buried; the sand is our only camouflage. We'll have to be extra careful. The contrast with our white hair will be obvious against the black desert."

"We just got free." Lumen collapsed and cried. She let out a string of curse words. "I can't go back in that line."

"Lu," Impulse said. "Dig."

"Don't you 'Lu' me at a time like this," she snapped.

"Dig."

Lumen rolled her eyes, but relented. Quickly digging shallow holes was their only salvation. After a few minutes, Tage realized it was taking too long.

"You guys," Tage said, "back up."

"What?" Lumen asked.

"Move," Tage said.

He'd never cast a Bolt Ignition with the purpose of it making a long scar in the ground, but this seemed like a cogent time to try. Concentrating on the angle of his hands, he threw a single bolt so that it got deeper as it skidded along the ground. Roughly five feet long, shallow at the beginning, but several feet deep toward the end of it. Dirt shot up with each additional bolt as the hole got deeper.

"Lumen," Tage said. "You first."

She jumped in the hole, lay on her stomach, then tented her arms over her head. Impulse shoved a large pile of sand over her, then jumped in and mimicked Lumen's stance.

"Can you breathe?" Tage asked.

"Yes," Lumen said. "For now."

Tage dug his heels into the ground and pushed on the mound. Stopping just for a moment, he got a fresh charge then pushed again. With Impulse covered, he still had to push what sand was left toward his spot and cover himself as best he could. He paused. In between beeps from the alarm, he heard the unmistakable sound of a shock craft. His heart thudded faster than he thought possible. The static rip of electric charge was close.

Since he had to cover himself, he had to lay face up. First, he covered his legs and midsection. Panic bubbled up in his throat. This was a bad plan. He had no way to completely cover himself. The scratching sound of the shock craft drew closer. He tucked an arm behind his head, creating a small pillow. He covered all but his eyes and nose with dirt. Desperately throwing dirt over his chest, he heard them just about overhead.

If he was discovered, the first thing he would do was scream and ask what they'd done with his friends. Play dumb. Keep them hidden. He would never let them down again. Capacity couldn't be too far away. He just had to get to her first.

Left with no other choice, he plunged his free arm into the sand, held as still as possible, and hoped for the best.

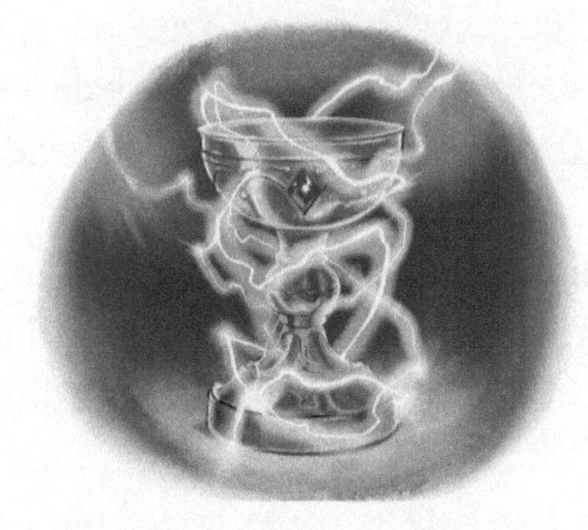

CHAPTER 17

• • • • •

Tage breathed shallowly so as not to disturb the sand barely covering his chest. He watched as the shock crafts zoomed past them. Once they'd flown overhead, he shifted just enough to follow the flight pattern. They hovered over the broken line where Tage had been for the last four months, then they dropped from the sky.

He waited, trying to hold as still as possible.

After a few minutes, the crafts rose into the sky again and continued down the line. He saw them drop from the sky for a few minutes, then rise again. He could barely see them, but they repeated the same pattern a third time. Had Tage gone that far? He wasn't sure. He'd turned around after getting Impulse, assuming Capacity was the other direction. But during this stop, Tage listened, and they seemed to be on the ground for much longer—that or anxiety was getting the best of him.

"What's going on?" Lumen asked, her voice muffled. "Tage? What's happening?"

"I think they're examining the disturbances in the

line. It looks like they stopped over our missing spots. And—" Tage sucked in a breath and tried to wiggle lower in the black sand. "Stay down. They're headed back this way."

He held his body as still as possible, unable to keep his chest from heaving. With each breath, little pieces of sand entered his nasal cavity. Breathing out his mouth was worse. Grits of sand settled into his already dry mouth. It was like a test to see how long he could take the irritant until he snapped.

This time, Tage closed his eyes and held his breath as the shock crafts zoomed over him like water on a hot plate. They were going much faster than before. Heading back toward Currentgrad, he assumed.

Three crafts had gone by. Was that all of them?

Were there three before? Or four? Think, Tage, what was it?

He tried to concentrate and recall this simple detail, but he was too exhausted and too clouded after months in the line.

"Tage?" Impulse asked. "How much longer do we need stay buried?" His voice grew higher. "I think I'm claustrophobic."

"I'm not sure, I think they're gone. Lumen, do you remember how many shock crafts you saw earlier?"

"Three," she said. "Tage, I can't breathe. I gotta get up."

"Okay," Tage said. "Let me get up first. I want to be sure."

Tage emerged, like a shock worm from a pulse dune. Since his hole was relatively shallow, he needed no assistance getting up. He spit sand from his mouth and wiped his face, trying to get the grit off. He ran up to the ridge where they'd met Lumen earlier. With a solid vantage point, he scanned the area. Reaching into the sand, he pulled a fresh charge from the earth to improve his vision.

He searched the area once more.

Nothing.

And silence.

No alarm.

"We're clear," Tage yelled. He ran back toward his friends. "Get up. We have to go."

He dug at Impulse's spot, helping him out first. Impulse nodded to him in thanks once he was free. Silently, he helped Tage free Lumen.

She stood and shook off like an extremely skinny wet dog.

"That was horrible," she said. "I think—"

"Wait." Impulse held up a hand, silencing her. He stood, pensive. "The alarms. They've stopped."

"Good," Lumen said. "That crap was annoying."

"I'm not sure if it's good or bad," Tage said. "Come on, I think Capacity is west. I saw the shock craft land past both my and Impulse's spot in the line."

"What about your parents?" Lumen asked slowly.

Tage shrugged in a loose gesture that he didn't feel. How much harder would it be for them to continue to Ohmstave with Koax not only left alive, but knowing Tel'el was in Currentgrad? Koax would want to exact his revenge on Tage's group as well as Tel'el. "They had escape routes planned, and a basement to hide in. I just hope that they're in Ohmstave to greet us when we make it there. I don't think they'd even guess at Koax putting us in the line." He repeated the words to himself again and again. Four months or more was a long time for Tage to be missing and for his parents to not send a party to even check the line. If they hadn't sent someone to check, how okay could they be?

He shook off the thought.

"We need to move," Impulse said. Again, Tage stared at his friend's emaciated body.

They ran quietly for a while, stopping to charge, and then continuing on. Tage loathed looking at each person on the line in turn, but to find Capacity, it was necessary. She had to be here somewhere.

"What's the plan after we get her?" Impulse asked.

After we get her. Tage had to keep this positive thought.

"We go to Ohmstave," Tage said. "And honestly, we're not that far. If we see Capacity or my parents, we can help them down and keep going. If not . . . we can't survive out here for much longer without help. That amp plant we drank from—"

"You had a drink?" Lumen yelled. "And you didn't bring me any? You guys suck!"

"Come on," Tage said as he started jogging. "This way, they're just up ahead. Anyway, the big amp plants, like the one we saw, only grow near Ohmstave. We're probably a day, maybe two away from it. I'm surprised they took us so far away from Currentgrad."

"I'm not," Lumen said. "Last thing they want is to have the assassins close to the overlord."

"Or the overlord wants to keep the powerline a secret and as far away from the soil chargers of Currentgrad as possible," Tage said.

Since Capacity was the one who had "fixed" the sparks in the overlord's drink, maybe it was more likely that she'd be the farthest from Currentgrad. Tage picked up hope and lengthened his stride.

Impulse ran next to him, his footsteps almost silent.

Tage wanted to beg their forgiveness. Tell them that he could have trained harder. Done more. Planned better or different—but he had to focus on getting them somewhere safe. A place where they could regain their strength and rebuild their lives.

They ran in silence until they came upon the outcropping of amp plants. Orange leaves, a stark contrast from the black earth, jutted wildly from the plant.

Lumen rested on her knees and pulled the thick leaf from the base. Tage and Impulse did the same. "Here goes nothing." She tipped the long leaf high above her mouth as she drained it of its moisture. "Ugh." She grimaced. "That sucker is bitter."

"Have a few, and bring the leaves or eat them, but we can't leave any trace behind," Tage said.

Their rest was only a few minutes, but after having the time to recharge, Tage felt refreshed, as if he'd slept for days. They raced close to the powerline, searching for Capacity. Nothing but humans. Legs buried to their knees, all strung up, arms splayed out and connected to each other by their hands, heads forward, chins on chest.

"Are they dead?" Impulse asked.

"No," Tage said. "They're in the same shock trance we were in."

"But they . . . I don't understand, how are they not electrocuted? Their skin not singed?"

"They're not touching the ground," Tage said. "It's insulated on their legs. Somehow it allows their body to act as a conduit, but it doesn't harm them."

"That's why he needs soil chargers," Impulse added. "We pull the charge from the ground, and the humans pass it to the small storage stations. I think your parents said something about that."

"Until the powerline is finished," Tage added. "And he's connected the two ends of the planet."

They could not allow that to happen. Too many

people had died already. Tage shuddered as he thought about the destruction he'd left in the line.

"The overlord is sick," Lumen said. "A real demented bastard."

"I killed them," Tage blurted out. "The humans. When I released myself from the line. I didn't know what I was doing." He felt Impulse rest his hand on his shoulder. "After they report this to the overlord, they'll be out, hunting humans to repair the line. It was selfish . . . but, I didn't know."

"I know," Impulse said. "Let's keep moving. We can get help. We can report to people with more resources than three disgraced soil chargers in their undergarments."

Tage led the pack once more. When they came upon Impulse's empty spot in the line, Tage examined it. The Surge Knights hadn't done anything to attempt to repair it. But what could they do? It wasn't like they had a few extra bodies on hand. No, they were there examining what happened to cause the disturbance.

The farther west they traveled, the rockier the terrain became. Tage remembered this. It had been a long time. A long time, indeed. The soft sands of the Charged Desert turned to porous, rocky ground. Like walking on enormous lava rocks.

"What's this?" Lumen asked.

"I've never seen anything like this before," Impulse said.

"I'd honestly forgotten about it," Tage said. "On this side of the planet, the ground isn't sandy until you get to the shore of the Saptex Sea."

"Yeah," Lumen said, "well, it sucks. I can barely draw a charge from it."

"Really?" Tage asked. "I'm pulling up a charge

almost constantly. I actually feel over charged." He drew energy down through his feet until he Arced, helping him to disperse some of the leftover energy.

"Huh," Impulse said. "I agree with Lu, I don't feel much of a charge."

"It's still electrified enough to electrocute a human if they were to touch it," Tage said. "Nothing out here is safe for them."

Lumen shook her head. "I can't imagine being so weak."

"They've adapted," Tage responded as they continued to move.

"What if they could harness the power, not with humans in a powerline, but somehow draw it up? Take all the electricity from the ground?" Lumen asked. "It might be a good thing for everyone."

"Yeah, it would change our world," Tage agreed. "But not all for the better."

They jogged in silence for a few moments.

"If the charge did disappear, we for sure don't want one person deciding who gets it and who doesn't. Besides, the humans have done just fine living with it. Their biggest obstacle is the overlord," Tage said.

"Well, and I like being charged," Impulse pointed out. "No charge sounds awful."

No charge sounded like the frustrating emptiness Tage had felt while in the line. He shuddered.

"Hey, look!" Impulse sprinted ahead. "There's a break in the line."

A break? "Do you see anyone?" Tage asked as he sprinted with his friend. "Capacity!"

"Capacity!" Lumen yelled.

But they saw no one.

On the farthest stop, the shock crafts had stopped for longer. Long enough to take someone from the line.

Capacity was gone.

They'd taken her.

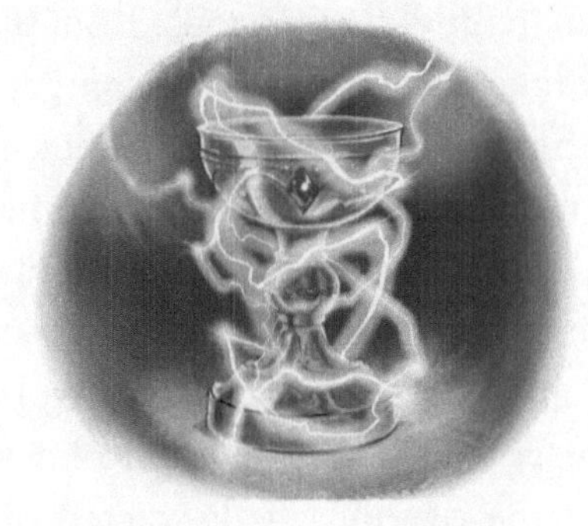

CHAPTER 18

• • • • •

Tage ran to the empty slot; two humans lay smoldering on the rocks on either side of what had to be Capacity's vacant spot. He fell to his knees and held his face. "They took her. The Surge Knights saw we were gone and they took her."

"Maybe she got out like you?" Impulse offered. "Capacity's smart."

"She is," Tage agreed. "But I saw them, the shock crafts. They only stopped at our areas for a few moments. I listened to them as I hid under the sand. They stayed grounded in this area for much longer. Then they rose up into the sky and flew back toward us."

"They took her back to Currentgrad?" Lumen asked. "Is that what you think?"

"We have to go get her," Tage said.

"Tage, stop," Lumen said. "You're being ridiculous. We need to have a plan first, and for crap's sake, we don't even know if they do have her. Maybe the humans rescued her? Maybe one of your parents was in this spot."

"If the humans could save people from the powerline, they wouldn't take an unknown soil charger," Tage said. "Plus . . . my parents would know to look for us in the line. It's been months, and they haven't come."

"Months," Impulse said softly. "My family . . ."

Tage's heart twisted at how helpless he knew Impulse would feel. Impulse had been ready to work as a Surge Knight to protect his siblings, and who knew what kind of punishment the overlord had exacted on them. Perhaps, with them being so young, he hadn't bothered. Yet.

As he scanned the line from where he knelt in the sand, Tage added, "I haven't seen my parents on the line either."

"Jail," Impulse said. "Like Capacity's parents."

"Maybe," Tage said. He looked back toward Currentgrad. "I don't know if they're still alive." It felt like he'd swallowed a brick. "Or if they're trapped there, or escaped, only to . . ." The possibilities were nearly endless.

"I'm not screwing around here," Lumen said. "I'm not sure if you noticed, but our last plan didn't exactly go off without a hitch. And now you want to beat down the doors to the Voltaic Dava, where we are clearly uninvited?"

"She's your best friend," Tage said. "How can you just abandon her?!"

"It's called survival, Tage. I learned from my mistake at the castle." She crossed her arms. "I can't bust her out or be her best friend if I'm back in that"—she pointed toward the powerline—"or dead. If you want to run there, be my guest. But you owe it to us to get us sanctuary in Ohmstave. At least until we can figure out what to do."

She was right. Of course she was right. They were

closer to Ohmstave, they had no food or supplies, and they were all weak from being trapped in the line.

"You're right," Tage said, feeling heavier with each passing moment. "We're wasting time."

"Exactly!" Lumen said. "I thought your giant human brain could figure this crap out. They know we're gone. The Surge Knights have probably already reported to the overlord and sent them back out to hunt us. We. Need. To. Go."

"I agree with Lumen." Impulse shuffled to continue forward toward Ohmstave.

"We're tired," Lumen added, her voice softening slightly. "We need to heal, and we need a plan. Look, let's just drag ourselves to Ohmstave, beg the weak humans to let us crash there for a day or two, and come up with a plan, okay?"

"Yeah. Fine," Tage said. "Fine, but only for a few days."

Impulse nodded.

"Do you remember the way?" Lumen asked. "Or is your big old brain failing you again?"

His human brain wasn't in the best condition, but he did know the way to Ohmstave.

"Follow me." Tage led them in a southwestern direction. The sharp rocks had taken over all the sand, and the uneven terrain forced his attention below. The occasional plant grew more frequent, but the rocky surface still undulated like the dunes in the Charged Desert. The charge was lower here, allowing more vegetation to grow. They were leaving the horror of the powerline behind them, but it would mean Tage no longer had the ability to look for Tel'el or Hayrah. Though there was a chance that a connection to Ohmstave and the humans would have gotten word as to where his parents were.

Tage ran, his friends with him. Every step was like a thousand dull needles being jammed into his feet. But left with no choice, he kept moving. Occasionally, he'd look over his shoulder and see the purple, swirling sky, but no shock crafts. He knew it was dumb to look; he'd hear them before he saw the craft.

"How's your charge?" Tage asked.

"It's getting to be normal," Impulse said.

"I guess," Lumen said. "It feels like someone keeps turning the faucet off and on for no reason. It's irritating. But getting better. Yours?"

"It feels weird," Tage said. "Definitely different. Are you guy sucking up charge constantly through your feet?"

"Yeah, just a trickle. Same as before." Lumen shook out her hands.

"No, not like that." Tage stared at the ground. "But it seems like now, I get fully charged with either my feet or my hands. I've never been able to draw a full charge from my feet before."

"No one has," Impulse's face twisted in confusion. "Not even a Surge Knight can do that."

"I know," Tage said. "It's weird."

"Well, lucky you." Lumen bent at the waist and plunged her hands in the ground. "I still have to do it the old-fashioned way. I can only top off through my feet. Like everyone else, Tage."

"Do you think that's why you were able to store enough charge to blast us out of the powerlines?" Impulse asked.

"Maybe." Tage shrugged. "It's the only explanation. I honestly don't know what happened."

He was hoping their charge was constant, like his. No longer intentionally sucking it up, but rather a current that constantly flowed. No reserve to fill, no limit to the amount of current allowed in the body. But theirs wasn't, and he couldn't explain why his charge was suddenly different.

After the first mile, his feet stung. A few miles after that, he simply Arced rather than walked. Big, long leaps allowed him to jump ahead of his friends, then wait for them to catch up. Arcing ahead felt as easy as running—in some ways easier. He could float rather than push on his sore feet. He took in the landscape. It had been so long since he'd seen the black rock and orange amp plants. The rare times he had left Currentgrad, all that could be seen for miles was black sand and an occasional plant.

The sky darkened, and dusk was settling into deep purple. The relief from the suns helped Tage breathe again. He knew the air was still hot, but there was so much reprieve in the slight temperature change that he drew in large lungfuls, which helped ease some of the aching in his chest. He knew they'd made the right decision in going to Ohmstave, but he also felt like a traitor leaving Capacity, and possibly his parents, in the hands of Koax.

"Should we stop?" Tage asked.

"For the night?" Impulse asked.

"Yeah?" Tage wasn't sure what the best move was, and he was decision weary.

"I don't think that's a good idea," Lumen said. "Maybe just a little break. The overlord will be pissed when he finds out what happened. He'll probably come looking for us himself." She wrung her shaky hands.

"True," Tage said. He sat on the rocky ground and rolled his neck from side to side. "And I'm sure he's assuming we're going to Ohmstave."

Impulse sat without a word, his head turning as he took in their surroundings.

"Dang." Lumen stretched her legs out in front of her. "It's so weird out here. Like another planet. Is it like this in Ohmstave?"

"No," Tage said. "It's sandy right outside the city, on the shore of the Saptex Sea. But just beyond that it's like this, pulse dunes as far as the eye can see. And lots of amp plants. They're a staple for the humans."

"Ew." Lumen made a face. "No shock worms?"

"Rarely," Tage answered. "Too dangerous. No one wants to get electrocuted while hunting them. They eat ferals too. They even grind their bones up and make a type of bread out of it."

"Double ew." Lumen stuck out her tongue. "They eat giant rats?"

"Yep." His mouth watered just thinking about food from home.

"Aside from disgusting food," Lumen said, "what is Ohmstave like?"

"It's a wooden fortress on stilts above the Saptex Sea," Tage said. "They harvested wood from the rubber trees and built the entire city out of it. Everything from the walls to the ground we walk on is wood."

According to the little pieces of history Tage had been able to learn, the ground slowly charged, and as it grew more and more dangerous, the humans began to build a safe haven. They could see the writing on the wall. Soil chargers thought they were nuts, even objected to them harvesting so many rubber trees for their city. But in the span of fifty years, the water dried up, the sea turned to latex, and the ground had become electrified.

Tage had always known there was more to the story, but the history of both Ohmstave and Currentgrad had always focused on the war between the two cities and learning about the terraregions and the ocean on fire that took up all of Far Side—the opposite side of the small planet.

Lumen picked up a few rocks and then slowly let each drop to the ground. "I've never seen a human, like a real human, before. Have you, Impulse?"

"Yeah." His voice was soft. "In the powerline."

Lumen bowed her head. "Well, they don't count. They were barely alive."

"They look just like you and me," Tage said. "The only difference is they don't have a web between their fingers or black fingertips, and their hair is different. Some have red hair, others yellow, but mostly brown or black." Tage thought back to the friends he'd had in the couple years he attended school in Ohmstave. Would he know them again if he saw them? He wasn't sure.

"That's so weird," Lumen said. "I didn't even notice that back there. But I can kind of imagine . . . speaking of which." She pointed to his head. "Are you going to keep bleaching the color out of yours?"

Tage gently touched the ends of his white hair, knowing the dark roots had to be inches long by now. "Jeez, I'd kind of forgotten about that. No, I suppose not."

"You look ridiculous." Impulse laughed.

Lumen grabbed the ends of his hair. "There's like four inches of black sprouting from your head, then it's white on the bottom."

Tage smiled to himself. It had been ten years since he'd seen his black hair. "Then I guess I'll have to cut it. Speaking of which, Lumen, your hair is way past your shoulders."

"I know." She tugged on it. "It's too long. I need to rebraid it."

"I think it looks just fine," a deep voice boomed.

Tage felt a sharp, cold point in the small of his back.

"What have we here?" the voice echoed into the night.

Just once—just one time—Tage would like for the worst possible thing to *not* happen to them.

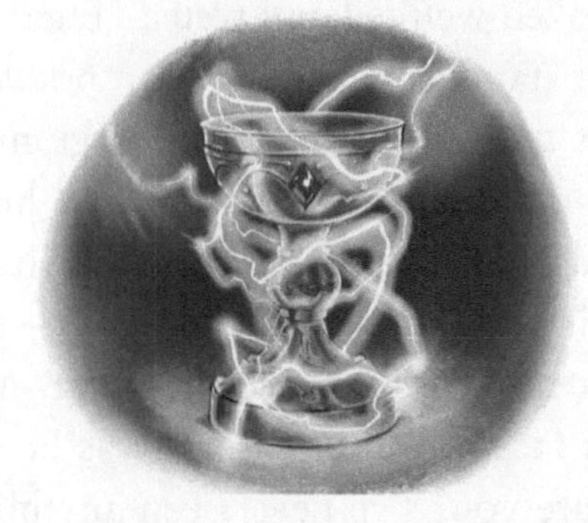

CHAPTER 19

• • • • •

"Bind 'em."

Tage winced as a coarse rope dug into his wrists. "Who are you? Are you with Overlord Koax?" He scanned the area the best he could and found half a dozen soil chargers who had snuck up on them.

Exhaustion was Tage's only excuse for allowing this to happen. But he knew these types of people. If ever there was a time when his brain, and the knowledge of Ohmstave, Currentgrad, and the small groups in the desert would help them, it was now.

"Lookie, lookie, someone stole their mama's cookie," a smaller man said. His hunched back stood higher than his bald, slumped head. He placed an arthritic finger under Tage's chin and stared at him through milky-blue eyes.

How old was this guy?

"High-low, high-low, is he human, I don't know?" The small man laughed.

Tage glanced at each soil charger in turn. Seven of

them, who looked well fed and rested. Tage, Lumen, and Impulse didn't stand a chance—at least not yet.

"Excellent question, Duit." The large man stood in front of the bound soil chargers, crossed his arms, and smiled in the dark. He was taller than Tage by a full head. His white hair was full and slicked back—soil charger, no doubt, but he was thick and muscular. A broad scar across his tan face pulled unnaturally as he squinted his eyes. "What are you? I've never seen anything like it. A new abomination from Overlord Koax?"

"What is he?" Lumen spat. "Who are you? Untie us."

"Blacknails," Tage muttered.

"Very good!" the man said. "You know a rogue soil charger when you see one. But please, call me Key."

"Why are you doing this to us?" Lumen asked.

"Excuse me?" His face contorted, deep and weathered lines from the suns now shining stronger than before, and his voice darkened. "We are the last rogue soil chargers. 'Blacknails,' as the freak over here so kindly called us."

Tage cringed.

"We had just set up camp today, after a long journey, and we heard an alarm in the distance, followed by shock crafts." He started pacing, his hands behind his back. Ursogen skins had been patched together to form his simple sleeveless shirt and pants, which stopped at his knees. The feet of the soil chargers watching them were also wrapped in leather.

Tage would have agreed to anything for some patched-together animal skins for his feet.

Key continued. "Normally, we'd never confront another soil charger. We say live and let live. Isn't that right?" He turned to his friends and they nodded in agreement. "But you"—he pointed to Tage—"are something else. Different."

"Frutant, nutant, he's a mutant," Duit said. Clearly, the old man had spent far too many days under the desert suns.

"I'm not a mutant," Tage said, then turned to Key. "Or a freak!"

"How did you get out of the powerline?" Key asked. "Or did they let you out? To hunt us?"

"Tell us how you haven't been put in the powerline first," Tage said. "I mean, how have your people not been caught by the overlord?"

"Okay, I'll play," Key replied. "The reason we've lasted so long is because we are always prepared and had our black camouflage on top of our tents. Because we have men like Duit here, who has been roaming the desert his whole life. We weren't spotted, this time. But we never take unnecessary risks. Our entire clan, the last rogue soil chargers, would have been put into that powerline if we would have been spotted. I sent out Duit and a few of my other associates to investigate the cause, and we found you three and a broken powerline. Is this the overlord's plan? To draw us out?"

"No," Tage said. He raised his hands in surrender. "Of course not. We were in the powerline, I was semi-conscious—we all were, I think. And I was able to store a little bit of electricity each day. Then, I saved enough and blasted off the metal couplers. Once I got out, I found Lumen and Impulse and used a Bolt Ignition to shoot off theirs as well."

"Impossible. We've tried that," Key said. "It doesn't even char the metal."

"It worked for me." Tage shrugged. "Maybe you did it wrong."

"And your hair." Key approached Tage and yanked

on the end of it. "Why is it sprouting black from your head, but white on the bottom?"

"Deaky, weaky, freaky," Duit said.

"So what?" Lumen rolled her eyes. "Maybe he's just due for a visit with a hairdresser."

"Because I've been stuck in the powerline for four months." Tage gritted his teeth, ignoring Lumen.

"And that changes your hair color?" Key raised his eyebrows. "No, that's not it. But I see you have the web and black fingertips. And what's most curious is you were Arcing without the aid of biotech. Arcing on its own is incredibly rare, but without biotech? Impossible. Pray tell, is this a new type of Surge Knight?"

"You saw me Arc?" Tage gasped. "How long have you been following us?" All of his energy and focus had been behind them, toward Currentgrad and the powerline. Not at possible threats from small factions of rogues ahead.

"Untie us," Lumen growled, "and we'll tell you. How about that?" She jerked her hands back and forth, trying to loosen her bindings.

"Hmm," Key said, tilting his head to the side as if deep in thought. "I think I like my way better. Are you spies for the overlord?"

"No," Impulse said. "We hate him. Tage, come on, tell him."

"Fine," Tage said. "The overlord took away our Surge biotech. Ripped it from our bodies piece by piece. And no, we aren't spies for him. I don't know why I can Arc without biotech. Something in that powerline changed me, triggered something. It's like I have more charge than ever. Maybe it's because I'm half soil charger and half human. Happy?"

I can get out of this. I don't want any more blood on

my hands. I'm sick of hurting my friends because of my selfishness. Tage kept his breathing even and his gaze on Key's.

A few grumbles and whispers passed within the group.

"Impossible!" Key said.

"Little crewmen fell off a boat, little human drowned in a moat," Duit said. "Black hair sprouting from your head, say goodbye because you're all dead!"

"Can you shut that one up?" Lumen nodded at the hunchback.

"Half human, half soil charger," Key said slowly. "That can't be. They die at birth."

"Believe it or don't," Tage said. "I don't care. I'm alive. Now let us go, we have business to attend to." A heavy hand smacked across his face, knuckles first. Tage spat blood. "What's your problem? We've done nothing to you." His outburst was once again met with a backhand to the face. The flesh-on-flesh contact boomed in the silent night.

"I will not have a freak like you speak to me like that. And do you really think we'd let you go back to the Voltaic Dava and report us?" Key turned to his thugs. "Let's bring them back to camp."

"No. Please." Lumen's eyes welled with tears. "I can't be captive again."

"Strong ones live, weak ones cry, and all the others, they shall die," Duit sang.

"SHUT UP!" Lumen screamed, her words echoing in the still night.

Key calmly walked up to her, standing only inches from her nose. "Never speak like that to us again. Do you understand me?"

Lumen straightened her posture and shook her hair from side to side. "No."

Never breaking eye contact with Lumen, his right fist struck like a cobra onto Impulse's face. It knocked Impulse to the ground, where he lay motionless for a moment. "Next time, that will be you."

A single tear trickled down Lumen's cheek, but she remained otherwise stoic and silent.

"Get them back to camp," Key ordered. "And then we can sort this all out."

Impulse groaned, rolled onto his side, and stood.

The three walked, hands tied behind their backs, sharp pulse-dune-tipped weapons pointed at the base of their spines. Lumen kept whispering to Impulse how sorry she was, and he accepted her apology. Tage watched as Impulse's eye continued to swell until it was fully shut.

Aside from Duit, the soil chargers were big and strong. They obviously trained their muscles regularly. Now he understood why the Blacknails were so feared.

Tage walked, continually sucking up charge through his feet to keep him going.

"How's your eye?" Tage whispered to Impulse.

"It's okay," he responded.

"Your other eye is going to match if you three don't shut up," Key said.

As they walked, Tage noted the shift in their direction, careful to reorient himself. Luckily, they weren't headed too far off from the direction of Ohmstave. He just needed to figure out a way to get them out of this.

Except he wasn't sure what "this" was. After a mile or two, they crested a ridge. At the bottom was a round campsite, dug nearly person-height into the rocks, lit dimly with small red bulbs strung around the perimeter. It looked big enough to hold hundreds of people, but based on the inactivity inside, Tage guessed it held far less.

"We used to be two hundred strong," Key said, as if

reading Tage's thoughts. "But Overlord Koax's powerline has greatly diminished our numbers. The overlords of the other terraregions either don't fully understand the powerline or don't object to it, so we have no options other than to stay nomadic."

"That's just it," Tage said. "We want to defeat Koax, and we have a plan. Look, we already got out of the powerline on our own. No one else has been able to do that."

Key eyed him and continued forward down the hill toward the camp. Tage slipped on the loose dirt and nearly lost his footing without the use of his arms to retain his balance. As they got closer to camp, his stomach rumbled. He took a deep breath—the smell of wormsteaks made his mouth water. Right outside the perimeter of camp was a thick, long wooden T and metal cages, attached with chains that sat firmly on the ground.

"What now?" Tage asked. "What do you want from us?"

Key simply grunted in response.

"Please, let us go," Tage begged again. "We'll put as much distance between us as possible. We're not going back to Currentgrad." At least not yet.

"You led the overlord to us," Key said. "And then you spout some tale of how you were able to store current and blast yourself out of the line. Don't you think others would have done that if it were possible? You had help! Don't think we haven't tried to blast our friends or family out. It's clear what you are. An operative. Your modifications are evident. For that, you must die."

Four hands closed on both sides of Tage, lifting him off the ground.

Die? Not out here in the desert. Not without taking Koax into death with him. Or saving his girlfriend and parents in the process. Just being killed simply for escaping? Tage could not allow that to happen.

"No," he protested. "Stop, it's not like that."

He struggled from side to side, unable to free himself from their grasps.

"Tage," Lumen yelled as they pulled her away. "What do we do?"

Tage had to formulate a plan. Before he could blast them with a charge, he was thrust into a metal cage. His back hit the wall with such force, his head bounced against it. Loud ringing in his ears sent a splitting pain through his skull.

"Hands," Key said.

"What?" Tage shook his head from side to side, trying to regain his composure, still disoriented from the powerline.

"Stick your hands through the bars."

They complied.

Maybe I can negotiate my death for their freedom.

"Discharge."

With seven soil chargers standing at the ready, and more in the interior of the camp, they had no choice.

They complied again.

Tage grabbed at the bars for balance as his cage was pulled into the air by the chains above. The metal kinked and rocked as a lever pulled. Not high, just high enough so he couldn't reach out for a charge. All three cages dangled.

"We'll be back after we discuss your situation with the others," Key said. "Then this will all be over."

Discussion? There was a chance then . . . a chance that while they discussed, Tage could get his friends out of this mess. He had to. He could not fail again.

Six of their captors turned toward the center of the dim red lights.

"Enjoy your time, despise my rhyme," the hunchback said, his milky eyes reflecting the red of the lights.

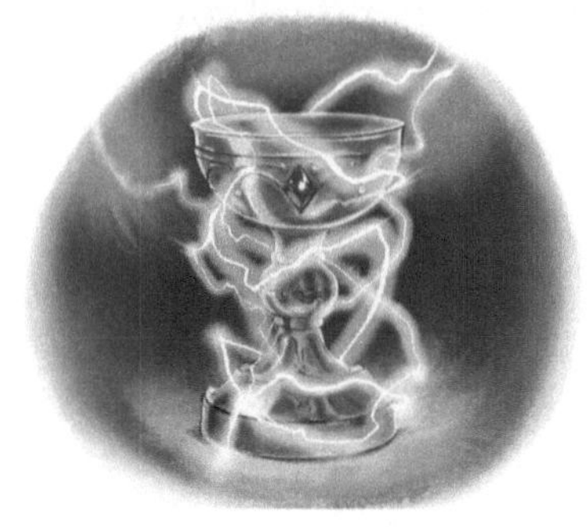

CHAPTER 20

· · · · ·

Lumen was on Tage's left, Impulse to his right.

The cloud cover was so thick, no stars shone through. The vast, empty sky seemed fitting.

"Tage," Impulse whispered, "what do we do?"

"Yeah, use your big human brain to get us out of th—this." Lumen's voice cracked on her last word. "This is bad, guys, this is totally—"

"Hang on," Tage said, grasping his head with his hands. "Just let me think."

He stared off into the distance. They were just outside the perimeter of camp, in a makeshift prison.

Lumen sat, took a chunk of hair on the side of her head, and began rebraiding. Tage watched her nimble fingers as she began weaving the ends back through the plait, thus tying it off. What an interesting skill, most likely learned through practice. Lots of practice. She grabbed another chunk and began the same process. Another braid was finished impossibly quickly.

Tage had to focus.

"These cages," he said. "This wasn't spontaneous . . . They must imprison people regularly."

"Well, of course we keep cages!" Key rounded the corner. "But we normally don't set them up unless there's a threat. Of course, after you three were spotted, and this one Arcing,"—he pointed to Tage—"I ordered a few Blacknails to hook some up while we captured you."

"Cool story," Lumen said as she continued to work her fingers through her hair as if she hadn't a care in the world. "We don't work for Koax, or any other overlord, for that matter. We need to go. The humans are expecting us in Ohmstave."

Key laughed deeply, as if someone had told the most fantastic joke. "You missed your calling, smart-aleck! You're a natural-born comedian."

"Is that so?" Lumen said as she once again wove the ends of her hair back through her braid.

"Uh," Tage interrupted, "Lumen isn't lying. I'm half human. After leaving the desert, that's where I was raised." He swallowed, his memories threatening to drag him under. "Mom and I would sometimes spend days in the desert, just to feel the charge. Her name was Hayrah. Maybe someone you know knew her?"

Key's expression didn't shift. "We'll be sure to deposit your bodies into the Saptex Sea." He ran a hand over his slicked-back hair. "Or maybe outside Currentgrad, since it's obvious you were created there." He walked over to Impulse and stared at him. "I'm just waiting to see what you and smart-aleck have hidden. Tage must have been the prototype."

"We're just soil chargers," Impulse said.

"Too bad," Key said, then turned to walk away.

"Wait," Tage called. "Where are you going?"

"Back to the meeting." Key looked over his shoulder and smiled. "Lots of questions that need to be answered."

"Like what?" Tage asked. "We lived in Currentgrad. We can tell you that Impulse has five younger siblings. That our other friend is being held prisoner. We don't know what happened to Lumen's parents. We've even been inside the Voltaic Dava Castle."

"Not those kinds of questions," Key said on a sigh. "More like, how you were made. Basically, we're deciding between a dissection and vivisection." He walked away, as if he'd said they were deciding between breakfast or a midnight snack.

Tage grasped the bars. They had to find a way out. Had to.

"No!" he yelled. Key stopped but didn't turn around. "You don't understand. We're out here because we tried to kill the overlord! He caught us and put us in the powerline. We can help each other!"

"If that were true, the overlord would have killed you."

"Why won't you listen to me?!" Tage ran a frustrated hand over his face.

"Silence, freak!" Key continued walking and rejoined the group.

"Tage?" Lumen leaned forward, staring at him through the bars. "Do you know what a vivisection is? Because I don't. But I do know what a freaking dissection is, and that requires death!"

Tage shook his head. He was well aware of the actions of both, but adding to the hysteria wasn't going to help. He looked around the camp again, as if to find answers. While his vantage point wasn't great, he could still see Blacknails gathered around a small fire—a span of dark material rested just above, most likely to help hide the flames. Maybe forty of them, give or take. Some drank from wooden steins, others from glasses filled with crimson liquid. More patched-together material created a large circle that covered the entire dug-out area—the center left open, aside from the square over the fire. Smaller structures built of metal and wood scraps appeared to work as possible separations of the different families and supplies. These people used everything they touched. Moved often. They would not be easy to convince.

"Okay," Tage said. "They're definitely going to kill us." He swallowed hard. "What they're probably figuring out right now is how. They aren't sure what we are or how they can hurt us without hurting themselves. If I had some charge, I could get us out of here! I can't believe it's come to this, I really thought I could reason with them." Tage released another sigh. "Maybe get them on our side."

Dropping to the bottom of his cage, he squeezed a foot through the bars and dangled it. He grunted as the bars tightened while he forced his leg through.

"Tage, stop," Lumen said. "It's no use. Your legs aren't long enough."

Tage pulled his leg up, lay on his back, and breathed deep.

"My charges, they really are stronger," he said. "When I'm on the ground, it's like I'm constantly sucking up charge like when I was in the powerline, as if there's no limit to the amount I can fill. And the ignitions, they're stronger, more powerful."

"I noticed that," Impulse said. "You had sparks dripping from your fingers earlier."

"I did?" Tage asked. "Why didn't you tell me?"

"We were running. I was tired." He shrugged. "Didn't seem important."

"Touching," Lumen said, rolling her eyes.

Tage had never in his life felt emptier. Weaker. It was as if his insides suddenly didn't fit together. He craved charge more than food. More than water. More than anything.

"That's it!" Tage jumped up.

"What?" Lumen asked.

"Impulse, you're taller than me. Can you reach the ground?"

"I can try, but Tage, my ignitions aren't as strong as yours."

"Force your leg through and see if you can reach," Tage said.

The months of being stuck in the powerline finally had an upside. Impulse's once-strong, muscular body had become nothing more than bones and loose skin. He pushed his leg through the bars until his bony knee hit them. Impulse shimmied to the left and right to get the kneecap past the bars. Squishing himself as far against the bars as he could, his toe still dangled above the dirt.

Tage's heart sank, but still . . . if Impulse could just find a little more stretch . . . "You're so close!"

Impulse grunted as he continued to reach with his foot.

Tage stood and grasped the bars again. "Lumen, help me."

"Help you what?" she snapped. "We would have better luck walking up to the Cathos pole and sticking our tongues on it."

Tage furrowed his brow. "Swing. Match my rhythm forward and back, forward and back, like a swing set. Impulse, when we dip, try to suck up as much charge as you can. Let me know if it's working, and we'll do it for as long as it takes for you to get a full charge."

Tage gripped the bars on the front of his cage and planted his feet; Lumen did the same. They rocked their hips and counteracted their inertia with their weight. It was wobbly and slow going at first, but once they found their rhythm, the entire contraption swung together back and forth. Tage didn't need Impulse to tell him he could reach the ground. The euphoric smile on his face told him as much with each forward dip.

"Stop," Lumen said in a loud whisper. "Someone's coming."

Impulse struggled to pull his leg back through the bar and remained seated. The contraption itself swayed slowly as Tage and Lumen did their best to steady it.

"What's going on over here?" a Blacknail asked. His long, white hair flowed down the middle of his back.

"Let us out," Tage said. "Please. We're uncomfortable."

"If you think you can tip this over, be my guest," the man said. "You think you're the first who's tried?"

Tage stared at him silently.

"These cages are impossible to get out of. Didn't you think it was odd we didn't leave a guard with you? We don't need to. You can't escape."

"I'm warning you," Tage said. "You'll regret this."

"Funny that you're threatening me." He laughed. "Let me give you a little advice: Keep it quiet. I wouldn't piss off Key if I were you."

He turned to leave, but Tage saw the fear in his eyes. The best advantage they had was this group being unsure of what Tage was. Once the soil charger was out of sight, Tage started rocking again. Lumen joined.

"It's now or never," Tage said. "They're probably sending someone right now to watch over us. They're scared."

"Ugh," Lumen grunted. "It's so hard to get this thing moving."

"Keep it up, Lumen," Tage said. "You're doing great."

Sweat dotted his brow as he rocked back and forth.

"I'm getting some charge," Impulse whispered.

The chains creaked louder as the contraption rocked harder. Lumen's new braids swung as they shifted.

"Okay," Impulse said. "I'm charged. Which ignition do you think will melt the lock? Bolt?"

"I think Bolt is the right choice, but your target is wrong."

Impulse furrowed his brows.

Tage grinned. "Cast any ignition at me."

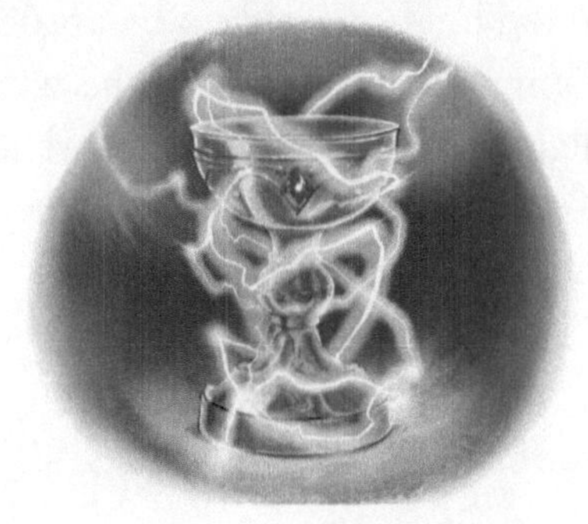

CHAPTER 21

• • • • •

Tage held out his hands proudly. "I mean it, right at me."

"I can't." Impulse shook his head. "We're not Surge Knights anymore. We can't just absorb ignitions. We weren't in the program long enough to learn that."

"Maybe, maybe not." Tage thought of how simple running through the desert had been. How Lumen and Impulse had needed to pause to recharge, but he'd been drawing more energy than he needed in his running steps. "I think I can, guys. And if it works, I'll be charged."

"And if not," Lumen said, "you'll be severely hurt or dead. Tage, we're so weak from that stupid powerline. It's not like you can just bounce back. Remember that Surge Knight at practice with Flux?"

"Yeah," Tage answered.

"He's probably dead," Lumen said.

"You don't know that," Impulse said.

"We have to try something," Tage said. "The reality is we'll all be dead if I can't get us out."

"Tage," Lumen protested. "You know that isn't how

it works! You don't get charged up by absorbing an ignition. It just dissipates, like a fart in the wind. And only
elite Surge Knights like Charuss can absorb an ignition! It
takes years of practice."

"I can't explain why," Tage said, "but something is
different inside me. My body is efficient with electricity.
It's almost become innate, or an instinct."

"Let me try the lock first," Impulse said. "Where's the
harm in that?"

Tage shook his head.

"Tage," Impulse said slowly. "I can't hurt you."

"You won't," Tage assured him. "And they'll hear
your attempt. We have one shot and no time. I know mine
has the best chance of working. Hit me with a Current
Ignition. I need the shock. Let me absorb your charge,
then I'll blast open my cage with a bolt. It only takes me
a few seconds to fully charge, and I'll blast both of your
cages open. At that point, I'm sure they'll be on us like
stink on ursogen poop." He smirked at Lumen. "Then we
either make a run for it or fight. They might be too afraid
of us to fight when we escape the cages."

"Are you sure?" Impulse asked.

"Yes!" Tage pleaded. "Please, hurry, we're running
out of time." He slipped his hands through the bars and
pointed his palms at Impulse.

Impulse stepped to the back of his cage, as if to lessen
the blow. He pointed his hands at Tage's open ones and
squeezed his eyes shut. "Please forgive me."

A bright Current Ignition cut through the evening
darkness directly at Tage. Like a rainbow of white light
connecting the two boys, Impulse shot the current at
Tage until his charge was depleted. Tage's body sparked
and swam with the influx of power. He expected to smell
burnt flesh, at least a little, but didn't.

Suddenly, he arched his back and slammed into the other side of the cage.

"Tage!" Lumen yelled.

"Ah!" Tage screamed.

"No, no!" Impulse shouted.

But it was too late.

Tage thrashed around in the cage, causing it to sway wildly. The chains clanked from all the commotion.

"He's overcharged!" Lumen said.

"How do you know that?" Impulse asked.

"I don't, I just figured that's what happened."

"There's current all over his body!" Impulse yelled.

Thin streaks of electricity encapsulated Tage's chest, arms, and legs.

Tage's pupils dilated, the hair on his arms and legs stood on end, smells became heightened, and his pulse raced. He could hear everything his concerned friends were saying.

He sat up straight, back stiff.

Tage Gradient was fully charged.

"Tage?" Impulse opened his eyes. "Did it work? Are you okay?"

"I'm better than okay," Tage said, shaking his hands. "I'm charged. You did it, Impulse!"

"Great," Lumen said. "Now let's bounce."

Tage had one chance. And while the charge from Impulse felt a bit weak, he still felt it. It had barely faded; Tage was able to use it, recycle the energy.

He pointed his fingers point blank at the lock and shot a single Bolt Ignition. The charge flowed from his shoulders down his biceps, through his forearms, and out his hands. The smell of burnt metal and metallic electricity filled Tage's nose. Small sparks bounced back from the metal, singeing his arm hair. Momentarily blinded from the bolt, he closed his eyes. The door clanged onto the ground and sent Tage's heartbeat into overdrive.

"He did it," Lumen whispered. "I don't understand, but it worked."

Tage jumped from the cage, catching the edge of the mostly melted door when he landed. Heat shot up his foot for a moment. He plunged his hands into the charged soil and sucked up charge in both his hands and feet.

Like a dry riverbed getting its first rain in years, his body filled with delicious electricity. He'd only been without charge for a short time, but in this dire situation, his body craved it. Needed it. Demanded a full charge.

To his left, he could hear a commotion and yelling. They were coming, and he'd be ready. Still crouched, he blasted both the other doors simultaneously. Lumen and Impulse jumped down to draw up charge, then stood facing the incoming onslaught.

"Follow my lead," Tage said.

Key led the group, and held his arms back to stop his army. Duit followed closely behind. He clapped slowly. "Nicely done. I bet you think this makes you special?"

"Not special," Tage said. "Strong. Now let us leave in peace."

"You may love the overlord," the hunchback said, "but he is something we abhor!" Tage had slowly started backing up when Key raised his hand and shot White Sparks directly at the three of them, causing them to scatter like hunted ferals.

"Ignitions fired," Lumen said. "I'll take the mouthy one."

Tage Arced forward into the middle of the fray. He blasted a Current Ignition from each hand directly into two soil chargers. The column of energy was encased by angry bits of wiry bolts. He held the ignition steady for fifteen seconds, then sucked up a fresh charge. The Black-nails fell to the ground, dead from the electric shock.

He stared at their fallen bodies. He'd just killed two men. *They forced my hand. I never wanted this.*

Ignitions streamed back at Tage. He Arced away to avoid them. As soon as his feet touched the ground, he began sucking up charge once more.

Next, he Arced and flipped backward, with his feet pointing at an oncoming group. White Sparks sprayed from his hands, burning anyone within range. The smell of bitter, burnt flesh made bile rise in the back of Tage's throat.

"We wanted to leave peacefully!" he screamed. "This didn't need to happen. I didn't want to hurt anyone!"

Looking back, he saw Lumen frantically charging and throwing anything she could to fend off the soil chargers. Impulse had backed himself into a corner and shot a constant spray of White Sparks. It wasn't effective at hurting them, but it prevented anyone from getting within point-blank range of him. They were severely outnumbered. He could see the fatigue on his friends' faces. They weren't drawing charge as quickly, and their ignitions weren't coming fast enough.

Heat burned up Tage's back and singed his clothes. He fell onto his hands and knees with the impact. The wind was knocked out of him. He lifted his head; a soil charger stood above him and kicked him in the chin.

The force of the kick, combined with Tage's frail body, was enough to flip him onto his back. The soil charger sat on Tage, pinning his arms down, grabbed his throat with one hand, and pointed his index finger inches from his face.

Blood dripped down Tage's lip. He coughed and gagged as his windpipe was crushed. He grabbed at the charged dirt, searching for an ignition in his body to throw. His eyes bulged, and his vision started to darken. Off in the distance, he heard screaming. But he couldn't make out what they were saying, only that they sounded terrified. Shrill screams. Horror.

He'd failed.

He had heard this was what dying was like. Where a person would come to a sudden peace about their end. The world slowed down, and he had a moment of clarity. He'd lost. Tage accepted his fate as his vision darkened.

Suddenly, the man released Tage's throat. Tage rolled to his side as he coughed. Tears had flooded his eyes, making it difficult to see. Everyone had fallen silent as they stared at him.

His right hand tickled, probably numb from that Blacknail sitting on him. To his surprise, a thick cord of current shot up from his hand like a beam to the heavens. Attached to it, high in the sky, like a kite outlined in electric lights, was the silhouette of something Tage had only seen once before in an ancient book. It adorned the back of his Surge Knight uniform—an eagle.

A very angry eagle.

Tage stared at the electric bird in awe. It had been many years since a real bird had graced the skies of planet Hadrain—certainly not in Tage's or his parents' lifetimes. It was at least thirty feet wide, with a sharp beak and outstretched claws on its feet. Tage guided the electrified eagle kite across the black sky using the string of charge attached to its form. The majestic ignition responded with precise movements. As it crackled across the horizon, it left a momentary imprint where it had been, like a fleeting memory. He didn't have to consciously direct the beast—it curved and swooped almost as if it had the thought before Tage.

Someone shot a Current Ignition at Tage, narrowly missing him.

"A Volt Foil!" Key yelled.

Instinctively, Tage pulled the electrified beast toward the earth, where it swooped at a group of soil chargers. Screams erupted and people ran and ducked for cover. The giant winged beast blinded those who were too close as it approached the earth. They were the lucky ones. It grasped a soil charger in each of its claws. Brilliant white-and-blue current engulfed them like a cocoon. He threw them into a tent. The Volt Foil's beak clacked rapidly until an unfortunate person's head landed between its jaws. Burnt hair was the first thing Tage smelled, then the head exploded under the force. Bits of blood, skull, and gray brain matter splattered anyone within ten feet. Tage pulled the current cord attached to his hand up to the sky and guided the eagle safely away from the remaining Blacknails. His kite of electricity cackled and sizzled above them, casting an unnatural light in the evening sky.

"Please," Key said, "we surrender."

Tage opened his mouth but couldn't find the words. What he'd just done was nothing he ever wanted to do. Moreover, this was something he didn't know he or anyone was capable of doing. The eagle was supposed to be a myth.

"Tage." Lumen ran to his side. "You casted a Volt Foil."

"I know," Tage said. His chest heaved and his legs shook beneath him. "I don't know how, but I did."

"Don't take us to Currentgrad," Key pleaded. "We just want to live freely."

"I told you," Tage said, frustration dripping off every word. "I'm not working for Koax. He didn't create me. At least, I don't think he did . . ." He trailed off as his body became heavier. The Volt Foil felt as if it were draining more than just his charge. "I never wanted to hurt any of you, but you forced my hand. I need your word you will let us go and never follow us."

"Done."

"We will let the rest of you live. I will not destroy your camp or harm another person. I'm half soil charger. Lumen and Impulse are soil chargers, just like you. We must stick together, or at the very least, not kill each other."

Silence blanketed the group for a moment.

"I'm sorry," Key said softly. "We were scared. What are you?"

Tage ignored his question. First, he'd already answered, and second . . . Tage wasn't quite sure what was happening to him.

"How can we be assured you won't come after us for revenge?" Impulse asked.

"We'd be fools to come after you again," Key said, staring at the Volt Foil in the sky.

"If we cross paths again in the Charged Desert, do not attack us, but welcome us as allies," Tage said. He loosened the electric lead holding the bird so it flew high above them. "We are on the same side."

Key nodded. His eyes were directed at the ground, sad, defeated. Humiliated.

"I hope to see you again," Tage said, stealing a glance at his creation in the sky. "But next time as friends. And with news we killed Overlord Koax."

"May we ask something of you?" a woman cried out, desperation in her voice.

"As long as you can promise three wormsteaks." Tage let out a pathetic laugh and shook his hand, releasing the Volt Foil. It crackled and sizzled away.

The gravity of what he'd done was settling in. He'd never seen a Volt Foil Ignition in all his life. He had no tech. He wasn't a Surge Knight. His abilities made no sense, but if he continued to practice, he knew they would help him win.

Tage nodded. "Yes, of course you can ask, but I can't promise an answer." By now, both Impulse and Lumen flanked his sides.

"If you defeat him, will you return to the powerline and release our people?" the woman asked.

Tage nodded again. "Of course. I hope I can teach you how and we can do it quickly. Together. But if I'm the only one who can do it, I'll personally release each person."

The woman erupted in tears and fell to the ground. He couldn't fully understand what she was saying in between sobs, but he gathered it was about her children. He approached the woman and gently rested a hand on her back. She flinched. He didn't know what to say, and suddenly felt uncomfortable surrounded by the Black-nails. He backed up, body drained and exhausted, and rejoined his friends.

"Goodbye for now," Tage said.

"Wait," Key said with a smile. "You made a request, which we are in a position to honor."

"What?" Tage asked.

Key turned toward the fire. "You're forgetting some-thing."

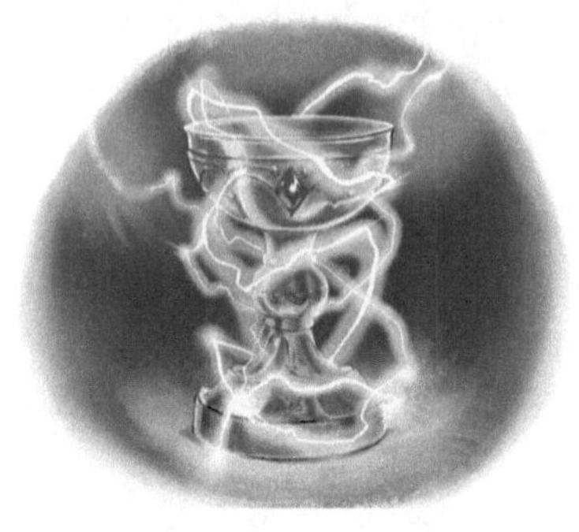

CHAPTER 22

• • • • •

After being nearly certain that they would die at the hands of their captors, Tage, Lumen, and Impulse now sat a few miles outside of the Blacknail camp with food the rogue soil chargers had prepared.

"That was insane," Lumen said through a mouthful of food.

"Yeah," Impulse said between bites of his wormsteak. "And thanks for getting us something to eat."

Tage bit into his own steak and said nothing. Asking for steaks had been a joke, but he was happy they had them. They hadn't had a real meal since the marketplace, on the day they'd attempted to kill Overlord Koax. His body still felt impossibly heavy after creating the Volt Foil—as if he were made of lead.

"How did you learn how to throw the Volt Foil Ignition?" Lumen asked. "That was the craziest crap I've ever witnessed."

"I don't know," Tage said. "Come on, guys, we need to hurry. Plus, I still want to eat my steak while it's hot."

Holding it with both hands, he took a bite like it was a sandwich. He grunted. "It's been a really long time since I had solid food. The texture almost hurts my teeth."

"Mine too," Impulse said. His steak was nearly gone. "Those Blacknails can cook a good steak."

Tage looked to his own hands and back at Impulse. He used to be so big; he needed this. Plus, Tage didn't have much of an appetite after what he'd done.

"Here." He handed his food to Impulse. "I'm full. Take mine."

Impulse's eyes grew wide. "Are you sure?"

Tage nodded, feeling only slightly stronger than he had before. "Please, we really need to speed up."

"Fine," Lumen said. "I'll run if you quit trying to change the subject."

He leaned back and lay flat on his back, muscles sore, as if he'd just spent the afternoon lifting ursogen.

"I'll try to explain it," Tage said, his words sounding slurred with exhaustion.

"Whoa, whoa, whoa," Lumen said. "What the heck is this?" She pointed at Tage.

"I'm exhausted," he said. "I felt stronger than ever when I threw the Volt Foil, but the second I released it, I felt half dead. Worse than when I got out of the power-line. I thought if I kept telling you guys to hurry, it would motivate me. But honestly? I need a minute."

"Take all the time you need," Impulse said. "We'll keep a lookout."

Tage closed his eyes and blackness enveloped him. The dirt beneath him seemed to cradle him as his body gained much-needed rest. He shouldn't allow himself to sleep, but it dragged him under.

A small tug on his arm jolted Tage awake.

"Welcome to the living." Impulse chuckled.

"I fell asleep," Tage said as he sat up. At least he felt more like himself—the soil below him hummed. How much time had they lost? "How long was I asleep?"

"Uh, like five minutes," Lumen said. "I just finished my steak, and it was freaking delicious!"

"Five minutes?" Tage asked. That couldn't be right. "I feel completely rested."

"Yep," she replied. "It's called a power nap. Remember how I used to do them in class? I swear by them. Now"—she reached down, grabbed both of Tage's hands, and helped him up— "let's hear about this Volt Foil."

"It was instinct, I suppose," Tage said. "I thought I was dying—my throat was getting crushed—and somehow, something deep inside me cast the ignition. Almost like a last-ditch effort to live, you know?" He thought about Capacity, trapped back in Currentgrad, and his parents, wherever they were, and guilt overwhelmed him. "Why couldn't I have done this in the chamber? I could have saved us. Saved Capacity."

"Yeah," Lumen said, "that would have been useful. Saved us a lot of time. Thanks for nothing, Tage." She laughed.

"You weren't that powerful then," Impulse said. "And it's not like you planned to do it tonight to save us."

"You're right." Tage kicked at a rock. "Something changed in me when I was in that powerline. I don't know if the powerline did it to me, or if it awakened something that was always there. I feel different. I *am* different."

"But how?" Lumen asked. "Impulse and I are the same. The powerline didn't change our charge. You can do all five ignitions!"

"I realize that," Tage said. "It probably has something to do with my human side. Maybe having the electricity flow completely through me connected something?"

"What did it feel like?" Impulse asked.

"The Volt Foil?" Tage wasn't even sure he'd be able to put his experience into words. "Power. It felt like I picked up a massive boulder with nothing more than my pinky. It felt both heavy and light at the same time. Both reckless and completely in control. The electricity coming from my hand felt like a cord—like flying a kite, but with control. I was the wind. Almost as if I shared a brain with it. When I swooped it down, I only moved my hand, but in my head, it did whatever I was thinking."

Tage stared back at his friends in the near blackness, shocked expressions painted on their faces. His face warmed.

"I know you guys want answers, but how can I explain something I don't understand myself?"

"I know, buddy," Impulse said, resting a hand on Tage's shoulder. "We don't think you're a freak—"

"I do," Lumen interrupted. "But you're *our* freak." She placed a hand on his other shoulder.

Tage shimmied both their hands off him. "Whatever."

"Oh, come on," Lumen said. "That was awesome, and you know it. As long as you can figure out how to do one without being on the verge of death, before or after, we're golden."

"Can we stop talking about this?" Tage asked. He had to focus on their next steps. The edge of the sky had begun to brighten with morning, but they still had hours before the suns would appear.

"Lighten up, Tage," Lumen said.

"Lu," Impulse said.

"Fine." She rolled her eyes.

"How much farther?" Impulse asked.

"To Ohmstave? I'm not positive," Tage said. "Maybe

a few more hours? The Blacknails didn't really take us too far off course."

They ran.

"I wish we had an ursogen," Lumen said. "It would make this so much easier."

"Shh," Impulse said. "Do you guys hear that?"

Tage stopped and held a hand up to his ear. "No, I don't hear anything."

"It was probably nothing," Impulse said. "You're right, though. We should run again."

The friends once again broke into a run. Tage had to remind himself that the sooner they made it to Ohmstave, the sooner they could gather supplies, make plans, and rescue Capacity. And learn what happened to his parents.

"Tage?" Lumen matched his strides. "I—I just . . ."

"What is it?"

"I'm sorry," she blurted out.

Thinking of all the things that they'd gone through, Tage couldn't imagine what she could possibly have to apologize for.

"Sorry for what?" He felt his forehead wrinkle.

"At the castle. When I outed your parents. I—I . . . panicked. He was torturing Capacity, and she was screaming and—"

"And it was one of the options given to us when we were planning," Tage said. "The hope was that Overlord Koax's hatred of Tel'el could possibly help us escape."

Tage was sure it had done the opposite—once Tel'el's name had been mentioned, Koax had no longer attempted any type of civility. Not that Tage expected much after attempting to assassinate him.

"I'll be honest," he said. "I was mad at first. Even though I knew it was one of the avenues we could take. But after . . ." *How I failed.* "After what we've been through, really thinking about how impossible it is to train for that type of situation, I'm not angry now. I understand."

"But your parents." Lumen sniffed. "I probably got them killed." Tears streamed down her face. "I didn't know what else to do."

"Lumen." Tage slowed to a walk, and both Impulse and Lumen followed suit. He put an arm around her, ready to repeat words his parents had told him again and again as he'd grown up. "Mom and Dad knew the risks of this operation. And I'm sure they were prepared. They weren't sitting ducks. Trust me."

"Let's keep running," Impulse said.

The sky began brimming with greater lightness on the horizon. The soft lavender was always the most beautiful at dawn. They paused again and again for Lumen and Impulse to draw more charge. Tage sucked it up continually, but stood quietly, pretending to need the break as his friends replenished their stores. In the early morning, ferals scurried around the rocks, their singed hairy bodies a blur as they ran in and out, hiding.

"Tage?" Impulse asked.

"Hmm?"

"The ground. It's sandy again."

"Oh." Lumen paused. "We didn't get turned around, did we?"

"No," Tage answered, squinting at the horizon, where a few tips of rubber trees could be seen in the distance.

"Yuck." Lumen sneezed. "Who farted?"

Tage's heart fluttered. "That's the sea! We're almost there."

Lumen's footsteps continued to move steady and even. "It smells like a giant turd."

"Well," Tage said, "what did you expect from a liquid-latex sea? And before you ask, yes, the city smells like that. But you'll get used to it."

"Ugh," Lumen groaned. "No one should ever get used to that."

More rubber plants began to spread through the sandy ground beneath their feet.

"Hurry," Tage said. "I want to tell you guys a few things, what to expect, basically. They wear clothes made of rubber normally. When they leave the city they wear the cribriform suits. We wore the same cribriform suits we used in training with Flux. But, theirs are more robust. The latex-insulated suit covers everything and is the only way they can walk outside of Ohmstave. Outside the fortress, along the high gates, there will be guards. Brutes, actually, guarding it with guns that shoot liquid latex. If they're under attack, they'll send in the special forces, the Rubber Naiads. They are usually women, and they're terrifying. They wear a rubber suit and goggles with a special mask that has a tube for breathing under the Saptex Sea. There's access to the sea from inside Ohmstave. That's the access point for them—they jump in, swim under the gates, then emerge. The intruder never sees them coming."

"Geez, Tage," Lumen said. "This is getting weird."

"No weirder than us using charge to heal ourselves." *Or my Volt Foil.*

"True," Impulse said. "Did they look like that?"

Tage had been concentrating so hard on recalling old memories that he nearly walked right into the Saptex Sea.

The slight hill they'd been climbing had hidden the fortress walls, but now that they'd crested the hill, Ohmstave—the wooden city fortress—spread out in front of him.

"Whoa," Lumen breathed.

"You lived here?" Impulse asked.

The suns had risen behind them, casting the wood in a golden glow. Home. Well, one of them. The desert had also been his home—as Currentgrad had. What a complicated thing to never fully belong anywhere one went.

Dark and shimmering, the top of the Saptex Sea now glinted in the light from the suns, making its presence far more known than just minutes before.

When Tage had left this place, more than ten years ago, he wasn't sure he'd ever see it again. Split logs with spired ends made up the outer walls. He could just make out slight movement near the top of the city wall—a guard, no doubt. They'd have to approach with caution.

"We're here," Tage said, right before he was doused with liquid rubber.

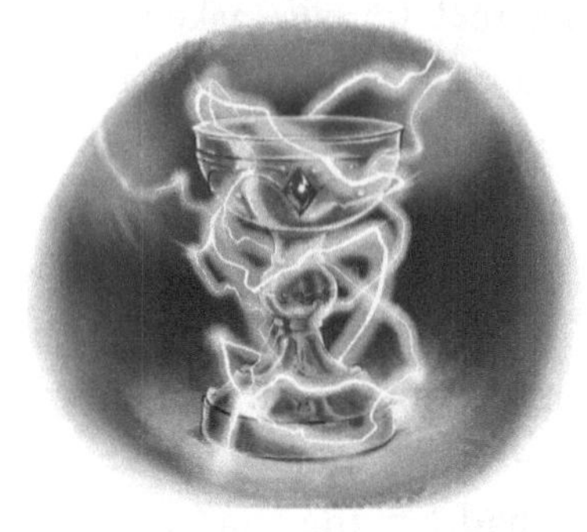

CHAPTER 23

• • • • •

At first, Tage instinctively cringed and tried to wipe the rubber from his eyes. Then he lay down and instructed his friends to do the same. He welcomed the feel of latex on his skin—the rubber meant one thing.

He was home.

"Stay down!" a voice boomed from above.

He knew that voice.

Fahren. Fahren had been the one to send Tage, Tel'el, and Hayrah to Currentgrad. He'd helped collect the poison. Assisted in setting up the plan that Tage had ruined. But at least he would know Tage. At least he had a connection here who could possibly aid them in their return to Currentgrad.

"Let me sort this out," Tage said to his friends. "Cooperate until then. Especially you, Lumen, don't say a word."

As the rubber started to harden, Tage peeled it away from his face. He stared at the sea. Like clockwork, three Rubber Naiads emerged from the latex sea, guns in tow.

"Don't move," one of them said. Her voice was high pitched but commanding.

"We won't," Tage said. "Please, let us in, it's me, Tage Gradient."

"I know, but your name means nothing to me," she said, as she aimed her weapon at his head.

"It should," Tage said. "Please, just ask Elder Fahren. He knows."

"Stop talking." She poked him with the barrel of her gun.

"What business do you have here?" Fahren yelled. His voice was above them. Tage assumed he was perched high behind the fortress walls.

"Can I answer?" Tage asked the Rubber Naiad.

She nodded. "Yes, but don't move."

"We've come for sanctuary—"

"Your sanctuary was revoked when we saw a living and breathing Koax at our gates," Fahren interrupted.

"Please, Elder Fahren!"

Silence.

"I failed." Tage knew what this meant. Ten years of planning. Ten years of Fahren doing everything in his power to keep anyone from acting against Overlord Koax, to prevent further paranoia. So Tage could infiltrate the castle with fewer guards and protections. None of those efforts had paid off. He'd failed so many people. Tage swallowed. "My friends and I failed, but we beg you to take us in."

Silence.

Had Tage led them all this way for nothing? Tel'el had always promised Tage that they'd be welcomed, even if he was unsuccessful. But now? Fahren had to know that allowing them sanctuary might provoke attack. Were they worth the risk? Did Fahren already know about the failure? Had his parents been in contact? But if they had, wouldn't someone have come looking for Tage and his friends?

He held his breath.

"Bring them in," Fahren said slowly.

Tage craned his neck, but saw no sign of the human leader.

"On your feet," the woman barked.

Tage stood and peeled the rest of the rubber off his face. He looked to his friends, and they followed him. The tall, wooden spires rose high into the air, just as he remembered. Leafless trees pushed from the sea's floor, and rubber leaked out of large, knotty holes in their trunks, keeping the sea full of the thick material. Tops of rubber trees pierced through the Saptex Sea's surface like arthritic fingers reaching toward the purple electric sky.

A drawbridge lowered, allowing them into the city. But something was off. He sucked in a sharp breath and looked closer at the walls. Charred. A recent burn.

Most likely from a Bolt Ignition.

"What happened there?" Tage pointed to the scar on the wall.

"That's why you're not welcome here anymore," the Rubber Naiad said.

"Were you attacked? Who did this?" The tip of the gun pressed hard into his shoulder blade. "Was it Koax?"

"Stop," the woman said.

Tage stiffened. Only a few feet separated them from the drawbridge. She peeled the rubber off Tage's fingertips. He looked to his side, and the other Naiads were doing the same to Impulse and Lumen.

"Discharge."

"Of course," Tage started.

"No talking."

204

Instead of throwing an ignition, he forced the charge out, letting small bolts of electricity fall from his fingertips. They danced around his feet, then fizzled out. He turned to Impulse and Lumen, hoping they'd do the same. Impulse followed suit. Lumen did not.

She closed her eyes and drew in a deep breath. Then she unleashed White Sparks. The sparks bounced on the ground until the energy dissipated and burned off.

"Huh," Lumen said. "I didn't think I'd be able to cast anything after having the rubber on me."

"We didn't leave it on long enough," the woman said. "If we left it on a few more minutes, you'd be stunted for a while. Maybe forever." She placed rubber mittens over each of their hands, then secured them with a tie.

"Wait," Tage said. "I'm pulling up charge constantly. I don't know why. But I need to discharge again when I'm on the plank. It's the only way." Being the only half human, half soil charger on the planet, there was no one to talk to about his peculiarities. For him, there was no normal—he'd proven that again and again.

Tage put one foot onto the wooden bridge, then the other. The texture immediately brought him to his childhood—evoking long-forgotten memories of a less complicated time. A smile emerged on his face. A wooden fortress, built over the edge of the Saptex Sea.

"Hurry up," the woman said.

Tage turned his back on the city, leaned over the edge, and released the current back into the Charged Desert.

As he was led by the Rubber Naiad into the city, he stopped. Buildings with boarded-up windows shocked him. A new layer of old boards had been used to repair cracks in the fortress's exterior, making the walls stand even taller than he remembered. The humans inside stared at him from the safety of their home, hidden behind curtains, peeking out from behind them.

Scared.

Suddenly, his stomach swirled. The gravity of his failure weighed on him like a pulse dune on his chest. The humans, once a proud population, now cowered inside their own homes. Fancy shops and nice homes were replaced with vacant buildings and boarded-up stores. Had the population dwindled that much? Tage knew the answer. He'd seen the powerline. Thousands had been captured and forced into it. He should have realized that with so many humans attached on the vast line in the desert, the numbers here had to have dwindled. He just . . . he hadn't been fully prepared.

He closed his eyes and sucked in a sharp breath. The bitter scent of latex was now more prominent than ever. He didn't know where his parents were, but hoped that Fahren had heard something from them. Anything.

All the plans—all the years of work—and he was about to face Fahren as a failure. His girlfriend was missing, and the entire city of Ohmstave had been reduced to fearful humans living in shacks. All hoping he could save them.

No. Tage shook his head. This was because of the overlord. But still, Tage should have been the first step in the humans claiming freedom from fear, rather than making them more afraid as they gave refuge to fugitives.

"You don't need to lead us to the Elders' Council," Tage said. "I remember where it is."

The woman didn't respond, but continued to chaperone them. The other two Naiads, who had been silent up until this point, brought up the back. After living amongst the larger and broader soil chargers for so long, the three Naiads looked impossibly small.

Tage followed without comment.

They crossed the center of the town, and off to the left was the building. The Elders' assembly hall, where Tage and Hayrah had met Tel'el for the first time. Fahren had stood and charged his makeshift family with the plan to take out Koax. Tel'el had been bloodied and battered; Hayrah had been young and beautiful. Tage had been a mere child.

He walked into the building, and the familiar herbal scent enveloped him. Not unlike the apothecary he had recovered in with Proxy—no wonder that place had put him at ease. On one hand, he couldn't help but feel the excitement of being home, seeing the Elders, especially Fahren. But on the other, he knew they'd be disappointed in his failure. Disappointed was probably not a strong enough word. Koax would double his efforts after the attempt on his life—Tage had brought greater danger to everyone on Hadrain.

The smooth wood of the building created a warmth he'd missed with the metal, concrete, and brick of Currentgrad.

"Take seats," one of the Naiads said. Three weapons were still pointed at them, and Tage had no doubt they'd all be shot with latex if he wasn't cautious. The rubber had never irritated him, but Impulse and Lumen had already been through so much.

"The Elders have been called," one of the women said. "You will wait here. We will have a weapon trained on each of you."

They sat at the end of the table closest to the door they'd come through, still in their filthy underclothes, bruised, charred, sunburned, and starving.

The Elders filed into the room and took their seats on

the far side of the table—leaving several seats between them and the three soil chargers.

Tage could hardly breathe. These had been his people for years. He still felt more of a kinship with them than he ever had with the soil chargers. Though, he'd been fighting first for the humans, and second, for the soil chargers to better understand the world they lived in.

Impulse leaned in toward Tage. "What's going to happen?"

"I don't know," Tage said. "We can only be honest and hope for the best."

"Oh, that's comforting," Lumen growled. "You said they'd take us in, Tage."

"I know what I said, and they will." He hoped his words weren't a lie. "I just need to fill them in, okay?"

Lumen rolled her eyes and crossed her arms. Frustrated, she stood. "Can someone take these stupid mittens off me?"

Fahren walked into the room, and Tage stared at the old man. He was weathered and looked ancient. It had only been a decade, but somehow, he'd aged a century. He wore a loose rubber gown painted light blue. Tage stared at the sunken eyes and gray beard of the man. His sloped nose accented his deep-set eyes.

Tage's heart sank. He'd expected a look or words of kindness from Fahren, not the glare the old man gave them.

"Sit," Fahren commanded Lumen as he strode to the head of the table. "You will show us some respect."

"Ugh," she said, then plopped loudly into her chair.

"Welcome, Tage," Fahren said.

"Elder Fahren." Tage leaned forward, resting his hands on the table, the rubber mittens still covering him. "Thank you for allowing us in the walls."

"It's Minister Fahren now," he said. "Ministers only serve for eight years. I was voted in a few years ago."

A promotion that put more pressure on a man who had carried the weight of protecting Ohmstave as an Elder for years.

Fahren stared at him, his eyes boring holes into Tage. Taking a moment, Tage looked at the other faces in the room—a few older, a few appearing to be only slightly older than himself. Though, with how many humans there were on the powerline, he shouldn't be surprised that there were so many young faces in the group of eleven Elders.

"As I mentioned, we failed," Tage said. "He put us in the powerline and—"

Fahren raised his hand. Tage stopped talking.

"Please inventory his biotech." Fahren said to another Elder.

The man parted Tage's lips. "No metal denture." Another lifted his hands. "No rings either."

Fahren stepped closer, tenting his fingers under his chin. "Check his spine."

The man pushed him forward and rubbed his hand down the length of Tage's spine. "Not that I can tell. A lot of scarring, though."

"You have some explaining to do." Fahren stared at Tage and his two friends. "I'm quite displeased about seeing you in this condition." The proceedings had begun. "It pains me to see you are without Hayrah and Tel'el. Have they perished?"

Tage bowed his head. So they hadn't been in touch—not even using one of the few spies. Of course he'd been trying to prepare for the worst, but Tage felt the weight of failure press on him again. "I'm not sure."

Fahren raised an eyebrow. "Not sure?"

Tage forced himself to look Fahren in the eye, grateful again that the humans had made him their leader—at least, he thought he was grateful. "We . . . I—" But Lumen cut him off.

"We've been strung up in a powerline for four months, old man," Lumen said. "Sorry we don't have the latest gossip." She stood. "I don't need this. I'll take my chances in the desert."

"Sit!" Fahren yelled.

"Lumen!" Tage shouted. "Stop it. What are you doing?"

"I'm leaving." Her chin jutted out. "I don't need to explain myself. This was your deal, not mine. I didn't let anyone down." She turned to Fahren. "And I certainly don't need to give him any answers. We risked our lives for humans we've never met, to hopefully change our world. We've suffered in the desert, strapped and only half aware . . ." Her words petered out as tears grew in her eyes. "My family . . . I need to find . . ." Lumen sobbed. She couldn't find the words. The weight of her world had come crashing down.

Two Brutes stood in front of the door—large humans recruited as guards.

"Lumen, please." Tage rested a mittened hand on her arm, but she flinched away. "Just wait a minute, okay? Let me sort this out."

The three Naiads were all aiming at Lumen, ready at the command of probably anyone in the room.

"If she wants to leave, she may go," Fahren said. He stroked his long beard. "One less mouth for us to feed. However, the rogue soil chargers are practically extinct. Most have been used for the powerline, and the rest have conformed to a city in one of the terraregions. She'll be hard-pressed to find a Blacknail tribe to join."

"Yeah." She folded her arms. "We met them last night. Or should I say we were attacked by them last night."

"Attacked?" Fahren leaned forward, as if studying her.

"Yeah, but Tage fought them off using—"

"Uh, I'm sorry, Elder Fahren," Tage interrupted. "Please forgive us. We're hungry, tired, and confused. Lumen isn't used to the human culture. But give us time, please, I beg of you."

Lumen's brows pulled together in confusion as she looked down at Tage.

"Please," he whispered.

"For the love of two suns, Lu," Impulse mumbled. "Just sit back down and maybe they'll feed us or free us."

After glancing between Tage and Impulse, Lumen finally sat, her mouth still twisted in annoyance.

"Let me explain what happened," Tage said.

He described everything in great detail. There would be questions, and he had no answers—wasn't sure he ever would—but he would at least try to answer them. As he recounted the Surge Knight Ceremony, a bubble crept up in his throat. Capacity had been there for him when he needed her, and now, when she needed him, where was he?

Tage squinted his eyes. "We think he has Capacity, maybe my parents too. We have to go back and finish what we started."

"No," Fahren said. "You've done enough. If the over-lord returns—"

"Returns?" Tage asked. "You mean he was here? Before?"

"Young man. You will not interrupt me again," Fahren said. He sat even straighter up in his chair. "He was here last night, looking for you three. Lucky for you."

"Lucky?" Impulse asked.

"The bald one speaks," Fahren said. "And yes, after that confrontation, we knew to be on the lookout for you three."

"So you already knew we were in the powerline?"

"Yes." Fahren nodded. "I wanted to hear your side of the story before I passed judgment. And if he hadn't told us you broke out, we would have killed you when we saw you on our shore."

Tage sat back. "But you sent me there. You asked us—me—to attempt this mission . . ."

Fahren released a slow sigh. "Tage, you have walked through the streets of Ohmstave. You have to understand that we cannot risk trusting anyone."

Wait . . . something else crept into Tage's thoughts.

"You can kill soil chargers? How?" Tage asked, leaning farther forward. "That had been our biggest block before."

And if they had the tech, why hadn't Tel'el been told? Tage? Had Fahren given up on their mission?

Fahren nodded. "The guns the Rubber Naiads shot at you have the option of heating the latex. When under attack, they activate that function and spew out boiling latex. It adheres to the skin and burns down to the bone. Two Surge Knights burned alive last night before the overlord retreated. He was convinced you were here. But he wouldn't dare burn the place down. They don't have the plans to extract water. This planet is cursed without us."

Lumen's jaw dropped. "Oh shi—"

"Not now, Lumen," Tage said. "That's incredible! What else have you come up with?"

"Excuse me," an Elder said. She puffed on a long pipe. Feathers of smoke rose to the ceiling. "Before we go into that, perhaps we should know where their loyalties lie."

"We're here, aren't we?" Tage asked. Months in the powerline, and his best guess was that his half-human genes had given him the ability to break free, otherwise they'd still be there. They had risked their lives at the request of everyone in this room.

"You had nowhere else to go," the Elder said.

"We always intended on coming here," Tage said. "Heck, they got involved and risked their lives to help me with the plan. They put everything on the line and have nothing. You always promised there would be safety here." Tage stared at Fahren. "You promised that if we were willing to risk our lives, we would find protection."

Fahren's expression didn't change. "For you."

The woman Elder looked sideways at Tage, then blew out another long puff of smoke.

"I needed them," Tage said. "Things changed in Currentgrad, we had to adapt."

"And yet, even with three additional soil chargers, you still did not accomplish a successful assassination," Fahren said.

Every failure crashed in on Tage again. Flashes of Koax implanting the tech into him, Capacity, Lumen, and Impulse pounded through his thoughts. Hours of training in a basement. Living a lie for all of his growing up years. Being given the burden of knowing there was a good chance he would die at the age of sixteen. Impulse had siblings back in Currentgrad who were hopefully in hiding, but were almost definitely starving. Capacity's parents were in prison, and she was who knew where.

"Yes," Tage said. "We were unsuccessful, but you have technology you didn't have when we were given this task. Was it not worth the risk to bring us weapons? To get word to Tel'el? Perhaps we could have improved upon our plan. You had the power to give us a better chance of success—"

"Enough," Fahren said quietly, but with a stern note in his voice that Tage was sure no one questioned. "Materials are scarce. The weapons were needed here."

"We're willing to go back," Tage said. "Fight again and save Capacity . . . She was integral to our plan." Tage had just forgotten the very basic principle that a soil charger left individual imprints. Fahren was correct. He had to make things right. "We only need to be here for a short time. Until we're strong. Is that asking too much?"

The Elders shared glances. A few whispered to one another. Fahren studied the faces of the Elders seated on either side of him. A few short nods were presented. A few shrugs.

Fahren sat for a few moments, the silence thick in the room.

Lumen shifted to one side and then the other.

Tage glanced at her and whispered, "Please, just wait."

She held all the same frustrations Tage had. They'd tried. They'd risked so much. Been tortured by their implants, the powerline, and the trek across the desert. They'd earned some respect and care.

Fahren folded his hands together on the table. "How do you propose your next move?"

"I'm . . . I'm not sure," Tage admitted. "I have ideas. Maybe you can help me with that?" Tage tried to meet the eyes of every Elder in the room. "We could plan together."

"Do you need medical attention?" Fahren asked.

"No," Tage said. "Just something to eat, drink, and a bed. Can we talk about this tomorrow?"

"And a shower," Lumen piped in.

Fahren stroked his beard and paused. "I suppose. As I'm sure you saw, there are several empty houses."

"I did." Tage shook his head. "I can't believe it."

"Believe it," Fahren said, his voice hardening. "The last ten years have not been good to us, Tage. Our hopes rested with the poison and the chaos that would follow. We have a few quiet spies in the city, but we must kill the overlord for them to act."

That task had been forefront on Tage's mind since the age of six. He would not give up after one failed attempt. He knew more. Was stronger. Had a somewhat better idea of how to proceed, how Currentgrad and the Voltaic Dava worked. He would not fail again.

"We will," Tage said. "We will plan, and we will make sure we succeed."

"Wait here," Fahren said as he stood. "I'll have someone come lead you to a designated home for the three of you to stay in. But make no mistake, there will be a Brute outside your door."

"Okay," Tage said. Whatever he had to do to get food and a shower, he'd do.

The back door of the vast room opened, and the Elders began filing out. "She'll be in soon," Fahren said.

The last of the Elders left the room. The Naiads had backed against the wall, but each still held their weapon.

"Great," Lumen said as she flopped back in her chair and crossed her arms. "Prisoners again."

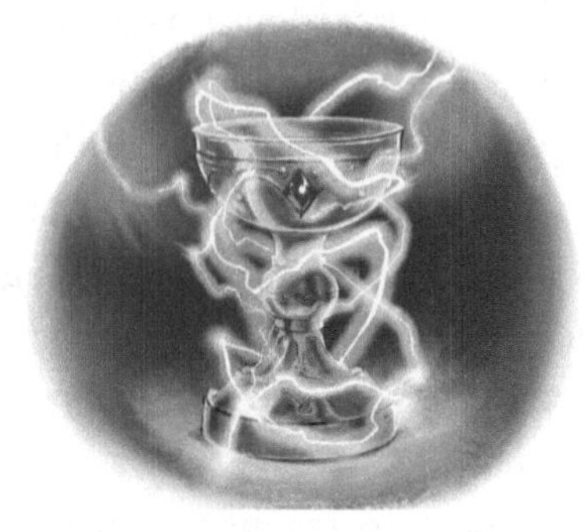

CHAPTER 24

• • • • •

A petite girl walked into the room. Long, brown hair danced at her waist. But the most interesting feature on her was her crystal-blue eyes, which matched her latex dress. Tage searched his brain. He thought he knew her from school, but he'd been six . . . Samara . . . Yes. They'd played during recess. She'd been very agile, if he remembered right.

"Hello," Samara said. "I'm here to take you to your house."

"Samara?" Tage tilted his head to the side, still studying her.

"Yes," she said, her cheeks flushed. "You remember me?"

"Yeah," Tage said. "I mean, it's fuzzy because it's been so long, but yeah, I remember you."

"Wow." Lumen crossed her arms. "She must have made quite the impression."

"She was kind to me," Tage said. "Not all of the kids

were nice. It was far easier for me to blend in with the soil chargers than to blend in with the humans."

He held his hand up to showcase his webbed fingers and black fingertips, but the stupid mittens were still on him. Tage glanced back at the Naiads.

One stepped forward and reached out. Lumen immediately put her hands out first for the woman to take the mittens. The Naiad slipped one off at a time, still eyeing them warily.

"The last thing we want to do is hurt anyone," Tage assured them, wondering if there was any point to assurances.

Impulse and Lumen released a long sigh and rubbed their hands together after the mittens were removed. Tage gave them an apologetic glance.

The Naiad who held the mittens crossed her arms. "We will be watching you closely."

"Oh, will you?" Lumen said. "Kinda creepy, don't you think?"

Tage cut Lumen off. "We'd expect nothing less. You have to keep everyone safe, and if it makes them feel better . . . we'll deal."

Impulse shrugged. Lumen scowled.

"Follow me," Samara said as her blue eyes found Tage's again. "The Elders have assigned a place for you to reside."

"Thank you." Impulse reached his arm out. "I'm Impulse."

Samara stared at his hand, eyes wide. The webbing wasn't so drastically different, but the black fingertips and nails would startle most humans.

"We can't hurt you," Tage said as he reached out and took her hand in his. "I mean, we can, but we won't. Touching us won't electrocute you. We have to throw an ignition for that to happen. And we discharged before we came within the city walls."

"Of course," Samara said as she gave Tage's hand a squeeze before shaking Impulse's. "I'm sorry. We get very few soil chargers staying here since, well, you and Hayrah."

Hearing Hayrah's name was like a fresh knife in the chest. Wherever Hayrah and Tel'el were, they weren't in a place that would allow them to communicate to Fahren. They were gone—in the powerline, or in prison. There was only the smallest chance they could have hidden in the basement, but knowing Overlord Koax's paranoia, Tage's house had been burned to the ground.

Samara dropped Impulse's hand. "It's nice to meet you, and thank you for all that you've done for us."

"I can't believe we've been afraid of them. Little humans." Lumen scoffed before sauntering out the door.

Impulse followed, and Tage walked out with Samara. He leaned in close enough to whisper. "We've been through a lot," he explained. "You'll have to forgive Lumen."

Samara blinked up at Tage as they followed his friends outside. "I can't believe—I just never thought I'd see you again."

"Yeah," Tage said, his thoughts still spinning. He knew they were coming to Ohmstave, but the reality of being back in the place where he'd spent his childhood was both nice and overwhelming.

As he peered at the familiar wood that made up the path under his feet, the large border wall, and the wooden buildings, Tage breathed in deeply. "I never thought I'd see this place again."

"Well." A slight smile played on Samara's pink lips. "I'm glad you made it back."

218

"Show-er?" Lumen urged, impatience on each sylla-ble. She folded her arms, and Tage was certain she was flexing what was left of her muscles after the powerline. "And any chance we could get some clothes? I've been in these undergarments for a very long time."

"Yes, of course." Samara smiled up at Tage once more, and then at his two friends in turn, before starting up the wooden path.

"My, my," Lumen said as she stepped next to Tage. "You seem to have a fan."

"Stop it," Tage said under his breath. "This isn't easy for anyone."

"You've been here before," Lumen snapped. "I feel like I'm in enemy territory."

Tage nodded once to show he understood. He'd always had the knowledge of what the humans and Ohm-stave were really like—Impulse and Lumen were just learning. He'd have to give them some leeway.

Samara turned down another path. Tage, Lumen, and Impulse followed, while a Brute stayed a few feet back. At least the Naiads with their latex guns were gone.

Tage looked around the city once more. The old wood had been maintained just as dutifully as when he was here as a kid—but it was all so empty. A city set up above the ground might seem crazy to a soil charger, but to the humans, it was their only option. Even the slight charge of the desert here was enough to hurt a human in just a few steps.

Now, Tage's bare feet padded against the hard wood. It felt dead after the energy from the desert, but there was also something calming about treading on paths he'd walked as a little boy. Sulfur bubbled up below him, stinging his nose. They walked around the corner, and

Tage paused, taking in another empty section of Ohm-stave.

"I don't think I'll ever get used to seeing so many boarded-up homes," Tage said.

"It's okay," Samara answered. "Minister Fahren only had us board them up to keep the maintenance low. We still go in and clean the houses weekly and keep them in tip-top shape. He was convinced you'd succeed and our population would rebound."

Tage's heart sank. The pit in his stomach had become a permanent resident.

"I'm sorry," Impulse said. "We've let everyone down, but we know more now, and we're going to try again."

"I know." Samara's face was stoic, and her voice was both low and flat. She seemed broken with this issue. No happiness or sadness—all emotion had been stolen from her in her short life. "This is the best spot for you. No neighbors. We're all—" Samara's gaze landed on each of them in turn. "We've all suffered losses at the hands of people who look like you. It's going to be a hard thing for some to see you around."

"Well, we are bigger," Lumen said with a smug grin.

Samara's return smile was faint. "Yes. You are."

Lumen's grin widened and she stood a little taller—dirt clung to her hair and her face, dark streaks from the desert sand covered her legs and undergarments. Same as Tage and Impulse.

"I feel faint," Impulse said. "And look at my poor arms." He stretched out a bony arm.

"With no charge, you'll gain that back in no time," Tage said. At least he hoped. Soil chargers generally healed up quickly, which was good—they'd all need to be at their best to go back to Currentgrad.

Samara pulled a key from her pocket and wiggled it

into the door. A loud click followed by a door swinging on squeaky hinges welcomed them into their temporary home.

Aside from the creaky door, the inside was pristine. The floors had been polished to a high sheen. Not a speck of dust dotted the room. The house opened into a living space that led into a kitchen.

Samara pointed to the stairs on the far side of the living room. "The upstairs loft has a large bedroom and bathroom. There are two bedrooms on the main level—they share a bathroom."

Tage breathed in deeply. Sulphur, latex, wood, and . . . food?

"This will do," Lumen said as she slowly moved across the main living area. "I'm the girl. I call the loft. You two slobs can share the bathroom down here."

"Great," Tage said, not caring in the least. He looked forward to actual sleep—sleep that wasn't tainted by being held as part of the powerline. And even in the weeks before the assassination attempt, he hadn't slept well. He couldn't wait to fall into bed.

"There is some feral stew on the stove," Samara said as she moved into the kitchen. "My mother made it when she heard of your arrival." She quickly removed the lid and did a quick stir. "It should be ready anytime."

Tage breathed in the familiar scent of his youth and watched Samara—the only connection he had to a time before Currentgrad. He was supposed to be welcomed by Tel'el and Hayrah, or have ridden across the desert with them on the ursogen. Instead, he was here with only half his party. "How is your mom?" he asked.

Samara crossed the room and took his hands into her own, once again peering up at him, her attention unwavering. Tage had forgotten how emotionally-driven the humans were. "She's really thankful you're back, Tage."

Tage squeezed her soft fingers before letting her go.

"Why?" Lumen asked, frowning. "He failed. We all failed."

"He tried," Samara said, her attention flashing to Lumen. "And that counts for something. We'll take care of you."

"You're a lot kinder than I expected," Impulse said shyly.

Samara peered up at him. "I hope that's what you find here."

Impulse gave her a short nod before wandering to the kitchen, breathing deeply.

"Thank you," Tage said as he rested a hand on Samara's shoulder. He half expected her to flinch, but she didn't move.

"Okay, that's enough," Lumen said. She pulled Tage's arm until his hand fell from Samara's shoulder. "One, we're not staying long, so stop getting attached. Two, he has a girlfriend, and three—listen up because this one is the most important one—"

"Lumen!" Tage rubbed his forehead, thinking of the new char marks on the walls of Ohmstave.

"No, I'm not done. Three, we're going back to Currentgrad not only to kill the overlord, but also to save Capacity. His girlfriend. Girlfriend. Got it?"

Impulse rested against the counter, his arms folded, watching. "Lumen, calm down."

"I . . . I . . ." Samara swallowed hard, but her eyes were full of tears.

"Lumen, really," Tage said. He pulled her a few feet away from Samara. "That's how humans act. They're nice. Accommodating. They bond."

"Soil chargers aren't?" Samara asked, her voice barely audible.

Lumen narrowed her eyes. "I don't know. We do have emotions, but we end up mostly angry."

"I'm sorry," Tage said to Samara. "It's . . . it may take a few days for us to settle in."

"Please forgive us," Impulse said. "I think we're just weary."

"Of course," Samara said. She turned quickly, rushing toward the door. "If you need anything, I'm on the corner we passed. Just two houses down."

She ran out the door, slamming it behind her. Tage spun to face Lumen. "That was beyond rude. Even for you."

"Mm-mm." Lumen shook her head from side to side. "That girl has a crush on you."

"Whatever." Tage rolled his eyes. "It doesn't matter anyway. She doesn't know me. I barely remember her."

"Maybe it doesn't matter to you," Lumen said, "but it does to me. Capacity is my girl. I've got her back. Always. And it seemed like you were a little too comfortable and cozy."

"Did it seem like that to you, Impulse?" Tage asked. "That, after not knowing what happened to my parents, I might find some comfort knowing someone from my youth? That I might fall into the human ways I was first raised with?"

"I'd like to get cleaned up and out of these undergarments," Impulse said. "I don't have anything to say about you and Samara."

"You agree with Lumen?" Tage threw his hands in the air. "There's nothing there. End of story, end of discussion. Maybe I knew her before, but I was six when I left. Six. And since then, I've spent just as much time with her as you have."

"Maybe we're just not used to the human culture," Impulse said, his attention on Lumen. "I'm going to get washed up." He walked back toward the hallway.

"Fine." Tage sighed. "But keep in mind that humans are driven by feelings and empathy. Not power. The electricity stunts our emotions."

"Our?" Lumen asked. "Now you want to be a soil charger? It seems like you've been full-fledged human since you got here."

"Whatever," Tage said.

Stomping down the short hall to his room, he considered his encounter with Samara. Capacity was being held. He couldn't even allow his thoughts to go beyond that. She'd been perfect and unexpected, and he'd let her down in the worst way possible. He'd pray to the two suns or the gods of charge or whatever it took to keep her alive until he could get to her. That was all the emotion he had room for right now. Samara was one of the few kids who hadn't called him Shockey or Blacknails. That was the extent of their relationship.

The shower turned on in the room next to Tage.

A knock at the front door broke Tage's concentration.

"What should I do?" Lumen called.

"Answer it," Tage replied, then he walked back to the living room.

Lumen jerked open the door. "Yeah?"

"Hi," Samara said softly. "I'm sorry we got off to a bad start."

Lumen said nothing.

"Anyway," Samara continued, "here are some clothes for you. My mom is a seamstress. She sized you up during the Elders' Council and pulled a few things from her clothing store. Please take them. I hope they fit."

"Thanks," Lumen said, her voice low and suspicious. "What are they made of?" She heaved them over her shoulder.

"Rubber," Samara said. "Everything is made out of rubber."

"I don't know if we can wear these," Lumen said.

"It's not liquid." Tage leaned against the wall. "You should be okay."

"Well . . ." Samara pressed her lips together, her eyes shifting back and forth, but never quite landing on Lumen. "We can figure something else out if that doesn't work."

Tage started toward the door before Lumen said something rude or stupid, or both.

"Thank you," he said.

"I'll see you three tomorrow." Samara smoothed her blue dress, the rubber squeaking under her palms. "There is a man in town who can help you heal. And I'd like to show you around. Especially you, Lumen. Maybe it will help you have a better understanding of Ohmstave and us in general."

"Thank you again," Tage said.

"And just a few more minutes for the stew," Samara said as she stepped back.

"Thanks for the clothes." Lumen patted the stack on her shoulder.

Samara smiled, but it didn't reach up to her eyes. "Sleep well."

Lumen closed the door behind her and tossed the clothes to Tage. "That was weird."

"No," he said. "That was nice."

"They're being a little too nice. Suspiciously nice," Lumen said over her shoulder.

"What's your deal?" Tage said. "You've always been snarky, but now you're just mean."

Lumen whirled around. "I'm angry."

There was no way to respond to Lumen when she was like this. Tage would talk to her after she got sleep and food.

Lumen grabbed a dress from the pile of clothes and stormed off. She stomped across the room and then climbed up to the loft. She stomped her foot twice and yelled down, "Impulse! Don't use all the hot water!"

This was ridiculous. Maybe Tage wouldn't wait. He walked to the bottom of the stairs. "Why are you so mad?"

"Are you serious right now?" Lumen came to the railing at the top of the loft. "Why don't you use that giant brain of yours to figure it out? Or maybe use the human empathy that you think us soil chargers are so devoid of."

Tage scrambled to make sense of what she'd said. "You think the humans think they're better than us?"

"I think *you* think you're better than us."

"I—"

"It's not just that, Tage," Lumen said. "My entire life has been wiped from me. When this is all over, I'll either be dead or cast out into the Charged Desert alone. The humans won't accept me here."

"They already have."

She shook her head and played with a long braid. "Not really. The Naiads weren't happy about leaving us alone, and they've put us on a practically empty street or path or whatever this thing is that people walk on in front of the house. And don't forget, there's a Brute guarding the door, keeping us in!"

"Do you regret getting involved?" Tage asked. He wouldn't blame her.

"Yeah, I kind of do."

"Aside from the pain you've gone through, I don't regret having you join us," Tage said. "That powerline is disgusting. It's an abomination, like the drudges. If Overlord Koax completes his mission in finishing the powerline, then we will become as oppressed as the humans. You know that."

She shrugged and folded her arms.

"Not only that," Tage continued, "you would have been doomed to a life as a Surge Knight. What kind of life is that?"

"What kind of life is this?" Lumen yelled as she gestured to the wooden walls around them.

"It's a chance," Impulse said. He stepped into the room, wrapped in a towel. Green, like most of the fabric here—woven tightly after shredding the leaves from the rubber trees. "It's a chance that lets us fight against Koax instead of for him. And, Lu, no matter what, you have me too."

She frowned. "I think I'll have my go with the shower now." She looked at Tage, opened her mouth, then clamped it shut and disappeared from sight.

"She's just scared," Impulse whispered. "We did the right thing."

"Thanks, Impulse. I think so too." But Lumen was also a little right as well. She'd been dragged into this, and nothing was going to plan.

Tage tossed an outfit to Impulse and headed for the other bathroom. He stood with his undergarments still on, letting the shower rinse months of dirt off him. Using the small soap, Tage scrubbed his undergarments and then his body.

Clear water ran from the showerhead. In Currentgrad, the water wasn't this clear. It had to travel all the way from Ohmstave in pipes and picked up sand and debris once it reached Currentgrad. Here, though, the warm water trickled down his neck and back. Stretching his neck from side to side, he watched months of filth drip off him.

He stood there for a moment, lost in the comforting feeling of the hot water. No cares, no worries. Closing his eyes, he faced the water and rested his head on the wall.

Once he finished, he dried off and stared at his face in a small mirror. He had about four inches of dark hair growing from his roots—the human side of him showing. Not needing to burn his scalp with bleach was a relief. Here, he could have his dark hair. Half dark. Half light. Half charger. Half human. He'd keep his hair like this. His cheeks were sunken, his skin leathery and dark from the months in the sun.

His lips were cracked and dry, and he ran a finger over them. *Where are you Capacity?* He let his eyes fall closed. He would go back for her. He would not let Koax keep her—he knew she was alive. Koax would use her as bait. If he'd wanted to send a message to Tage, he'd have killed her and left her in the desert for Tage to find. That wasn't what Koax had done. All Tage could hope for was that she wasn't being tortured. Though, he wasn't sure what kind of torture could be worse than the powerline—the intense feeling of being aware and unaware at the same time.

He shook his head. They needed strength, rest, and a plan. A better one. With more contingencies when things went sideways, as he was sure they would. But he'd die before he let anyone keep Capacity from him.

"Hey!" Impulse called. "This isn't terrible!"

Tage felt his lips pull into a smile as he slipped into the familiar latex clothes. The texture took some getting used to, but he swung his arms back and forth, enjoying the stretch of the material.

Tage walked into the kitchen to see Impulse, still in his towel, curled over a bowl. Lumen slurped another one next to him. Impulse nudged a bowl in Tage's direction. He took a big bite. He hadn't realized how raw his throat had become until the salty broth coated it. Tangy amp plants and herbs tickled his taste buds. "I forgot how good this was."

"This thing is weird." Lumen pulled at the collar of her dress. "How do they live like this?"

"You'll get used to it," Tage said.

She rolled her shoulders again. "It feels like I'm suffocating, like I'm wearing those horrible gloves over my whole body."

Tage hadn't felt that stifled by the mittens they'd worn when they first arrived.

Lumen lifted the bowl to her lips and slurped the last drops.

Impulse snorted. "Nice."

She slugged his shoulder. "Hey. I need the protein. I can't believe how skinny I've gotten."

"Proxy warned us about this," Impulse said. "Only being fed gruel really stole our muscle tone. I'm still so weak."

"Yeah," Tage agreed. "It sucks. But if we get enough food and don't charge, we'll regain our strength in just a few days. Oh, that reminds me. The humans will probably be a little unnerved at how fast that happens. It takes them months to gain muscle tone."

Impulse's brows shot up. "Months?"

"Lame," Lumen added and then paused, staring at Tage. "But you're halfsies, so what about you?"

"Me?" Tage asked. "I don't know. I guess we'll have to see." So far, Tage seemed to have the best qualities from each side.

"Guess so," she said. "This soup isn't half bad."

"I grew up on it," Tage answered.

Impulse yawned. "I could sleep for a month."

"I need my undergarments to dry," Lumen whined as she tugged on the latex dress. "I don't know if I can deal."

"Just sleep naked," Impulse said. "I do."

"Too much info," Tage shot back with a smile. Amazing what some food and a shower could do.

"I'm gonna go crash," Impulse said as he rubbed his stomach. "My belly is full and warm."

Lumen rinsed her dish in the sink. "So there's really not a water shortage?"

Tage shook his head. "There really isn't."

She kept the faucet on. "So . . . I could let it run . . ."

"Yep," Tage said. "They have really good purifiers here, so they recycle the water, and they separate the water from the Saptex Sea. We won't run out."

"I may take another shower tomorrow," she said, once again tugging at her dress. "And the next day and every day until . . ."

"Until we go back?" Impulse asked.

Lumen turned to Tage. "When will we go back?"

"As soon as we're strong and have a plan," Tage answered as he stood and rinsed his bowl, shutting off the water. He tucked the rest of the soup into the small cupboard in the floor that brought up cool air from deep underground.

"A solid plan," Impulse added.

But Tage had used a solid plan before—the problem was he'd had only one way to kill Koax. When he went back, he'd need to be far more clever. Think with his mind rather than brute strength or poison. Tage would have to use every skill in his arsenal to take down Koax.

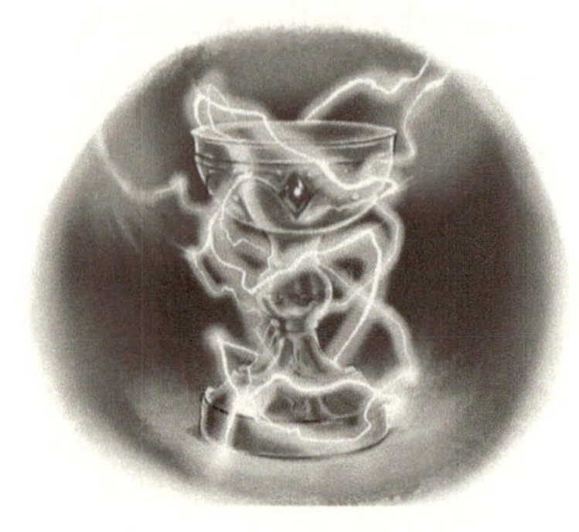

CHAPTER 25

• • • • •

For the first time in months, Tage awoke on his own. He rolled over on the comfy mattress and blinked the sleep out of his eyes. Flat on his back, he stared at the ceiling and wished this all was over. Wished Capacity was next to him, in their own home. Free of the overlord. Free of expectations and big plans. He wanted to be past all the difficult roads ahead, and through to the other side. Alive. Happy. Content. Rebuilding the world he lived in—or allowing someone else to take up that task.

"You boys up yet?" Lumen yelled as she stomped down the stairs.

"I'll be out in a sec," Tage answered.

He stepped onto the floor, and pins and needles shot up his legs. The long trek coupled with rebuilding muscle had taken its toll on him. But the floor was firmer under his feet, and he felt far lighter than he had the day before— his muscles had clearly been rebuilding themselves as he rested.

He walked into the bathroom, running his hands over

his growing arms. As soon as he stood in front of the mirror, he was met with a far different picture than he'd seen the day before. His cheeks were no longer sunken. His shoulders weren't as broad as they'd been before he'd been stuck in the powerline, but they were far more muscular than they had been the day before.

"This is fantastic." Tage gently touched his arm, then looked down to his thick legs. He'd been right—he really did have the best traits of both humans and soil chargers. Would all half human, half soil chargers be this way? Imagine what could happen on Hadrain if they all tried to live together.

Tage headed back to the living room to see Impulse almost double the size he'd been the day before. The last visual remnants of their failure would soon be erased. It couldn't happen soon enough.

"Morning," Impulse said to Tage.

"Impulse,"—he grinned—"you're looking healthy."

Impulse stood taller than the day before. No longer hunched, his back was thick and straight.

"I feel great," Impulse said. "I'm honestly surprised my clothes still fit. The rubber is pretty stretchy, but it makes me feel like I'm suffocating. A little. I mean, I don't want to be a pain but . . ."

"I cannot wear this." Lumen came down the stairs with the yellow material of the latex dress clutched between two fingers. Her hair was braided in a circle on her head again, and she was back in her undergarments, only slightly cleaner than they'd been the day before.

"I'll talk to Samara," Tage said.

Lumen shot him a look, but he wasn't about to let Lumen take the lead on the latex-wardrobe issue.

Twisting his arms from side to side, Impulse had a

faint smile on his face. "I missed these arms," he said softly.

There was no way Impulse didn't also miss his family, wonder how they were, or count the minutes until he could check on them.

"This will probably freak out the humans," Tage said as he again flexed his legs.

"Then I guess they'll just have to deal with it," Lumen said. "I feel so much better today, but a little sore. It is weird, though, right? Why are we rebuilding so fast, faster than before? We were charged a majority of the way here."

"Maybe because we've only been truly charged the last few days? In the line, we were the conduit, but we didn't hold it. Our muscles weren't damaged, just atrophied. If anything, it may have acted as a break from the previous charge," Tage said.

"Makes sense," Impulse said. "I can't think of a time in my life I even went a couple days without charging."

Lumen shrugged. "I'm just happy we're not ruined. The quicker we heal, the quicker we can get out of here."

"Is there any soup left?" Tage asked. "I'm starving."

"Nope." Lumen flicked the back of Impulse's head. "This one ate it all in the middle of the night."

"Sorry," Impulse said, his face reddening. "I woke up starving."

"It doesn't matter." Lumen walked to the kitchen. "That sneaky human broke in this morning and left a basket of bread inside the door."

"She didn't break in," Tage said. "Humans don't lock their doors like we did in Currentgrad. I mean, they probably lock the empty houses to make sure they stay clean, but they sort of live communally." He removed a cloth covering from the basket and was greeted with the smell of warm, freshly baked bread. "Bone bread—this stuff is great. Let's eat it while it's hot."

"Bone. Bread." Lumen neither said nor asked.

"They make a type of flour from ground up feral bones," Tage said. "Trust me, it's good. Plus, it'll help us heal, and it's the only food we've got."

Impulse took a small loaf the size of his hand and shoved it into his mouth. He smiled at Tage while nodding.

"Good," a small voice said. "I see you found the bread."

Tage whipped around.

"Geez," Lumen said. "Ever hear of knocking, Samara?"

"Sorry," she said. "I forgot. Are you guys ready? I need to take you to see Brakdern."

"Brakdern?" Lumen asked. "Who's Brakdern?"

"The healer . . ." Samara said, her voice trailing off as she glanced at each of them. "I think he should check you over to make sure you're better before you go."

"Oh." Tage glanced at Lumen, who stood in her undergarments again. "The latex seems to be . . ."

"Feels a little like I'm suffocating," Impulse responded as he peeled off the shirt. "I'll just put my old undershirt back on. It's fine. Thank you for the clothes."

"Oh." Samara's fine brows tugged downward. "Yes. Of course. I thought it would be all right, but I can see how it might not be very comfortable."

"Really," Impulse said with a small smile. "This was unexpected and kind, it just . . . suffocates a little."

Samara's cheeks grew pink.

Tage shrugged. "I mean, I know some clothes are made from skins, and some from the rubber leaves used for towels and sheets and the linen . . . is that still a thing here?"

"Yes," Samara answered. "Tage, you can keep the latex clothes that were made for your friends."

"I mean, I'd pay to see you prance around in the yellow dress." Lumen smirked.

"How much?" Tage asked Lumen with a smile.

"You'll just have to . . ." Samara licked her lips. "I'll have something for you to wear tonight."

"Samara?" Impulse took a small step forward. "Thank you again. You've been very kind."

"Anything to help," she responded.

"Yeah. Okay." Lumen clapped. "We're all happy and getting along. Now, what are we up to?"

"The healer, yeah?" Tage said. "And thank you for the bread. I've missed this stuff." He ripped off another chunk and put it in his mouth.

"Yeah . . ." Samara trailed off again as she stared at the three of them. "What happened to you guys? You're bigger than yesterday . . ." She took a small step back.

Lumen's smirk grew, and she drew her shoulders back. Tage knew she was just trying to put on a show of her strength—which wasn't at all necessary for Samara.

"This is normal," Tage said. "When we have proper food and rest, we can bulk up quickly. Since we were all healthy before the powerline, our bodies are trying to return to that state. Our homeostasis."

"And," Lumen interjected, "since we weren't technically charged the entire time, our muscles weren't permanently damaged. Just atrophied from lack of movement. The charge flowed through us; it wasn't stagnant." She winked at Tage. "See, I can be smart too."

"You're a very complicated bunch," Samara said with a light laugh. "Follow me." She darted her crystal-blue eyes toward the door and tucked a stray piece of hair behind her ear.

Tage walked silently next to Samara. Her long hair was formed into a plait down her back, which swished as she walked. He noticed her balling her hands into fists and releasing them over and over.

"Are you okay?" Tage asked softly.

"Yes," she answered quietly. "It's nothing."

"Hey," Lumen said, pointing over her right shoulder. "What's down there? It looks a lot more interesting than this alley."

"That's the marketplace. We'll go there after."

The narrow alleyway was illuminated by the purple sky above.

"I can't get over this place," Impulse said in his quiet voice. "So impressive."

Samara smiled at him over her shoulder, and Tage glanced between the two of them, wondering when Lumen would start giving Impulse a hard time about being friendly.

They twisted and turned down obscure alleyways.

"Is this a trap?" Lumen whispered.

"Yeah," Impulse said. "Fatten us up and then eat us?"

Tage snorted his laugh, reveling in the smells and sounds of home.

"Here," Samara said as she stopped.

In a corner between two buildings was a small door. Without knowing where to go, anyone would have missed the entrance. No window, no outline, just a wooden handle. The door couldn't have been more than two or three feet wide.

"What's this crap?" Lumen asked. "What are you trying to pull?"

"N-nothing," Samara said. "This is where we come

when we get injured. Our healer. He calls himself Brakdern."

"Okay." Tage reached for the handle and opened the
door. "After you."

Samara smiled, then entered with Tage following.
Lumen was last. Once she closed the door, they were
plunged into darkness as they walked down the stairs.

"Samara," Tage said, "is there a light?" He pressed
his hands against the wooden walls for balance as he nav-
igated the narrow stairway. They came into this dank hole
to be healed? The first pricks of unease trickled through
Tage, and he held his breath for a moment to try and
heighten his other senses.

"Just a few more steps and you'll be able to see."
Samara didn't even pause as she continued down.

"Is this a joke?" Lumen coughed. "Ugh, what is that
smell?"

"I think it's sulfur," Impulse answered. "How much
farther?"

A thin sliver of light ahead was a welcome sight,
but something felt off to Tage. The bitter scent of latex
was overwhelming, and the heat had become more than
uncomfortable. Sweat dripped and pooled in his latex
shirt.

"Brakdern?" Samara called. "I'm here with the soil
chargers. And Tage."

And the *halfsie*, he said to himself, repeating the word
Lumen had used.

Finally, at the bottom of the wooden stairs, Tage
scanned the cluttered room. If he hadn't known better,
he would have thought they had crawled into a junkyard
cave. A small wooden ball rolled around the room high
above them on a rickety track. It chimed a soft ring as it
went.

Piles of books were stacked precariously up to the ceiling in one corner. In another, a rusted trunk full of random parts overflowed onto the floor. Tage recognized some of the equipment right away.

Biotech.

Another wall had shelves from floor to ceiling—similar grow lights to what Hayrah had used in Currentgrad to grow things like tomatoes. Here, Brakdern had a very strange assortment of plants, most of which Tage had never seen.

A portly man wearing only a red rubber loincloth stood near the entrance, arms crossed above his pale, fat belly. The man's black hair was slicked back, pulled into a tight bun. Brakdern squinted, his eyes almost getting lost in his cheek pads.

"So, this is him?" Brakdern took a step toward Tage, arms still crossed.

Samara nodded.

"Tage Gradient," Brakdern said, then nodded toward Impulse and Lumen. "And these are your wayward friends?"

"Excuse me?" Lumen eyed him. "Wayward?"

Brakdern laughed, and his stomach fat rippled. "Come on. Have a seat. I'll get you fixed up."

"We heal quicker than humans," Tage said. "We should have our full muscle mass back in a day or two."

"Then you don't need my help?" Brakdern asked as he swiped the back of his hand over his forehead.

"No," Tage said. "I mean, yes, we do. I . . ." He eyed the biotech in the corner again. "I just wanted you to know."

"Where are we?" Impulse asked.

"The infirmary, my boy." Brakdern slapped a thick

palm onto Impulse's shoulder and led him to a wood bench. "Where did you think we were?"

"We walked down so many steps, I thought we were under the city," Impulse said.

"Very good!" Brakdern smiled, his face shiny with sweat.

"What?" Lumen said. "How are we under? That doesn't make any sense."

"We're only inches above the Saptex Sea," Samara said. "The heat from the sea, plus the humidity, is a better atmosphere for the herbs to grow. It's only fifteen feet lower than the houses, but it makes a big difference."

Lumen rolled her eyes, then whispered to Tage, "If this is the infirmary, what happens when people are too sick to walk down all those stairs?"

"I make the occasional house call," Brakdern said. "I have excellent hearing."

Lumen took a deep breath then released it, nostrils flared. "Can you fit up those narrow stairs?"

Brakdern winked.

"Please sit," Samara said.

Tage was careful to sit in the middle of the bench and leave room for Lumen to sit next to Samara. If she did have a crush on him, he didn't want to give her the wrong impression.

Brakdern sat on a wheeled chair and slid up to them, hands on his knees, leaning forward. "Well, what do we have here?" He squinted again. Tage expected him to point out his differences, but he didn't. "Looks like you are in need of current hazel for your bruises and cuts, black gentian for weight gain, and maybe some pulse-dune powder for the fatigue." He leaned in closer and stared into each of their eyes. "Yes, definitely pulse-dune powder."

Walking over to a bar, Tage half expected him to pull drinks from behind the counter. Instead, he placed three jars, some cloth, and a mortar and pestle on the counter. He whistled as he ground up two of the herbs into the black bowl.

"These house calls . . ." Lumen twirled her braid. "Do you wear more clothes for them?"

"You must be the comedian of the group." Brakdern chuckled. "Sometimes yes, sometimes no. Down here, I like to be comfortable. It's hot." He poured a clear liquid into a wooden bowl. "Make yourselves useful. Dab the current hazel onto any cuts or bruises you see."

Samara jumped up, retrieved the shallow dish and cloths, and placed them on the ground in front of Impulse. "Use a new rag each time you dip it into the solution," she said.

Tage removed his shirt, looked at Impulse, and shrugged. Impulse did the same.

"There's a dressing screen over here," Samara said to Lumen. She led her to an accordion screen on the opposite side of the room. "I'll bring you a cloth once you've disrobed."

Samara plunged a cloth into the solution and wrung it out. Tage followed suit. The blue rag was softer than he expected. He ran it up and down his arms and shoulders. All cuts and nicks, large and small, burned with each pass. It smelled of alcohol, with a slight floral scent.

"Is your skin on fire?" Impulse asked.

"Yes," Lumen yelled from behind the screen. "This better help, because it sucks."

"At least we're not charged," Impulse said. "Can you imagine how much worse this would hurt with our senses heightened?"

"That's a thing?" Samara asked. "Like, you have better senses when you're charged?"

"Yeah," Impulse said. "Does that seem weird to you?"

"I guess . . ." Samara shrugged lightly. "I'm just learning."

"Thanks," Tage whispered to her, "for being nice."

She nodded, but immediately turned away when Tage and Impulse tugged their pants down. He'd forgotten how shy the humans were with their bodies.

Tage removed his pants and repeated the process. Each little cut and trauma stung; not a terrible pain on its own, but like a thousand little pinpricks, whereas the shower had soothed the wounds. Well, that and he'd been so exhausted, he probably wouldn't have even noticed the current hazel. He ground his teeth in irritation, then shimmied into his rubber clothes once he was finished.

"Yep," Tage said, "that was terrible." He turned to Impulse, who was fully dressed—if you could call wearing underwear dressed. "Lumen, we're decent again, you can come out."

She rejoined them on the bench. Somehow, her scowl was even more pronounced than before.

"Tage," Brakdern said, "how does it feel to be back?"

"Nice, I'm happy to be here." Tage blinked and peered around the unfamiliar room. "I'm sorry, but I don't remember you."

"You wouldn't," Brakdern said. "I was one of the rare rogue humans until a few years ago. I lived solitarily, only coming to Ohmstave a few times a year to barter my herbs and medicine. But once the desert became too dangerous, Elder Fahren offered me a job and safety here. Well, he was still an Elder then."

"Do you miss it?" Tage asked. "Living in the desert?"

"Every single day." His gaze was fixed on the concoction he'd created and was busy stuffing into small pills. "But I still get out. That was one of my terms." He looked up at Lumen. "I even fit up and down those stairs. The cribriform suits work just fine in the Charged Desert."

Samara shuddered. "I don't like wearing those. But I don't leave Ohmstave, except to check on the ursogen, but that's just on the outskirts."

"Never?" Lumen spurted.

Samara just shook her head. "I'm curious, of course, but—"

"The desert," Tage piped in. "Is that where you got the biotech?"

Brakdern grinned widely. "I'm glad you noticed, and yes, I scavenge."

"What would a human need with biotech?" Impulse walked to the bits and pieces piled on the shelves. He picked up a spinal LED light and turned it over in his fingers.

Tage's mind started to spin as he looked at the shelf of Brakdern's finds. There were a lot of parts there. Rings. Lights. Uniforms. Dentures . . . a little bit of everything. Tage glanced at his two friends, remembering the difference from being without and then with the implants. Now, he didn't feel much different than he had with the tech, but he could tell that Impulse and Lumen weren't as powerful without.

"I'm a collector," Brakdern said flatly. He walked to the group on the bench. "Take two pills three times a day for the next two days. It'll speed up your healing, weight gain, and muscle growth. Rest as much as possible."

"Thank you, Brakdern," Samara said. "We'll get out of your hair now."

Tage leaned forward, and more pieces started to fall into place. "How familiar are you with the placement of biotech?"

"Very," Brakdern said.

"How?" Lumen folded her arms and squinted at him. "How would you know about the placement?"

"I don't just find the biotech on the ground," Brakdern said. "I mean, sometimes I do. Sometimes it rests around skeletons, but sometimes I remove the tech from the bodies of dead Surge Knights."

Samara gasped.

"What's the big deal?" Lumen asked. "They're dead. And they're not your people anyway. I'd think you'd be glad to know there are dead Surge Knights out there."

"I'd rather not see anyone die," Samara snapped back.

Instead of a nasty retort from Lumen, she actually smiled in a way that almost looked like approval at Samara's reply.

Impulse nodded in agreement.

"Remember how humans are different?" Tage whispered.

"Oh right." Lumen snapped her fingers. "The human emotion thing." Her attention went to Samara. "Samara, they're dead. It's okay."

"But . . ." Samara's attention jumped from person to person. "But even to take it off their bodies? That doesn't bother you?"

"At least this way, the overlord can't recoup his tech and reuse it," Impulse offered. "It makes sense to me."

"Why are you asking about this anyway?" Brakdern asked.

"Because I think I figured out part of our plan." Tage took a long breath in. He'd need his friends on board, and he'd need to make sure it was safe, but if they wanted their power back, this was the best way to do it. "Brakdern, can you make us Surge Knights?"

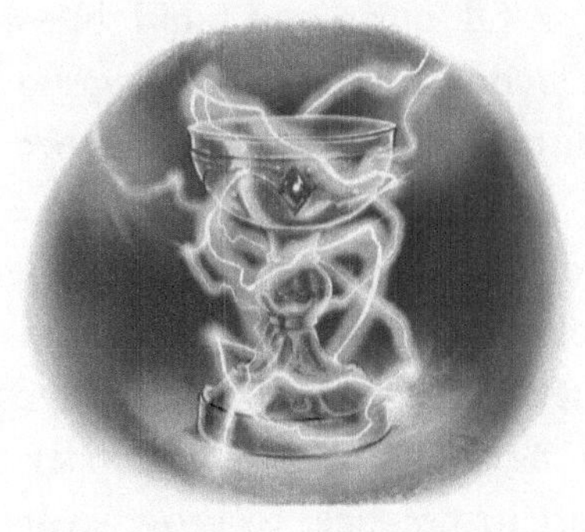

CHAPTER 26

• • • • •

"Excuse me?" Lumen screamed. "Been there, done that, have the scars and permanent nightmares to prove it."

Impulse rubbed his forehead but didn't speak.

Brakdern sat on the chair once more, and it squeaked loudly under his weight. "Hmm." He looked up and to the left, lost in thought. "Maybe."

"No," Lumen said. "Not again. No way—"

"Hold on," Tage said. "Let's just talk through this first."

Samara had backed herself against the wall.

"Tage," Impulse said quietly, "I'll do whatever I need to do to kill Overlord Koax. But I need to know the plan first. I've never felt pain like that in my life—both having it placed and taken out. I don't know, man."

"Let's not get ahead of ourselves," Brakdern said. "I'm not sure I can even do it, or if I even have enough parts." He stood, padding over to a trunk. "Samara, grab a pen and paper and help me inventory the tech."

Samara leapt to attention. Tage still couldn't quite

figure her out. Kind, quiet, and timid, but so giving—she jumped when it counted. She'd been a good friend to him when he was little, and already, she was becoming a good friend again.

Tage nodded his head toward his friends to come closer. "The plan is . . . well . . . I was thinking . . ." But he'd only gotten as far as getting his friends their power back. They'd have the whole trek back through the Charged Desert to practice, to grow stronger, and they had determination on their side. How many of Koax's Knights had been forced into service? If Tage could get more Knights on their side, the odds would be in their favor. At least enough to come in and surprise everyone enough to take out Overlord Koax.

"You're not even sure." Lumen folded her arms. "So typically male. Can I say that? I don't care. I'm saying that. Your only plan is to make us as powerful as we were the last time we failed, only this time, we're short Capacity."

Tage flinched. Swallowed. Every piece of his insides twisted as he thought about what Capacity and his parents might be going through.

"And you want us to go through that procedure without a proper plan!" Lumen yelled. "Plus, this place isn't exactly clean. I don't want him bolting crap onto me."

"I promise I won't mess up," Brakdern shouted from the corner.

Impulse and Tage chuckled; Lumen turned bright red. Tage wasn't sure if it was from embarrassment or anger. Probably both.

"Regardless of the plan, we need you two to have the power of a Surge Knight," Tage said.

"You're not going to get the modifications?" Lumen

folded her arms and raised an eyebrow. "How convenient."

"I'm not sure how or why, but I'm stronger now than when I was a Surge. You've seen it." He held Lumen's gaze until she turned away. "I don't want to mess anything up or jeopardize it. The Volt Foil will be our ticket to freeing Capacity, our parents, and killing the overlord."

"Volt Foil, eh?" Brakdern whistled.

Samara's wide eyes said that she had no idea what they were talking about, which was probably best.

"There has to be another way." Lumen leaned back against the wall, already looking defeated. Inside, she had to know this was their best chance.

Impulse pulled her in for a hug. "I don't want to do this any more than you, Lu. But you're strong. Look at the Blacknails, they almost killed us. We need to be better. Stronger. We're not enough as just soil chargers."

"Overlord Koax made the process as brutal as possible to prove his power," Tage reminded them. "Both when he put the tech in and when he pulled it out. This time"—he looked at Brakdern, hoping the guy would confirm his guess—"we'll have Brakdern to do it gently, using painkillers throughout."

Lumen pushed Impulse so he was an arm's length away, then pulled him back in and held him. She sniffed a few times against his shoulder.

"I can give you some 'medicine' that will make it less painful," Brakdern said, making air quotes. Tage figured it was best to not ask what he planned to use to make the process less terrible.

"Think about our families," Impulse whispered. "Even if all we do is get them out, we have to go back. We have to try."

Lumen pushed him away once more, wiping her tears.

"Okay. Fine. You're right. We need to get out of here immediately anyway. The humans are rubbing off on me. Emotions are a drag."

"Brakdern,"—Tage walked toward him—"do you have enough for two Surge Knights?"

"I do," he said. "I'm fairly confident I can do it, but are you guys sure?"

"We think so," Tage answered.

"Go home, eat, and rest," Brakdern said. "I need to talk to the Elders first, then I'll decide if I am willing to modify you."

"It's the only way. But yes, we'll go talk about it, and you can discuss it with your people," Tage said. "We can't go against Surge Knights if we're lowly soil chargers."

"I know," Brakdern said, holding up a hand. "Go. Rest."

"Thank you," Samara said. She grabbed Tage's hand and pulled him toward the stairs. "They're staying at the Rondeouxes' house—find us there."

Brakdern nodded.

Once back on the street, Samara took them to the marketplace. It was much smaller than Tage remembered. But it still echoed of a time before. The wooden streets were polished and kept clean. Beautiful rubber sheets were draped in between buildings to protect them from the suns. But the bright sunlight still shone through the various colorful sheets and created a kaleidoscope on the ground.

Merchants traded for food, wares, and clothing. It was all very orderly and dignified. Nothing like Current-grad. No haggling for prices, no five-finger discounts. Aside from the occasional mention of a lost loved one, everyone seemed happy. Or at least tried to be. A small glimmer of sadness crept into their eyes, but they had become pros at hiding it. It was as if the humans woke up every day and decided to play pretend.

Pretend they weren't being hunted outside the walls. Pretend Overlord Koax wasn't going to bust through the gates at any time and set the town ablaze. Pretend the soil chargers would never figure out how to get water from the Saptex Sea. Pretend everything was okay.

Impulse asked questions about everything, and Samara led him around the market. Tage sat on a bench and let his eyes fall closed, wishing Capacity were with him. Could feel the wood under her feet. See where he'd lived as a child.

"Ugh." Lumen flopped next to him. "Everyone's too nice. It's weird. I mean, I'm getting some looks, but seriously."

Once they'd had enough sightseeing, Samara took them back to the house.

"What did you call this place?" Impulse asked. "Ron something?"

"Rondeoux." Samara turned to him. "That was the owners' last name." She pushed past the door and led them in.

"They're out there?" Impulse nodded toward the entrance.

"Yes," she said. "They had no children; they were newlyweds. I think they were out hunting for ferals and never came back. We assume they're in the powerline. But they'll be back. Once you defeat the overlord, that is."

"You're really putting a lot of faith in us," Lumen said wryly. "Bold."

"It's not bold." Samara's bright eyes clouded with tears. "It's hope. That's all we have. Keeps us going, I suppose. Anyway," she continued, "I'm going to bring you some food and very simple linen clothes with draw-strings for growth."

Tage laughed.

"If you bulk up any more, your clothes will burst at the seams." Samara pointed at each of them. "I think a loose sleeping gown will be most comfortable. Or, like I said, drawstrings."

"Good point." Impulse gave her a smile. "Your thoughtfulness reminds me of my oldest little sister."

"I only make good points." Samara forced a smile. "And you must miss them."

Impulse paused for a moment before nodding.

"Anything else?" Samara asked, her attention still on Impulse.

Tage stared at her a moment—all the kindness and time she'd given them had been far more than he expected for a group of fugitive failures. "No. And thank you, Samara."

Her cheeks flushed, and she scurried out the door.

They sat on the two wooden couches, staring at each other.

Lumen squinted. "You really think Brakdern can change us into Surge Knights?"

"I do," Tage said. "Humans are far more emotion-driven. He wouldn't agree to it if he wasn't sure he could."

"Would he care if he accidentally hurt or killed two strangers?" Impulse asked. "Soil chargers?"

"Yes," Tage said. "Humans consider all lives valuable, soil charger and human alike. This isn't a done deal anyway. We still have to see what the Elders say."

"You better hope he succeeds," Lumen said. "If not, it's *our* blood on *your* hands."

They'd already spilled a lot of blood for Tage's mission.

The friends sat in silence for a while. Lumen took another ages-long hot shower. Impulse dozed off. Tage let his plan rumble through his head. They couldn't just go running in there. He'd need to talk to Fahren to see who Tel'el's sources were. Their best plan would be to get into Currentgrad undetected, find allies, and plan from there.

With two small knocks, Samara returned with roasted feral, mashed amp plants, and three sleeping gowns. She was shortly followed by a man with broad shoulders whom Tage would know anywhere.

"Dad!" Tage yelled. He ran to him, nearly knocking him to the ground with his embrace. His heart fluttered; hot tears streamed down his face. "I can't believe it. How?"

"Tage, my boy," Tel'el grunted as he patted Tage's back.

Tage leaned back and took in his dad's appearance. His threadbare and tattered white shirt hung loosely off his frail body.

"What happened to you?" Tage asked.

"I've been charged nonstop for over four months. Some of it was a dirty charge from ferals and shock worms." Tel'el leaned against the wall. "I've damaged my body. But I'm alive."

"You need food," Tage said as he helped his dad to the table.

Samara bustled into the kitchen, dished up the feral roast and mashed amp plants onto four plates, and set the table.

"Mr. Gradient," Lumen said, "is my dad with you?"

"No." Tel'el fell into his chair. "I think he's in hiding. I couldn't get to him."

"You think?!" Lumen asked, a little too harshly.

"I should go." Samara started toward the door.

"No," Tage said. "Stay. You can fill the Elders in, I'm sure they have questions."

"I've already spoken to them." Tel'el waved his hand as he breathed in deeply over his plate. "It's all been settled."

Tel'el's arm shook as he grasped his fork. Samara sat next to him on a bench and took the fork from his hand. Tage studied the girl. Her compassion was beyond anything he could understand. She cut small bites of the meat and fed Tel'el.

Tage swallowed. Too many questions rattled his mind for him to speak—most of the questions, he was afraid to have the answer to.

"Thank you, Samara," Tel'el said. "It's moments like this I remember why I loved Ohmstave so much."

"Of course," she said. "I'm going to get Brakdern. Surely, he has something that will help Tel'el." She nodded and left quietly.

Tage swallowed and asked the one question that would encompass everything rattling in his mind. "How bad was the fallout after we failed?"

"Let's sit and eat," Impulse suggested.

"Bad," Tel'el whispered, his hand shaking a little less now that he'd had a few bites.

Tage swallowed, and exchanged glances with Lumen and Impulse—both of whom sat in front of untouched plates and stared at Tel'el.

"I'm sure you all have a lot of questions," Tel'el continued. "The night of the assassination attempt, your mother and I were at home. We'd been anxiously awaiting any type of disturbance at the Voltaic Dava—knowing you were waiting for a window to use the poison."

Tage's heart hammered as he thought about the nights they stood in the passageway, hoping to not be caught watching, hoping for the food to be left—even for a moment.

"After three or four days, I don't remember now, I was anxious. I thought maybe there was a hiccup and went to the basement to review the plan. Look for cracks in it. Without warning, I heard a crash and tried to go upstairs to find out the source. Something had been knocked onto the trapdoor and I couldn't lift it. I listened as they bound and cuffed Hayrah and took her away. They searched the house for me but never found the secret basement. I waited for days but couldn't get out. I was running out of food and water, but finally after a week, people came into the house and started looting. Eventually, someone stole whatever was on top of the door, and I escaped in the middle of the night."

"They took Mom." Tage rested his head in his hands. Why hadn't his mother just stayed in the basement? Why hadn't she run?

"Your mother is dead, Tage," Tel'el said flatly.

"But . . . no . . ." Tage shook his head. The entire room spun. "But you said . . ."

Tage felt the weight of several hands on his back, but continued to stare forward, stunned.

"What about my family?" Impulse asked, his voice shaking.

Tel'el shrugged his bony shoulders. "I don't know."

"And Capacity?" Tage asked.

Tel'el slowly shook his head. "I didn't hear about what happened to her. For all I knew, she was still in the powerline with you."

Tage put his face in his hands and breathed deep.

Tel'el continued. "I could hear the conversations

above when I was trapped. The looters commented that I was a coward for running and leaving Hayrah behind to take the punishment. The overlord killed her because she wouldn't give up my location. He would have killed her regardless."

Tage stared at nothing, memories racing through his mind. Previously, he thought not knowing his parents' fate was torture. But this? This was much worse. Had they simply killed Capacity too? Tage had hoped they were keeping her alive to lure him back, but what if they'd decided that was too much trouble?

His stomach turned and his eyes fell closed as he thought about sitting on top of the swing set with her. Thought of how she'd kissed the corner of his mouth just before they'd deposited the poison. She couldn't just be gone, could she?

"At first, I tried to find you four in the powerline. But it's so massive . . . I resorted to plan B. I infiltrated the other terraregions, making secret alliances with soil chargers, trying to convince them what the overlord is doing is wrong. Most of them are blind. They believe his propaganda—that there is too much charge in the desert. That it's dangerous, and only a few chosen ones can leave their cities. They believe the powerline will solve everything. The isolation of staying in their cities has become their detriment. No one has seen the powerline for what it truly is or how he'll control the entire planet once he harnesses the energy."

"Did you show them?" Lumen asked. "Take them to it?"

"No." Tel'el slammed down a fist onto the table. Forks clanked. "I tried, but they're scared. Overlord Koax has every terraregion convinced everything outside the city is too dangerous, the powerline forbidden. After several weeks of gaining their trust, I got a few soil chargers from each region on my side. A small army."

"What do we do?" Impulse asked softly. "Will killing him do any good now if there are so many believers?"

The pain in Impulse's eyes showed his fear. Tage had lost his mom. Impulse was facing the idea that his actions may have terrible repercussions for his younger siblings—soil chargers who hadn't yet had a full chance at life.

"This ends now," Tel'el said, his voice deep and face dark from traveling through the desert. "I'm going back and killing the overlord no matter what it takes."

"Good," Tage said. "We have a plan, or the beginnings of one. How many others do you have connections with?"

"No." Tel'el lifted his head and stared at Tage. "You're not going. Absolutely not. I already lost your mother; I'm not losing you, too. It's too dangerous."

"We both have family and friends in Currentgrad," Lumen said. "All of us do."

"There was a small miscalculation that led to our failure," Tage said. "We have to see this through."

"No." Tel'el drew in a long breath. "If I hadn't failed all those years ago, we wouldn't be in this situation."

"If you hadn't failed, I wouldn't have been adopted. I wouldn't have been your son." Tage lowered his head. "Plus, you need us. We need as many as we can get. We have a medicine man here, Brakdern, who thinks he has enough tech to turn Lumen and Impulse back into Surge Knights."

Tel'el glanced at his friends before his eyes rested on Tage. "Not you?"

Tage opened his mouth to speak, but nothing came out.

"He doesn't need it," Impulse said. "Tage cast a Volt

Foil, he was Arcing without tech, and he saved us from a group of Blacknails."

"You what?" Tel'el coughed before searching Tage's eyes with his own. "How?"

"I don't know." Tage had no answers for what he was or what he was able to do. "Something snapped in me when I was in the powerline. I feel connected to the energy. My body craves it. And I have no limit—it just flows through me at all times. I never get charged; I stay charged. Old energy flows out as a fresh charge fills the void without any conscious thought. I just keep gaining power."

"My boy!" Tel'el beamed. "I've never been prouder of you in my life."

"This isn't a developed talent," Tage said. "I just . . . do it."

Tage stared into the old man's eyes. The last four months had taken decades off his life, weathered him. But Tage recognized the glimmer in his eyes. His puffed-out chest. Full smile, despite his obvious physical pain. He stared at the only man who had been a dad to him, knowing he'd lost his mom. His own death, Tage had been prepared for, but in all the years of training and preparation, he hadn't been fully prepared to lose his parents—he'd assumed that if they were killed, it would be because he'd failed and been killed himself. Of course, the possibility had been out there, it just hadn't felt real. And now, Tage had yet another reason to want Overlord Koax dead.

"This means we're coming, right?" Impulse asked. "Back to Currentgrad?"

Tel'el slowly nodded.

A knock was followed by Samara and Brakdern. So again, she had remembered to knock—she just hadn't waited before coming in. The thought gave Tage a brief moment of much-needed lightness.

Tage turned his attention to the door where Samara and Brakdern were walking through. Once again, Brakdern only wore a loincloth. He lumbered in, waddling like a shock worm climbing into a pulse dune. In one hand, he held a heavy medical bag. The other pulled a trunk on wheels.

"What do we have here?" Brakdern said.

"Oh crap." Lumen made a face as she stared at the trunk. "Are we doing this biotech thing already?"

"Later," Brakdern said. "You made such a big deal about the stairs, I thought I'd make a house call just for you. Even dressed up for the occasion." He twisted from side to side, his red loincloth flapping about dangerously.

"Really?" Lumen crossed her arms, raising an eyebrow.

"Yep." He fiddled with a leather cord around his neck. "Now, onto the real business: I'm here for the newbie. You three need to take your pills and rest. You'll need it—even you, Tage. I spoke with Minister Fahren. In light of the new information, he's agreed the biotech is the best solution. I'll be back later tonight to perform the transformation."

"Here?" Lumen yelled.

"You said you wanted a house call." Brakdern winked. "Go on, get some rest."

"He's right," Tage said, poking at his dinner. "Let's finish the food and sleep."

They ate quickly. Tage didn't even bother reveling in the familiar food—anything familiar reminded him of Hayrah's death. After they finished, Lumen and Impulse went to their rooms without another word. Tage sat with his dad as Brakdern poked, prodded, and eventually administered medicine.

Tel'el yawned. "Is the medicine supposed to make you drowsy?"

"A little," Brakdern said. "Both of you, rest. Please. I'll be back in a few hours for the biotech installation."

"You can have my bed." Tage stood and motioned for his dad to follow.

"The couch is just fine," Tel'el said.

"Get up," Tage insisted. Tel'el followed him into the bedroom and stumbled onto the bed.

Tage sat on the edge, like Tel'el had done when he'd first moved in with Tage and Hayrah. Back when Tage could see the confusion in Tel'el's eyes, the warrior probably having no idea what to do with a kid. But Tage thought of all the years they'd spent together, and knew he'd been lucky.

"When will we go to Currentgrad?" Tage asked. He covered his dad with an ursogen hide.

"I need to leave soon," Tel'el said as his eyes drifted closed. "I need to round up my army from the various regions. We'll meet you outside the walls of Currentgrad. We'll decide on a time tomorrow. The place we had set up for your exit."

"Promise you'll wait for us."

"I promise," was the last thing Tel'el said before drifting off to sleep.

Tage wandered back out to the living room and gathered an ursogen hide from the back of a bench before wrapping himself up and lying down.

Hayrah was gone. Capacity was hopefully still a captive—words he never thought he'd think. But Tel'el had gotten some sympathizers. Their numbers were bigger, and they were angry. They had a lot to fight for the first time they'd tried to kill Overlord Koax, but now they'd been trapped, tortured on the line, heard and learned so much more about the world they lived in. Would their numbers be large enough to make soil chargers see past Koax's lies?

More than ever, Tage hoped whatever genetic gifts had been given to him by both his human and soil charger parents would be enough to add an element of surprise to their attack.

They had to be cautious. They needed escape routes. They needed more warriors. He would not let Hayrah die for nothing. Would not let Capacity be held for nothing. So much injustice. Determination deepened Tage's resolve. He had to work smart. Work hard.

He could not fail again.

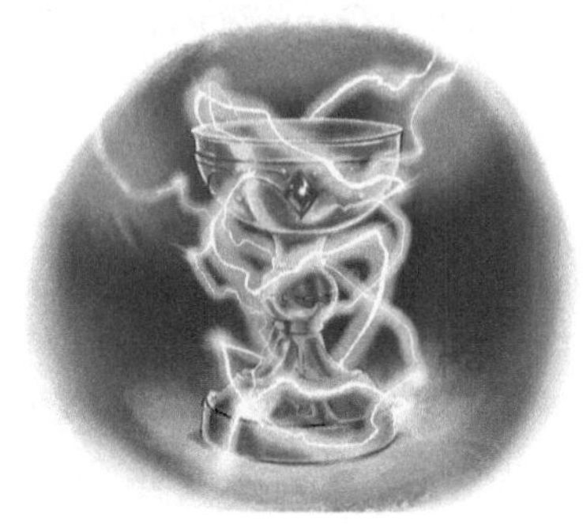

CHAPTER 27

• • • • •

Tage awoke to a gentle nudge that he'd felt hundreds of times growing up. Tel'el whispered something he couldn't quite understand in his sleepy fog.

"Hmmm?" Tage rolled to his side, then sat up.

"The man, Brakdern, is back."

"Oh. I guess it's time." The edges of his lips pulled down. "I thought I was at ho—Currentgrad for a minute when you woke me."

Tel'el sat on the edge of the bench next to his son but said nothing. Tage studied his dad's face. No improvement; if anything, he looked worse.

"Dad, are you okay?" Tage gently touched Tel'el's trembling arm. His white shirt looked like a moth had feasted on it after rolling in soot. Linen pants hung loosely off his bony hips, the hem on the bottom frayed from fire or electricity.

Brakdern had opened the trunk next to the table and begun sorting the Surge Knight pieces.

"I'm fully dependent on charge now," Tel'el replied.

"Like Overlord Koax and Charuss. I'm weaker without it. Unless there are red pots full of charged dirt here, I need to get out to the desert soon or I'll become sick."

"You look sick now." Tage stood, then helped his dad to his feet.

"I am," Tel'el said. "Someone should be here soon to escort me out of the city walls. I guess they still don't fully trust me. But they will after all is said and done."

"I'll walk with you," Tage said.

"No, your friends need you. This surgery, the placement of the tech," Tel'el whispered. "Tage, it might not be a success."

"I know." Tage stared at the ground. "Maybe we should leave them behind. I'll go with you. I'm stronger anyway." He could make up for some of the pain they'd both already suffered.

"We need them," Tel'el said. "My army is small. I've had a chat with them both already. Lumen and Impulse, especially Impulse, understand what's at stake."

"They knew before," Tage said. "When we recruited them for this mission in the first place, they were ready and understood the risks. And they've had to live with failure, just like me." Only Tage had trained for longer. Was far more to blame than either of them.

"I know." Tel'el's eyes were like steel—hard and determined, despite his hunched body. "Like I said, I talked to them both separately and together. They have given up so much already, I didn't want them to walk into this unless they were fully committed. And that's why I'm having this conversation with you."

"Committed?" Tage shook his head. "They aren't thrilled with the idea of being transformed again, but they'll do it. We know it's our best chance. We have to save

Capacity and kill the overlord. Impulse is just hoping his younger siblings are safe. We all have a lot on the line.”

“That’s not what I mean,” Tel’el said. “I mean committed to the understanding that you might”—he cleared his throat—“die.”

“I know.” Tage thought he’d understood that risk the entire time. Perhaps it was youth, or arrogance, but deep down, he’d always allowed a sliver of hope that he’d be successful. Of course, he’d said he was prepared for death, even to himself, but under that understanding and bravado was a deep-seated feeling that he was invincible. That invincibility had disappeared. Now, after failing once and looking into his dad’s worried eyes, knowing the overlord had already killed his mom—Tage understood he could ultimately be the overlord’s sacrifice.

“Everyone has to be committed to take out the overlord—Charuss, too, if possible. We were all naïve with the poison,” Tel’el said. “We thought that more numbers would mean a greater chance for success, but in the end, we didn’t kill Koax.”

Tage swallowed.

“Your friends could die during the procedure,” Tel’el said. “Brakdern will be kinder and use medicines that Koax didn’t use, but Koax has far more practice.”

“I know.” Tage’s voice cracked. If only they could charge the same way he did. But pausing during battle to recharge, needing to wait until their charge was depleted, only being able to use one ignition—as normal soil chargers did—they’d lose for sure. The risk was worth taking.

“The Surge Knights might find you on the way to Currentgrad; capture you or worse.”

“I know, Dad.” Hot tears stung Tage’s eyes.

“If we’re lucky, we’ll make it into the city. But even

then, they'll be waiting. It could be over in a matter of minutes. They know we are coming."

"I. Know." Tage balled his hands into fists, tried to control his heart, steady his breath.

"Capacity might already be gone," Tel'el said.

"Fine!" Tage finally cracked. "She might be dead, I might die, Lumen might die, Impulse, too. Heck, you already look dead. This whole thing is probably going to fail. Okay? Happy? We know. We understand. But we have to try."

Tel'el sat silent, and Tage wondered briefly if his friends could hear.

"You don't understand what being in the powerline does to a person," Tage continued. "It changes you. The faint recognition of who you are, of being trapped but unable to do anything about it. We're already broken. At least let us try to exact some revenge. Save the humans. Save Capacity, her mom Relay and her dad Aeocag, Impulse's family, Lumen's parents and as many as we can from the powerline. Not only that—if we don't, the humans will become extinct!"

Tel'el slowly nodded and patted Tage on the back. "Then it's settled. I've made some arrangements for you. Brakdern has two pet ursogen he's agreed to donate to the mission. You three take them. That's the only way you'll get to Currentgrad in two days."

"Two days?" Tage asked. "It must be a hundred miles to Currentgrad. Can the ursogen cover that kind of ground so quickly?"

"Yes, easily." Tel'el nodded. "You'll even have time to sleep at night as well."

But wait. "Brakdern keeps ursogen here, in the city?"

"No," Brakdern piped in, "just outside the city. Keep 'em caged on the shore of the sea."

Tel'el and Tage stared at him.

"Well, we *are* in the same room," Brakdern replied. "Also, I don't plan on allowing anyone to die while I'm inserting tech."

Tage's attention dropped to the wooden floor. "How will you make it to Currentgrad?" he asked Tel'el.

"I've got my own ursogen waiting for me at my first stop," Tel'el said. "That's the easy part. Now, Brakdern's ursogen look a little emaciated since the charge isn't as strong on the edge of the sea. But give them a few hours in the Charged Desert and they'll beef right up."

"Why does Brakdern have ursogen in the first place?"

"I can answer that one, too," Brakdern said with a grin. "I use them when I scavenge. Actually, one of them was Tel'el's. Ping was just a baby when Tel'el used him to get to Ohmstave when the first assassination attempt failed."

"I turned him loose," Tel'el said. "Told him to go home and . . . he did. I didn't realize where he'd been all this time."

Samara knocked twice and stepped inside. "Are you ready, Mr. Gradient?"

Lumen jogged down the stairs. "So, you ready to fillet some soil chargers, Brakdern?" Her attention turned to Tage. "And are you ready to watch this crap-fest?"

"Come on, Dad." Tage stood. "I'll walk you to the door."

"Ready?" Samara asked Tel'el again.

"See ya on the flip side, Gradient." Lumen smirked.

Tel'el nodded.

Impulse shook Tel'el's hand. "See you in a few days, Mr. Gradient. Thank you for coming here and setting this up."

Tage hugged his dad, whispering goodbye to him.

264

"You wait for us," Tage said. "We'll be there as soon as Lumen and Impulse are healed."

Tel'el patted Tage's shoulder in response and left with Samara, who threw an apologetic smile-frown Tage's way.

Tage gathered with his friends in the living room. Lumen swayed from side to side, eyelids heavy. Impulse sat staring forward.

"Are you two okay?" Tage asked, though it was a stupid question. How okay would Tage feel if he were about to get tech again? "I think I should just go. You guys stay here."

"No way!" Lumen shouted. "This stuff's great!"

Tage held a finger up to his lips.

"I gave them a mild sedative," Brakdern said. "I can't have them completely out of it, but I wanted to spare them a bit of the pain."

"Oh," Tage said.

"I'm going," Impulse said. "Lu and I want to find our families. So we're going, and you can't stop us."

Tage smiled. He hoped it wasn't just the sedative talking. He knew his friends, and he knew they would follow him to the ends of Hadrain.

Brakdern held up metal dentures in front of his mouth and smiled. "Now, who's ready to get some biotech?"

Silence. Tage furrowed his brow.

"Lumen, you want to go first?" Tage asked.

"I—I don't think I can do it," Lumen said, leaning against the counter in the kitchen.

Lumen held the back of her index finger up to her nose. She had a sour look on her face. "I want to do it . . . but does he know what he's doing? And what if I get paralyzed?"

"I wore my lucky loincloth!" Brakdern shifted. "You

won't be paralyzed, probably. Heck, you might even want more done." He held up a strange-looking piece of tech. "I got this off a downed shock craft. I could install it if you want."

"I think I'll just stick with the basic Surge Knight biotech, thanks," Lumen said, voice thick with sarcasm. "Tell me again where you got this crap from?"

"The overlord dumps his dead Surge Knights in the desert all the time. I think he's hiding their deaths from the general public." Brakdern smiled sheepishly. "I scavenge at night a few times a month. You'd be surprised at the things I've found. Without the ursogen, I'd never be able to cover that kind of ground so quickly or haul so much back."

What was killing so many Surge Knights? Tage sat back. Koax? Something else? Or was Koax occasionally yanking the tech out and inserting the disloyal into the powerline?

Tage hadn't ridden on an ursogen since he, Hayrah, and Tel'el first crossed the desert together when he was six. His heart twisted again at the loss of his mother. No one as good and determined as Hayrah should ever have to die.

"I can go first," Impulse offered.

"No." Lumen stepped forward, her face unreadable. "For sure I'd wimp out if I had to watch before it was done to me."

"You just tell me if you need a break," Brakdern said. "I'll give you some watt leaves to smell. They should help your body relax, which should also ease the pain."

"Ready?" Tage guided Lumen to a long coffee table.

"Lie here." Brakdern pointed. "Facedown."

Tage grabbed a stack of papers. "Here, put your face on these."

"Thanks." She lay facedown, resting her forehead on her folded arms.

Suddenly, all the straps that Tage had hated seemed like a good idea, as did the cradles that allowed them to hang. They weren't at all set up for this.

"What can I do to help?" Tage asked Brakdern.

Brakdern pointed to the rows of hardware lined up on the table. "Hand me the stuff when I need it."

Samara walked through the door with a heavy bucket in tow. "Well, your dad is off to another terraregion. Here." She handed the bucket to Brakdern. "Just as you requested."

The obnoxious scent of sulfur filled the small room. Latex sloshed onto the wooden floor as Brakdern dipped both of his large, meaty hands into the bucket, covering his fingers and palms with latex all the way up to his wrists. He continued to dip after each layer hardened, creating a sort of rubber glove for each hand.

"Now I'm ready," Brakdern said, examining his hands.

"That's pretty clever," Tage said. "Is that for sterilization?"

"No," Brakdern admitted. "I'm not worried about germs. I'm worried about getting shocked."

Of course. They'd discharged, but soil chargers could always have small amounts of residual charge. Brakdern needed to be careful.

Tage knelt near Lumen. She shivered.

He leaned down to her ear. "It'll be okay."

"I know," she said. "Samara, help a girl out, will you?"

Samara stepped to the other side of the table and unbuttoned Lumen's sleeping gown down to her waist. Tage turned his head slightly, examining her scar-covered back. His heart dropped into his stomach. They were about to add to those scars.

"Lumen," he said. "I'm so sorry, your back. The scars."

"Yeah," she said, "pretty, aren't they? At least the keloids will be an easy map for Brakdern to follow."

"Do you have the patient prepped?" Brakdern asked, as if he were a world-renowned surgeon.

Tage looked at him with a raised eyebrow. "Um, yes, I suppose . . ." His voice trailed off to a near whisper.

"Yeah, the patient's prepped," Lumen said. "Just get this over with."

Brakdern pointed, and Tage handed him a gnarly-looking vertebrae LED.

"If the overlord can do this, I can do this," Brakdern said, turning it over in his hands, trying to figure out the orientation. "I think we'll start with this one."

"Which way does it go?" Tage asked.

Brakdern looked at him and then down at Lumen's back. "I think this way."

He held the piece against Lumen's spine near the base of her neck, orientating it with her existing scars. He swiped the area with discharged current hazel and then reoriented the tech.

"Does it really matter?" Lumen asked.

"Absolutely," Brakdern replied. "Screwdriver."

Tage handed him the tool, and he started screwing in the vertebrae piece. This time, everything was mounted on the outside of the skin. At first, Lumen didn't squirm or say anything. She just gripped the sides of the table with white knuckles, her fingernails breaking and cuticles tearing.

"Breathe in deeper," Brakdern commanded, and

Samara grabbed a few more leaves and set them on the paper near Lumen's face.

The paper shifted wildly under her as she attempted not to move. She started screaming, and the entire house filled with the sound of terror.

"I thought the sedative would help?" Tage asked worriedly.

"It only takes the edge off!" Lumen spat.

"Here." Brakdern handed Samara a small rubber mouthguard. "So she can bite it instead of screaming."

"Go faster. Go faster!" Lumen said through gritted teeth. She clamped down on the hard rubber mouthguard.

Tage grimaced. He knew the pain she was experiencing. He handed another LED light to Brakdern, who continued. A swipe of current hazel, and then another light.

"I'm sorry, my dear," Brakdern said over and over with each turn of the screwdriver.

Blood trickled down her sides. No sawdust box to catch the crimson drops. By the time Brakdern passed the midpoint of her spine, Lumen was breathing rapidly and devoid of energy to scream. She was pale. Blood pooled in the small of her back. Samara's tears were small rivers.

Once he placed the twenty-four vertebrae biotech, Brakdern asked, "Can you sit up if we help you?"

"I think so," Lumen managed to answer.

Her eyes were closed, and it seemed to Tage that she was only moments away from blacking out. Tage held her limp arms and Samara helped hold her head as they lifted her into a seated position. She retched all over the floor and then screamed in pain.

"I told you this was a stupid idea," Lumen said.

Tage frowned.

"What now?" Her voice shook.

"We have to get the rings on," Tage said.

"Can we . . . can we . . . can we . . . skip the . . . the denture . . . the metal teeth? I really don't want that in my mouth."

"I wish we could." Tage shook his head. "But the overlord, I asked him, he said it was like a circuit breaker. It allowed the charge to flow."

"We could skip it and have her check her tech in the desert," Brakdern suggested. "But if a circuit breaks, then there's no power. I'd suggest we do it."

Samara wiped Lumen's sweaty hair out of her face with a cool cloth. "It'll be okay."

"Thanks. You know, you're not so bad," Lumen said. "Do the rings first, Brakdern."

Tage helped Brakdern by placing the ten toe rings on. He harpooned the tops of her feet with each wire connected to the steel-forged rings. Despite the numbing agent Brakdern had used, each time Tage stabbed her skin, she let out a string of curse words. Brakdern added ten rings to her fingers. They didn't have to be as forceful as Koax had been, but the rings did have to be tight.

"Please lean back," Brakdern said. "This is the last part."

"I can't." Lumen's eyes crashed shut. "I can't do it."

Tage's insides were in knots, making his knuckles white as he flexed and unflexed his hands. But it would all be worth it in the end. It had to be.

"I don't know if I have a denture that'll fit your small mouth," Brakdern said as he pulled out five sets of dentures that had been embedded in another soil charger's gums. Tage ran his tongue over his teeth, remembering the ache of the new dentures, the taste of the metal in his mouth.

"Just do it." Lumen sighed as a tear slipped down

her cheek. "I didn't go through all this only to not have it work."

Brakdern tossed a smaller one up and down in his palm. "Ready?"

Lumen parted her lips, but just barely. Brakdern slowly pushed in the silver denture, and Lumen responded by fully opening her mouth. With one swift move, he shoved it into her gums.

"You okay?" Tage asked.

She moaned, and then passed out.

"Brakdern?" Tage asked.

He gestured loosely to her. "I'm surprised she stayed awake for as long as she did. Strong girl."

"Guess this means it's my turn." Impulse stood and stretched.

Tage held Lumen upright before carrying her up to her room and laying her on her stomach. Brakdern had created a small mound of pillows near her hips, allowing her spine to curve and to prevent her vertebrae from fusing. Tage covered her with an ursogen-skin blanket and whispered, "Thank you."

When he returned to the living room, he stared at Impulse.

"How is Lu?" Impulse asked.

"She's going to be okay . . ." He thought of the look on her face just before she fainted. "Fine. Just resting. Or passed out, I'm not sure which." He looked over his shoulder, then back at Impulse. "Are you ready?"

Impulse set his jaw and squared his shoulders. "I am."

"Are you sure you can do this?" Samara asked, her face only now dry of tears.

Impulse shrugged. "Yeah. I'll be fine."

"Denture or no?" Brakdern asked.

Impulse nodded. "I don't wanna risk it either. I want it all. Every piece of tech. Just like Lu."

Brakdern made a face at the offending pieces and nodded.

Both Brakdern and Tage used small hammers to slowly alter the denture to fit into Impulse's mouth. Impulse was unwavering until after the denture was placed. With all the hardware bolted onto him, he quietly passed out.

How could it be that Tage didn't need to go through this? He was the reason they'd had their tech torn out, and redone. His failure was once again causing his friends pain. Of course, he had to focus on succeeding where they'd failed, but listening to Impulse breathe in deep, sleeping breaths as his blood trickled to the floor, the horror of a second transformation twisted Tage's stomach. If he thought for a second that the tech wouldn't hinder him, he'd have gone through the transformation simply as an act of solidarity, but the freedom he'd felt after releasing himself from that line was like nothing he'd experienced.

Tage crawled on the floor, attempting to put himself far enough under Impulse that he could lift him. He pushed upward, but did more grunting than moving his friend.

Brakdern laughed.

"I think I'll need your help with Impulse," Tage said through a smile.

"No problem," Brakdern said, picking up Impulse's legs. "Whew, he's huskier than he looks."

Finally, Tage was able to stand and they shuffled back to Impulse's room. At least he'd taken the room closest to the main living area.

Brakdern left as soon as they deposited him on the bed. Tage lingered for a minute, watching the makeshift Surge Knight breathe. Then Brakdern returned with a couple of clear vials and syringes. Tage watched him insert the needles into the solution and fill the syringes. He plunged them into Impulse's bicep.

"Antibiotic and painkiller," he said. "I gave it to Lumen before you took her up. I'll be back later tonight to check on them. For now, let them rest." Brakdern guided Tage out of the room.

"I can stay and clean their wounds while they sleep," Samara offered.

Tage wasn't sure if he responded; he only ached at the pain they had endured. It wasn't fair, and Tage would have gladly traded places with either of his friends had it been possible—the thought only made him feel slightly better.

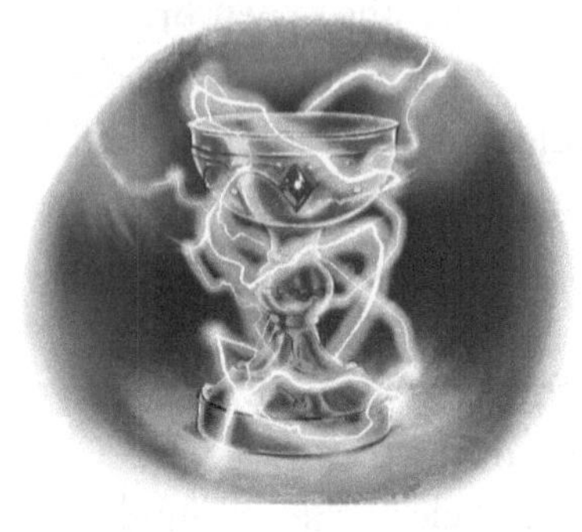

CHAPTER 28

• • • • •

Samara shimmied into a white cribriform suit over her clothes. The suit was a solid latex onesie from head to toe, with a zipper in the front. Once zipped up, she tucked it into the vertical rubber flap. The only opening was around her face.

"The old cribriform suit." Tage chuckled. "It's like a glove for your entire body."

"It works," Samara said, her face tight. "We can't keep the ursogen inside the gates, too dangerous."

"I figured." Tage rolled his head from side to side, still thinking about his friends sleeping off yet another transformation. "Does anyone else use them?"

"Mostly Brakdern and the Naiads," Samara said. "We've used Ping in the past for construction or hauling trees out of the sea."

Tage nodded and followed her through the city to the gates. She spoke to a guard, and within seconds, they lowered the drawbridge to allow passage.

"Be careful," a large Brute said. "If the lookout even

thinks he sees a shock craft or disturbance, we'll sound the alarm. You'll have sixty seconds to return or you'll be locked out."

Samara nodded.

Tage glanced behind them as they stepped past the wall.

"They'll be asleep for a long time yet," Samara assured him. "Even with your superpowers."

The lightness in her voice at the end helped his shoulders relax.

They walked on the wooden bridge over the Saptex Sea and to the edge of the shore. Tage placed a foot onto the ground, and delicious charge flowed up through his feet, swelling his nerves. Even as a Surge Knight, he had to consciously take up charge, but not now. It ran through him like blood in his veins.

Tage offered a hand to Samara, guiding her off the platform. She leaned back; the fear in her eyes was obvious.

"I'm not a conduit," Tage assured her. "I can't hurt you unless I'm trying."

"I know." She stood on the last board of the bridge. "Will you check the soles of my feet before I step down? I tested the suit before I put it on, but . . ."

She sat on the edge and Tage lifted each foot, running his hands over the rubber.

"Off the bridge," a Brute yelled at them from above. "We need to close it immediately."

"You're good." Tage took a step back.

Samara drew in a deep breath and held it in until both feet had left the walkway. Her white cribriform suit was a stark contrast to the desert.

"Okay?" Tage asked.

She just nodded in response.

He breathed in deeply, the charge from the ground flowing through him, energizing every piece of his body. In this moment, he felt as if they might succeed. As if he'd hold Capacity again soon. Help Tel'el finish what he started. Bring Impulse back to his family. Help Lumen reunite with hers. "I'm whole again."

"What does it feel like?" Samara asked. "To have so much energy running through you?"

Tage took a few steps in silence, relishing in every piece of his body being fully alive. "It's like every sense is heightened. Every smell. Every sound. I swear I can pick out individual cells in my body. I'm aware of everything. My heart, each grain of sand on my feet."

"Is it . . . hard to throw those bolts?"

Tage felt the current and threw a short Bolt Ignition back into the sand.

Samara jumped.

"Sorry." He shook his head. "It's not hard. It's as easy as skipping or walking." Especially now.

He glanced back at the walls of the city, but the guard just frowned. Good thing Tage had done something small.

"I'm sorry about your mom," Samara whispered.

His eyes welled with tears so quickly, he swiped at each. "Thank you. Tell yours I'm sorry we failed." There was nothing else to say.

Samara lifted a shoulder, twisting the suit. "We all hoped . . ."

"Yeah." Tage frowned.

"Can I ask you something else?" Samara led him around the east side of Ohmstave.

Tage nodded.

"Are they close?" Samara stared at their feet in the sand. "The drudges. Are they close to fixing their brains so they can problem solve?"

"They aren't good with critical thinking." Tage chose his words carefully. "But they've created incredible things there. It's not out of the realm of possibility."

Her eyes met his. "You think it's only a matter of time?"

"Yes," Tage said.

"Once that happens . . ." Samara said. Her voice cracked and she swallowed loudly. "Tage, you must succeed. All we have to offer is our ability to extract water from the sea, and once they—the drudges—learn how to do that, it's over. We already live as prisoners, but he'd have an endless army."

"I know." He stared at the ground.

"It's the only reason the overlord hasn't completely killed us off, isn't it? If the drudges can be trained to get the water, then we're done. And who's to say he won't just kill us anyway?"

"Hadrain needs you," Tage said. "Without you, the entire planet dies. The far side is covered in fire. There are only three terraregions left, and we hope there will be enough chaos after Koax's death that we can convince them the powerline is a terrible idea."

He shrugged at her. "Here we are, worried about one overlord harnessing all the electricity in the world, when in reality, the humans have all the power. You control the entire water supply."

"For now," Samara said.

"Last I saw, the drudges were profoundly dumb," Tage said.

"But who's to say the overlord won't grow impatient?" She kicked the dirt, fine bits of dark sand pluming around her small feet. In her anger, walking had become a slow jog. "What if he just starts sacrificing a few soil chargers? Making them the ones who engineer the sea to separate water from it? They'd lose their ability to charge forever, but it wouldn't kill them."

"He doesn't know *how* you do it," Tage said. "In the past, the humans he captured either didn't know themselves, or refused to give up that information. I heard him ranting about it at several town hall meetings. He hates the humans and doesn't understand their loyalty."

"Do the soil chargers hate us?"

Tage stopped and grabbed Samara's hand. "Look at me. I don't know about the other terraregions, but yes, in Currentgrad, some do because of the overlord's propaganda. But things were getting restless when I left. People have been cooped up within the city walls for too long. You guys are prisoners because the desert could kill you. But they are prisoners of the overlord. He's convinced them it's too dangerous to leave. That only the Surge Knights can roam about to hunt and keep them safe. People speak out, but they're captured and put in the powerline. Once we stop the powerline and kill Koax, we have a shot at peace moving forward."

Samara continued walking.

"I think he knows the walls are closing in, and that's why he's so desperate to finish the powerline. Then it won't matter who rebels. He'll have all the electricity, and the other terraregions will be at his mercy."

A tear slipped down Samara's cheek. "Please, Tage. I beg you."

"I know," he said. "Trust me, I know more than ever how dire things have become."

They walked in silence for a few minutes, following the curve of the wooden walls separated only by a river of bubbling rubber.

"Tell me about your girl."

Tage let his eyes fall closed for a moment. "I didn't

mean to get involved with anyone. The whole time I was there, I knew my purpose, but—"

"Romantic," Samara said.

Tage shook his head. "My attachment to her made her a target."

Samara sniffed. "I'm sorry."

"But she's lithe and strong and so much more capable than she believes herself to be." He drew in a long breath. "I have to save her."

The pungent scent of hot dung, static, and beast sweat filled the air. Ursogen.

Tage raced ahead to the tall, reinforced cages. The ursogen trotted up to the fence and poked their snouts through. Aside from the tuft of hair around their jowls, their bodies were hairless. Smooth, gray bodies were free of scabs, unlike the ursogen in Currentgrad. Brakdern had taken meticulous care of the beasts. Their skin sagged a bit, hungry for better land, more charge, but that was an easy fix. He reached the slats, past one's broad head, raised a brow at the long teeth, and pet its stubby, charred ear.

"Is he injured?" Samara asked. She stood a few feet behind Tage.

"Injured? Oh, no. Their ears are always a little burnt. Sometimes, when they're fully charged, sparks will drip out of their claws and ears. It doesn't hurt them. But I'm sure Brakdern is very careful when they're in the strongest part of the Charged Desert."

"Are they vicious?"

"No," Tage said. "This is the thing with the ursogen: As long as they're charged, they're happy. And they can go forever. Unlike humans, the charge doesn't hurt them. It feeds them."

"Kinda like you?"

"I guess," he said, shrugging. He never thought he'd ever compare himself to one of the broad, hairless beasts. Another snout came over the top of the door, breathing in deeply, taking in their scent.

"We usually view anything with charge as hostile."

"Naw." Tage reached in with his other hand and pet the second one. "They're good. When they're fully charged, they're incredible. Their skin is almost transparent, and you can see the electricity flowing and coursing through their bodies."

Samara's head rested to the side as she studied the creatures. "How does one control a beast like this?"

"Step back," Tage said. "Like this."

A thick column of light encased by bolts of electricity emerged from Tage's hands and directly into the faces of the ursogen. Immediately, he felt their glee and appreciation—their willingness and excitement to be out in the desert again.

"Tage, stop it!"

"What?" He dropped his arm, releasing the current. "It's a Current Ignition."

"That's so mean." Her brow wrinkled. "Why did you do that?"

"They like it." Tage raised his hands in defense. "I don't know how Brakdern controls them, but this is the way we do it."

"You shoot them in the face with electricity?"

Tage laughed. "You've got it all wrong, Samara. It's like I just gave them a drink, or a snack. Look at them."

The ursogen licked the bars, searching for more current.

"See? They need current. Now, they'll obey me. When I come back with Lumen and Impulse, they'll remember me, be happy to see me. I promise."

"You're sure you didn't hurt them?"

"Positive." Tage studied her worried face. "They're fine."

"Do they want more?"

He nodded.

"Okay." She stepped back.

Once again, Tage sent them a gentle current, and the two large creatures leaned into it, their round ears cocking forward, their long teeth showing as they licked the air, the charge, their lips. He found himself grinning, almost feeling their happiness at having someone know how to feed them.

"Okay," she said. "It's just . . . strange. We do everything we can to prevent charge, so it feels so off or wrong when—"

"Yeah," Tage agreed. "I get it."

Samara's attention began darting around. "The suns are going down."

Glancing up at the darkening sky, Tage shrugged. "Guess we should head back." But as he felt the current move through his body, he could no longer imagine facing something that made him afraid out here.

"Actually,"—Samara looked frantically from side to side—"do you mind if we run? Being out here in the dark frightens me."

"I can make us some light," Tage said as he released White Sparks, creating a trail bouncing on the sand in front of them.

Samara stopped walking, her eyes reflecting the sparking light. "I'm afraid, but it's also kind of beautiful."

Stretching both arms forward, he called to the guards. "I'm just doing a demonstration! I won't get the sparks near you!"

Even in the dimming light, he could make out their

frowns. He turned away from the Saptex Sea, urging Samara to stand slightly behind him.

"Okay," she whispered.

Tage shivered, paused, and sent two brilliant arcs of White Sparks into the air.

He felt her take a step back from him, but when he turned, she was watching the sparks slowly fizzle out as they bounced along the desert. "It's terrifying." She forced out a light laugh. "But yeah. It's a little beautiful, too."

The surge of pride was a thoughtless thing to allow himself to feel while his friends suffered.

"Let's get you back," he said.

She didn't move, but instead studied his face. "You are endlessly fascinating, Tage Gradient."

"And you are endlessly kind," he replied. "I don't think I could ever fully thank you for how you've treated us, made my scared and tired friends feel welcome."

She gave him a slight shrug before picking up into a jog and heading toward the entrance.

Tage ran a step behind Samara, while his heightened senses allowed his vision to scout farther ahead. He saw a flash of light far in the distance. Maybe lightning, maybe not. They were smart to head inside. But Tage also knew he'd need to get away from Ohmstave before Koax came back. Koax would come with an army. Tage needed to be in Currentgrad with his dad, with the help his dad had found, and in a place where they could use the element of surprise rather than Koax using the same tool.

Within a few minutes, they were at the gates and the Brutes lowered the bridge. Tage placed both feet on the wood and discharged onto the shore—his body now feeling empty and tired.

Instead of stepping back as he expected, Samara

stood behind him and watched the bolts disappear into the sand.

"A little less afraid each time," she said.

Tage chuckled briefly.

"Does everyone's look about the same? The energy things, I mean," she asked.

"Well, Capacity throws the most beautiful White Sparks you've ever seen, and Impulse's Current Ignitions are far wider and stronger than mine. Or they used to be."

He and Samara ran across the bridge and into safety. The bridge creaked and popped as the Brutes pulled it back up, sealing them off from the outside world. Samara immediately pulled the top half of the cribriform suit down.

"Thanks," Tage said to the Brutes as he walked past them. They stood tall, chests puffed out, as if they were saluting him. A definite shift from when he'd first arrived. "I guess Minister Fahren has convinced everyone we really are here to help. Makes me wonder if he'd have had the same effect if he were still an Elder."

Passing through the streets, Tage caught a few people staring at him. But not as a freak, more like a celebrity. Word had spread, and the stakes had never been higher.

As they approached their house, Brakdern was exiting with an ice pack over his left eye.

"Brakdern," Samara gasped, "what happened?"

"Everything is fine." He laughed. "Turns out Impulse comes up swinging when you wake him."

"He did?" Tage asked. "That's so unlike him. Lumen, I could see, but not Impulse. He's our gentle giant."

"I think he's a little discombobulated, that's all." Brakdern shrugged.

"How are they?" Samara asked.

"Sleepy. I gave them some medicine and put them back to sleep. They'll be ready in the morning. They shouldn't be too sore, just hungry. Did you see the ursogen?"

"Yes," Tage said. "You've taken very good care of them. Which one is Ping?"

"He's the bigger of the two."

"I didn't know they could live to be over ten years old. They usually only live for a few years in Currentgrad." Although, they were treated quite differently there.

"Oh yes, they can live up to fifty years." Brakdern's smile faltered. "I'm going to spend the night in the stables with them. I might not see them again."

"Thank you." Tage gripped Brakdern's hand, shaking it. "I appreciate your sacrifice. And I'll try to bring them back. I promise."

"It's all right. Ping is coming full circle. He left with your dad, and he's going back with you." He nodded. "But I am rather fond of them, so yes, bring them back if you can." He turned to Samara. "Come on, Samara, I'll walk you home."

"Thanks for the distraction," Tage said. "It felt good to get some charge again."

Samara smiled in return. "And thank you for helping me feel safe in a place I never feel safe."

He nodded once as she and Brakdern started up the path together.

Walking into the house, he took a deep breath. Spicy herbs and medicine made Tage's nostrils flare. He checked on his friends, who slept peacefully, then went to his room.

Lying on his back, he stared at the wooden ceiling. The weight of their small world was on his shoulders. He thought of Capacity, hoping she was alive. Of his mom, whom he'd never see again. His heart ached for her.

Then, he thought of Overlord Koax. His wicked smile when he placed the biotech. The pleasure he took when ripping out the tech just a few days later. And finally, the powerline.

"Sleep well, Koax," Tage said out loud. "I'm coming for you."

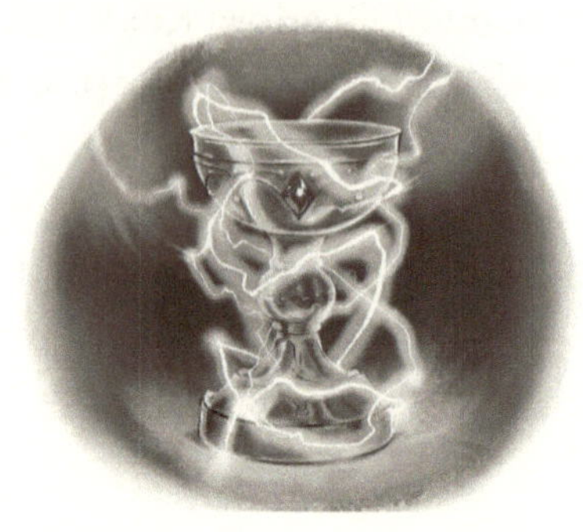

CHAPTER 29

• • • • •

Tage was the first to wake the next morning. He showered, knowing it might be his last one ever. The hot water steamed up the small bathroom, and he welcomed the warm, humid air. When he emerged from the shower, the undergarments he'd worn in the powerline and when he arrived in Ohmstave were lying on his bed. They smelled of lavender. Just like Capacity. The holes had been patched, and the hems restitched.

Once he was ready, he was met with Samara waiting in the kitchen. She greeted him with warm bread and fried feral.

"Morning."

"Good morning." Samara offered him a plate. "Fried feral. I know it's more of an evening dish, but I wanted you to be full."

"Thanks," Tage said. He brushed his wet hair off his shoulders as he sat.

"I'll wake the others," Samara said. "Then I have one more thing for you before you go."

It was still early; the sky was still violet, but would soon drift to a light lavender. Tage took a deep breath, savoring the delicious spread before him. The crusty bread released a bit of steam as he broke it in half. Crispy, salty feral crunched between his teeth.

Lumen began slowly stepping down the stairs.

"Hey." Tage wiped his mouth with the back of his hand. "How are you feeling?"

"Better than the first time we did it," Lumen said, shuffling into the room. "The overlord probably severed some nerve endings, so it wasn't as bad this time."

"Or it could be the pain and healing pills Brakdern gave you," Samara offered.

"Must be," Impulse said as he entered the room. He sat in front of his plate, lifted up the feral, and hesitated.

"What's wrong?" Samara pinched her eyebrows together. "You don't like it?"

Lumen snorted. "I've never met a meal Impulse didn't like. Maybe his teeth are sore."

"Teeth?" Impulse smiled wide; his silver dentures gleamed. "What teeth?"

"Right!" Samara rushed over. "This is your last dose of pills. Brakdern says you'll feel completely better in a few hours, but you need to take it with food."

Lumen snatched a pill from Samara's small hand and dry swallowed it. Impulse nodded in thanks as he took his.

"Weird," Lumen said. "My fingers are pretty sore, but the rest of me feels decent. Thanks again for the food."

"Please." Samara dished up the remainder of the food to them. "Get full. The next few days won't be easy, according to what Tel'el said."

"Do I have time for a quick shower?" Lumen asked.

"Take it," Tage said.

Lumen lapped up the juice from her meat with her bread, then shoved it in her mouth. As she walked away, she cursed loudly.

"What?" Tage asked.

"Uniforms! All this tech is useless without the Surge Knight uniforms. We'll never get into Currentgrad."

Tage opened his mouth to say something but couldn't find the words. She was right. They'd come this far and would fail over something as stupid as ursogen-hide clothing.

"It's all right," Samara said. "That was the other thing I brought for you. Brakdern not only took the tech when he scavenged, he took their uniforms as well."

"Wow." Impulse stopped eating, focusing his attention on Samara. "Thank you."

"Thank Brakdern," she said. "You'll have to go through the pieces and see what fits and which pieces are part of the uniform. They're on the couch. I hope your undergarments will work as a base layer. If not, feel free to use anything I've brought over."

"I meant to thank you for that," Tage said. "That was a nice surprise."

"You humans are a little too nice, you know that?" Lumen asked. She picked up her white tank top and long white shorts. "I'll hurry."

Tage studied Samara as she sat at the table. Her face had a sad smile painted on it. It looked like she'd lost ten pounds on her already small frame, her skin was sallow, and her once bright crystal-blue eyes seemed dull.

"We appreciate everything you've done for us," Tage said.

She smiled, lids heavy.

"Here." Impulse handed her some bread. "You look like you could eat."

"Are you sure?"

Impulse nodded.

She quickly stuffed the chunk into her mouth.

"Samara?" Impulse sat back. "Why don't you rest a minute while we pick out our gear?"

Sucking in a breath, Samara nodded. Tage watched them study each other for a moment.

His heart flipped just thinking about sitting with Capacity in the same way.

Tage and Impulse inventoried the pieces and found more than enough gear to outfit themselves. First were the long suede pants; as soon as he slipped them on, he was thankful for the undergarments the humans had repaired. Leather on skin wasn't a comfortable combination. Next, he slipped on the leather sleeves; they attached with straps over his solar plexus. Then came the rubber back piece. Tage missed his eagle. This one had the initials E.H.K.J. scrolled on it.

"How do I look?" Tage asked.

"Like a Surge Knight," Impulse said.

"Too bad you don't have that scary bird on your back piece," Lumen said, walking into the room. Her wet hair had been rebraided and was free of flyaways.

"I'm gonna shower." Impulse stood. "I've never had access to so much water. I can't get enough."

"We'll dig through the rest of the stuff," Tage responded.

Tage helped Lumen pick out the right sizes from the box of clothes. Most of her items were slightly big, but they'd do. Once she was dressed, they rummaged through everything and picked out the largest ones for Impulse.

"Why don't you help Impulse?" Lumen asked. "I'm going to talk to Samara."

Tage made his way into Impulse's bedroom.

"Are you ready for this?" Tage asked.

"I am," Impulse said.

"How do you feel?"

"Strong."

Impulse finished getting dressed, and they met the girls in the kitchen. They were standing, and Lumen had her hands resting on Samara's shoulders. Lumen was actually smiling, and she pulled Samara in for a hug.

Tage cleared his throat.

"Oh, hey." Lumen's face reddened. "You guys ready? That took forever."

One-and-a-half humans and two-and-a-half soil chargers walked in silence toward the gates. The sun was fully out, and the lavender sky swirled above them. As they got closer to the entrance, Tage noticed a commotion. It was early, yet most of Ohmstave's citizens were up, lining the streets.

"What's going on?" Tage asked. "Did something happen?"

"It's nothing," Samara said. "We wanted to wish you three off. Thank you for what you're about to do."

"Finally, they trust us," Lumen said.

"We failed before," Impulse said. "We could fail again."

"We understand." Samara smoothed her rubber dress. "We are still thankful for your sacrifice." She quickly hugged all three.

As they got closer, the people parted. Loud cheers and thanks flooded them from each side. Some offered food, trinkets, and clothing. They politely declined them all.

At the end, Fahren waited for them, his long robe sweeping the floor. "Mere days ago, you entered our city as outsiders. Today, you leave as heroes."

The crowd erupted.

"We thank you and bid you good luck and farewell!"

The drawbridge creaked open before Tage could respond. They waved goodbye and walked out of his hometown. As the gate slammed shut behind them, Tage turned to his friends.

"Well, that was weird," Lumen said.

"They're desperate, more than when we arrived," Tage said. "I have a feeling Fahren came clean with them about how dire things really are."

"We must succeed," Impulse said.

Tage started toward the ursogen. "We will."

"Good, because when we come back,"—Lumen smirked—"I want a parade."

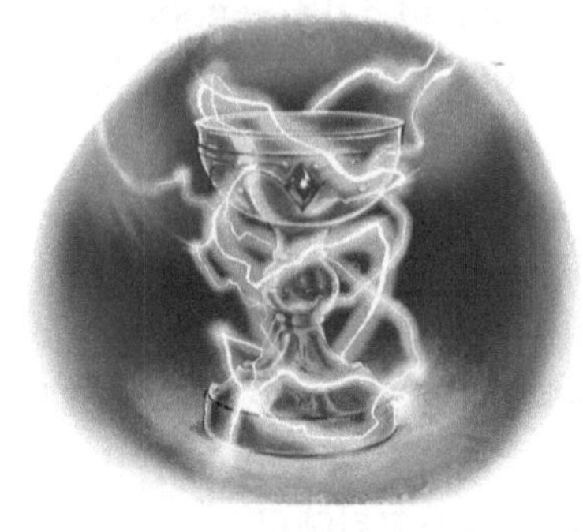

CHAPTER 30

• • • • •

The ursogen immediately came to the edge of the enclosure when Tage got close, their giant noses pressing against the bars, showcasing their long teeth. After blasting them in the snout with a Bolt Ignition, he opened the gate and led the two beasts into the Charged Desert. They watched the ursogen's loose skin become taut as their muscles grew with charge.

"I feel ya," Lumen said as she crouched, pressing her hands into the desert.

Impulse followed suit. "Oh yeah . . ." He nodded with his eyes closed. "That's the good stuff."

"You two feel okay?" Tage asked as he cinched up the flat woven blankets onto the backs of the ursogen. He rechecked the supplies now resting in bags that were attached to the blankets. Food. Water. A few ursogen skins. Running his hands over the familiar woven material, Tage glanced behind him at maybe his last-ever glimpse of the stilted city of Ohmstave.

Tage patted one of the ursogen on the shoulder, just

now able to see the electricity coursing under its skin. "You guys ready?"

Lumen leapt on top of Ping. "Come on, Tage. Time's a wastin'."

He followed her, climbing on in front when she scooted back.

Impulse rode the smaller ursogen.

The beasts scratched at the dark sand with long claws, eager.

Tage nudged Ping with both legs, and Ping sprang forward, his paws lightly padding on the coarse rocks and sand as he sped through the desert.

Holding on to the tuft of hair by the jowls, Tage kept his body flat against the beast. Lumen held onto his waist and pressed herself against him. Wind rushed through his hair. His eyes watered as the beast sprinted across the desert. He stared at the ground, a blur of black soil.

Finally, after his arms shook with weakness, and the suns were high overhead, Tage guided the animal to a stop. The second his feet touched the sand, he let the fresh charge swell in his body. The two ursogen immediately began sniffing and digging in the sand—maybe after shock worms or something.

"Moment of truth?" Lumen crouched, grabbing the sand with both hands and letting her eyes fall closed.

Impulse followed suit, just not closing his eyes. He stood. "Maaaannnn, this feels good," he moaned. "Worth the pain. Worth it. To feel this fully charged. You don't feel like this without the implants."

Tage turned his attention to Lumen.

She leapt from her crouch, pushed her hands in front of her—and a small trickle of electricity fell from her hands back into the sand. "Oh . . . Tage . . ." She looked at her palms in horror.

The world around him spun. This couldn't be right. "Just keep trying."

Impulse did the same. Tage held his breath, but Impulse's ignitions both dribbled back onto the sand.

Had they missed something?

"Tage . . ." Lumen trailed off again.

"Just keep trying," Tage urged. "Maybe . . . Maybe . . ."

He could not have begged his friends to undergo this again only to have it fail.

Impulse grabbed the sand again. "I can recharge without fully discharging. That's something, but I can't really do anything with the charge."

"You're doing something," Tage said, his heart thundering. "Try again." He counted the biotech coursing down Impulse's spine. *Uh-oh. No lights.*

Lumen sat and watched her fingertips fizzle again and again. Suddenly, a bolt shot straight ahead, arcing before finding its home in the black sand.

"Woot! Take that!" She shot Bolt Ignitions from both hands into the desert. "Take that, you psycho mother—"

"All right!" Tage interrupted with a laugh. "Can you do sparks on the same charge? Something else? Can you recharge without discharging?"

Lumen turned toward Tage, a smug smile on her face. She stretched her arms high in the air and rained White Sparks straight into the air. They bounced off her skin and uniform, taken up by the desert soil like dry ground in a rainstorm. "I've got style." She twisted to the side, striking a dramatic pose and arcing Bolt Ignitions both in front of and behind her. "Check me out."

"Thank the Anoths and Cathos," Tage released on a breath.

"Look out, you shriveled old man!" Lumen yelled,

jumping higher into the sky than any human would've been able. White Sparks rained down on her, pulsing through the air around her like a halo—definitely her strongest Ignition. "No—"

"Great job, Lumen!" Tage said. "Was it worth it?"

She pulled back her lips and flashed her silver denture. "Dang right!"

Impulse pulled back his own lips, showing off the metal gleam. "At least I make this look good," he slurred.

"How are you, Impulse?" Tage asked.

Another weak dribble fell from his fingertips to the ground.

Impulse slipped off the rubber plate on his back, sleeves, then white tank top, folded them carefully, and placed them on the back of Ping, who only snorted briefly before continuing to paw around in the sand. "Watch my lights as I charge." He plunged his hands into the soil. "Are they all lighting up?"

Tage watched as the red light near the bottom of his spine lit up first. Lights blinked to life, working up his spine, then abruptly stopping at the base of his neck.

"Do you see that?" Tage pointed.

"Hmm." Lumen reached out and touched one of the unlit bulbs. "Oh! I think I know what to do."

Impulse's top two lights flickered again and Tage frowned.

"You trust me, right?" Lumen asked Impulse.

"Yes," Impulse said carefully, as his eyes narrowed. "Lu, what's going on? Are they lighting up?"

"Sure," she said with a slight, obviously fake smile. "Mostly. Be still."

He groaned and got to his knees so she could adjust the lights.

Tage stared at Impulse's back. He'd healed up remarkably well—especially considering how short a time it had been since he'd gotten the new biotech implants.

Lumen wiggled the top light.

Impulse's spine stiffened, and he grunted. "What are you doing?"

"I think they're a little loose," she said. "Tage, find him something to bite on. I need silence while I work."

"Lumen, I'm not so sure you should mess with those." Tage started toward her.

"If a fat, sweaty human wearing a loincloth can do it,"—she shot him a disdainful look—"I'm pretty sure I can figure out a loose bulb or two."

She pressed on either side of the first bulb. Blood trickled down the left side, and the light flashed on. Then she repeated the process on the one below it. Impulse gritted his metal prosthetic loudly the entire time, hands plunged into the desert.

"Yes," she said. "See? I knew I could do it. It was just a loose connection. How do you feel?"

"Actually,"—Impulse stood, craning his head one way and then the other—"I feel more complete." He discharged, then sucked up a fresh charge. "Here goes nothing." A shot of light burst from his palms and onto the ground. "That felt . . . right. Good. Yes, I'm good."

They'd done it. Both Lumen and Impulse had their full capability back. "Thank the suns." Tage collapsed onto the sand, letting himself rest on his back after being crouched forward for so long, relaxing now that he knew that at least his friends would have a fighting chance with their abilities.

"If I'd have gone through all that—having Mr. Loincloth cram metal into me—for nothing, I'd be so pissed," Lumen said with a smirk.

Staring at his hands, Impulse smiled. "I'm gonna get my family."

"We're gonna get—" Lumen swallowed. "We're gonna get Capacity. I try not to think about what she might be going through, but . . ."

"I know," Tage whispered. He'd kept his thoughts mostly off of her as well, unable to fully process what Koax might have dreamed up for her. What his mom might have gone through in her last moments.

"Well, that got dark." Lumen opened her small pack. "Time for another snack."

But Tage's human side couldn't let go quite so easily.

Their lives were dim at the moment. The same nearly insurmountable task of finding a way to kill Overlord Koax was ahead of them. Saving Impulse's and Lumen's families. Capacity. They had Tel'el and whomever he was able to find to help. Would it be enough? Plus, the overlord knew they would be coming.

"Breakfast kept me full forever," Lumen said after she hopped down. "I'm usually hungry before noon."

"Me, too." Impulse sat in the sand, running his fingers through the coarse grains.

"I didn't know how common feral was," Lumen said as she tucked a braid behind her ear. "They sure eat a lot of it."

"It's not common. It's a treat to them," Tage said. "Didn't you see how thin Samara had gotten while we were there? She was already skinny, but missing a few meals made her gaunt. They sacrificed their food for us. They have nothing to offer, nothing to give, yet they gave us all they could."

The friends sat silent for a moment. The tidiness of Ohmstave was only a testament to how the humans cared for one another. The soil chargers didn't have that same sense of deep emotion, which was why Currentgrad felt so dirty in comparison. Koax didn't bother to pay anyone to care for the city.

"Well, now I feel terrible." Impulse laid down a bag with food and water. "I ate so much."

"I don't," Lumen said as she tossed a small bite of dried meat into her mouth. "If we fail, we die. I think a few nice meals were the least they could do."

Tage said nothing but shot Lumen a glance. He unwrapped his sandwich and found a note. It read: *The humans of Ohmstave are grateful for your bravery. Best of luck. —Fahren.*

"Did you guys get a note?"

"Yeah." Lumen chuckled. "Humans."

"I thought it was nice," Impulse said.

Tage's stomach swirled and flip-flopped. He struggled to eat lunch but did his best. Impulse and Lumen didn't seem to have the same reservations.

"Can I just say how glad I am our tech works?" Impulse asked.

"Speaking of which," Lumen said as she pointed at Tage, "you need to practice your Volt Foil."

"I will," Tage said. "Tonight."

No matter what, they had a lot of distance to travel to get to Currentgrad.

"Okay," Tage said. "Let's ride."

They spent the rest of the afternoon on the ursogen's backs as the beasts ran across the desert. The clouds in the purple sky churned above them. An electrical storm to the east rained down thousands of lightning bolts.

Tage told the story of how Tel'el used the carcass of an ursogen to save himself from a ferocious electrical storm after his failed assassination of the overlord ten years ago. The storm had both saved and nearly killed him. He spoke of how his dad had acquired Ping and arrived at Ohmstave. How he met his dad and Hayrah, then traveled the same trek they were following now to Currentgrad.

Only this time, they weren't going undercover. The plan would be swift and precise.

"I wonder how different things would be if he had succeeded?" Tage asked.

"It's getting dark," Impulse said. "How late should we travel?"

Tage scanned the sky. The electrical storm still boomed in the far distance, the sky the darkest of purples, nearly black.

"Let's go to that outcropping of pulse dunes," Tage said. "We can take cover behind them and rest for the night."

He gently kicked the ursogen in the ribs, and it picked up its speed. Tage's hair blew behind him in the wind. Closing his eyes, he took a deep breath. Dry, electrified air.

They tied the ursogen to the porous rocks and removed the packs from their backs. They sat on the inside of the semicircle of black rocks, resting their backs against them.

"Lu," Impulse said, "will you pass me a sandwich?"

"Sure."

Tage stared up to the dark sky full of stars. He ate in silence, counting his heartbeats as he chewed.

"We'll go at first light," Tage said. "If we get to Currentgrad early, we can rest then. I'd rather be early than late."

"Where exactly are we meeting Tel'el and his brigade?" Lumen asked.

"There's a spot where we used to sneak out," Tage

said. "I'll show you tomorrow." He hoped Tel'el had better ideas of how to kill Koax. Any type of ignition, Koax could simply absorb.

"Tage." Impulse fiddled nervously with his wrapper. "I think it's time. It's the only unknown weapon we have. They know we can do White Sparks, Bolts, and Current. They've seen you Arc, but they don't know about the Volt Foil."

"I know," Tage said. "But I don't want to scare off the ursogen."

"They're tied up," Lumen reminded him.

"If they're spooked, they can easily break free of the rocks." Tage stood. "I'm going to Arc toward the electrical storm and do it there."

"Why?" Impulse asked. "Tage, we don't think you're weird because you can Volt Foil."

"No." Tage shook his head. "It's not that. I can Arc faster than I can run. And if I'm near the storm, it hopefully won't draw that much attention from watching eyes. Out here? The massive electrical bird will stand out. And I really worry about startling the ursogen. If we lose them, we'll never get to Currentgrad in time."

"Well, look at you." Lumen whistled. "Didn't you just think of everything?"

"Yeah, yeah, my big brain. I get it." Tage rolled his eyes and hoped that he could draw the Volt Foil again. "Watch from here and make sure the ursogen don't get spooked."

Impulse nodded. At least he could count on him. Lumen? Not so much. She'd be staring and waiting for the show.

Tage started running, bare feet pounding against the Charged Desert. He closed his eyes, focusing on the charge. His body lifted in a long, swift arc, concentrating on length versus height. He covered fifty yards in a matter of seconds, the ground below him flying by as fast as it had while riding the ursogen. This time, he wanted to see how high he could go. Like a geyser of liquid latex erupting under his feet, he shot thirty feet into the air. A waterfall of electricity connected him to the ground and guided him forward. He landed and immediately Arced forward. Fast.

He landed again and squinted behind him, but he could only make out the faintest edges of the dunes they'd rested behind. He hadn't meant to go quite so far. The angry wind from the storm penetrated his Surge Knight uniform, drying the sweat on his body. His skin broke out in gooseflesh. He stared at the powerful storm for a few moments. All that voltage being deposited into the earth. Recharging it. The same power the overlord wanted all for himself.

He Arced away from the storm and landed on his knees. He sank both hands and feet into the sand. Sucking in a deep breath through his nose, then releasing it through his mouth, he concentrated on the current in the ground. It coursed up and out of him, but he grabbed it with his mind. He lifted his right hand from the ground, picturing the giant, predatory bird that had saved him, feeling the feathers, the strength, the lift of the air under its wings. The freedom. An ignition shot out of his hand like a cord into the sky.

Attached to that cord was an eagle.

It flew high above, like a piece of discarded paper fluttering lazily in the wind. Its outstretched wings spanned over thirty feet. Its beak was the size of a small ursogen. Tage pulled his hand toward the ground, and it followed by swooping a non-existent enemy. He pulled it back up, then down. It mimicked his every move, diving dangerously to the ground, then back up high into the sky. Tage could feel the flex and pull and freedom of being the bird, but was also anchored by the power that held him to the ground, supplying the energy for the Volt Foil. It flew from one side of the sky to the other with frightening agility.

Tage laughed, feeling a lightness he hadn't felt since . . . maybe ever. "The overlord can't beat me."

He wiggled his fingers and released the bird into the electrical storm. It sputtered a few times before dissipating into the swirling bolts of lightning. Staring into the sky, his chest heaved, and his heart thumped against his chest. He stumbled once, but felt the energy below his soles in the sand.

Tage stood, wiped a sheen of sweat with the back of his hand, and walked a few feet, charging through his soles, before he focused on his Arc Ignition. Instead of being thrust up and forward, he skidded and fell face first onto the ground. Coughing, he spat dirt from his mouth. He sat, arms propped up on his knees, trying to calm his breath. Just as he'd feared, the Volt Foil zapped him of energy. Energy he couldn't fix with current.

The Volt Foil would have to be his last resort. He'd only have one chance to get it right.

CHAPTER 31

• • • • •

Tage stumbled through the desert, the charge seeping into his feet not giving him enough power to even keep his vision solid. He knew the general direction of the camp, but it took Lumen's and Impulse's voices to help direct him.

"Where on Hadrain is he?" Lumen said.

Impulse chuckled. "He moves fast. He's probably just goofing off."

"Here," Tage said, but his voice came in a whisper. "Here," he tried again, only slightly louder.

"Tage?" Impulse called.

As he squinted, he could just see their forms in the dark, hear the quiet pawing of the ursogen. "Yeah," he croaked, a little louder this time. He should be stronger by now. Recharged.

"Nice of you to join us," Lumen said, grinning until she tossed a few White Sparks, lighting the desert around him. Her grin fell. "What the heck happened to you? You look like ursogen crap."

"Thanks." Tage raised a hand in surrender. "The Volt Foil—it takes everything from me. Maybe in time, with more practice, I'll rebound better."

"Newsflash," she snapped, "we don't have any time."

"I know." Tage stared at the ground.

Lumen handed him his pouch of water.

"Thanks."

"He'll get it," Impulse said. "I trust him."

"Yeah." Tage drained the canteen. "I need to sleep."

Tage rested his head on his pack, and sleep found him quickly. His dreams immediately turned to nightmares. Surge Knights. Red lights. Overlord Koax. The changing of the lightning in his chalice. The days of waiting for the window to deposit the poison. Knowing that ten years of preparation had just been lost. His tech being yanked out. Knowing his friends would be next. The powerline. The endless awareness and fogginess. Ohmstave. Each moment built upon the next. Capacity. The ursogen. The Volt Foil. The exhaustion.

"Sick!"

Tage jumped from his dream and onto his feet. "What?"

"Ugh," Lumen said, swiping at a cheek with both hands. "The ursogen just licked my face. What a crappy way to start the day."

Tage stared at the faint purple sky. "Good boy, Ping."

"Excuse me?" Lumen wiped thick saliva from her face. "Hey, Impulse! Wake up."

He grunted and rolled over, eyes still firmly pressed together.

"It's late." Tage squinted at the sky. "We would have slept the day away if Ping hadn't woken you. And hey, it means he likes you."

Lumen's face twisted in disgust.

"You've made a friend." Tage slapped her arm in jest.

"Great." She rolled her eyes. "Well, I don't want him to get the wrong impression. You and Sleeping Beauty"—she pointed to Impulse—"can ride together."

• • •

By early afternoon, all pulse dunes and amp plants had been replaced with the empty, barren Charged Desert Tage remembered from his trek to the city as a kid.

"This is familiar," Impulse said wryly.

"Yeah." Lumen dismounted and picked up a handful of black sand. "I never realized how ugly the Charged Desert really was until now. The pulse dunes and amp plants really break up the landscape by Ohmstave."

"It's not like we spent much time outside the walls, Lu," Impulse said.

They'd only ever gone to the walled-off grounds sanctioned for students to play with charge. Just another way for the overlord to scare them into believing the Charged Desert was too dangerous for just anyone to roam.

"True." Tage also hopped off his ursogen. "Come on, Lumen, switch with Impulse. Let's give the big guy his own for the rest of the way."

"Fine." She rolled her eyes. "Didn't you leave Currentgrad pretty regularly?"

"Not really," Tage said. "I'm familiar with some of the tunnel systems, but my parents did most of the intel outside the city. That way, if anything happened to them, I'd still be around to carry out the plan."

"Huh." Lumen waited until Tage was firmly on the ursogen before she swung a leg over, and the friends once again moved toward the city—a little slower now that they had to start keeping an eye out for patrols.

"We're supposed to meet Tel'el and his people near a secret entrance?" Impulse asked.

"Yeah," Tage said. "But we might need to wait for them just inside the tunnels."

"Huh," Lumen said again. "Why are there tunnels in the first place? It seems like an obvious breach of security. And you know how paranoid Koax is with security. Doesn't fully make sense."

"The tunnels . . ." Tage cringed. The truth would come out now. "They're not exactly tunnels. More like . . . a water system."

"Is that where our fresh water flows in?" Impulse asked. "From Ohmstave?"

"No." He scratched Ping behind the ears. "It's the opposite."

"Opposite of what, Tage?" Lumen gritted her teeth. "Opposite of fresh?"

"It's sort of . . ."

She was very likely going to kill him before he had a chance to reach the city.

"Where the wastewater flows out of the city," Impulse finished. "Am I right?"

Tage swallowed once before nodding, watching Lumen out of the corner of his eye.

She folded her arms. "Nope. No way. Thank you for playing, but Lumen is out."

"I know it's not ideal," Tage said, forcing himself to watch her stiff glare. "But it's not sewage, that's a different pipe." A corner of his mouth quirked upward. "Much smaller. We'd never fit."

"Oh good, I'm thrilled you're choosing the wastewater over the raw sewage simply because we can't fit. Great plan, Tage," Lumen said.

Nervous laughter fell between them as Tage read

her frustration and thought about being so close again. Thought about Ohmstave and how much was riding on their success. "It's gross, but not that bad. It's mostly water from sinks, and food. Mostly rotten food they want out for compost. And some trash—not everyone in town follows the rules of rubbish, and that's why the pipe is so big. It's actually a tunnel."

"Was this our original escape plan?" she yelled.

Tage made a tiny motion by pinching his fingers nearly together. "A little bit, yeah."

Lumen shook her head. "Worst, Tage. You're the worst."

"Hey, guys," Impulse said quietly. "Hush up. We're almost there."

Tage glanced up to see the top edge of a corner watchtower.

"Ah crap! Now what?" Lumen flicked Tage's ear. "Your human brain didn't take the watchtower into account."

"It won't matter," Tage said. "We're dressed as Surge Knights on ursogen. We have a few bags. They'll assume they're full of worms and we were out hunting. Guide the ursogen toward the gates, and once we're fifty feet away, follow me. When we're close enough, they won't be able to see us from the watchtower. The wall will block their view, and we'll veer to the side."

Impulse pushed out a breath. "And they won't warn the gate we're approaching?"

"Why would they?" Tage asked. "They're not looking for Surge Knights, they're looking for intruders. They let the guardsmen tending the gate do their own thing. They'll spot us, see we're in the proper uniform for Currentgrad, then ignore us. Trust me, that's how my dad and my mom . . ." His heart dropped into his stomach. "H-how they used to get in and out of the city."

"Well, let's cover up those black roots, brainiac." Lumen broke the tension. "Last thing we want is you getting us caught for something so stupid."

Tage realized in that moment how much Lumen's humor—and brutal honestly—had gotten him through some of the hardest times. "Thanks," he said.

She wrapped the thin, white sleeve that held the bread they'd greedily eaten at lunch over the top of his head. "It's not big enough so I'm going to have to hold it for now. We'll need a better solution when we get there."

Tage led the pack. They kept their heads down in case the guards recognized their faces, although Tage doubted their binoculars could see that much detail. As they got closer, Tage raised a hand to the watchtower. Someone from the tower raised one back. He kept his eyes on them as best he could until they were out of view, hidden by the massive stone wall. Soon, the only thing he could see beyond the pulse-dune wall were the spires of the Voltaic Dava, jutting straight up into the air like black nails reaching high into the sky to pluck out its prey.

He made a hard left to the corner of the pulse-dune wall, then followed it all the way down until he was just inches from the next corner. The massive ursogen's feet kicked up black dust.

"Here," Tage said. He dismounted, and his friends followed suit. The white cloth fluttered to the ground. "Now it's just a waiting game."

"Not for long," a familiar voice said from around the corner. "Tage, my boy!"

He ran to his dad and gave him a long hug. His thin, frail body felt sharp against Tage. "Have you been waiting long?" Tage asked.

"No," Tel'el said, "not too long. I've already gotten the others into Currentgrad and hidden. They're ready."

"Great," Lumen said. "They, uh, your friends, they go in that way?" She pointed to the tunnel. Water trickled out along with bits of food and trash. "'Cause if there's another way, I'll take it."

"Yes," Tel'el answered. "I led them up there earlier."

"Okay," Tage said. "Then we'll follow you."

"No," he said. "Not this time. Tage, you know the way, and I need to handle something first."

Tage shook his head. "It's been months since I've used the tunnel."

"I was worried about that. Here, take this." He handed Tage a piece of rubber. "It's a map; follow it to the church. It's likely to be empty; if not, the pastor won't give you much trouble. Meet me in the marketplace, blend in. I've got my men and women placed strategically."

"Then what?" Lumen asked. "What are we supposed to do once inside? This plan sucks."

"We've got to draw him out," Impulse said. "The overlord."

"Exactly," Tel'el said. "We won't really know what to expect until the last moment. You'll have to trust me. Follow my lead."

"Dad," Tage said, "it seems like this is a bad plan, or no plan at all. Follow your lead? Follow your lead to what? All the planning we had last time, and it still wasn't enough. All the planning you did the first time wasn't enough . . ."

"I have a plan." Tel'el smiled, but the smile didn't reach his eyes. "I can't tell you. You just have to trust me."

"But—" Tage started. "I'm going to use the Volt Foil."

"Use it when I give you the signal," Tel'el said. "He hates me the most." His dad paused for a moment. "I love you."

Tage swallowed. "This isn't a plan."

Tel'el shook his head. "When you see drudges gather in the square, you use everything you have. That'll be the signal. Run to the tunnels, and I'll have people there to help you."

Tage glanced to the side to see Lumen and Impulse sharing a glance.

Reaching out to touch the ends of Tage's bleached hair, Tel'el smiled faintly again. "Pull your hair back. It's the first thing they'll go for if you're fighting hand to hand."

Tage nodded once. Why was Tel'el keeping him in the dark?

"Actually," his dad said, "when you're at the church, find a way to cover your hair entirely or shave it. It's a dead giveaway—"

"Told you," Lumen smirked.

"I have to go; I'll see you in the marketplace. If not there, then at the church." Tel'el smiled and ran back around the corner with the two ursogen.

Tage stared at the opening where his father just left. Surely, he'd find a way to give them more information.

"So?" Lumen asked. "Are we going through with this?"

"Okay," Tage said, shaking his head. "Follow me."

"Great!" Lumen said. "I can't think of anything more soothing than soaking my body in garbage."

Tage reached up to the lip of the tunnel, then hesitated. Capacity was so close. Koax was so close. Tage turned to his friends. "Get a charge, then be quiet for a minute, okay? The tunnel goes under the castle. I'm sure they can't hear us, but they check it on occasion for security. That's why everything that leaves the city goes under the castle. No matter how gross it is,"—he looked at Lumen—"be quiet."

He attempted to fill his charge, but his body simply remained full. He pulled himself up into the stone tunnel. Face first, his chest lay flat on the rushing water. Years of runoff had created a slippery moss layer. Turning his face to the side, he did his best to keep the water out of his mouth, eyes, and nose. The fetid smell made Tage's lunch bubble up in the back of his throat. He swallowed hard and tried to clamp his mouth shut, breathing hard through his nose.

Once completely up, he stood and shook his hands in a lame attempt to dry them, but the greasy water clung to him. A half-eaten wormsteak floated near his shin. Chunks of bread and other food items skimmed the fatty, cloudy surface of the ditch they stood in. He turned, looking a few feet down on his friends, and waved Lumen up.

Impulse gave her a boost, so only her bottom half got wet. She wasn't forced to enter it face first like Tage.

Lumen opened her mouth to say something, but Tage's eyes grew wide and he put a finger up to his lips. She opted for sharing her disgust by dramatically gagging.

Tage nodded toward the opening and put a hand out for Impulse, who waved it off and instead lifted his massive leg up, so his foot was inside the entrance. He clamped either side of the wall with his hands, then used his remaining leg to catapult himself upward into the cave. He stumbled, splashing the water, then fell onto his hands and knees.

Impulse mouthed, "I'm okay." Then Tage waved them forward, looking at the map, away from their only source of light. Bits of food, trash, and debris constantly nipped at his shins. At least, he hoped it was just food. Occasionally, something hard, probably discarded bio-tech from a botched surgery, would hit him.

Snapping his fingers together, Tage created a constant small spark as a guide for their light. Each snap seemed to echo louder and louder in the large tunnel.

I can't believe we're back. I hate this place, but I don't belong in Ohmstave.

The darkness seemed blacker than any night he'd ever experienced. His hands shook. Strange shadows danced on the wall from the sparks from his hands.

Tage advanced forward. He looked over his shoulder at his friends, who were following, wide-eyed and panicked. His chest heaved. Disgusting water splashed around him; the scent inescapable.

Their steps echoed, and the splashing water coated them. Tage looked over his shoulder once more; his friends were a few feet behind. He turned forward again, toward the church, and smacked into something hard.

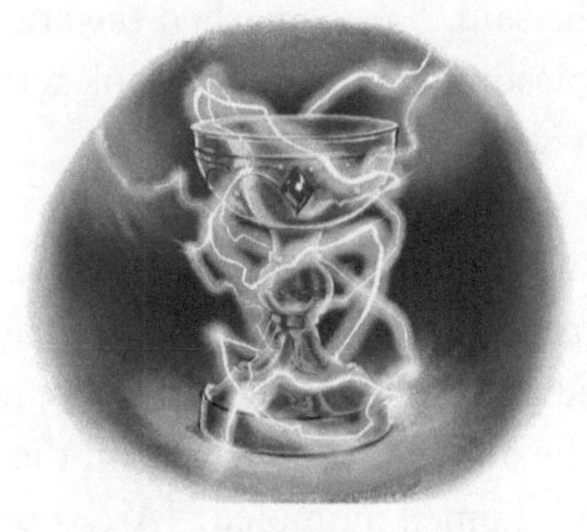

CHAPTER 32

• • • • •

Tage bounced off the surface and onto his butt. Completely stunned, he shook his head. Pain blossomed in his nose from where he'd bloodied it on whatever he'd run into. The putrid water was replaced with the heavy scent of copper. Blood rushed down his face.

"Tage," Lumen whispered, "are you okay?"

"What happened?" Impulse helped Tage to his feet.

Tage blinked slowly and widely. "I ran into a low-hanging pipe." His moan echoed through the tunnel.

"Shh!" Lumen said. "What in the name of Anoths and Cathos is wrong with you? Shut up!"

"It's fine," Tage said. "We're way past the Voltaic Dava. We're at the center of Currentgrad. One tunnel heads east, one west. Past these are many offshoots. Here, hold the map so I can see which way we need to go."

Impulse held out the map. Tage snapped his fingers a few times, and Lumen gasped.

"What?" Tage looked wildly over his shoulders.

"Tage," she said. "You smashed the crap out of your nose. You're bleeding. It's bad, you look terrible."

She stared at him, and he frowned.

"What? It's true."

"Focus, Lu," Impulse said.

She shrugged.

Tage stared at the map once more. "We need to go up. There should be a ladder somewhere on the wall I hit."

"Ran into," Lumen mumbled. "Are you sure we need to go up?"

"Yes," Tage answered. "We should be close."

He felt along the sides of the slimy walls until his hand clasped the rung of a ladder. He leaned in close and got a better look, then jiggled one of the rungs. Rotten wood.

"Try to stand on either side of the rung, not right in the middle. They're pretty soft," Tage warned.

He went first, slowly but carefully, stepping on the sides of the rungs. He held on to the support beams that went straight up instead of grasping the middle of the rung above him. Each step was a step closer to Koax. To Capacity. To finishing what he'd been training for since he was a six-year-old boy, leaving Ohmstave for the unknown. Tage paused, reaching above. They had to be close to the top. There were only a handful of rungs, but feeling around in the wet and in the dark used every ounce of Tage's strength.

Reaching up again, his hand touched metal. He felt around until he grasped the handle, then twisted until the pressure released.

"I found the trapdoor," Tage said as he climbed another rung and shoved his shoulder upward. "I just . . ." He grunted. "Need . . ." He pushed with all his strength. "To get it op—"

Tage's foot came loose, and he swung downward, desperately clinging to the rungs above. His foot landed on something, making a sickening crunch as it broke his fall.

"Tage!" Lumen yelled. "What the—"

"I'm sorry!" he called down. "Lumen, I'm so, so sorry. Are you okay?"

"Seriously," she cried. "I think you broke my face. Move, Impulse, I'm getting down."

"I'm sorry," Tage said quietly. "The door is really stuck."

"I'll get it," Impulse said.

"Fine," Lumen replied. The sound of her creaking her way back down the rungs filled the small space. "I'll wait down here until you jokers have it open. I plan on living today and would like to have a face that isn't completely busted."

Impulse led the way up the ladder. Tage snapped his fingers together, creating a small light for him. Once at the top, Tage crawled up next to Impulse and placed his palms against the door.

"Good thing you're so tall," Tage said. "I'm two rungs higher than you, and you can still touch the top."

Impulse said nothing.

"On my count," Tage said. "One, two, three, push!"

His ladder rung bent and groaned under his weight but stopped short of snapping. The metal and stone tile above moved slightly with a loud scratching sound. Stone against stone.

"Almost there," Tage said.

A stream of light pierced the darkness. Tage squinted and put his fingers along the open edge of the tile. Impulse did the same and they both pushed. The stone slid loudly across rock. Faint light flooded the tunnel as they dislodged it completely.

"Yes," Impulse said. "You go first, Tage."

They crawled out into the middle of a small room—the entire floor was stone. Two wooden desks sat haphazardly near the side. Light came from a small, mottled window. The office space was more like a storage closet. Dust covered the lamps, and, aside from the two desks, there was no other furniture. Tage couldn't have asked for a better entrance point to Currentgrad.

He hoisted himself up and sat on the edge, listening. Putting his finger up to his lips while he looked down at his friends, he whispered, "I don't hear anything. I think we're safe. This is one of the back rooms of the church. Be careful of the missing rung I broke." He reached a hand down into the hole and helped pull Impulse out, then did the same with Lumen.

"Guys, come help me," Tage said.

He bent down and grasped the edge of the metal and stone that covered the secret door. All three helped replace the stone, but left a corner up in case they needed easy access to it again.

"This will be our meeting place if we need to escape," Tage said. "I know what Tel'el said. But if it's a losing battle, it's not cowardly to leave with your life."

Impulse nodded, but Tage saw rage in his eyes. The gentle giant was no more; sweetness had been sucked out of him long ago. His family was here, too. Probably suffering because of Impulse's betrayal of Koax.

"We need to find something to cover or cut your hair." Lumen grabbed an end of Tage's hair. Hers was still up in braids—they were messy but functional.

"Yeah," Tage said. "But we need to hurry."

At that moment, the door swung open. A pastor walked into the room.

Tage's eyes connected with the soil charger's, and his went wide.

Well, he'd thought this had been a safe spot.

CHAPTER 33

• • • • •

The three of them froze in place.

The pastor's wide eyes shifted and paused on each of them in the small space. His tall, ornate hat hid his hair, but his bushy brows nearly reached the bottom edge of the spire-shaped hat.

"Um . . . um . . ." Tage was at a loss for words. "We're . . ."

"Who are you? What are you doing in here?" the pastor asked. His words were slow and careful. He cocked his head sideways, staring curiously at Tage. "What are you?"

Tage absently touched his hair.

"Hey . . ." Lumen chuckled lightly as she stepped forward. "Pastor Bundle, it's me, Lumen Nal."

The pastor raised an eyebrow. He adjusted his billowy robes and pulled at his shoulder, then removed the stiff, ornate hat, inlaid with gold stitching. Sparse, wiry white hair hung from the top of his head. The right side of his face drooped, like a candle had melted it.

"Lumen, my child, what are you doing here?" Then he looked at Impulse. "Impulse, is that you? I hardly recognized you. What are you doing here?"

"We—we came back because . . ." Tage stuttered. He hadn't gone to any church.

"Several months ago, I heard you three and another girl, Capacity, had broken some cardinal rule that was punishable by jail." His words came out slow, deliberate, and sad. "Lumen, I was most disappointed to hear you had done something so offending. Though I expected you'd eventually get into a little trouble. You've always been more mischievous than others."

Tage shot Lumen a glance. Any information would be useful. "What did they say we did to be put in jail? I'm Tage Gradient, by the way."

"I know who you are," the pastor said, his voice still calm and quiet.

"Oh. Uh. Okay." Tage glanced at his friends, wondering what the next move should be.

"I never heard what the infraction was," the pastor said. "I heard the news through the congregation. The official statement was the four of you would spend your lives in jail. Nothing more."

Tage opened his mouth, but the words were lost with anger. He needed to feel the pastor out. The last thing he wanted was to take out a holy man if he didn't need to.

"Children, I've heard nothing of a pardon or release for you." The man wrung his hands, his face twisted in worry. "If the Surges catch you or the overlord finds out you're here, you're going to be in terrible trouble."

"Is there anyone else in the church, Pastor?" Tage asked.

"No, it's just me. I heard loud scratching sounds on the stone floor, and I came to see what the sound was.

What, pray tell, are you doing here?" the pastor asked again.

"We came to get Capacity, among other things." Tage stared at his friends, then back at the old man. "The overlord put us in jail, but jail isn't what you think."

"Is that so?" The pastor limped toward them, his right arm tight to his body.

Tage tensed his muscles.

"Yes," Impulse said. "Jail is a powerline. A human and soil-charger powerline."

"What?" he gasped. "The rumors cannot be true."

Tage nodded. "We were placed there—it's a soil charger, a row of humans, and then another soil charger. The line goes for miles, trying to connect Anoths and Cathos."

The pastor stepped back. "I had hoped . . . I had hoped the leadership wasn't quite as corrupt as it appears."

"Well," Lumen said slowly, "it's true. The overlord shoved us in that powerline of his. We were held there for months. Tage boosted us out. If we or—I mean if *someone* doesn't stop him, he'll connect the two poles, and control all the power on this hemisphere of Hadrain."

"Truly." The pastor shook his head, eyes full of tears. "The powerline is—is real?"

"I'll never forget the sight of those people for as long as I live," Impulse said. "I must have thanked the gods a thousand times that we were hardly within sight of it on our way back here."

The pastor clutched the tall hat in both hands.

Tage slowly stepped forward. "There are thousands of humans and soil chargers, and without arresting us all for almost no reason, he won't be able to finish the powerline."

"Why? Why would he do that to some of his own?" the old man asked.

Silence. The three fugitives stared at each other.

"If you're worried about me turning you in, please don't fret." He released a long sigh. "It's not my place to pass judgement. Nor do I get involved in police matters. Their laws do not match with those of the gods."

"Like we said, the overlord is using the humans and soil chargers to connect the poles of Hadrain together." Tage paused. "He uses them to suck up the charge from the ground and store it. Pastor Bundle, they've been driven to near extinction. Once the overlord figures out how they extract water from the latex of the Saptex Sea, they'll be a race of the past."

"But you"—the pastor turned to Lumen—"and Impulse are still Surge Knights?"

"Yes and no," Impulse said. "The overlord took great pleasure in ripping the tech out before making us slaves in the powerline."

Lumen balled her fists.

"It's a complicated story," Impulse said. "Lu and I had the biotech reinstalled. We knew we'd need it for this."

"Ah," Pastor Bundle said. "A final reckoning."

"Are you going to turn us in?" Tage asked.

"No." His laugh was laced with sadness and disappointment. "It is out of my control. Overlord Koax has done some deeply questionable things. Even has a following who worship him, and not our gods. It was bound to happen." He looked down once more, then painted a soft smile on the left side of his face. "I will thank you in advance for keeping the violence away from the church."

"Of course," Tage said, eyeing the old man and the door. "I'm sorry, but how can we trust you aren't going to alert the Surge Knights the moment we leave?"

"Is a man of the gods' word not enough these days?"

He shuffled and sat on the edge of one of the two desks. "Come, have a look."

The old man pulled his hair to one side and loosened his robe, exposing his back. Brown age spots littered the pale skin. But as Tage leaned in closer, he saw big, thick scars on his spinal column from his neck to his shoulder.

"I used to believe that being a Surge Knight meant keeping soil chargers safe from the human monsters. I attempted to join the Surge Knights when I was twenty," Pastor Bundle said. "The surgery gave me a stroke, leaving my right side mostly numb. I accepted it was part of my fate, the gods' will, and found myself here."

"Dang," Lumen said. "How old is the overlord?"

"Lu!" Impulse scolded her.

"What? It's a valid question."

"Over one hundred fifty," Tage said. "I know that much from our intel."

"He was old when I was young," the pastor said. "The artificial life he has comes only through constant high doses of electric current. Through his connection to his Surge Knights. He must be close to two hundred years of age."

"Wow," Tage said, his mind spinning.

"But I digress." The pastor tightened up his robes, then stood. "I've lived the fate the gods have bestowed upon me. And now, you are doing the same."

What else could Tage possibly learn from this man? And would his new knowledge be at all useful? He wasn't sure yet.

"Do you know where Capacity is being held?" Tage asked.

"Last I knew, she was in jail with you three." He picked up his tall hat and turned to leave. "Good luck to you. But I must stay out of this. I need to pray."

"Wait, Pastor Bundle?" Lumen smiled widely. "Do you have any clothes we could wear, or a disguise or something like that? We definitely don't want you to be implicated, so we could just say we stole them from the church if we ever get caught."

"As I said, I must stay out of this," he said. "But if you were to stumble upon a wardrobe, it would most likely be in the west wing of the church."

The old man clasped his hands together and bowed at them before shuffling out of the room. They waited a minute, then followed him out.

"I guess we have his blessing?" Tage asked.

"Yeah," Lumen said. "I feel bad getting him involved."

"It's okay, Lu." Impulse put an arm around her. "It'll all be over soon. Come on, I'll lead the way."

The three of them slowly moved through the church, the layout foreign to Tage. Instead of using the power from the desert, candles were lit and rested in holders on the walls, making flickering shadows as they passed. Another reason Tage felt they could trust the pastor.

"Did you know he was slated to be a Surge Knight?" Lumen asked.

"No," Impulse said quietly. "But his story makes me even happier that our bodies still work."

"West wing." Lumen gestured with a flourish.

Tage pulled on a large metal ring handle. The hinges groaned under the weight of the massive door as he pulled it open. He coughed at the musty scent. Down both sides of the long hallway's walls hung thick, colorful robes. Some had religious hats hanging with them, and others had shawls.

"Should we all wear the full garments?" Impulse asked. "Hats included?"

"I think so," Tage said. "The Surge Knights might be looking for us. We're wanted, after all."

Tage passed out the heavy robes, then slipped his on over his uniform.

The heavy material felt odd draped over his shoulders, covering even his uniform. He stuffed the matching hat onto his head, making sure that every strand of his dark roots was covered. Lumen put a shawl over her head, and Impulse wore a stiff hat that was in the shape of an upside-down teardrop.

Tage's hat flopped over to one side as he adjusted it. "How do I look?" he asked.

"Like an idiot," Lumen said. "But that's nothing new."

Tage smirked. At least she was keeping a sense of humor throughout the ordeal. He took one last look in the mirror to ensure his black hair wasn't peeking out before they headed to the entrance of the church.

"What's going on outside?" Impulse asked. "Why did Tel'el say to meet in the main square?"

"He has a plan," Tage whispered. "That's all I know."

"Let's get our friend," Lumen said through gritted teeth.

Stained-glass windows were mounted high above. Specks of color reflected down onto the wooden pews lining the room, making the entire chapel look magical.

Impulse pushed the heavy, old double doors open, and they exited onto the streets of Currentgrad.

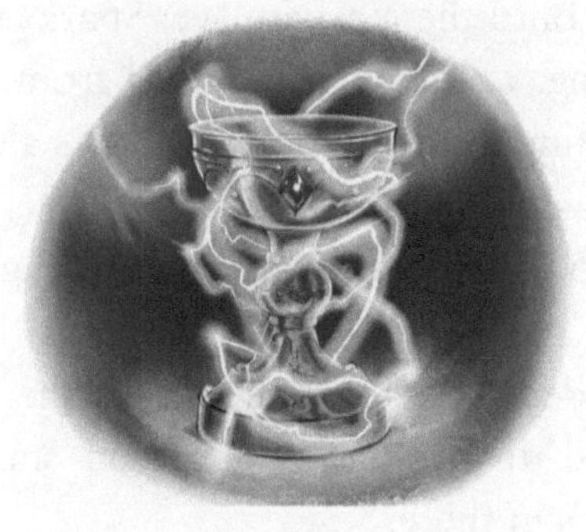

CHAPTER 34

• • • • •

Tage stopped, taking in the marketplace. The purple sky was darkening, and electric lights shone brightly. It was the same as he remembered, but so different than Ohmstave. Gone were the orderly and polite humans sharing their bounties, living like a community. Now chaos ruled. Soil chargers haggled over food, wares, clothing, jewelry—anything you could think of. Some yelled loudly, while others took five-finger discounts.

"I don't miss this," Tage said.

"Me neither," Impulse agreed. "What would Samara say?"

"The humans are oppressed, but so are the soil chargers, look." Tage pointed to men fighting over a thick piece of ursogen hide. "We're all pitted against each other."

"Where's your dad?" Lumen whispered.

Tage scanned the marketplace, pausing on the castle in the north. The Voltaic Dava towered over the streets. An illuminated courtyard lit up the entire castle. Tall spires cast shadows onto the marketplace. Sparks spewed from exposed wiring, and current coursed from long, skinny antennas, casting more ominous shadows along the front of the large castle.

Impulse took a step forward toward Tage. "Hideous, isn't it?"

Tage nodded. He stared at one of the stained-glass windows, and an outline of a person stared back. "I wonder if she's in there?"

"Maybe," Lumen said. "Makes sense if he's trying to lure you here to save your girlfriend."

"Seriously," a soil charger said, walking past Tage. "The church missionaries are here again."

"Ignore them," another said, then yelled, "Hey! We don't need your religion."

"Is that so?" Lumen crossed her arms.

"What have your gods done that the overlord hasn't?" The man's face contorted.

Tage's balled fists were hidden by his long robes, but his rage was evident on his red face. The two soil chargers laughed as they walked away.

"Forget them," Impulse said. "We need to find Tel'el."

"Shh!" Tage said. "Don't say his name. Just look for him."

"What's he wearing?" Lumen asked.

"I don't know," Tage said. "Last we saw, he was in the clothes he wore when we were in Ohmstave."

Tage's heart raced. Why hadn't he thought of asking Tel'el what he'd be wearing? A pool of sweat formed under his robe and Surge Knight uniform. He walked slowly, trying to keep a look of calm and serenity on his face. Avoiding prolonged contact, he did his best to search out his dad.

"Tage," Impulse said. "Twelve o'clock. That's him. He's dressed like an ordinary soil charger."

Tage darted his eyes through the crowd until his eyes were locked with the familiar ones that had brought him comfort most of his life. His dad nodded to the left, then broke eye contact and disappeared around the back of the marketplace, toward a residential area.

"Nod at people as you pass them," Impulse said. "And follow me; they'll think we're going to proselytize in the neighborhood."

No one paid them much attention as they walked through the bustling crowd—aside from a few snide remarks here and there.

"Hello, sir," Tage said to his dad. "Would you be interested in hearing some scripture?"

"I would," Tel'el replied. "Please, join me for some tea."

Tel'el hopped up onto a porch, then opened the front door to a dilapidated house. Tage followed, turning back only when the rotted wood groaned under Impulse's weight.

"What are you doing?" Tage whispered once inside the abandoned house.

"What am I doing? What are you doing?" Tel'el waved his hand up and down the length of Tage. "I said cover or shave your hair, not steal robes from the church. I almost didn't recognize you."

Lumen's brows danced. "Wicked, huh?"

"Sorry," Impulse said, his gaze shifting to the floor.

"No, we're not sorry," Tage said. "We did our best. What are you doing? Why did you bring us in here? We could get caught."

"Did you see the drudges?" Tel'el asked.

"What? Yeah, there were a bunch wandering around." Tage ripped off his hat. "What's the plan?"

"We need to split up. Catch a drudge's attention, then have it follow you to the middle of Currentgrad, right outside the courtyard of the Voltaic Dava. I'll be waiting. Bring me a dozen or so. Once I have enough, I'll create the diversion I need to draw out Koax."

"How do we make them follow us?" Lumen asked. "I've never had a real conversation with a drudge before."

"You two need to lose your robes; they'll think you're Surge Knights. *Discreetly* tell them they are instructed to follow you by order of Overlord Koax. They'll follow. Tage, since you have to stay covered in your robes, you'll have to say it's under the orders of the church. Most are very dense, so they shouldn't question you. If they do, tell them you're mistaken and move on to another drudge. Do this one at a time. We can't have a herd of drudges all leaving the marketplace at once."

Tel'el's attention turned toward Impulse and Lumen. "Your families are being hidden in the empty school on the far north side of town."

Impulse released a long breath and stared at the ceiling for a moment. "Thank you," he whispered.

Lumen stared silently at the ground. Tage watched the dirty floor moisten with her tears.

Tel'el tapped Impulse on the shoulder. "I'm happy at least one part of our initial plan worked out."

"What's next?" Tage asked.

"Impulse, Lumen," Tel'el's tone softened, "can you give us a minute?"

"Of course," Impulse said. "Come on, Lu, let's round up some drudges."

As they left, Tage studied his dad's face. Weathered

and broken, the last few months had taken a severe toll on him.

"Tage, my boy," Tel'el said, then embraced him in a hug. "You're so brave, and wise beyond your years." He kissed the top of his head. "I think you should keep your hair like that. Half white, half black." He barked out a laugh.

"My hair?"

"Yes, it's an outward representation of your inside. You've taken the best from both your human and soil-charger sides and become something unstoppable." He pressed his forehead against his son's, stared into his eyes, and cupped the back of his neck. "Tage. You're special. No one can stop you unless you let them. You're a gift from the gods."

"Dad." Tage's stomach flipped and tightened. "What's going on?"

"Everything." Tel'el smiled, and a tear slipped from his eye. He hugged him once more, then released his embrace. "I need you to know that no matter what happens out there, you keep your eye on the prize. We must kill Koax."

Tage's heart began to skip. "Is there something you're keeping from me?"

"I love you, Tage. You weren't my son by blood or birth, but you were mine just the same."

Tage folded in his lips, pressing them together to suppress his tears. This wasn't just a declaration of love.

It was a goodbye.

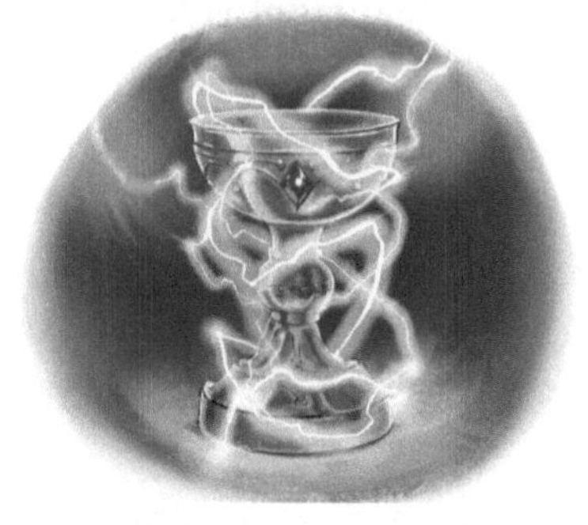

CHAPTER 35

• • • • •

Rounding up drudges was harder than it sounded. Mostly because aside from varying widely in features, they also had a wide range of intelligence. Meaning zero to minimal.

The first drudge Tage encountered had three eyes, and its nose was more of a snout and was pulled to the side of two of the eyes. This one had all its limbs, but six fingers on one hand, and four on the other. Save for a few scraggly hairs, the gray, bald head shined in the electric light. The lower jaw jutted out unnaturally, exposing its black gums.

"Excuse me, drudge," Tage said. Two of its eyes focused on him. The third looked past him. "By order of Pastor Bundle, your assistance is needed."

"I not answer to pastor." Snot bubbled out of one nostril.

"No," Tage said. "Of course not. It isn't an order, simply a request."

The abomination tilted its head toward an armored shoulder, confused.

"Come, other drudges await," he said.

Tage released a pensive breath, shoulders back, walking away from the marketplace and toward the church, robes flapping in the slight breeze. Then he veered a hard left toward the courtyard outside the castle. Relief washed over him when he saw the drudge had in fact followed him.

Leading the drudge to Tel'el suddenly made his hands shake. He still didn't know the whole plan. And being out in the open like this, so exposed, felt like a suicide mission. Maybe it was. Maybe it always had been, and that's why they'd failed before. Him and Tel'el.

Tel'el stood still, stoic and unmoving, until Tage finally closed the gap.

"Sir," Tage said, scrambling for what to call him, "your drudge."

"Not pastor," the drudge grunted.

"Very good!" Tel'el said. "I'm not the pastor. It's very important you stand right here until I give you orders. The overlord has a very special plan for you. Don't move a muscle. Do you understand?" The drudge neither moved nor responded. "Excellent! You're a very good drudge."

Tel'el placed a hand on Tage's back, leading him away.

"Am I the first?" Tage whispered.

"Yes. Lumen and Impulse must be having trouble; I hope they didn't get caught."

Tage cursed under his breath.

"Tage, please." Tel'el frowned. "Keep your composure, now is not the time to crack. Hurry."

"I'm sorry," Tage said. "I will."

He walked as quickly as he could without drawing attention to himself and made his way back to the marketplace. Two men had gotten into a fistfight. A drudge lumbered and grabbed one of the men, tossing him to the ground. He made a sickening crunch when he landed, his neck bent completely to the side. Eyes dead. Then the drudge picked up the aggressor with one hand and dragged him away. The man screamed and kicked but was no match for the drudge's strength.

Tage's hands shook. He'd forgotten how savage they could be and how strong they were. All brute, little brains. A deadly combination. Craning his neck, he looked for a drudge that seemed less involved, one shuffling around aimlessly.

Behind him, another commotion erupted. A tent collapsed, and jewelry crashed down to the cobblestone. Rings and bracelets went flying. A drudge had walked through the tent and continued toward another, seemingly unaware of the destruction it had caused.

"You'll do just fine," Tage whispered.

The soil charger next to the jewelry merchant desperately tried to scoot his table out of the drudge's way. Tage placed his hand on the bare shoulder of the drudge, sending a cold shiver up his arm. Dead flesh.

The drudge halted immediately, but Tage was stunned. He thought he'd touched or been touched by a drudge in the past, but he didn't remember them feeling ice cold. This was a new drudge.

Regret washed over him; people stopped to look as they passed. The chaos wasn't out of the ordinary, but a man of the gods resting his hand on the back of a drudge most certainly caused stares. He withdrew his hand as if he'd put it in a firepit.

"Drudge," Tage said softly. The beast stood two feet taller than Tage. It turned slowly. A cyclops. The worst kind of drudge. Angry, unpredictable, profoundly dumb, but a killing machine. "Follow."

"Thank you, sir. Please pass my thanks onto Pastor Bundle," the merchant said.

Tage placed his palms together and bowed at the man. The ground behind Tage tremored as the drudge followed. He had to walk slowly, for fear of the drudge getting distracted by something else. Every few feet, he'd feel the shaking stop and see the drudge veering off.

"Drudge," Tage said. "Come."

After garnering plenty of stares, he finally left the marketplace and was out in the open. He'd have to find a new part of the market to harvest drudges. The attention was too great now.

The sky was full dark now. Tel'el waited patiently in the shadows between the housing units, just outside the courtyard. Tage breathed a sigh of relief; he couldn't wait to dump this drudge. It made him nervous in a way he couldn't put into words.

"Drudge, stop," Tage said. It halted. "This man has orders from Overlord Koax."

"Overlord." The drudge snorted.

"I'll take him from here," Tel'el said.

"Have you seen them?" Tage whispered.

"Yes, we have five," Tel'el said. "Go."

Tage walked back, going up and around toward the marketplace, instead of from the bottom. Just a few steps outside the bustle, he met Lumen. She'd taken a more aggressive approach to gathering drudges. Hers had its arms bound behind its back and looked more like a prisoner than anything. Not good. Her eyes met his for a moment, then she straightened and kept moving forward.

"Move it along, drudge," Lumen said.

"What are you doing?" Tage asked.

"They don't listen well to women without a little

coaxing," Lumen whispered as she passed. "Stop stalling, drudge."

Tage huffed. This was the worst thing she could do. He needed to go back in, but wanted to talk with her first. Looking back and forth from the shadows and the marketplace, he trudged forward. Tel'el would deal with this.

He hoped.

It wasn't long before he ran into another drudge. This time, he took a different approach. He placed a hand on its right shoulder and simply guided it away from the marketplace without saying a word. Another cold shiver worked its way up Tage's hand, chilling him to the bone. It was like the opposite of delicious electricity coursing through his blood.

He removed his hand from its shoulder and placed it in a more inconspicuous place near its low back. Still, cold death radiated off it. As he was nearing the exit, he managed to snag another drudge. He quickly walked to the courtyard with the two drudges. Once he was close, Lumen intercepted him.

"This is enough," she said. "Nice job on getting two at once."

"What the heck was that back there?" Tage asked. "You could have blown the entire plan."

"Yeah, well, I didn't, did I?" She pushed one of the drudges hard toward the small gathering they'd created. It stumbled, but quickly regained its balance. "And Tel'el made me stay back after anyway. Said I was a liability. Geez, you two think alike. You'd think he was half human too."

The other ten drudges were sitting quietly, waiting for a command. Tel'el stood in front of them, hands at his sides, staring hard at them.

"Dad," Tage said. "You've got to tell me what's going on. Where's Impulse?"

"He's hiding near the housing units," he said, never taking his eyes off the drudges. "You two need to join him and watch what happens. Do not come back into this square until Koax is here. And he'll be here. I promise you that."

"W-what?" Tage sputtered. "Dad. How?"

Tel'el winked. "Here comes the fun part." He looked at the drudges. "Stand." The drudges stood. "By order of Overlord Koax, follow me." Each one followed Tel'el as he walked. Once they'd mostly straightened out, Tel'el took a hard left. They followed.

Tage and Lumen ran fifty yards before they spotted Impulse. Tage hid behind a house, craning his neck to watch. "I didn't realize they were so easily swayed to do anyone's bidding."

"They're not." Impulse joined them. "Only for Koax, that's why they listened."

"Why hasn't anyone in Currentgrad used them like we did?" Lumen asked.

"Why would they?" Impulse said. "Remember how brainwashed we were?"

Tage glanced at his friends, knowing that it probably killed them to not be seeking out their families the second they arrived.

"I guess." Lumen shrugged her shoulders. "Man, was I missing out."

"Shh," Tage said, "look!"

Tel'el had guided the twelve drudges into walking in a constant large circle. Arms splayed wide, he was now in the center of the drudge merry-go-round. His clothes hung off his thin body.

"This isn't good," Tage said. "What is he doing?"

Droves of soil chargers exited their homes and the marketplace to watch the spectacle. Tel'el shot White Sparks straight above him. Small bits of light rained down on him as he moved toward the Voltaic Dava.

Then he started singing.

"He's trying to lure Koax out, but he's . . ."

He's gone mad.

Surge Knights converged on him. Their uniforms were not as pristine as Tage's had been. Sloppily placed bio-tech and small, shrunken, overcharged bodies confirmed the overlord was churning out subpar Surge Knights after another attempt on his life. Rush jobs. Lazily trained soldiers.

Tel'el ducked, sinking his hands into the charged ground. The Surge Knights were only a few feet away. Tage clenched his fists. Sweat pooled on his back.

Tel'el jumped up, blasting a Current Ignition at the drudges, moving in a circle to get each one. All twelve of them burst and popped as their skin exploded from the heat. Three Surge Knights fell back, arms and faces burned.

For a moment, everything stopped.

Tage held his breath.

"Stay back!" Tel'el yelled. He sunk his hands in the ground once more. "Your fate will be worse than mine if you even mess with a single white hair on my head." Surges looked to each other for answers. "I believe the bounty on my head belongs to Koax."

"Your dad's trying to get arrested," Lumen breathed.

And then what? What?

"How dare you," a Surge yelled. "No one disrespects the overlord like that. Get him!"

The Surge Knight shot a single Bolt Ignition at Tel'el. His slight frame easily dodged the bolt of electricity. It bounced on the ground before hitting a brick wall and charring the edges.

Tage's attention was suddenly pulled to high above the wall adjacent to the castle. A thick Current Ignition came hurtling down at the Surge Knight who had shot at Tel'el. The beam of electricity hit him square in the back. His spine arched, pieces of tech melted from his body, and his eyes were wide with surprise before he fell lifelessly to the ground.

"You imbecile!" Overlord Koax yelled. "The foolish soil charger is right. He is mine and mine alone to have."

Tel'el's plan had fallen horribly into place. Koax would come into the square. For an execution. Tage's heart twisted. He'd already lived through his mother's death, Capacity's captivity—so many things. Why this? Why did Tel'el have to draw him out this way?

"Ah." Tel'el rested his right arm in the crook of his left and held his chin with his hand, black fingertips still smoking from the earlier blast. "There you are, come to greet me yourself. This city sure has deteriorated in the last few months."

"Tel'el," the overlord spat from on top of the fortress wall. "I never thought I'd get the pleasure of seeing your face again."

"What ever do you mean?" Tel'el jumped to the top of a lone pulse dune in the sandy square. He innocently pinched his eyebrows together, cocking his head to the side. "Why, I lived under your nose for ten years. I shook your hand, even volunteered my son to become a Surge Knight. And what a fine Surge Knight he became. One of the strongest you'd ever seen. So strong, he nearly—"

"Silence!"

Tel'el jumped from atop the pulse dune. Tage instinctively cringed, expecting his old bones to break upon impact. He landed softly, as if he'd only jumped a foot or two.

"He was a fraud like you. A failure." Koax stalked slowly toward Tel'el. By now, half the city had come out and was jockeying for a spot to see Tel'el's execution unfold. "Neither of you could get the job done."

Gasps and murmurs erupted through the crowd. Some people started yelling "Who?" and "Why?"

The overlord lifted his chin in Tel'el's direction. Charuss came barreling out from nowhere and stunned Tel'el with a small Bolt Ignition. He grabbed Tel'el before he could fall and held him steady.

Tage's heart leapt into this throat. He lurched forward, but Impulse grabbed his upper arm, holding him in place.

"We have to help him," Tage growled.

"No," Impulse said again. "He said to wait, not to interfere."

"I can't just stand here." Heat rushed up Tage's neck, settling in his eyes. "I can't watch and do nothing!"

"Tel'el made me promise," Impulse whispered, tightening his grip. "He has a plan. If you mess it up, we may never get Capacity back. The humans are depending on us."

"Do not shoot him again," the overlord's voice boomed. "This is not your fight, Charuss."

"But he tried to kill you," Charuss said. "So did his bastard son."

Unable to quiet the huge crowd, the overlord ran a frustrated hand down his face. "Ten years ago, this disgrace joined our Surge Knight Program," he announced. "The rumors you heard were true. He pathetically attempted to assassinate me. I felt bad for the weakling and simply banished him to the Charged Desert to live out his pathetic life. I could have killed him, but as a fair ruler, I chose to let him live." He turned to the crowd. "As you know, living in the Charged Desert is nearly impossible, and incredibly dangerous, but I still gave him a chance, which was more than he'd given me."

"That's not true," Tel'el yelled.

Charuss grabbed his hair and yanked it back. Tel'el yelped.

Tage jumped forward, but Impulse again held him back.

"It's not true? Are you not alive? Tsk, tsk, *liar*," the overlord said. "Such a shame. You had a chance to live and chose to come back for seconds. Or is it thirds?" He whipped around, robes fluttering, and scanned the crowd. "Where is he, the half human?"

Tage heard the low rumblings and disbelief from the soil chargers about a half human amongst them. He looked to Impulse, who shook his head again. Tage opened his mouth, but Impulse clamped a broad hand over Tage's face and brought him to the ground.

"You're going to get us all killed, and nothing will change if you don't let Tel'el speak," Impulse whispered through gritted teeth. "If you go up there and kill the overlord, the entire city will turn on us. They'll blame the humans, and the rift will be worse than ever. Tel'el said to wait until Koax came into the square. We will wait."

Tage's shoulders relaxed. The entire plan became clear. They'd kill Tel'el, and in their relaxed celebration, Tage should strike. A single tear streaked down his dirty cheek. He looked up at Impulse and nodded.

Tel'el was going to get the overlord to admit to every-thing. And sacrifice himself in the process.

For once, Tage wished he'd been wrong. The last few moments he'd had alone with his dad in the shack had indeed been a goodbye.

CHAPTER 36

• • • • •

"Hold him," the overlord said. He disappeared into the castle for a few minutes. Whispers from the crowd became loud arguments. Some feared a half human was amongst them; others argued if one even existed. Then the conversations turned to why someone would want to kill the overlord. Why risk their life? What was the Voltaic Dava hiding?

Tage felt the tension in the crowd. Maybe they weren't all mindlessly following him after all.

"Bring me the traitor," the overlord's voice boomed once again up on the pulse dune wall. "Or she'll take his punishment."

Before Tage looked up, he once again felt Impulse restrain him and a hand clamp over his mouth.

Capacity.

She stood between two Surge Knights who held her up.

Tage's eyes grew wide and his heart thumped, but he was helpless.

"What have you done to her?" Tel'el asked.

"Remember," Lumen whispered harshly. "Remember when Tel'el said it was okay to strike."

Leaning on a Surge Knight, Capacity seemed too weak to stand on her own. Pallid skin sagged over her emaciated body. Dozens of cuts and bruises littered her pale skin. Her once-thick hair was now reduced to a few tufts that jutted wildly from her mostly bald head.

Voltage torture.

But worst of all was her eyes. Dead eyes. She stared off into space, unfocused.

"Bring me the half human, Tage," he yelled at Tel'el below. "Where is he?"

"He's in the powerline," Tel'el said. "Where you put him."

Gasps and even a few screams echoed throughout the courtyard. Then Tel'el doubled over, a black singe mark burned over his side. Charuss smiled, satisfied with his work.

"Charuss!" Koax yelled. "Do not touch him again. Go find the traitor and his friends. I know they're in here somewhere."

"I told you," Tel'el said. "They're in the powerline. The one you created to steal the power from Hadrain. The one where you've enslaved poor, innocent soil chargers and humans alike."

"They are not innocent," Koax snapped.

"So you admit it?" a brave soil charger yelled from the crowd. "The powerline is real?"

"Who dares question me?" Overlord Koax yelled. "Who?"

Silence.

"Humans must be managed." He paced along the rock wall, arms behind his back, robes flapping in the wind. "Remember the water shortages we experienced?" He paused, looking to the crowd.

"The dirty humans withhold water from us," a Surge Knight near Tage yelled.

"Precisely," the overlord said. "I vowed to protect my people. Never let something like that happen again. The other terraregions had made backdoor deals with them, and it prevented us from getting the water. The humans were out of control. So I placed a few, select humans in jail. To teach the bad humans a lesson. We haven't had an issue since. Water is minimal, of course, but—"

"Then why not lock me up?" Tel'el yelled. "Why would you let me go? Because you didn't! I escaped, and you know it. I outsmarted you. The humans have never withheld water. You lie! If—"

Tel'el's entire body stiffened as a Current Ignition struck his right arm, the bright light still attached to the overlord's hand, like string connecting them. Then Tel'el's arm ripped clean off his body, the heat cauterizing the wound immediately. A blackened arm lay limply on the charged soil.

Tel'el screamed, then grabbed his side where his arm once was. He threw his head back in pain. Veins pulsed out of his neck as he yelled.

Tage squeezed his eyes shut, biting his lip to stifle a cry.

Dying would have been simpler than watching Tel'el be toyed with this way. Would Koax not come down? When should they make their move?

"Is there anything else you'd like to say?" The overlord smiled. "Like where your traitor son and his degenerate friends are?"

"Why?" Tel'el asked. "You have me. What do you want with those kids?"

"Those *kids*," he snapped, "destroyed my beautiful powerline. It will take months to fix what they've ruined!"

Murmurs broke through the crowd.

The overlord's eyes fluttered from side to side, as if looking for a way to walk back his words.

Tage had to listen to the human part of who and what he was. He had to be smart. If the soil chargers were confused by Koax and his plans, they wouldn't all be fighting against Tage, Lumen, Impulse, and whomever his dad was able to find. He'd need to wait until the mumblings of confusion turned into mumblings of anger.

"My dear people." Koax smiled and pressed his thin fingertips together, two notably missing. Tage reveled in his handiwork. "There's something I must tell you. I did place four young adults into jail. Our old jail was expensive and such a waste of precious water. Always the innovator, I created a new jail that serves as a jail for the humans, too. It's a powerline. They were placed there because they tried to poison me. Kill me. It was the third attempt on my life in a decade. First Tel'el failed in killing me, then a pathetic attempt by a weak human, and then Tel'el sent his son and his derelict friends."

Murmurs and whispers grew to all-out shouts.

"Why?" someone yelled. "Is that where my son is?"

"He's lied to us for years! He can't be trusted!"

"The humans have never withheld water!" Tel'el yelled loudly. "You've tried to make them your slaves. Please"—Tel'el turned to the Surge Knights guarding him—"tell them what he's done."

"Silence!" Koax screamed.

He shot White Sparks at Tel'el, singeing his entire body. The too-familiar scent of burnt flesh and hair filled the courtyard. Tage had never seen anyone throw White Sparks that far. A pit formed in his stomach. His dad was dying, and the overlord was stronger than he'd realized. And still, Koax hadn't come down. Would he? Would Tage's Volt Foil succeed where others had failed? Would he create his eagle, only to die on the street in Current-grad?

Tel'el fell to the ground, rolling from side to side. Writhing in pain.

"Please!" Tage broke free of Impulse's grasp. His robes fluttered in his rush to join his father's side. "I am a man of Anoths and Cathos. Let me read him his last rites."

"No," Tel'el whispered. "Not yet." His eyes were full of tears. "Let me get a confession. Don't let me die in vain." He spat blood. "Please."

"Out of the way," the overlord yelled. "A man of the gods is no use to you."

Tage furrowed his brow. "I beg of you," he said, keeping his head down. "Allow me to pray with the misguided soul one last time."

"Quickly," the overlord responded.

"I love you," Tel'el whispered softly.

"I love you, too."

"It's him!" Charuss yelled. "Tage!"

Tage turned to see Charuss aiming with an outstretched hand. Tage launched himself into a roll, just in time to avoid a Bolt Ignition. It sizzled past him and made contact.

With his dad.

The ignition meant to kill Tage entered Tel'el's body and shocked his heart. It was enough to extinguish his life. Tel'el slumped. Lifeless.

"You fool!" the overlord yelled at Charuss.

Tage stared, frozen in disbelief. Tel'el lay on his back,

motionless, eyes open, a gaping hole where his midsection once was. Time stopped.

Two hands under his arms pulled him to his feet.

"Tage Gradient!" the overlord yelled.

Out of the corner of Tage's eyes, he saw Impulse and Lumen creeping toward them. Tage shook his head, but they converged on the unsuspecting Surge Knights anyway. Two quick blasts to the base of the Surges' spines and they collapsed. Dead.

The crowd gasped.

"What's going on?"

"Why did they kill one of their own?"

Impulse and Lumen stood as if they were guarding Tage.

"What is this?" Charuss asked. He stood only a few feet from them and splayed out his arms. "Everyone, you see? They're wicked."

"Tell them, Charuss," Tage said loudly so everyone could hear. "Tell them how you take great pleasure in watching Koax rip biotech out of Surge Knights. How you taunt and laugh at those stuck in the powerline even when they are members from your own community who were sent to jail for made-up crimes. But instead of jail, they got dragged out there to suffer forever. Tell them how you hunt innocent humans like worms or feral and place them in the powerline."

A bright bolt of electricity erupted from Charuss's palms. Tage thought about trying to absorb it for a moment, then ducked, pushing his two friends to the ground and avoiding the blast. Surge Knights descended on them before they could get up.

From Tage's vantage point, all he could see was a sea of white hair. Panic set in his mind. Angry shouts spread throughout the crowd.

Lumen kicked wildly. "No!" She shot White Sparks at point blank range. Tiny bolts of electricity rained down, burning not only those holding her, but also herself. Impulse was physically fighting off three Surge Knights. Bare knuckles to the face—nothing they'd seen in battle.

Tage jumped to his feet and ran into the crowd.

Surge Knights and soil chargers had flooded the courtyard. Some fighting to get in, others to get out. A city divided. Some still believed in the overlord. That was fine, Tage would persuade them. He'd gotten this far, what was a little more convincing? He'd charged the pastor to spread the word—maybe more would learn what was really happening in Currentgrad, Ohmstave, and with the powerline.

Tage kept his head down while doing his best to find his friends. Twisted braids on a head he'd know anywhere bounced ahead of him. He ran quickly, then jogged alongside her, never making eye contact. Chaos reigned, like a bar fight spread into the street. Yelling, jostling, bodies crammed together shouting.

"Lumen," he gasped. "Where's Impulse?"

"I don't know," she said. "But I know he got away. Some soil chargers helped him get free. I assume they're the people your dad planted."

Now was the time for Tage to use every ounce of power he could find within himself. No matter the cost, he would not allow Tel'el to die for no purpose. Koax was never coming down without more incentive. Tage had to give him that incentive.

"Get out of here, Lumen," he grunted.

"What?" she asked.

"Go, I'll need you in a minute," he said.

Tage sucked up a full charge, then cast White Sparks high into the air as he sprinted toward the Voltaic Dava.

"Ko-oax," he sang, drawing out the word. "Come out, come out wherever you are!"

Tage felt a hot blast to his side. Without being prepared to absorb it, he took the hit directly. His armor took part of it, but it still knocked him down.

The crowd gasped, then silence fell over them.

Tage jumped to his feet as pain worked its way up his side and into his shoulder. He was surrounded, Charuss leading the charge.

"I should have known you'd return," Charuss said. His body looked almost as sunken in as the overlord's. "Foolish boy. But you're half human; I'd expect you to be smarter than that."

"Not looking so good, Charuss," Tage said. Two Surge Knights stepped closer, but stopped short of touching him.

"There are no rings," one whispered. "No lights . . ."

"How do you know you're not playing right into my hands?" Tage stared at the old Surge Knight.

"If your plan is to die, then yes, I suppose you could say I am." Charuss smiled, then snapped his fingers. "Everyone, please, your attention. Those who live here have had the benefit of safety granted by Overlord Koax. Now is your time to show your loyalty. We have betrayers among us. Two of them you may already know, Lumen Nal and Impulse Watt. Then there are three others dressed as imposter Surge Knights, but their uniforms are darker than ours.

"You may have seen them during the commotion earlier," Charuss continued. "They are among us right now; I can feel it. Look around, call them out to us. We must send a message. We will not tolerate this sort of attack."

"Here's one! The girl!" someone yelled.

Surge Knights ran toward the voice, retrieving Lumen.

"The imposters, all three are here," another yelled out.

"Yes," Charuss said. "Excellent, you will be rewarded for your loyalty. Where is the big one? Impulse."

There were a few grumbles, but no one announced his location.

"Someone must see him." Charuss paced with his hands on his hips. "If anyone here doesn't believe in the overlord as their leader and savior, then please, the doors are open. You may leave. For the rest of you, I assume you like the comforts of Currentgrad. The safety—"

"The Charged Desert is unsafe because of Koax," Tage interrupted.

"Where is Impulse?" Charuss boomed. For such a small, weak frame, his voice still sounded of a strong warrior.

Impulse walked out from the crowd and placed his wrists behind his back. Hands balled into fists, ready to accept his fate. A Surge quickly bound them together with a thick piece of leather. He walked over to Tage and stood oddly close to him. The yelling and small scuffles from within the crowd died down as their small team was gathered.

The three warriors Tel'el had recruited were lined up next to Tage, Impulse, and Lumen. But Tage hadn't yet pulled out his best weapon. They'd been set up to die in front of this crowd, but he wouldn't let his friends be killed—not while he was alive to save them.

He glanced up, trying to search out Capacity, but she'd disappeared.

"Excellent," Charuss said. "Thank you for making this easier on the both of us. Your death will be quick. Not painless, but quicker than Tage's fate."

Charuss nodded at the Surge Knights. They ran

behind them, tying their wrists together just as they had with Impulse. "Discharge!"

They all discharged and were forced onto stone steps.

"Do you see what happens to betrayers?" Charuss announced.

"Tage," Impulse whispered. "Open your hands."

Tage looked at him, confused, but did as he asked, turning slightly toward him. A sharp metal blade landed in his palms. He glanced at Impulse's wrists and saw he'd cut the leather and was simply holding it on to look like he was bound. That explained why he revealed himself with his hands balled up.

Brilliant.

"The overlord will be here any second," Charuss continued.

Tage tuned him out while he closed his eyes and concentrated on loosening his hands enough to cut the leather. He awkwardly sawed back and forth over and over, doing his best not to cut himself. His fingers dripped blood, but finally the bindings broke free. As Charuss continued to grandstand, he passed the blade to Lumen.

"You and that human brain of yours think of everything," she whispered.

"Don't thank me," Tage whispered back. "This was all Impulse."

"Silence!" Charuss said.

"Or what?" Tage asked.

Charuss's eyes narrowed on Tage. "It would be such a pleasure to kill you myself."

"But you can't," Tage said as he smiled. Koax wouldn't allow it. Especially not after Tel'el. Soon, his friends would be free, and Tage could unleash his eagle, giving them a chance to escape.

"Hate is what I feel for you," Charuss said. "And I want you dead. I can't kill you, but I can kill your friends."

"No, you won't," Tage said. "You can't do anything until Koax shows up."

"Stop calling him that! You will show him some respect!"

"Or what?" Tage repeated, his voice rising. "You're his minion, but you don't have any real power in the Voltaic Dava. Everything you do is for his bidding. You couldn't even stand up to him with the powerline. You knew what you were doing was wrong. And now, I hear you've stolen people from Currentgrad, innocent people from our city, and forced them into the line? Coward."

"I'm no coward," Charuss yelled. "It was my idea. He praised me. Said it was an excellent idea, then gave the orders. They weren't innocent. Taxes were raised, and they defaulted on them."

"You said it was a farm," someone yelled from the crowd.

"It *is* a farm. An electric farm!"

"Your idea?" Tage was surprised by this admission. "I didn't know you had independent thoughts."

"Young Tage," the overlord interrupted. He stood on a catwalk high up on the pulse-dune rock wall, holding Capacity close to him. The purple sky had deepened to almost black, swirling behind him. "If only you knew how independent Charuss truly is."

"Nice of you to join us, Koax," Tage called up to him, trying not to let his eyes focus too long on Capacity's frail and beaten form. Clearly Koax was using her as both a lure and a shield.

The crowd had grown restless. It was a mixed bag of people yelling angrily at Tage's disrespect and at the overlord, and demanding answers. Tage took the opportunity to sneak a glance at the three recruits and confirmed they'd all removed their bindings.

"Are you going to answer your constituents' questions?" Tage asked.

"Perhaps." Koax tapped his fingertips. "I think you're asking the wrong person the wrong question."

"How so?" Tage asked, and took a slight step off the stone and onto the charged sand.

"Before I announced myself, I heard you berate my number two. Charuss is loyal and strong. But he has a mind of his own. You're lucky he held back on you. Showed restraint this time."

"What do you mean this time?" Tage asked.

"Far be it from me to spoil Charuss's news," he said. His tone was more of someone not wanting to spoil a happy surprise. But Tage knew better. "Go ahead, ask him."

"What did you do?" Tage gritted his teeth.

"Which time?" Charuss smiled, metal dentures gleaming in the artificial light. "Capacity might be okay, one day. She's in a trance. Proxy can get her out of it, but I don't foresee that happening."

Oddly, relief washed over Tage. He'd seen the empty expression in her eyes and worried she had some sort of brain damage. She'd clearly been tortured, but he had hope it wasn't permanent. Back in Ohmstave, they had loincloth-wearing Brakdern, who clearly could work wonders. He squared his shoulders and stared at Charuss.

"Then there's the other girl in your life," he said. "Your mom, what was her name, Hyra? Hyttin? Either way, it doesn't matter—"

"You?" Tage screamed. "It was you?"

Tage shot a Current Ignition out of both palms. The columns of light both landed on Charuss's chest.

Tage screamed, holding the ignition. Sucking up charge through his feet, he walked toward Charuss. Bright light made him squint, but he never broke eye contact. Terror and surprise were frozen on Charuss's face.

He released the charge and stared at the broken body below him. Tage had obliterated Charuss's entire torso. The scent of Charuss's charred flesh hung in the air, the stench sticking to their sweaty skin.

Out of the corners of his eyes, he saw another full fight breaking out. Soil chargers versus Surge Knights, and most shockingly, Surge Knights against Surge Knights. The city had begun to turn against Overlord Koax.

"Stop!" the overlord yelled.

If anyone could hear, they didn't listen. There had been enough bloodshed so far. It was time to end it once and for all. Tage bent down and held his hands on the ground while Lumen and Impulse fought off Surge Knights near him. He filled every ounce of himself with energy. Electricity swelled every cell in his body, every blood vessel vibrated with charge. His nerves exploded with voltage.

The eagle rose into the sky.

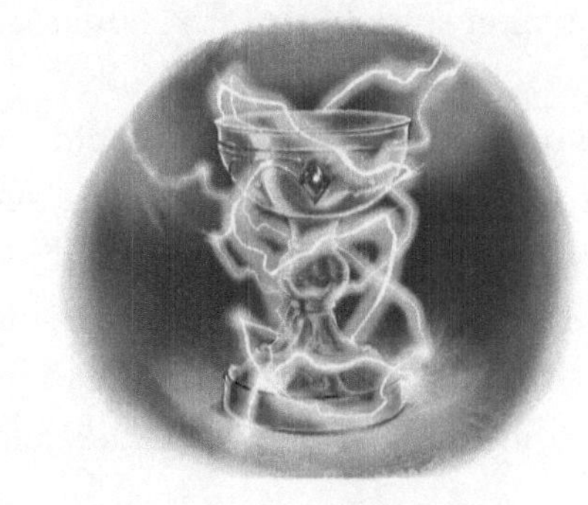

CHAPTER 37

• • • • •

For a moment it seemed like the fighting had stopped, frozen for just a second. Surges and soil chargers alike looked skyward with awe. The overlord cowered immediately and glared down at Tage.

Tage kept one hand on the ground, then waved his arm back and forth over the courtyard, waiting for the right moment to have the electric eagle swoop. He saw a group of roughly thirty drudges, completely unaware of the danger above, sneaking up on a group of soil chargers. He pulled his arm toward the ground, and the eagle swooped at the abominations. Its charged talons grabbed the heads of some, squeezing them until they popped. The beak chomped at the ones too scared to move, and its wings flapped, electrocuting the ones smart enough to try and run. In an instant, the entirety of the drudges were wiped out.

The bird cawed as he lifted it back high into the night sky. Tage immediately dove the beast into the Voltaic Dava. The main spire burst into chunks of stone and debris.

"No!" the overlord yelled. "How could you?!"

He shot a Bolt Ignition at Tage, but a Surge Knight with red lights lifted a shield, helping to redirect the flow. Then another new Surge Knight was at his side. The new Surge Knight stood behind the one who had just used his shield, also holding a shield between Tage and Overlord Koax.

Tage didn't let up. The Volt Foil demolished the top half of the castle. Pulse dune bricks, singed and smoking, toppled, raining onto the ground. Tage guided the large creature toward the overlord, blasting it into the walkway. A hole in Currentgrad's east wall gave way, and the catwalk collapsed. The overlord fell onto his back. As the walkway fell, the part closest to Tage crumbled to the ground.

The two Surge Knights holding Capacity backed up, pulling her with them. Tage didn't focus on them. Once he had Koax, he could get her.

Overlord Koax rolled to his stomach when he began to slide. He scrambled to find a handhold; his fingertips leaked current as he grasped at stone, trying to prevent himself from sliding toward Tage.

Tage smiled, his eyes dancing with the reflection of electricity from the bird. He continued the onslaught with the Volt Foil, lifting the large current creature into the air. The raw, three-dimensional image of power flew around above the entire city of Currentgrad.

The crowd screamed in terror. Pure chaos.

He slammed his hand down swiftly, and the eagle crashed down onto the wall again. The overlord's grip dislodged and he slid toward Tage, straight down the broken catwalk. Tage lifted his hand from the ground, and the

354

Volt Foil Ignition dissipated into showering sparks, falling onto the crowd in the courtyard.

"You'll never enslave another person—human or soil charger—again, Koax."

Before Koax could speak, Tage pointed at him, then blasted a Volt Foil directly at the ruler. Koax smugly held out his palms, in a hubris attempt to absorb Tage's Ignition. Shock and pure terror colored his face. The old man had no idea how strong Tage had become. The skin began melting off his body, dripping and burning his gray robes. Overlord Koax arched his back, his metal teeth clenched together as his lips melted away.

Tage still had charge. Some energy. The Current Ignition should have nearly knocked him out.

The ruler's clothes liquefied, his stringy white hair singed black, his eyes wide, and his metal teeth on display as his skin bubbled away from the heat. Tage squinted his eyes and switched his ignition to White Sparks. The overlord's body smoldered, and the charred body slid toward Tage's feet. Fueled by heartbreak and hatred, he couldn't let up.

Tage stared as the once-undefeatable ruler dissolved before his eyes. The overlord's charred corpse smelled of burned metal and rancid, cooked organs. Tage breathed heavily, his chest lifting and falling. A single tear rolled down his nose and fell into the smoking remains of Currentgrad's ruler. Next, he scanned the crowd. Everyone had stopped fighting. In unison, they gasped at the sight. In a mere moment, an entire new future had opened up for Currentgrad and the whole of Hadrain.

Burnt flesh and melted sinew, riddled with biotech, made up the pile that was once the powerful ruler. In the end, the overlord was nothing more than an abomination of his own invention. His own creature. Tage fell to his knees and threw up.

Everyone in the courtyard stared at Tage. No creature, man, or soil charger moved.

Tage regained his composure, climbed a pile of rubble caused by the Volt Foil Ignition, and stared at the faces below. "Koax has been defeated. His rule is over."

More soil chargers than not applauded. Currentgrad still had a long way to go to figure out how to move forward.

"All hail Overlord Tage," a Surge Knight yelled.

"No!" Tage shook his head. "Absolutely not. One person cannot rule over many. You need a council. Checks and balances. The humans, they are good. They've never withheld water from you, and they never will. They have a government that works. I will bring them back here. They'll help you set up a fair system that benefits all."

"What do we do until then?"

"I'll take most of the Surge Knights to remove the people from the powerline. We'll need volunteers to help Proxy. I'm sure we'll need a bigger triage center. The rest will help you rebuild. Everyone else, live. You're free. Go into the Charged Desert, or even go to Ohmstave. Pastor Bundle and Impulse will be in charge until I get back with the Elders Council of Ohmstave."

"And what if we don't want to live under this new rule?" someone called.

"Then leave," Tage said. "You have freedom. You can stay or go. Find a new terraregion. It's completely up to you. But I urge you to help Currentgrad rebuild."

A slow clap erupted from the crowd, then grew into a loud applause. Tage's breath was cut short. He saw hope on their shocked faces. Tears welled in his eyes; relief finally hit him. Jumping down onto the ground, he turned his back and wiped his eyes.

He'd done it—finally finished the mission that Tel'el had started more than ten years ago. Koax was dead. He'd have good news to report to the humans. Life was looking up. The changes in this city would take a long time, but at least they'd begun.

A hand rested on his back. "Capacity is with Proxy right now," Lumen said. "I sprinted to the two Knights who held her. They were new. Still in pain from the biotech. Not bad . . . recruits."

Without another word, Tage dashed toward the ruins of the Voltaic Dava.

"Tage!" Lumen called after him, but he pushed forward. "Tage!"

A few young Surge Knights sat outside the main doorway to the castle, but Tage sprinted past them, down the familiar corridor.

"Tage!" Lumen yelled again.

But he didn't stop until he stood in the doorway of the room where he'd healed from his biotech.

Capacity lay on a table, eyes closed, bony and thin.

Proxy hummed as she rubbed medicine on her scarred legs. Her eyes met Tage's. "She won't wake for a while."

Taking slow steps forward, Tage stopped at her bedside. "I'm so sorry," he whispered.

"Nothing is as simple as it seems," Proxy warned. "This city is used to leadership. If you don't find a way to govern soon, we'll end up with another Koax."

Tage closed his eyes. He hoped she was wrong.

"She'll sleep?" Tage whispered.

"If I'm able to keep her asleep for a few days, her body will have a better chance to heal," Proxy answered.

"We'll be moving the infirmary to the school on the far side of town—the empty one. Expanding."

Tage nodded once. Had Proxy known what was coming? Known that the defectors had been hiding there?

Lumen grasped Tage's shoulder. "Tage. We gotta get going."

Tage realized he couldn't do much more for Capacity at this time. He wanted to consult with Brakdern as well.

He leaned forward and placed a kiss on the corner of Capacity's still mouth. "I'll be back soon."

The two friends left Capacity with Proxy, and slowly walked back outside. She'd be okay. She had to be. Capacity was in good hands.

Impulse joined them. "I don't know how long I can keep the people here happy. Lumen's mouth is too dirty to talk to crowds, and I'm not good with words."

Tage allowed himself a small smile. "You can check on your family. Check on Lumen's too. I know she's been trying to play it cool, but I know she's just as eager to see her parents—even if they did think she'd die during the Surge Knight Ceremony."

Nudging Tage's arm, Impulse smiled, too. "I plan on doing just that."

Tage nodded and looked to the sky. It had faded from black to a dark purple dawn. He walked through the crowd. Most people stared, others gave their thanks or asked for him to promise he'd find their family member in the powerline. His limbs still shook from the effort of the Volt Foil, but it hadn't drained him as much as the first two times. Maybe he'd continue to grow in power as he practiced.

"Thank the humans when you go back," Impulse asked. "Thank Samara."

"Yeah," Tage said absently. Hopefully, he could talk

a lot of humans into coming back here with him—help teach the soil chargers how to be kinder, more thoughtful, use their system of governing for Currentgrad. Maybe one day, they'd all be able to mix. Tage imagined a time when halfsies like him would be common. Could they ever get to that point?

Small groups of people spoke; soil chargers in Surge Knight uniforms, their lights out, walked together. They were maybe unsure of where to be or what to do. Impulse could help give them jobs cleaning up the mess Tage had made with his eagle. Keeping angry citizens from destroying the castle, moving the infirmary to the old school. Glances were tossed Tage's way, small nods of deference greeted him as he passed. Thrust from obscurity into the spotlight wasn't something he'd really prepared for. Running. Hiding. Waiting—those were in his skillset. Being noticed was not.

Pastor Bundle stood outside the church and jogged over to them.

"Pastor," Tage began, "I hope it's okay that I volunteered you with Impulse to oversee things for a few days."

He nodded. "Of course. As long as it leads to lasting peace, I'm happy to offer my assistance."

"We have to go. We've got a long trek ahead of us," Tage said.

Pastor Bundle's brows knitted together. "Long? Why?"

Tage shook his head. The answer was obvious.

"If I may offer a bit of advice," the pastor said with a sly smile. "Take a shock craft."

"Of course." Tage laughed. The thought hadn't even occurred to him. "Then I guess we'll be back later today."

"Take her." Pastor Bundle nodded to a Surge Knight.

"She's got a good head on her shoulders, and has been driving shock crafts for years. She'll get you there safely."

Tage shook the pastor's hand. Shook the hand of a Surge Knight only a few years older than himself. "Trip," she said. "That's my name."

"Tage," he responded.

A corner of her mouth lifted. "Pretty sure everyone in Currentgrad knows who you are, Tage."

He'd gone from a kid who'd spent most of his life in hiding, to whatever he was now.

In just a few hours, he would be able to tell the humans they'd succeeded. He could bring them back here to help Currentgrad reform a government, and he could free thousands from the powerline.

"We did it," he breathed.

Lumen nudged his shoulder with hers. "We did it."

Trip nodded with them. "We finally have something to look forward to."

That was the center of it all, really. There was hope for things to come.

He walked to the gate where the shock crafts were stored with Lumen, Trip, and hope for the entire planet.

THE END

As a kid, Tyler H. Jolley always had a knack for storytelling. When he grew bored of old fables, he created his own exciting and unique worlds. Many years later, he still had so many new ideas and stories swirling in his head, but with nowhere to share it. That's when he put his pencil to paper and let the creative juices flow.

His debut novel, *Extracted*, came out in 2013 and swiftly became an Amazon Best Seller and Spencer Hill Press Best Seller. *Prodigal and Riven*, the second and third books in The Lost Imperials series were released in May of 2015.

After a brief hiatus he restructured and returned to writing. His Adventurous Ali series has received much praise. To date, he's released four in the series.

When he's not writing, you can find him at his orthodontic practice, mountain biking, or on the hunt for the perfect doughnut.

www.ingramcontent.com/pod-product-compliance
Lightning Source LLC
Chambersburg PA
CBHW051204190726
48288CB00006B/1800